ADAPTIVE

THE ELITE TRIALS

ADAPTIVE

BECKY MOYNIHAN

BROKEN
BOOKS

Published by Broken Books
www.beckymoynihan.com

ISBN-13: 978-1-7327330-2-2
ISBN-10: 1-7327330-2-3

Cover design by Becky Moynihan
Cover model by Neostock
www.neo-stock.com

To those with a dream:

Anything is possible if you believe.

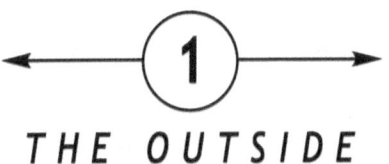

THE OUTSIDE

I stopped counting after three hundred steps.

Minutes ticked by, each holding the weight of an hour.

The urge to catch one last glimpse of Tatum City tugged at me. I resisted, just barely. My eyes traveled instead to my current company. Broad shoulders, tree-trunk torso, and legs so much longer than mine. His moving frame prowled with a wild grace only the self-assured, or cocky, could manage. And underneath that tough exterior was an even tougher interior: impatient, calculating, competitive, ruthless . . .

"Keep up," Ryker grumbled. His startling blue and black eyes narrowed on mine before they jerked forward again. "We have a lot of ground to cover. Bren has a solid two days' head start."

Rudeness was another quality of his.

If my tongue would cooperate, I'd grace my companion with a witty reply. But with that first step into the outside world, anxiety had gripped me. For eleven years, I'd been enclosed by walls. Too long. I had only ever wanted to feel freedom on my skin again. Now, the thought of unrestricted access to the entire world—and the world having access to me—sent paralyzing fear through my limbs.

I was out of my element, torn in two. My heart yearned to keep going while my brain reminded me of the dangers, of the safety the city offered. The city . . . *safe?* I held in a derisive snort.

Still, I might have turned around and begged the guards to let me back inside if it weren't for the dark-haired man in front of me who had strode through the gate and into the unknown with unwavering confidence.

I touched the twin daggers at my sides for the umpteenth time, casting a quick glance to the trees skirting the road. Any number of beasts could be in there, preparing to attack. Yet Ryker hadn't drawn his weapons, so neither did I. Showing weakness was new to me. My muscles still tightened at the thought of another human seeing my flaws. My scars. With one exception. A certain big idiot with teasing, albeit piercing, gold eyes.

Who are you, Brendan Bearon?

I thought I'd known him. Just thinking of Bren's large, gentle hands holding me close caused my heart to skip and my face to heat. I looked down, realizing I'd unconsciously pulled out the bear tooth necklace he'd given me. As a child, I'd been gravely wrong about him, then again as an adult. His mysterious dealings with Renold had cost me my freedom. Maybe my guardian had ordered Bren to toy with my affections, to screw up my one chance at winning Title of Choice. With an annoyed sigh, I shoved his image aside and hid the necklace once more.

How *could* I know him when I barely knew myself?

2

Then there was Ryker, another mystery. The only thing he and Bren had in common was their obsession with secrets. That and the Elite Trials. Both had wanted to win, but for what purpose? To become shallow, self-serving elitists? I had never found out, and now the reasons didn't matter. We were all on the outside, traveling far away from Tatum City, the cage of lies.

The city couldn't offer a better life, no matter what Supreme Elite Tatum said. Instead, it took. It grabbed the best parts of a person and tore them apart, leaving a greedy, bloodthirsty corpse behind. Those who didn't conform, who openly opposed the rules, disappeared. To this day, I didn't know what happened to them. With Renold's penchant for torture, I could imagine something painful.

It's all that remains of them, he'd taunted only hours ago after I'd opened the velvet box containing two severed thumbs.

The simple seamstress and hairdresser, who I'd known for eleven years to be nothing but loyal, had paid the price for my one intentional act of rebellion. Which I now regretted. Did they suffer? My brain refused to dwell on the possibilities, denied that they were . . .

A shiver raced down my spine, shaking my shoulders. I wouldn't think of what had happened to them, especially when I was feeling halfway unhinged. I picked up the pace in an attempt to distract myself from thoughts of my guardian and his sadistic ways. His control over me was stronger than ever now that he'd discovered another weakness of mine: my friends. If I didn't finish this mission and return, he would punish those I cared about, maybe even kill them.

I couldn't live with that, especially after reading Bren's cryptic yet all-too-clear message.

She is your sister.

Iris.

I should have seen it. The physical similarities. My gut hadn't warned me. Now, she was alone in a swarm of trainees and trainers, some who had a vendetta against me. Lars, in particular. Maybe he'd start hazing her again without me or Bren there to protect her. I grimaced as the prickling sensation at the base of my neck urged me to look toward the city once more.

But I didn't give in. Not a single wall or cage stopped my forward progress. My mum was out here, waiting for me to find her. For a moment, I debated taking my freedom and abandoning my mission.

And yet . . .

Stars, what kind of person would I be if I left my sister in the hands of that monster?

Deep in my brooding, I didn't realize Ryker had stopped until it was too late. I plowed into him. More like bounced off, actually. Ow. I gently touched the bridge of my nose where it had collided with the leather quiver strapped to his back. His head whipped around. "You really have a bad habit of running into me. For having won all three Trials, you're rather inept on your feet. How you survived is beyond me."

My jaw dropped and I blinked, slowly. Did he just call me a *klutz*? I sputtered out a laugh. "Well, that just goes to show

how much you know. I didn't win all three Trials. If I had, I'd be far away from here by now." Oops. Maybe I should have left out that last part.

His eyes narrowed. "You did win. It was an unfair ruling." My brows inched upward. That was the last thing I'd expected him to say. Noticing my look, he fully faced me. His voice was little more than a growl as he said, "And before you get any funny ideas, I am loyal to Supreme Elite Tatum. You'd better be too if you know what's good for you."

When I didn't reply, he moved his gaze to the ground. He crouched, touching an indent in the snow-covered road.

"What is it?" I squinted for a closer look.

Ryker stood, glancing to the north and shaking his head. "It's our target's footprint. He headed north, toward the old city."

I sighed. "Can we just agree on one thing? Our target is a person and he has a name—Bren. Let's use it from now on, okay?" He remained silent. Great. "Oh, and one more thing," I continued. "Why did Renold want you with me on this mission?

If he deviates from it, I want you to kill him, was the very last order given to me. Did Renold think me incapable of following through with my mission if Bren failed to follow his? Was Ryker meant to complete the job, to kill Bren, if I couldn't?

He started walking again, this time due north. My patience stretched thin, and I had to bite my tongue to keep a torrent of snarky words at bay. Finally, he said, "My orders are to track Bren and keep you alive. Apparently, Supreme Elite Tatum doesn't think you're capable of doing either on your own."

Even as I gaped at how accurate my guess had been, a growl formed in the back of my throat, nearly choking me.

You're pure reaction, Lune. It's incredible.

My jaw hardened as I tried to block out Renold's parting words. *Get a grip, idiot, you're stronger than this! Nobody can get a reaction out of you unless you let them.* Renold couldn't be right about me. I wasn't reactive. I could control myself. Really. My blunt nails dug into my scar-roughened palms. I barely felt the pricks of pain.

My shorter legs sped up until I drew even with Ryker. I tried not to glare as I replied, "If you recall, I beat you in the Rasa Rowe Trial. I think I'm quite capable of taking care of myself."

He snorted as if I'd said something childish. "You trained and competed in a controlled environment. Out here, there are no rules, no walls, no roof over your head to keep you dry. If the beasts don't get you, the people will; and if they don't finish you, nature will. It'll pick you apart, piece by piece, until only your ashes remain. You'll be begging me to return you to Tatum City by the end of the day."

His words both chilled my bones and heated my blood. He didn't know me at all. I snorted in return. "I give you permission to punch me in the face if you hear me begging to head back. I'll follow through with this mission, and only then will I return. Can I count on you to do the same?"

A grim smile formed on his lips. "You don't have to worry about me. I'll do what needs to be done."

Well, that wasn't ominous or anything.

We passed the next few miles in silence, the light dusting of snow turning into a steady fall. Soon, the ground was completely covered in a thin white layer of fluff, erasing any sign of boot prints—to my eyes, anyway. Ryker kept up the pace, gaze straight ahead, unwavering in his northern path.

How did he know where to go? I decided to ask. "How—?" He whipped a hand toward me, his fingers wrapping around my shoulder and digging in uncomfortably. My first reaction was to dislodge the threat. I grabbed his wrist and ducked underneath. He spun before I could jack up his arm behind him, and a second later, I found myself staring up at a cloud-filled sky, lungs burning as they tried and failed to suck in oxygen.

Angry blue eyes hovered above me, blocking my view of the falling snow. "What was that?" he hissed, then jerked his head to the side, peering at the line of trees next to the road. "Never mind, we have bigger problems. We're being watched."

My heart fluttered as I flicked a glance at the dense woods. "By what?"

"More like by whom. They've been following us since we left Tatum City, no doubt trying to decide if we hold anything of worth. If they don't relent soon, we'll need to shake them off our trail or confront them."

I didn't know how he knew that people were following us, but my burning curiosity would have to wait. "I'd prefer we not confront them if it can be avoided. Do you know how many there are?"

He paused, tilting his head like a dog. "At least two. Maybe three. Probably male. We have to get off this road, come on." He didn't bother offering me a hand up, already making for the tree line east of the road. Rude. Just plain rude.

My spine groaned as I stood, not happy with the way it had been slammed onto frozen ground. As I entered the dense woods, Ryker was nowhere to be seen. This teamwork thing was *not* going well. Doing my best to follow his fading footprints in the snow, I almost shrieked when a hand materialized out of thin air and pulled me behind a tree.

I knocked the hand aside and grabbed the front of Ryker's coat, jerking him toward me. "Don't touch me," I softly growled. "You might find yourself missing a limb next time you do."

He watched me coolly. "That makes two of us." His eyes shifted to my fingers still gripping his coat. I released it. "But if I have to *touch* you to keep you alive, I will."

My lips pursed as I smothered my need to have the last word. Control. *Control your impulses.*

Ticking his head in a *follow me* gesture, he slunk farther east, then crouched behind a fallen log. I joined him, unsure what the next move was. Several minutes dragged by. Nothing happened. I noticed the snow barely dusted the forest floor this far in. Pine needles and dead leaves covered the ground instead. Maybe our pursuers couldn't track us in here and had given up.

I leaned toward Ryker. "I think we—"

In the next instant, he exploded from our hiding position, his loaded bow aimed at a spot to the left of us. "Don't move," he snarled at something I couldn't see. I squinted into the gloom created by the thick, towering trees. A shape slowly emerged—a man, hands raised to show he was unarmed.

"Easy there, fella," he said in a drawling accent. "I'm not here to hurt you. I couldn't help but notice you two came from the walled city. It's not often people leave there. I thought maybe you could tell me a little bit about what it's like in there, hmm? It's such a curiosity, you know."

I could see the man fully now. Maybe mid-thirties. It was hard to tell, what with the heavy beard masking his features. There was an odd twinkle in his murky brown eyes. I didn't trust him. Apparently, Ryker didn't either, his fingers tightening on the bow. His voice was deep and gritty as he slowly ground out, "I said don't move."

The man sighed, lowering his hands, then flicked a glance over Ryker's shoulder. Warning bells rang in my head a second before my companion violently shoved me. I fell, my skull bouncing off the ground before I could catch myself. Bright lights obscured my vision but I managed to roll over, pulling a throwing knife from my belt in the process. The bearded man was closing in fast, a hunter's knife in his grimy hand, the tip aimed for Ryker's unprotected back.

I didn't hesitate to throw my knife. The blade glinted through the air before sinking into the man's thigh. He screamed and clutched his leg as he toppled over. I swiveled, looking for more threats. Behind me was another man, crumpled in a heap with an arrow sticking out of his chest. I wrenched my gaze away, fighting a ball of nausea in my gut.

Ryker advanced on the injured bearded man, an arrow aimed at his head. I scrambled to my feet, unsure if I wanted to interfere. Would he kill him? One look at Ryker's murderous expression and I knew he would. I carefully laid a hand on his arm.

"Don't," I warned.

He shook off my touch. Addressing the man, he asked, "Are there more of you?"

The man sneered, his only reply a spray of spittle. Thank the stars, it didn't reach us. Ryker lunged and stomped on the man's ankle. Bone cracked and he shrieked. I gritted my teeth, forcing myself not to say anything. "I'll ask you one more time," Ryker said, his voice smooth, like the calm before a storm. "Are there others?"

"No!" the man spat, panting in agony. His eyes shifted to the right.

"He's lying. There are more." I inspected our surroundings again. That's when I saw the shiny glint of metal spiraling through the air, straight for my head. I jerked out of its path, but not before steel sliced into my neck. I swiped at the cut and sticky wetness coated my fingers. My hand came away red with blood.

Injured already? Ugh.

Ryker pivoted, searching for my attacker. We saw him at

the same time. My eyes widened as Ryker prepared to shoot.

"No!" I grabbed for his wrist and foiled his aim. The arrow sailed harmlessly through the woods. I watched as my attacker took off, quickly disappearing from sight. A deep growl rumbled beside me and I froze, goosebumps pricking my skin. I peered into blazing pale blue eyes.

I willed my hand to stop trembling as I pointed a finger at Ryker. "First, you sound like a dog when you do that. Second, he was just a boy, barely a teenager. He didn't deserve to die."

He batted my finger away and stepped into my personal space. Warm breath hit my cheek as he snapped, "He almost *killed* you. Ever heard of self-preservation? If you don't stick up for yourself in this world, you'll be buried and forgotten before you know what's hit you."

I refused to back down, giving him a glare of my own. "I think your memory may be failing you. Just two weeks ago, I survived all three Trials. I even *killed*." I held in a wince at that, pushing back the guilt threatening to pull me under. "But where does it stop? Should we keep killing until humanity's wiped from this planet?"

He stepped back. "Sometimes I think this world would be a better place without us humans in it."

I blinked, weighing his words. Maybe he was right, but that wasn't the solution.

We both spun at a shuffling noise behind us. The bearded man was trying to sneak away, half crawling, dragging his wounded leg behind him. "Stop," Ryker barked, aiming an arrow at his chest.

The man stilled and held his hands up once again. "I'm no harm to you. It was just the three of us, no more."

"He's telling the truth," I murmured, flicking a glance at Ryker's white-knuckled grip. "We should let him go."

Muddy brown eyes briefly met mine, confused and calculating, before returning to the deadly arrow tip. "Your girl is smart. Maybe you should listen to her. Besides, I realize now that I made a mistake. I didn't see your tattoo earlier. That makes us—"

His last word ended in a wet gurgle. He clutched at the arrow lodged in his neck with fear-filled eyes. I stared as blood spurted from the new wound, for a moment not comprehending. Then I whipped my head toward Ryker. The first thing I noted was his calm, almost bored expression. Then I saw his unloaded bow.

My blood pumped hot and heavy, rage flooding me at the casual way he'd ended a life. I knew that the bearded man would bleed out in seconds, the arrow having pierced an artery. Surging forward, I shoved Ryker's chest. Not expecting my attack, he stumbled. His feet tangled in a tree root and he fell with a thud.

"Why?" I shouted as I kicked his leg. His grunt of pain sent adrenaline coursing through my veins. *Yes, feel the pain, you cold-hearted murderer.* "He was defenseless. Why did you kill him?" I kicked at him again, but this time, he was ready for it.

He grabbed my boot and yanked. My other foot slid out from underneath me. My tailbone took the brunt of the fall and I stilled as sharp rods of pain raced up my spine. *Crap, that hurt.* He was up and out of kicking range before I could refill my lungs.

With crossed arms, he glared down at me like I was a pesky gnat that wouldn't go away. He waited a beat, probably making sure I wouldn't attack him again. I arched a brow and placed one leg over the other as if settling in for a nap. Blowing out a breath, he held my accusatory gaze. "Here's what you need to know before you judge me: I was raised out here up until two years ago. You learn pretty fast that you can't trust anybody, especially the ones who stalk you through the woods."

His words struck a chord deep inside me. They reminded me of my first encounter with the Recruiter Clan eleven years ago. With Bren. Too bad I had been stupid and naive back then, my only thought on gaining a friend.

Ryker continued, jabbing a finger at the two dead bodies. "These men would have stolen our belongings at the very least. Killed us at the very most." His eyes narrowed on mine, darkening. "Then again, there are worse things than death."

My mind blanked. No, I wouldn't think about what *could* have happened if we'd been caught unaware. I might not make it through this mission, otherwise.

"So why couldn't you have just left him? He was injured and alone. There's no way he could have pursued us farther."

Ryker laughed humorlessly, shaking his head. "He's part of a larger group. The one you let get away will seek help. Soon, this place will be crawling with people bent on vengeance, and we don't need anyone describing our faces to them—namely mine. That's why he had to die, and that's why we have to leave. Right now. Let's go."

He repositioned his backpack and bow and stalked off through the woods, once again not bothering to see if I followed. My body remained frozen with indecision. Briefly glancing at the bodies, I steeled my spine, knowing there was no way I could bury them. Hopefully Ryker was right and their people would find them.

Ryker.

Goosebumps skittered down my arms.

Was I really going to follow a murderer?

He was unleashed. Wildly unpredictable. Not much different than the mutated beasts that I feared. Maybe I should grow a healthy fear of him as well. What if I got in his way and he decided to kill me next?

THE STRONG SURVIVE

My neck wouldn't stop bleeding.

I really needed to clean the cut but could barely keep up with Ryker's long strides as it was. We were traveling north again, this time off-road. Normally, I was steady on my feet, but with a hand pressed to my wound and tree roots hidden beneath the thin blanket of snow, I kept tripping.

Ryker stopped abruptly. I watched warily as his hands formed tight fists. Finally, I caught up with him and stood several feet away, just in case. I never knew what to expect of him, so a cautionary distance was a smart idea.

"Take care of your cut," he said. What? I didn't think he'd noticed. "Do it quickly before an animal smells the blood or more of those men find us. We're still in their territory."

A retort was at the tip of my tongue, but it vanished when my brain latched onto that last word. Territory. I unstrapped my backpack and rummaged around for the first aid kit. I hadn't expected to be needing it *this* soon. "Whose territory?"

I didn't think he'd reply, too busy chewing a hangnail on his thumb. But he muttered, "The Recruiter Clan."

My blood ran cold. They were *here?* So close to Tatum City? I supposed it made sense since they worked for Renold, but . . .

The kit almost flew from my grasp as my trembling fingers ripped the top open. Several tries later, I managed to secure a bandage, then shoved the kit into my pack in record time. "Done. Let's go." I stood and began marching north. Ryker didn't follow. I whirled and barked, "What?"

He remained still. Staring at me. Studying. Heat crept up my neck at the bold perusal. "They said you were tough," he finally replied. Was this his version of small talk?

"I guess it depends on your definition of tough," I replied, sarcasm leaking into my tone.

"They also said you were weak," he continued as if I hadn't spoken. "And I'm inclined to agree. You can't be strong without first being smart, and it was a stupid move not to clean your cut before bandaging it. Now, do it again the right way."

He just called me weak. And stupid.

I felt a shift inside of me, a spark that ignited whenever someone dared call me such things. Without the weight of Tatum City on my shoulders, I let the inferno build. Imagined fire bursting from my eyes, hurtling toward Ryker and burning him to cinders. His remains scattered over the snow. How was *that* for weak?

I blinked only to find the rude man still standing. Alive and whole. With a thump, my backpack hit the ground and I bent over it, seeking out the kit once more. *I'm going to flay and roast him.* With my teeth tightly clenched, I jabbed rubbing alcohol into the wound. *Then I'll feed him to the wild animals.*

After that, we traveled in complete silence. The rural landscape—whites and browns and emerald greens—gradually gave way to more and more buildings, mostly pale gray and crumbling. Deserted. Some were taller than Tatum House. The structures were eerie, missing their doors and windows. Creepier still were the large, once-colorful words looping across the exteriors. The sprawling script looked angry, as if warning us away. But their spellings made little sense to me.

B-A-N-K.

G-A-S S-T-A-T-I-O-N.

From the dark interiors, anything—or anyone—could be watching.

Exposed. We were too exposed.

All was silent except for two pairs of boots crunching on snow. The road was uneven where roots pushed apart the broken asphalt. Then there were the abandoned cars. Some were positioned in the middle of the street. When the Silent War happened, the one that destroyed the majority of life a century ago, the cars' owners had probably died right then and there. Every time we passed by one, I quickly peered through its broken windows, expecting to see a skeleton inside. My hands itched, desperate to hold my twin daggers or bow.

"Where is everyone?" I asked Ryker.

He whipped his head around, pinning me with a glare. We both stopped. And had a stare down. *I'm not looking away first, buddy.* After several seconds, he slowly exhaled through his nose and closed his eyes, as if I were the most annoying person on the planet and he couldn't believe his bad luck at getting stuck with me. *Ha! At least I won the staring contest.*

His reply came out hushed; I had to lean forward to catch all the words. "Rule number one out here: don't go looking for other people. If someone approaches you, find a place to hide until they leave. Most people live in groups, and if you stumble on the wrong one, well . . ." He snorted. "Use your imagination."

I stifled the urge to roll my eyes. He sounded just like my mum, spouting off cryptic rules. And then a thought zapped me. "Isn't Renold going to be mad that you killed members of the Recruiter Clan? They work for him after all."

A deep crease bisected his heavy brows. "It doesn't work that way out here. The strong survive. He has no use for the weak." For a split second, I could have sworn blue fire flashed in his eyes, then it was gone. He dragged a hand through his short-cropped hair. "Stay close. It's easy to get lost in this rat-maze city. And don't speak. We don't want any curious—or hostile—visitors." With that, he continued down the street.

I stared at his back. Then stuck out my tongue. He was so bossy. His head turned around yet again and I quickly pulled my tongue in. Those piercing eyes narrowed on my face. Did he catch me mocking him? My brow arched as I dared him to chastise me. He jerked his chin once, ordering me to follow, then strode off.

Two hotheads traveling together through dangerous territory. Nothing disastrous about that combination. No, not at all.

Minutes ticked by, then Ryker veered right, taking us in

a northeasterly direction. Did he have a compass inside his head? I was chewing a hole in my cheek in my quest to keep silent. Questions burned on the tip of my tongue, like how he knew where to go. I couldn't see a single footprint in the snow except ours.

I needed a break soon. My stomach growled, reminding me that it hadn't been fed since early morning. And then I'd thrown everything up when Renold had given me that blue box. I squeezed my eyes shut, willing the image of thumbs rolling across cement to dissipate before I threw up again. My lashes fluttered as I searched for the sun but only found a wall of puffy gray clouds laden with snow. It was mid-afternoon, I guessed.

We weren't making good time. Ryker wove in odd criss-cross patterns, sometimes circling around buildings before heading north again. I remained quiet, his dogged little shadow. If Renold wanted him on this mission, then I would put up with him.

For now.

But if he showed any signs of going rabid wolf on me, I would put him down.

Another half hour trudged by. With every step, my bladder reminded me of its fullness while my stomach reminded me of its emptiness. I opened my mouth to call for a break but no sound came. Warmth pricked my cheeks. For some reason, I was too embarrassed to tell Ryker that I needed to pee.

I cursed my stupidity. We would know all about each other's daily habits in no time, but I didn't want to be the first to admit basic human needs. Ugh. This was so idiotic.

Taking a deep breath, I charged off the path. A large stretch of land opened up, baring dozens of cars positioned in neat rows. I skirted around them instead of cutting through, still creeped out at the thought of skeletons lurking inside. To the left was a long, flat building with several gaping doors devoid of glass. I walked along the windowless side, making for a dense patch of foliage in the back.

The perfect place to relieve my aching bladder.

Just as I waded through the first bush, a guttural voice practically thundered in my ear, "What are you doing?"

In less than a second, my daggers were in my hands, aiming for Ryker. We both froze, eyes locked as the blades pressed against his throat in an X, one of them grazing his black moon and claw tattoo. With my heart tripping wildly, I said, "Let's get one thing perfectly straight: never sneak up on me."

At the threat, Ryker gave me a bored look as if I were holding dull butter knives to his neck. "I'll ask again: what are you doing? Because it looks a lot like you're trying to ditch me and I would heavily advise against that."

"I have to *pee*, you nosy pervert. And why can't I ditch you? Sounds like a solid plan to me. Thanks for the tip."

His lips curled into what could be called a smile. It was scary, whatever it was. "Because I'm your ticket back inside Tatum City, that's why. And I hear there's someone you left behind."

Had he listened in on my last conversation with Renold? Rage stole over me and I growled. His answering snarl almost made me wet myself.

With his face mere inches from mine, I could see his eyes swirling like storm clouds. We stayed like that, seething through bared teeth, forever. In reality, it wasn't more than half a minute, but it felt like time had decided to stop. Lucky me.

Finally, the words almost indecipherable, he ground out, "You scared of me?"

"No," was my immediate reply. Yet my heart flapped like a trapped bird.

He leaned into the blades and whispered, "You should be."

Crap.

With a casual glance at the deadly knives digging into his throat, he pulled away and strode back toward the road. As he turned the building's corner, I heard him say, "You have three minutes. If you're not back by then, I'm coming in after you."

That was so not going to happen.

I took off through the brush, still clutching my daggers in case I ran into something more unpleasant than Ryker—if that was possible. He did scare me, I begrudgingly admitted to myself. He had predatory eyes and they were currently fixated on me.

An ache pulsed over my heart and I rubbed at the spot with my knuckles. I had become so used to Bren watching my back. Now, I was alone and vulnerable. I missed him. His teasing grin, the way he watched me—not like a predator, but like he'd found something special he didn't want to lose. No. *No.*

He couldn't be trusted. Who knew what his mission was and to what ends he'd go to complete it?

And . . .

I might have to kill him.

Focus. Focus, you idiot. If you lose sight of your mission, you'll never see Iris again.

In record time, I finished emptying my bladder. There was no way I'd let Ryker catch me with my pants down. I buttoned them, then dug into my pack for food, unwrapping a chunk of bread. After shoving the bread partway into my mouth, I grabbed my two daggers that I'd stuck into the ground while squatting.

Keep your weapons close. Even closer when you're awkwardly peeing in the woods.

Then I heard a twig snap.

Silently pressing my back to the nearest tree, I listened for further movement. Was that Ryker? Had he been *spying* on me? A blend of anger and humiliation churned in my gut, hot and nauseating. Not a good combination. He would pay for this. I was going to make this mission impossible—

An animalistic growl from behind me sent goosebumps springing over my body. Nope, not Ryker. I was fairly certain of it. I peered around the tree and caught sight of a massive tan paw. Holding in a squeak, I hid behind the trunk once more.

No, no, anything but *that*.

A saber cat.

I hadn't seen the rest of the body, but I couldn't imagine

what else it could be.

Of their own volition, my fingers sheathed the daggers and unslung my bow. Old habits. Instinct. Thank the stars. I had never fought a beast with my knives before. Smarter to stick with what I knew. I waited for the inevitable claw of fear to take hold. There it was, climbing up my throat, settling right behind my tongue. I couldn't swallow, let alone speak. I could barely breathe past the bread still wedged between my teeth.

My hands shook as I prepared to shoot the mystery animal. Would one arrow be enough? Scurrying paws headed in my direction. *No, I'm not ready!* I leapt into the open, prepared to shoot, but the beast was already too close. A furry beige blur. It jumped. Paws as big as my head landed on my chest, and the heavy weight bowled me over backward.

The force of the landing ripped my breath away. I widened my eyes, horrified as sharp teeth descended. The canines should be much longer though. The animal—maybe not a saber cat after all—went for my jugular and I was too shocked to move. I heard the tearing of my fragile flesh as . . .

Wait. It was biting into my bread.

I tried shoving the animal's chest, but it was determined, tugging at the food as my head thrashed side to side. Enraged, muffled growls left my throat as I struggled to push the massive form off me and claim the remaining bit of bread.

In the midst of the chaos, some insane corner of my mind bellowed, *Foul beast! No one takes my food!* My boot lashed out and caught it in the belly. The animal snarled, baring dozens of pointy teeth.

Stars help me.

"Give it to him."

I froze. So did the beast. One of its black ears swiveled toward the sound of Ryker's calm voice. Why wasn't he shooting it? Didn't he see that I was about to become a meal?

"Give him the bread. He's just hungry."

What! Is he serious right now? Yes, the beast wants to feast on my flesh!

As my heart beat out of my chest, I slowly lifted a hand to my mouth. The beast zeroed in on the movement and I waited for its dark maw to chomp down on my fingers. Nothing happened. The animal waited, its yellow eyes filled with hunger and keen intelligence. I pinched the last of the bread between two fingers and offered up the morsel.

Before I could so much as twitch, the food was snatched away. Pressure eased from my chest as the beast stepped to the side, devouring my lunch. I finally took my first full breath. Air shuddered out of me as I realized how close I'd just come to death.

"You injured?" Ryker asked, still looking far too relaxed. He didn't even have his bow ready.

I shook my head. Though, I had no idea because I couldn't feel my limbs. What had just happened? How was I still alive?

He was staring at the beast now, so I did too. It was a . . . dog. A huge one. A mangy one. But still a dog. I wanted to slap my forehead. Then bury myself. What had Ryker thought of my reaction? He better not say anything.

He whistled and the dog's head snapped up.

24

"Are you crazy?" I hissed, and slowly rose to my feet in case he came back for seconds. The animal watched us, ears pricked forward as it finished the bread. From a distance, I noted the paws were more the size of my hands, not my face. I didn't recognize the breed. "What kind of dog is it?"

"Probably a mutt. Looks like a mix of German Shepherd and Alaskan Malamute. Maybe some wolf."

Wolf?

"Why is it not attacking us?"

Ryker shrugged. "I'm guessing he's someone's pet. Or used to be. He could have run away from the Recruiter Clan. Can't blame him."

"You seem to know a lot about dogs. Did you used to have one?"

I was surprised when his eyes shuttered, as if he were reliving a terrible memory. He cleared his throat, wiping away the dark expression. The abrupt noise startled the mutt and he danced farther into the woods, then peeked at Ryker from behind a tree.

"We should go. Nightfall is in less than two hours." With a last glance at the dog, he took off in the opposite direction.

Question and answer time was over. I must have struck a nerve. Did tough guy Ryker Jones have a weak spot for puppies? Nervous laughter pushed at my throat but I didn't let it out. I had a gut feeling that if I poked fun at him, I'd end up slow-roasting on a spit for dinner.

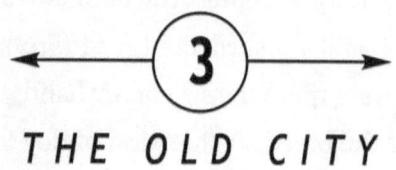

3

THE OLD CITY

We were practically jogging as the gray sky darkened.

Ryker's earlier swagger was gone, and he carried his bow now. We flitted from building to building, sticking to the narrow passes in between and ducking beneath the black windows. It was almost as if he was scared. Well, crap. If Tattoo Boy was afraid, then maybe I should be worried. I touched my daggers' cold hilts, their solidness reassuring.

We should be stopping soon and setting up camp, but he showed no signs of slowing. Finally, I couldn't take it any longer. "Shouldn't we stop for the night? The temperature is dropping and visibility is getting low."

Without comment, he rounded a red brick building. I followed, only to find him hunkered down behind a large, faded blue metal box. I sneered at the stupid color that reminded me of the Tatums, but crouched next to him. When I looked at his face, he was glaring at me. Nothing unusual there. "What did I say about talking?" he hissed. I could tell he wanted to yell instead.

"That you think I do it really well?" In reply, his jaw clenched. *Ugh, he has no sense of humor.* I refused to answer his bossy question. "By the sound of things, we're the only two souls passing through this city. What is there to be afraid of?"

He snorted softly. "Everything. This city comes alive at night. The last place we want to be is within the city's borders when its occupants crawl out of their holes."

Icy goosebumps rippled down my legs.

"If it's so dangerous, then why are we here? Why not skirt around it?"

"Because Bren came through here."

At the sound of Bren's name, my heart decided to skip a few beats. I ignored the feeling as best I could, focusing instead on the skepticism building in my gut. "How do you know?"

"I'm tracking him," he answered, an impatient edge creeping into his voice. Huh. He must not like being questioned.

"Is he leaving a special trail only trackers can see?" I snarked. Because I still hadn't spotted any signs of him.

"Something like that," Ryker said evasively.

My eyes narrowed. "How did you get so good at tracking?"

"How did you get so good at being annoying?"

Oh. Short temper. I curled my lips into a fake smile. "Everyone's got to have a hobby, right?"

His teeth ground together, like he was restraining them from ripping into me. A long sigh fled his nose. "You—"

"What deal did you make with Renold? What's in it for you?" I prepared myself for the inevitable brush-off. No one wanted to reveal their secret plans with the devil.

He laughed drily. "Don't ask questions you don't want the

answers to." And on that cryptic note, he peered around the metal box and tensed, as if listening to noises I couldn't hear. "The city's northeast border is two miles away," he said, his voice extra low. "Beyond that, there's a two-story white house that backs up to the woods. Our destination. If we get separated, meet me there. It's on Orchard Street."

"Separated?" I whisper-yelled. But he didn't respond, already up and moving. My heart thumped double time. Something strange was going on with this city if we were taking these precautions. And how on earth would I find *Orchard Street?*

Ryker made a soft chirping noise. He gestured at me to join him. I did, squinting through the growing gloom as something stirred in the shadows across the snow-dusted street. I strained to see what it was. Ryker tapped my shoulder and I immediately stiffened, whipping my gaze to his.

My breath hitched at the sight of his irises, almost glowing in their intensity. He pressed a finger to his lips and I nodded my understanding. Pointing at me, then up the street, he waggled two of his fingers and mimicked running legs. I frowned and shook my head, carefully backing up a step.

No way was I darting out into the exposed street with an unknown *thing* lurking in the shadows nearby.

Ryker bared his teeth and buried a fist in my coat. I almost squeaked in shock as he hauled me to the edge of the brick building. My stomach roiled a warning. *Danger.* He latched onto my arms, positioning me in front of him. I ached to ram an elbow into his gut and hide behind the blue box once more. "Northeast." His words were barely a wisp of air. "Two miles. White house."

I fiercely shook my head again even as I searched the street for signs of life. None. Only the shifting shadow across from us.

A sound like breaking glass burst the silence and I flinched. "Go," Ryker breathed. What? Blood roared in my ears. He couldn't be serious. "Now!"

With a not-so-helpful nudge, he forced me into the open. Just as I was about to whirl around and demand we stick together, the shadow thing stilled. Adrenaline zinged through me. I bolted. Not back to Ryker, but down the street. My trembling legs pumped as fast as they could while encased in heavy boots and carrying an even heavier backpack. I couldn't tell if I was being followed. My breaths and footfalls were peals of thunder. Too loud. Death tolls. I glanced behind me only to see a figure dart into the street.

It wasn't Ryker.

Air seized in my lungs. My instincts went haywire. *Run. No, hide. Run. Hide!* I kept running. And then the street ended and I wanted to pass out from panic. *Left or right? Left or right!* I went left. Northeast. Two miles. *Don't forget. Don't forget. Don't look back. Don't look . . .*

I looked back.

Another figure joined the first and, with a loud whoop, gave chase. *Stars, help me!*

It was the cackling noise that did me in. It sounded too much like Lars, and the thought of people like him out here, unimpeded by rules, scared me to death. I darted into a door-less building and was immediately doused in darkness. *Bad idea, bad idea, bad idea.* Ice coated my insides as I lurched forward, following through with my bad decision. Too late to turn around. The cackling drew closer. Glass crunched under my leather boots and I grimaced, trying to lighten my tread.

Blood thumped painfully in my skull. I quickly sucked in a breath, then another. The ache lessened. I bumped into a metal structure, maybe shelves, and latched on, using my hands to guide me along the cold length. All too soon, I came to the end. Beyond, nothing but dead air.

Then I realized the cackling and pounding of feet had stopped. I held my breath again, listening. Silence. Utterly . . .

Crunch.

I ducked behind the shelves and squeezed the bottom one until my fingers ached. Two human silhouettes framed the building's entrance, blocking my only way out. Trapped. I was trapped. Oh stars.

"You sure he went in here?" a deep male voice asked.

"Of course I'm sure," a tenor male voice snapped in reply, then cackled. "What, you don't trust me?"

"I trust that you'd dump rat poop into my food, Skervvy."

A man—I assumed Skervvy—guffawed. "Oh, ye of little imagination. I'd slip strychnine in your water. Much more en-tertaining."

"You're sick, Skerv dog. Now stop your yammering and find our target."

The taller, skinnier man gave a dog-like yip, then slunk

forward, glass grinding under his shoes. He sucked in a lengthy inhale. "Oh man, Thane. This one's fresh! Smells like snow and . . . flowers? Maybe apple blossoms. Do you think . . . ?" He hooted. "It's a girl, I'm sure of it! I get credit this time. You got the last one."

Thane, the stockier of the two, snorted, then shuffled farther into the darkness. "Doesn't work that way, dog. Whoever presents her to the boss gets the reward."

"Do you think she escaped?"

"What? No. You think one of those weak little slips could best one of us?"

"Hey, never underestimate determination and the wily ways of women."

Thane grumbled in agreement.

Something struck the metal shelving I still gripped; the friction jolted through my fingers. I curled into a tighter ball and slowly drew my right dagger. How could he smell me? I cursed myself for indulging in a hot, scented bath this morning. Had it only been a handful of hours since I'd mourned my fate of being stuck inside Tatum City? And now . . .

No. Despite the dangers, I was still glad to be outside of those toxic walls. The men were arguing in earnest now, their playful banter replaced with vile threats.

"I'm warning you, man. I know where you get your water."

"I swear, if you touch my water supply, Skervvy, I'll cut off your—"

"Shh! Did you hear that?"

Silence. Painful, ear-splitting silence.

Cackling laughter made me jump. "She's scared out of her mind. Her heart is hammering like a wee rabbit's."

"Which direction?"

More silence. I willed my heart to stop beating.

"Left. Toward the back."

"Divide and conquer?"

My heart jack-knifed in my chest.

"Divide and conquer," Skervvy agreed. "But she's mine, man. Fair is fair. I sniffed her out."

"We'll see," was the only reply as, to my left, Thane crept into the gloom and out of sight.

The faintly glowing and now unobstructed exit beckoned as the men descended, slowly yet surely boxing me in. But maybe I was faster than them. Maybe I could slip down the middle and bolt through the door and . . . and . . .

The wait was killing me. *Now. Go now!* I jumped up and hurtled for the front end of the building, hoping, pleading for a stroke of luck. For a—

A heavy weight tackled me to the floor. Pain zipped through my knees and hand as I braced against the fall. I whipped my dagger back and felt the blade connect. A man screamed—I didn't know which one. "She's armed!"

Skervvy.

I jerked an elbow into his face. He reared back, cursing up a storm, and I wriggled free. On my feet again, I staggered away, all of my focus on that patch of dying light. Almost there. Almost there. Almost—

From the left, hands shoved me. I collided with the metal shelves, and the world tipped. No, the structure was tipping. No, no, no! Gravity pulled me down. As heavy metal crashed with a resounding clang, my body bounced off the shelves. I wheezed in air, momentarily stunned. My coat had cushioned the impact, but I knew my ribs would be sporting a new bruise.

A set of hands—no doubt Thane's—grasped my backpack and yanked me upright. I clenched my teeth against the pain and brought my dagger up, but he whirled us around before I could thrust it in his face. He was behind me now, tightly gripping both my arms. Rage stole over me, heat flaring up and down my body.

"Drop the weapon, missy, or I'll have to hurt you," he purred in my ear, like he would enjoy doing so.

I stared at that patch of freedom, so close yet so far away, and let the dagger slip through my fingers. It clattered at my feet.

"Good. Now, don't mind me," he said, wrenching my arms back and gripping both wrists with one large hand, "but I'll need to search you for more weapons." And I let him. I remained perfectly still as his meaty paw, brazen and groping, trailed down my front. I didn't twitch a muscle as that hand traveled down, down, brushing my thigh. As his chest pressed up against my backpack, as his breath stirred my hair . . .

I struck.

My skull plowed into his nose with a sickening crunch. Thane shrieked and staggered back, dropping my wrists.

I scooped up my dagger, then charged for the exit. Just five more steps. Four. Three. Two. A sharp bite of pain lanced through my calf and I stumbled out of the building.

I didn't stop to check the injury. As I veered left down the deserted street, Skervvy's voice rang out in an eerie singsong, "I know your scent, girly! You can't hide from me for long. I'll find you!" His cackling laughter was the last thing I heard.

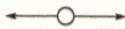

The night was pitch black. No sign of the moon.

If it weren't for the snow, I'd be walking blind. The faintly illuminated ground allowed me to pick my way through the city without smashing my head into buildings. Hours. It took me hours to reach the northeast borderline. Ryker had been right: the city came alive at night. On occasion, I'd see an orange flickering ball. I learned to avoid them at all costs. Black shapes hovered over those orange flames like bugs around a lightbulb.

More than once, a *pop pop pop* noise would rend the air. It had been over eleven years since I'd last heard that sound, but there was no mistaking the gunshots. I had briefly stopped to check on my wound—Skervvy had nicked my calf with a blade—but I didn't bandage the cut. I couldn't. The crazed man's final words batted at my mind and spurred me onward. *I'll find you!* I believed him.

Now, I stared with uncertainty at a rural stretch of weathered houses. I figured the faded green signs with words on them were street names, but I couldn't recall which one Ryker had told me to find. My heart sank. Besides, I could barely read, never having received more than a seven-year-old's rudimentary knowledge of spelling. Longer, complex words tripped me up. I was lost and the air was frigid. A headache had bloomed behind my eyes from all the chattering my teeth were doing.

Maybe this was my chance to be free of Ryker. He'd probably get me killed anyway. He had shoved me at those up-to-no-good hoodlums and then took off for who-knew-where. Somehow, I had to track Bren on my own. I would find him, convince him to complete his mission, then head back to Tatum City. To Iris, my sister. I couldn't let Renold have her. He would destroy her. She wasn't like me, raging and fighting to break free of injustice. Iris was soft-spoken and gentle. Meek. She wouldn't survive his torture techniques.

Resolve filled me. It warmed my insides, giving me the boost of strength I needed to turn from the row of houses and—

I came face to face with Ryker. His glaring eyes startled me so badly, a squeak slipped past my lips. He clamped a hand over my mouth too late. I flung his hand away, snarling, "Don't. Touch. Me."

His gaze narrowed even more, running along the length of me. I fought the urge to cross my arms. Those unnerving eyes latched onto my wounded leg before returning to my face. "Where were you going?"

I gestured at the houses. "I forgot which street the white

house was on." Better to admit that than my altered mission of excluding him.

"No, you were turning away. You were going to ditch me."

"So what if I was? You're the one who ditched *me* earlier."

He forced out a clipped sigh before reaching into his pocket. I stiffened, instinctively grasping my daggers' hilts. "I didn't ditch you. It was a test. And you failed."

Before I could see what he pulled out of his pocket, before I could make sense of the determined look on his face, a jolt of white hot agony streaked up my spine. It speared through my neck and bounced around in my skull. My body locked. Shook. I couldn't stop it. I couldn't move. The sensation was like being struck by lightning. Like being zapped with . . .

Ah crap.

My eyes rolled upward against my wishes. Helpless. I was helpless as my body lost control. Helpless as I tipped sideways, as I fell. Down, down . . . But I didn't smack into the snow.

No. Ryker caught me.

Then all went black.

4

RENOLD'S ORDERS

Click.

Click.

Click.

The metallic sound woke me. Was someone trying to unlock my dorm door? Out of habit, I reached for the knife underneath my pillow. Or tried to. My arms wouldn't cooperate. Neither would my wrists. They were being restrained.

As the realization sunk in, my eyes popped open. I waited for my surroundings to take on familiar shapes, but . . .

I wasn't in my barracks dorm room.

The room's walls weren't cement but a dingy, flaking yellow plaster. I quickly looked around—the action drove pinpricks of pain through my skull. My wrists were tied to the wood-slatted headboard of the bed I lay on. Bed. I was in a stranger's bed.

My breathing sped up. *Think, think, think. Where am I?* Renold would never allow a room in Tatum House to fall into such disrepair. There weren't even curtains. I inhaled sharply. The windows were boarded up. Trapping me. Making me a prisoner. Always a prisoner.

A scream got stuck in my throat. *Don't alert the*

kidnappers, you idiot. Free yourself! I fisted my hands, then pulled and twisted and yanked against my restraints. The delicate skin of my wrists burned, but I didn't stop. I couldn't. I had worked too hard, day in and day out for eleven years to contend in the Trials. No one would take away my chance at freedom. *No one.* Not even—

I gasped and a tear slipped down my cheek as memories came to me.

Bren. The Trials. My sister—Iris. My new title, Elite Guardian.

The mission.

My ultimatum.

It had already happened.

I was . . . I was somewhere else now . . .

"Took you long enough to wake up."

My head jerked toward the room's open door and there stood Ryker, holding a gun. His thumb repeatedly flicked a lever on its dull black side. *Click. Click. Click.* I doggedly tracked the movement as my brain tried to make sense of everything. At the next flick, it all clicked into place. Especially the memory of an electrical charge rendering me unconscious.

I suddenly couldn't breathe past the raging fire in my chest. "What did you do?" I rasped. My throat was dry and my tongue felt three sizes too large. I spoke anyway, more forcefully this time. "What did you *do?*"

He leaned against the doorframe. "What I had to. You were going to jeopardize the mission by sneaking off without me, so I followed Renold's orders."

I barked a laugh. "Orders? *Orders?* And what, pray tell, are these orders? Because Bren has an even greater lead now and my *orders* are to find him, not pander to your trust problems—" I cut off my tirade as he stalked toward me with the gun. My limbs shook at his menacing expression, one that had warned me again and again not to get in the way.

And here we were, me at his mercy as he took my measure and found me no doubt annoying and more trouble than I was worth. This was it. The end of my existence. I consoled myself with the thought that I had stepped into the outside world one last time. But that meant I couldn't save Iris. My eyes started to burn and I squeezed them shut. Ryker wouldn't see me cry. Or beg. Never that. I waited for cold metal to touch my skin. Waited for that thumb to flick off the safety.

Waited.

"What are you doing?"

I squinted an eye open. He was hovering over me like a hulking shadow, but the gun was gone. My gaze jumped to his. Was he going to strangle me with his bare hands then? Maybe he found me so annoying that killing me so intimately would give him lasting peace.

"Did you think my orders were to kill you?" he asked, his voice a touch less gravelly.

"Uh." *Should I answer that?* "Since you always look ready to kill me, yes, yes I did."

His face didn't change, but he tensed. So tense that I wondered if he was still breathing. Then, "My orders are to keep you alive. I told you that before. I don't have time to chase after you *and* Bren, so I was given permission to zap you if you strayed from the mission."

I ground my teeth together as I struggled with my need to spew sarcasm. "How does it work?"

"What?"

"The electrocution!" I shouted. So much for keeping calm. "You didn't touch me or point a volt gun at me. How does it work?"

"Keep your voice down," he snapped. I continued to glare at him silently. A moment later, his brows pulled together. "You don't know about the implant?"

Implant? I dug my nails into my palms. *Wake up. Wake up! You have to be dreaming!* I inhaled slowly. "What are you talking about?"

His expression morphed into shadow as he looked at the floor. "You, me, and Bren. We have chips lodged in the back of our necks. Practically fused to the bone, actually. They're insurance so we'll come back to the city when we've completed our missions. If we don't, the chips are installed with a kill switch. Your father wanted me to use the electricity on you as a warning. To remind you of your duties in case you were thinking of running away."

I gaped, completely struck mute.

Stars. There was no end to this madness. No escape. I was a ticking time bomb and Renold the detonator.

"Untie me," I demanded softly. My stomach lurched and I grimaced as a rush of saliva filled my mouth. "Untie me!"

Ryker's eyes were locked on mine now, boring holes into

my retinas as he gauged my sanity—and probably wondered whether I'd make a break for it despite what he'd just said. But he slowly leaned over me and unstrapped one of my wrists, then the other. I was off the bed in a flash, staggering for a dim corner as my gorge rose. A dry heave left me. Another and another as my body trembled and swayed. I placed a hand on the wall as my knees threatened to buckle.

When had Renold implanted a chip in my neck? It was too awful to think about, but I racked my memory anyway. I thought back to all the times I'd met with him in the big house's eerie sub-basement. Recalled every single torture device he'd used on my body—whips, electric rods, needles.

Needles!

Jabbed into my neck with such force, I'd almost passed out on more than one occasion. But there was that time, a couple months before I contended in the Trials, when a particular needle had felt close to hitting bone. It had left my neck sore and bruised for days afterward. I stopped breathing.

Stars above.

"The trouble is, I don't know if I can trust you," he'd said to me all those months ago. My heart hammered. Had he known? Had he foreseen this outcome? Had he . . . planned for it? Insurance. He had assured my loyalty by stripping away my choice. Either I did what he asked or he would kill me.

The discolored wall before me blurred.

"We don't have time for this." Ryker's sharp voice snapped me back to the present. "We've lost several more hours, thanks to your inability to follow simple instructions. You have ten minutes to pull yourself together and meet me outside. The bathroom's through there. It has running water."

I turned in time to see Ryker gesturing at a closed door across the room. Then he was gone, taking that ugly black gun with him. Through a clenched jaw, I hissed. Good riddance. After grabbing my backpack and a small electric lantern next to the bed, I stalked to the room's closed door and ripped it open. Sure enough, a dingy sink and toilet greeted me. There was even a mirror. I glanced at my foggy reflection.

Ugh. My dark auburn hair—almost black in the weak lighting—stuck out in a hundred different directions, having long since escaped the confines of its single braid. My pale skin was smudged with dirt, probably from running my hands along those grimy metal shelves. I finally looked at my eyes. *Her* eyes. My mum's. And now, they reminded me of Iris's, too.

My chest began to ache and I quickly shoved aside images of their haunting faces. I had a mission. Thinking about either of them right now would do me no good. I got to work cleaning myself up as best I could. The sink water ran brown for a full two minutes. While I applied a fresh bandage to the cut on my neck, a small, niggling voice whispered in my head, *Do you miss Tatum City yet? The comforts of hot water, a warm bed, and food. Familiar dangers that you know how to avoid. Turn back.*

I shook my head.

Turn back.

"No," I whispered, snapping the first aid kit shut.

This mission will be the death of you, Lune Avery. You

don't know a thing about surviving the outside world, the voice, born of my fears and self-doubts, insisted.

"I don't care," I hissed, even as my stomach twisted. "I'm not going back. Not until I complete this mission."

"Who are you talking to?"

I squeaked and whirled at the same time. Ryker stood just shy of the doorway, cautiously peering into the bathroom as if expecting to find an intruder. I glared at him, hoping he hadn't heard the pathetic noise I'd made. "I'm not talking to anyone. Are you hearing things? If your sanity is slipping, it's probably not safe for you to be out here. Maybe you should go back to Tatum City."

He straightened. His upper lip curled, revealing clenched teeth. "Nice try. But you'll have to do a lot better than that. Time's up, we're moving out." When he didn't retreat—just stared at me like a creep—I huffed and gathered my supplies. It was then, as I found my boots at the foot of the bed and started putting them on, that Ryker's actions fully hit me.

I yanked up my pant leg and, sure enough, the cut Skerrvy had given me was bandaged. My spine went rigid and I jerked around to face him. "You knock me out, half undress me, then touch my body while I'm lying unconscious?" Blood roared in my ears as I approached him. He had no right. *No right.* I stopped near enough that I could have easily rammed a knee into his groin. Somehow, I managed to keep both feet planted on the floor. "This won't happen again. You do *not* have permission to touch me, no matter the circumstances."

His watchful eyes took in my close proximity with cool

detachment. Maybe he didn't care about his manly jewels. "Two things: don't exaggerate and don't tell me what to do. You may have the superior title but 'Elite Guardian' means nothing out here. Your ability to *survive* is the only thing that matters from this point forward. Besides, your puny little self should be grateful that I cleaned out an incredibly dirty cut and kept you from frostbite."

"Grateful?" I snarled, fisting my hands. "*Puny?* Who do you think you are, bossing me around? What gives you the right?"

Something dangerous glinted in those eerie eyes. "I am your *Keeper,* so I have every right. That is *my* title—my duty and mission. That's why I'm out here, my tracking and survival experience aside. But here's the thing, *Princess.* I don't want to be out here. So go ahead. Keep complaining, keep running, keep slowing us down. Fail your mission. The sooner you do, the sooner we can go back."

A weight pressed down on my lungs, robbing me of air. A thousand biting words wanted to spit from my mouth, but in the end, all I could manage was a low whisper laced in warning. "Don't call me princess. Ever."

He leaned forward into my personal space. "Be a good girl and I'll think about it." In the next blink, he was halfway across the room. Right before exiting, he threw over his shoulder, "I'm graciously giving you an extra two minutes, then I'm leaving, with or without you. You'll regret it if it's the latter."

For a full minute, I stared at the spot he'd vacated. My thoughts whirled. Digested all that he'd said. We weren't just two hotheads unwittingly thrown together anymore. No. This was more than that. So much more. This was personal.

And before this mission was over, I really was going to kill him.

It was only midday on the second day of our mission when everything screeched to a halt.

"What is it?" I asked a crouched Ryker. He was staring at a twin set of strange markings in the snow that were several inches wide. The curious bumpy pattern stretched along the northeastern road up a hill and out of sight.

He swore softly. "Our target's not on foot anymore."

A flutter of panic churned in my stomach. "So what is *Bren* traveling on then?"

He shoved to his feet and followed the markings down the hill, not up. I didn't question him despite my burning curiosity. He was the tracker, not me. About a dozen yards off the road, hidden by trees and bushes, was a windowless wooden shed. Locked. Large boot prints trod the snow around the weathered structure. Bren's, I guessed. "Some kind of ATV," Ryker muttered, fiddling with the lock.

"Is that a mutated beast?"

He dropped the lock and glanced at me with an unreadable expression. "I forgot how painfully ignorant you insiders are."

He went on to explain what an all-terrain vehicle was but

I didn't hear him—the blood pounding in my ears drowned the words out. "You know nothing," I hissed.

Ryker stopped. His brows inched upward. "Is that so?"

"Yes, that's so. You spout the importance of details yet you think I'm an insider. Maybe I don't know anything about this contraption Bren has found, but I'm far from ignorant. I'm not like *them*." I was saying too much. I'd been doing that a lot the last few months and doing so had only heaped trouble on my head. But I was sick of the silence. Sick of the lies. Sick of people thinking I was a Tatum City Elite.

I expected him to sneer and stalk off. Instead, he crossed his arms and began speaking again, the tone of his voice almost smug. "I know you were born on the outside. I know you were kidnapped. I know you have unique abilities. I also know the Supreme Elite physically beats you. I know that you fear him more than you fear the mutated beasts that roam the land."

Every single word was a blow to my chest. I staggered back, struggling for air. How? *How?* He knew everything. My eyes widened. Stars above, did he know Iris was my sister, too?

His mouth tipped cruelly. "As I said, I'm your Keeper. And you're an ignorant insider because you are completely oblivious to the world around you and what is happening in it. You think the Elite Trials mattered?" He scoffed. "I failed the Rasa Rowe Trial, thanks to you, and that is why I'm out here *babysitting*. In the larger scheme of things, the Trials are simply a test of your abilities. Now get off your high horse, Princess. You're *exactly* like them."

I was being cracked wide open. My life, the deepest, darkest parts of me, were on full display. And he mocked me. Shamed me. Even blamed me. A hot ball of fury lodged in my throat. I envisioned two onyx horns sprouting from his skull, his eyes bleeding black. Ryker was the devil. Any moment now, he would throw back his head and boom with laughter. I was a bug beneath his boot, and with great pleasure, he squashed my body, splattering my innards and dissecting my limbs.

With a roar, I charged him. I aimed for his legs, but he wasn't as tall as Bren—more compact, muscular—and didn't tip over backward. He latched onto my backpack and flung me off him. I bounced off the shed but was already whirling with a throwing knife, my sights set on his heart. Then I froze.

The barrel of a gun was aimed at my head.

"Go ahead. Throw the knife. It'll be the last thing you do." His voice was deathly soft. The gun clicked.

I didn't lower my arm. "What will Renold do if you kill me? I might be *ignorant* but I get the impression that I'm needed. If you fail *your* mission, what are the consequences, huh?"

That deadly black weapon trembled ever so slightly. *Got you.*

"We can't kill each other," he bit out. "If we do, we'll be stripped of our titles. All deals will be forfeit. We'll spend the rest of our days rotting in a jail cell. Or worse."

Neither of us moved. We carefully took each other's measure. Would I really throw the knife? Would he really pull the trigger? Or were we bluffing? I wasn't entirely sure on either count. All I knew was that he had thoroughly wedged himself beneath my skin and I desired nothing more than to gouge him out.

"We'll never survive out here if we're constantly at each other's throats," I began. "Let's call a truce, at least until we find Bren."

The gun wavered some more, then vanished as he tucked it out of sight. "Truce."

That's all he said before turning on his heel and stalking back toward the road. I sheathed my knife and trudged after him. I didn't know what his plan was now that Bren had an ever bigger lead, and I didn't ask. The questions could wait. My gut told me that if I opened my mouth anytime soon, he would only further insult me. And my exposed heart couldn't handle anymore at the moment.

Why did he know so much about me? A sick feeling slithered in my stomach. Was he watching me? Stalking me? I was following him into the wilderness, alone and far from civilization. And not only did he have a gun but the ability to electrocute me on a whim. I touched the smooth skin at the base of my neck, probing, searching for a lump. Nothing. Nothing at all. Whatever had been injected in me was beyond my reach.

With Ryker several strides ahead, I allowed a handful of tears to trickle down my face, then silently brushed all evidence of my misery away.

TRACKER

"Keep up!"

I clenched my teeth for the umpteenth time. He was the bossiest person I'd ever met. "Barking won't get me to move any faster. You do realize I'm carrying a heavy backpack, right?"

"Pretend I'm Elite Instructor Drake then."

My eyes narrowed on the back of Ryker's head, and I caught a glimpse of his black tattoo before it slipped beneath his coat. I squinted some more. "Nope. Not working. Your swagger is all wrong. Too preening."

He sighed his irritation, then jabbed a finger at the sky. "You see that?"

My gaze swept upward. "Yes. It's gray and boring. Thanks for the sightseeing tour."

The sound of him growling under his breath made me smirk. *How does it feel to have me underneath your skin? Annoying? Good.* After a few more steps, he replied, "The weather is about to worsen. By nightfall, it'll be snowing again, harder this time. The tracks will be buried."

Oh. I picked up the pace without comment.

Sure enough, the first snowflake splattered on my cheek

an hour later. Surrounded as we were by oak and pine trees with no buildings in sight, worry squirmed in my gut. The temperature would plummet soon and my toes were already chilled to the bone, along with my fingers, despite the woolen socks and gloves I wore. I doubted Ryker had another safe house stashed away out here somewhere.

Or did he? I didn't know a thing about him, I realized, which made the worry in my gut writhe. He was right about one thing: I should have spent more time studying my enemies. Instead, I had allowed Bren to distract me, to dominate my waking and sleeping hours. To wrap himself around my heart. And now . . .

And now I was weak. My lips pursed. I wouldn't let my guard down again. The cracks in my heart couldn't be healed, but I could fill them in with steel. I imagined the hot molten element settling into the vulnerable dips and valleys, swallowing them whole, drowning out the pain and suffering. Leaving the organ stronger. Harder. Impenetrable.

Bren wouldn't get in again. He couldn't be trusted. A heart shouldn't be given to an untrustworthy person. The more distance I created between us, the more I could face my upcoming mission, whatever that entailed.

But could I really kill him? I might be able to remove him from my heart, but the thought of Brendan Bearon removed from this world sent a pulsing ache through my chest.

Ryker suddenly broke into a steady jog.

"What are you doing?" I yelled, launching after him. I wouldn't be able to maintain this pace for long. I wasn't used to this form of exercise.

He angled his head so I could better hear him over our pounding feet and shuffling gear. "We need to cover as much ground as possible before the tracks completely disappear. We can rest later." With that, he jogged faster.

In a matter of minutes, gusts of cold air heaved in and out of my lungs. I couldn't control the wheezing noise that left my mouth between breaths. But I wouldn't stop. Ryker was the key back to my sister, and I wouldn't give him an excuse to call me puny again. Soon, though, I fell behind. He was but a blurry speck on top of the hill. *Another* hill. I glanced behind me, belatedly realizing why this trek was wearing me down so fast. We were climbing. As in up-a-mountain climbing.

Ryker dropped out of view as he crested the hill, and that's when it happened. My boot caught on something hidden. I pitched forward, nosediving into the snow. Stunned, I laid there for several seconds. Icy wetness trickled down my neck and bit at my cheeks. Still, I didn't move.

Then I snickered. I must look ridiculous, so I chortled harder until my body shook with laughter.

"Are you injured?"

I raised my head, clumps of snow falling off my forehead as I peered up at a barely-winded Ryker. Ugh. So not fair. I attempted a straight face before answering, "No."

He frowned. "Then what are you doing?"

I flashed an impish grin, then pushed my arms and legs through the thickening snow. "Making a snow angel."

His expression was perfect. Slack-jawed and bug-eyed.

If the man looming above me had been Bren, he would have joined in, but apparently Ryker didn't do snow angels. He reached down and hauled me up by my fur-lined hood. When I was on my feet, he pulled me close, close enough that his warm breath fanned my cheeks as he snarled, "What is wrong with you?"

I shoved his chest and he released me. "What's wrong with *you?*"

He looked to the sky and growled through his teeth like an animal. Payback was all too easy with him. "You're going to screw up this mission, I know it. The Supreme Elite never should have allowed you to step foot outside those walls."

I crossed my arms. "Are you questioning the Supreme Elite's decision?"

In the fading light, his piercing eyes shone brightly. He knew what I was doing. There was no way he could argue that point. "I'm questioning your intelligence. It's only a matter of time before your dumb luck runs out. And I'm not going to take the blame when you wind up with a frostbitten finger or nose. You do realize if that happens, you have to cut off the dead tissue?"

At that, my whole body shivered. I shoved my fists into my armpits for warmth. "Don't worry your inflated head about me. I can take care of myself."

He snorted but didn't comment, even though I could tell he wanted to. Once more, he trekked up the hill. I paid more attention to my steps this time, placing each foot in the boot prints he made. To keep from thinking of the chill sinking deeper into my skin with each passing minute, I focused on the mission. My task was easy enough, in theory, and so was Ryker's. Find Bren, make sure he completed his mission, then return to the city. But so many things could go wrong.

"What is Bren's mission?" I asked a brooding Ryker. His annoyance at my earlier antics was all too obvious. We had lost several more minutes of daylight, and the tracks were no longer crisp but fuzzy around the edges.

"I don't know," he grumbled, like the not-knowing annoyed him further. Maybe he wasn't used to being left in the dark. I was more than used to it.

"And why would Renold need me to kill Bren if he doesn't complete this mystery mission? Can't he just activate the chip's kill switch?"

Ryker shook his head, and I thought he muttered, "So ignorant."

"What was that? Did you just say I'm brilliant for coming up with such an astute observation?"

He rolled his shoulders back as if trying to shrug the questions off. But he answered, albeit mockingly, "I'm assuming you don't know what your Elite Guardian title means?" Before I could come up with a witty reply, he continued. "The Supreme Elite is entrusting you with the safety of Tatum City. But first, you must prove your loyalty."

What do I value more than anything?

"So you're saying this is a test? Of my loyalty?" A test to see if I would do my duty and return, or run away with Bren. Because he knew. Renold knew how I felt about the giant idiot with honey-gold eyes. *Used to. Used to feel. Not anymore.*

"Maybe you're not completely stupid," Ryker said.

"Thanks. It's unfortunate that you are," I shot back. Ugh. He brought out the worst in me.

An hour later, the tracks were gone. Still, we pressed onward and upward. My calves burned, especially the wounded one, and my toes were numb. But I didn't worry about frostbite. Not yet. My stomach was an empty pit, though. I was used to two, sometimes three solid meals a day, and I'd barely eaten more than bread for a day and a half now. And yet, the thought of Ryker's insults if I complained kept my mouth shut.

You cannot break me. You cannot break me.

So busy chanting, I didn't see him stop. I plowed into his back. Again. Traveling on an incline, the action knocked me backward. My butt plopped into the snow. I was too tired to care how stupid I looked as I crawled to my feet again, brushing wet snow from my backside. Great. Now I couldn't feel my butt.

Ryker didn't even glance at me. Jerk. "We should set up camp," he said. I stared, waiting for instructions. When he continued to scout our surroundings in silence, I offered to collect some sticks for a fire. A few steps later, he halted me with two terrible words: "No fire."

I whirled. "What? We'll freeze!"

"Not if you take the proper precautions. It won't be pleasant, but we can't risk a fire and attract unwanted attention. There are too many unknowns out here. Things that are hungry and wouldn't think twice about slaughtering us to get at our food supply. And that's just the animals."

Stars.

"Want to head back yet?" he taunted.

The question set my blood to simmering. "Not unless I'm in a body bag."

"I could scrounge one up if you'd like."

"Don't bother. I wouldn't want to inconvenience you some more. So what's the plan?"

He pointed to a small clearing off the road. "See that outcropping of rock?"

I squinted into the gloom and pelting snow. "No. Do you have night vision like Bren?"

At that, he stiffened. "How much did he tell you?"

Goosebumps raised on top of my already goose-bumped flesh. "Not nearly enough."

His shoulders relaxed a fraction of an inch. "I can see better than you, smell better than you, hear better than you, but more importantly, I am faster and far stronger than you. That's all you need to know."

As he headed for the outcropping, a thousand words pleaded to be expelled. Only a handful made it out at a soft whisper. "You have a very large ego."

"Heard that."

"Which must mean you have a very small—"

His narrowed eyes landed on mine. The words died on my tongue. "The sooner you set up your tent, the sooner you can feel your toes again."

I blinked. How did he know my toes were numb?

Anyone could have guessed that. And tent? There was no way I had a tent in my backpack. I decided to check anyway, just so he wouldn't call me stupid again. My numb fingers fumbled at the straps, then struggled with the zipper. Finally, I rummaged around inside. Water bottle, food, spare clothing, first aid kit, small electric lantern, sleeping bag. Bren's book.

I shoved that to the very bottom of the pack. But no tent. Just a silver wad of slippery fabric. I pulled the mystery item out and held it up. "This?"

"Let me guess. You don't know how to open it." With that, a silver single-person tent snapped open in front of him, making me jump. Impossible. How did the material become so rigid?

As my gloved fingers poked and prodded at the unassuming fabric, I heard Ryker get to his feet. No, no, no. I tugged on it, first gently, then with a vengeance. He was *not* going to help me. I could open a dumb tent.

"Snap it." He was hovering over me now with arms crossed. I slapped at the material and he groaned. "Like this." As he bent over to grab the infuriating thing, I yanked it out of reach. In doing so, the tent magically popped open. Right into his face.

He grunted as the inflated material forced him back. And then the most amazing thing happened. He tumbled into the snow. I held my breath, having no idea what he would do. His expression shifted from surprise, to horror, to—

Uh oh. He was gearing up for a "let's insult Lune" moment. I beat him to it. "Do they put labels on these things?

56

Like, *Warning: don't put your face in the tent while it opens.* My mum said they used to for the stupid people who couldn't think for themselves. You know, before the Silent War . . ."

"You think this is funny?" Steam practically shot out of his nostrils as he picked himself up and knocked the snow off his pants.

I shook my head. "Yes." Did I just say that out loud? Oops. I bit the inside of my cheek.

"If you think you're so smart, you should have no problem fending for yourself the rest of the night. Have at it." With that, he grabbed his backpack and strode to his tent, disappearing from view.

Ouch. I was on my own.

After zipping myself inside the makeshift shelter, I flipped on the lantern. When I discovered that its yellow body emitted a weak strain of warmth, I tore off my gloves and wrapped my hands around it, moaning softly. So good. Soon, sharp pricks of pain jabbed my fingers as feeling rushed back into them. Not so good.

I laid out my sleeping bag and tucked myself inside—boots, coat, and all. They were damp, but I couldn't bear the thought of shedding any layers.

As I sat there chewing on dried meat, a bone-deep exhaustion hit me. What with being zapped unconscious, sliced in the neck and leg, and wading through miles of snow uphill, my body had reached its limit. But when I laid down, even with the warm lantern propped close to my face, I couldn't stop shivering long enough to drift asleep. I also couldn't stop thinking about predators lurking just beyond the tent. What if a saber cat, my oldest fear, found me while I was sleeping?

An hour passed. Maybe two. A headache pulsed at my temples as my teeth chattered incessantly. My whole body shook, no matter how tightly I curled into a ball. Outside the tent, frozen tree limbs clacked together, sounding eerily similar to twigs snapping underfoot. And so, I spent my first real night in the wild awake, cursing Ryker, hating Renold, and blaming Bren for my pathetically miserable state of existence.

Worst of all though, I wanted to go back.

I wanted to go back to Tatum City.

"How'd you sleep?" The taunt raised my epic crankiness level.

"Screw you," I said, my voice flat, toneless. I wrestled with the tent, trying to wad it into a messy ball. From the corner of my eye, I watched Ryker break his tent down and tuck it neatly inside his pack. My lips tightened. I wasn't going to ask for his help. Last night had been the most miserable experience of my life. I could barely stay awake and the headache still pounded unmercifully, further sapping my energy.

Ryker had no idea he stood on incredibly thin ice. I was in no mood for games this morning. At least the clouds had stopped spitting snow and the sun decided to show. But the light only magnified the ache behind my eyes.

"Bend it."

"I'll bend *you*," I muttered.

He huffed an irritated sigh, then stomped over to me. I was too numb, too slow to yank the tent out of reach. He took it from my floundering fingers and twisted the two sides in opposite directions. Like magic, the rigid material deflated, allowing him to crumple the sleek fabric into his palm. "See? Bend it. Remember for next time."

Next time. Right. How was I going to endure another night of this miserableness?

A shiver racked me from head to toe. I winced.

"Take a pain med. Here." He tossed a rattling object at me. They gave him a whole bottle? My eyes slowly slid to his—it took me a moment to focus. He was studying me neutrally. Not concerned. Not mocking. Just . . .

My chin jutted out. "No."

"Why not?"

"Because I don't need it. A headache doesn't warrant treatment."

He snorted. "You insiders are so lame."

I stilled. Even the blood in my veins slowed. "Excuse me?"

A corner of his mouth twitched. "You heard me. Your ideals are pointless. Why suffer needlessly? For pride and glory? You're a bunch of arrogant fools."

I bared my teeth and hissed, "I'm *not* one of them!"

"Then stop acting like one."

"I'm not—" I growled in frustration, which only sent my head spinning. "Fine. You know what? I'll take a stupid pill."

His mouth twitched some more right before he turned away and began strapping on his gear. "Make that two pills or you'll never get through the day. We won't be taking breaks. I can only scent his trail for so long before it grows cold."

Scent his trail? Is this guy for real?

"Are you part bloodhound?"

He coughed, shaking his head. "I'm no more dog than you are."

There were *so* many things I wanted to say about that comment, but this conversation was worsening my headache. Minutes later, we were all set to go, and I did indeed choke down two pills—the pain was that bad. My muscles were still clenched against the morning's chill, but the sun's warmth helped take the edge off.

The world was all blue skies and sparkling white wonderland. If I hadn't just experienced the worst night of my life, I'd marvel at the pure beauty. But my brain felt untethered. One moment it was floating, the next knocking from the inside out as if ordering me to lay down and rest already. I couldn't, though. Time was of the essence and I didn't think Ryker would stop even if my brain exploded from the painful pressure.

No. There was only one thing to do. Walk.

But, stars above, why did it have to be uphill?

6

NIGHTMARES

For the third time in the last half hour, I heard a twig snap to the left of us. I watched Ryker carefully, expecting him to pause, maybe even investigate, but he continued to scale the ever-steepening road with unwavering strides.

You can't hide from me for long. I'll find you.

What if we were being followed again? What if Skervvy had sniffed me out and was waiting for the opportune moment to stick a knife in my back?

I chewed on my lip, hating the thought of sounding paranoid, but self-preservation won out. "So I met a couple of creepy dudes the other night in the old city," I began nonchalantly. Ryker tensed but didn't stop. "I think they might be following us."

That got his attention. He snorted, shaking his head like I'd said something stupid. Again. "We're not being trailed by humans."

A second passed. Then another and another. All the different ways I could murder him in his sleep flitted through my mind. Why hadn't I thought to pack a fork? I ground my teeth together before taking the bait. "Then *what?*"

He shrugged. "I'm guessing it's the large wolf dog you

shared your bread with. He knows you're an easy target and is probably looking for seconds." My hands formed fists. Or tried to through my gloves. "I could be wrong though. Might be a saber cat."

That did it, he needed to die. He was worse than Lars!

"What are you doing?" he asked.

I looked up in time to avoid another Ryker collision and halted unsteadily beside him. He studied me quizzically, completely oblivious that I was plotting his death. When he continued to stare, I followed his gaze to my hand, which was clutching one of my gold daggers. When did that happen? I twirled it slowly before sliding the blade into its sheath. "Nothing. Nothing at all."

His days were numbered. My body craved his demise more than I thought.

"Why saber cats?" He turned and resumed trudging up the slope, missing the dark scowl I threw at him. Did he know *everything* about me?

"You know I'm not going to tell you that, right?" At his silence, I glibly added, "What are *you* afraid of?"

"Obnoxious questions."

"Well, then I'll make sure to ask as many of them as I can. Here's another one: what's with the moon and claw tattoo?"

His laugh was clipped. Annoyed. Maybe even a touch angry. "You spent all those months training with Bren and he never told you his past?"

I sucked in air too quickly and had to muffle a cough. "He—he has one, too?" I wasn't about to admit how little I knew Bren. That he hadn't willingly told me about himself. That Renold had conditioned me not to ask questions. But the moment I'd left the city, my question filter had broken.

"No, but he knows what the tattoo is for. It's our clan's mark. All you need to know is that it means 'nocturnal predator.'"

Our clan. *Our.*

I blinked slowly as my brain took its sweet time registering his words. Then images flashed through my mind faster than I could process. Bearded men. Pirates. Tattoos. A younger me, gagged and bound. Kidnapped. Betrayed. *I didn't see your tattoo earlier. That makes us . . .*

Made them *what?*

Clan. Tattoos. Kidnapped. Clan. *Our clan . . .*

I froze midstep. "No," I breathed. My heart thundered. Adrenaline rushed through me. "Not again. No. No, no, no."

"What's wrong?"

I startled as the deep voice penetrated the whirling storm of memories. My eyes met my captor's, confusion momentarily stunning me when I realized they weren't gold but a pale blue with black rims. Not Bren's eyes. Ryker's. Apparently they had more in common than I thought. *Way* more. I hadn't considered until this very moment that Ryker's tattoo could be the same as the tattooed men who'd kidnapped me.

Say hello to your father for me, Renold had said to him right before we'd left the city. What did that mean? Maybe Ryker's *real* mission was to take me to his father. His *clan.* And then what? All of my old anger and bitterness roared to the surface. No way was I going to be blindsided and kidnapped *again*.

I had an arrow nocked to my bow and pointed at his heart in the span of a breath.

He moved toward me and I pulled the string taut, halting him in his tracks. His lips pulled back, baring his teeth. "What's gotten into you?"

My fingers spasmed, almost releasing the arrow. Ryker growled low in warning. Blood pumped loudly in my ears. Two words drummed against my skull, over and over until I had to expel them or I'd explode. "Recruiter. Clan."

I released the arrow.

For a split second, pure elation filled me as I watched that arrow tip slice toward my kidnapper. I was stronger now. Wiser. I wouldn't make the same mistake twice.

But that moment of time quickly became bone-chilling dread. Faster than I could track, Ryker twisted his body. The arrow soared skyward and vanished into the midday sun.

I gaped in disbelief. Ryker's jaw dropped, too, mirroring mine.

"You shot at me." The statement almost sounded like a question. Either way, I didn't respond. I couldn't feel my tongue. He took a slow step down the hill, but I was still too shocked to react. To realize I'd just lost my window of escape. He lunged. With speed, trajectory, and superior weight on his side, I was screwed. We collided, skidding and rolling in the snow several feet before he pinned me beneath him.

My least favorite position. So I executed my favorite

move. I kneed him in the groin.

As he grunted, I shoved him off me, then sprang to my feet. He did too, despite his slightly bent frame. He glared and slipped a hand inside his pants pocket. Alarm bells clanged through my skull, but I was fixated on one thing. *Escape. Escape. Escape.* I whipped my bow staff in an arc and struck his cheek. He tumbled backward.

I turned and flew down the hill, tripping more than once. *Get away, get away.* I wouldn't be kidnapped and imprisoned, ripped from everything I knew all over again. Asher. Iris. Freedom. And yes, my traitorous heart cried, even Bren. If Ryker dragged me to his clan, chances were I'd never see their faces again. Never feel their touch. Hear their voices.

"Stop!"

There was an extra dense patch of trees ahead just off the road. If I left the trail and kept up the pace, maybe I could—

A rod of fire streaked down my neck and spine. I screamed as I lost my footing and pitched headfirst toward the ground. My arms shot out, breaking my fall, and I quickly tucked into a roll. The entire time, my body trembled and jerked as electricity pumped through me. The pain in my skull intensified until black spotted my vision.

Snow crunched nearby. The agony switched off.

Before I could collect myself, hands grasped my bow and tore it away. My wrists smarted as they were forced together. I blinked to clear my sight and Ryker's irate face came into view. He wasn't looking at me but at my wrists as he wound something around them. My breath hitched. He was binding my hands together.

I wrenched my arms out of his grip. Lightning quick, his nose was inches from mine. A growl rumbled in his throat. "Don't. You want me to shock you again? I will. Gladly."

At my silence, he unsheathed my daggers and tucked them out of reach, then resumed securing my restraints. I noted a shallow cut across his right cheek. I should have struck harder. "Why are you doing this?" I hissed, then clenched my jaw as a fresh jolt of pain cleaved my brain. The headache was back.

"You're a flight risk and apparently have a death wish. You're giving me no choice but to protect you from yourself."

"What? *Myself*? You're the one kidnapping me!" My voice had risen but I didn't care anymore. Better that a wild beast find and eat me than get carted away to another city ruled by a madman.

"Kidnap? Are you insane?"

"Yes, I'm the crazy one. Why would anyone want their freedom, right? Now, where are you taking me?" Maybe he didn't know about my hidden pants pocket currently concealing a knife. I could stab him in the back. Seemed fair, considering.

"I'm taking you to *Bren*, remember?" He pulled back, eyeing me like an extra limb had sprouted from my forehead. At least he didn't look ready to murder me anymore. "I'll ask again: what's gotten into you?"

I struggled into a sitting position, and when he didn't stop me, lurched to a stand. He followed suit, casually dusting snow off his pants. Yet I knew, by the taught line of his shoulders, that he was anything but relaxed. "I'm not stupid, Ryker. You're from the Recruiter Clan. They *kidnap*. It's what they do. Does Renold know what you're up to?"

Suddenly, nausea burned in my gut as another puzzle piece clicked into place. "It was *you*, wasn't it? You're Renold's eyes and ears. You told him about my weaknesses. About my fear of beasts. About how close Bren and I had become." Everything made sense now. The way he'd lurk nearby, materializing out of the shadows. He had been watching me. The desire to scratch out his eyes and feed them to the birds sizzled through my veins.

He could have done any number of things, but laughing definitely hadn't crossed my mind. "Yes, that was my duty, Keeper, remember? Even before the Trials, I was appointed to look after you. As for the Recruiter Clan, do you think I would have killed those clan members if I were still one of them? Your problem is that you don't *think* before you act." Reaching down, he picked up my bow and slung it over his shoulder. "You won't be needing this anymore. Oh, and the next time you raise a finger against me, I'm chopping it off."

From that moment on, I refused to speak to him. We traveled for hours, sometimes on the road, sometimes taking shortcuts through the woods. Always upward. Without the use of my arms, I stumbled and fell often. Ryker never once looked back. I hated him. On my hate scale, he ranked somewhere between Renold and Lars. If he kept this up, he'd pass Renold in no time.

Dusk came early, a warning sign that another storm was approaching. We set up camp after I tripped over a rock and almost bashed my head in. Ryker grumbled about my lack of coordination and poor eyesight, but I didn't snark back. I simply popped open my tent—not an easy feat with your hands tied—then shut out the world.

"Lune. Wake up."

My brows furrowed. I was about to bark at Ryker to go away, but the distinctly feminine voice had my eyes opening wide. Who . . . ?

"Did you think you could get rid of me *that* easily?"

My exhaustion vanished and I bolted upright. "Catanna," I breathed. My old nemesis. The girl I'd wanted to befriend who had chosen to hate me instead. A shudder shook my shoulders. She only came to me when I was at my weakest. How had she found me? Something wasn't right. She shouldn't be here. "Where are you?"

"Come and see."

Her falsely sweet words drifted on a wind I couldn't feel. As I exited the tent and steadied myself on a large boulder, I realized I couldn't feel anything, not even my own body. A shadow moved in my peripheral and I changed course, trailing a patch of fog that surrounded a dark shape. Catanna.

"This way," she whispered, her features bending and morphing, never solid. Never whole.

I followed. She may have tried to kill me more than once, but her company was preferable to Ryker's. I waited for the stirring in my gut, my innate warning system. I felt fine though. She wasn't a danger to me. "How did you escape Tatum City, Catanna?"

Her laugh was friendly, but I knew better. "I should have listened to you, Princess. You got exactly what you wanted. Freedom."

"But . . . but I didn't. I'm not free. It looks like you are though. How?"

She turned toward me—at least I think she did. The fog still hid her from view. "I'll show you. Just a little farther now. Come." Her form silently swirled, drifting past trees and jutting rock shelfs. We climbed. I slipped more than once, maybe even injuring myself, but the possibility of freedom kept me going. It was worth the pain.

At last, after what felt like hours of scaling rocks and tree roots, she stopped. Her silhouette shifted, pulling aside fog wisps until a narrow path formed. "Come here." My feet obediently carried me forward, pausing just shy of the fog. "You want to know how I gained my freedom?"

I nodded. My heart thumped against my ribs in anticipation.

She smiled. I couldn't see her face, but somehow, I knew that she did. "Will you do what it takes? Anything?"

Air caught in my throat. She had asked me that once before. Would I do anything to be free? Would I kill again, on purpose this time? I swallowed the lump of guilt threatening to choke me. "What do I need to do?"

The shroud that was Catanna receded, revealing a dark, trickling stream. Sound returned. Thundered in my ears. Why was the water so loud? My body moved, responding to a silent command. My boots sunk calf deep into the water that rushed faster than I'd first anticipated. I expected it to be cold. But there was nothing. No feeling.

I stepped to the edge. The edge of what? My captivity? Catanna was behind me now, cutting off my retreat, forcing me to face my fate. I raised my chin. *Show no fear. I am not weak.*

"There's only one way to be free," Catanna whispered in my ear. I leaned forward, away from her. I couldn't help it. I didn't like people at my back. As my foot inched past the edge, seeking purchase in the stream bed, she gave me her answer: "Death."

I gasped and jerked awake. Cold punched my body. After wildly glancing around, I had one unbearably long second to realize that I was teetering over the lip of a waterfall. Then I swayed, thrown off balance as one of my legs dangled over empty air. I instinctively tried to pinwheel my arms and correct my precarious position, but they strained fruitlessly, refusing to spread wide. I looked down. My wrists were still bound together.

All it took was a small gust of wind and I knew it was over. A scream lodged in my throat as I tipped forward and plummeted to the inky darkness below.

Water had been a comfort to me for as long as I could remember. But, once again, Catanna was trying to turn my strengths into weakness. Even in my dreams, she knew how best to hurt me.

Not this time.

As the life leached out of my body, at least I was wrapped in water's familiar embrace. If only waking nightmares weren't my achilles heel. I had been able to control them while locked inside a room at night, but out in the wilderness, I was vulnerable.

Reactive.

I hated that word.

"Lune, wake up."

The world tilted. I fought to remain where I was, the spot peaceful somehow, but my body was numb to the bone. "Go . . . 'way, Cat—anna." The words chattered out of me, breathy and weak. Not the strong ending I was going for. "Y-you . . . can't w-win."

"You're certifiably insane," a male voice muttered.

I knew that unpleasant timbre. It belonged to the one human I never wanted to speak to ever again. "No," I groaned aloud, willing my legs to propel me away from Ryker. In the state I was in, he'd probably trigger the chip in my neck as a mercy killing, and I didn't want to go out that way. "L-leave me."

"I was right," he said with a grunt as he heaved me into

his arms. The water relinquished its embrace and I bit back a whimper. "You really do have a death wish."

A shiver racked my body from head to toe as the chill night air hit me full force. "S-stars. L-let me go."

"Good. You're still shivering. That means you have a fighting chance at surviving this."

I moaned my protest, wanting to be left in peace where I could think about Catanna's words. What if death *was* the only way to be free? Maybe if I stopped fighting the inevitable, I'd get what I always wanted. No one would even miss me. I had pushed Bren away, had left Iris to fend for herself, had robbed Asher of the extra food supply his family desperately needed. Had—had whipped Freedom and betrayed her trust. Had disobeyed my mum who'd probably forgotten all about me by now.

Blackness crowded my guilt-laden thoughts, numbing the pain and sorrow and regret. But the thought of giving up, after all these years, weighed heavily on me. As much as I wanted to sometimes, I didn't think I could, like my very DNA was formed of stubborn determination. Even now, as the last of my strength trickled out of me . . .

"Lune, wake up! You're stronger than this. Hypothermia isn't going to be the death of you."

I whimpered as something struck my cheek.

"You feel that? Good. Stay awake, you hear me?"

"D-did you just s-slap m-me?"

"Yes."

I cracked my eyes open so they could shoot beams of fire

at Ryker's stupid face, but he wasn't above me. In fact, I wasn't in his arms anymore. When had that happened? The dark room spun and I squeezed my eyes shut again. Wait. Room? What was happening to me? Was I in another waking nightmare? Ryker was here, so that made sense.

"Open your eyes or I'm going to slap you again, Lune." Something clattered nearby and I obliged out of curiosity. In the near pitchblack, I thought I saw Ryker shoving wood into a fireplace. The sight of him made me want to unapologetically speak my mind.

"You're a rude, inconsiderate jerk." The true statement slurred out of me, smooth as honey.

"I know. I've never pretended otherwise." He glanced at me, then swore softly. "You've stopped shivering." He rifled in his pack and pulled out a box of matches. A moment later, the fireplace glowed orange. "You've moved onto the next stage of hypothermia."

That should have concerned me, but I just felt detached. Tired. Numb. "Sucks to be me."

"It's going to suck even more when you find out what I have to do next."

"Go ahead," I muttered. "Can't feel anything anyway."

"Stay awake, Lune," he snapped, and that's when I decided my name sounded wrong coming from his lips.

"You're not allowed to say my name, Tattoo Boy."

His brows ticked upward. "Is that so, *Lune?*" Before I could retort, he unzipped his coat and shucked it off. His shirt quickly followed, then his boots and socks, leaving him only in pants as he looked down at me almost smugly. "Well, that's too bad, Lune, because I'll say your name a thousand more times if it'll keep you awake."

My mouth dried at the sight of his sculpted chest. Before I could look away in embarrassment, my eyes snagged on another tattoo. Several of them, actually. The fire illuminated his skin just enough to reveal their locations but none of the details.

Ryker cleared his throat. Heat should be flooding my cheeks after getting caught staring, but none came. "Your turn," he said.

My gaze flew to his. "But . . . No. No way."

He came at me, and I could do nothing—*nothing*—as he got to work peeling off my clothing now stiff with cold. Well, I could still speak. "I swear, if you don't stop touching me—"

"What? You'll do what exactly?" He tugged my arms free of my coat, then started rolling up my shirt.

"I'll kill you. I'm going to kill you, Ryker." Something stirred in my chest as he slid the shirt from my body, exposing more skin than I'd ever shown another. Only a black bra and bear tooth necklace kept my upper body from complete nakedness. I knew what I was feeling then. Panic. I gasped for breath, the sound weak and shallow.

At the noise, he paused with his fingers inches away from my waist. "I'm not going to hurt you." I looked up to find him studying me carefully. His voice, though still gruff, softened. "I'm trying to save you, and this is the only way I know how."

I couldn't make sense of his expression and didn't bother

trying. In that moment though, I knew he was asking for permission. A part of me didn't want to give it, but the rare show of open emotion in those unsettling eyes had me rethinking my stubbornness. And then the craziest thing happened. I nodded.

I'm going to regret this.

His fingers resumed their course, unbuttoning my pants and pulling the soaked material from my frozen legs. I could barely feel any of it. Just a whisper of touch. The room darkened as he unrolled something—a sleeping bag. I knew my body was being tucked inside, knew he wedged his body in with mine, but my thoughts scattered, drifted to the edge of consciousness.

"Lune, stay with me."

"Can't," I mumbled. Sleep dragged my eyelids shut, filling my bones with lead.

The last thing I heard was my name spoken again and again . . .

7

ESCAPE

Warmth.

Everywhere I touched.

I could feel my toes again. My legs. My arms. My nose, which was currently pressed against something soft and deliciously warm. I breathed in deep. A smoky, earthen scent assailed me. Rich and heavy, but not unpleasant. I ran my fingers over the smooth surface my cheek rested on. Not a blanket then. It was too warm, too firm yet supple. Too . . .

My eyes snapped open. Oh stars. Ryker. I was sleeping on Ryker. I was petting his *chest!* What was wrong with me? I must have lost my mind. There was no other explanation. Mortification unlike anything I'd felt before burned its way up my neck and consumed my face.

Escape. *Escape!*

I shifted, slowly reeling in the wayward leg that had curled itself around Ryker's. I bit my lip to keep from screaming in frustration. What had happened? Why were we—?

"Don't even think about running again."

At the voice so close to my ear, I jerked upright. Then I noticed my state of undress. And shrieked. "What in the—? How did—? Get out! Get out, get out!" I shoved him away from me, which didn't really work since we were stuck inside a single-person sleeping bag. I continued to push and kick and shout at him until he eventually crawled out, taking his sweet time.

I clutched the bag's thick material to my chest, shaking with rage and . . . disgust. Yes, that was it. How dare he! Taking advantage of me in my—

"You're welcome."

I looked up at him sharply. "What, why?" I snapped. "I didn't give you permission to—"

"Yes, you did."

"What? No, I would never. I loathe you! What delusional part of your brain thinks you can—"

"You almost died last night," he interjected, crossing his arms over a very naked chest. "After you ran away in the dead of night without your supplies—which was really stupid, by the way—I found you half frozen in a river. A *river*. With your hands still bound. What were you thinking? I had to warm you up the fastest way I knew how."

My stomach bottomed out as memories swarmed me then, ones I immediately wanted to forget. How was I going to explain that I hadn't been running away? That Catanna had . . . Nope. Ryker could think what he wanted. I wasn't going to tell him about my nightmares. He already thought I was insane.

Time for evasive tactics.

"So, where are we exactly?"

His jaw slackened. He shook his head, then turned and

snatched his shirt off the floor. On his right shoulder blade, a large, intricate tattoo in shades of gray caught my eye. A rose surrounded by thorny vines. The rest of his back was a patchwork of scars, some long and thin like mine, others round and raised.

I glanced away as he faced me again. "We lucked out last night when I stumbled across this deserted cabin. By the looks of it, no one has set foot inside for years. Maybe decades." He tugged on his boots and coat, making for the door. "I'll be right back. Might want to get dressed."

I did. As soon as I heard the crunch of his boots fade away, I scrambled for my backpack that he had thankfully brought with him. How had he carried a wet me and two heavy packs? *Note to self: don't engage in a wrestling match with Ryker.* I whipped on a fresh set of clothes while my body started to shiver without the extra heat. Stars, had I really slept with him all night?

"I need a shower," I muttered. "A really hot one. Or cold. Maybe both." An itch formed beneath my skin that I couldn't scratch—a craving to pummel a certain tattoo-riddled jerk—so I began picking up my discarded clothing. Wait. I froze as last night became a crystal clear memory. "Ryker undressed me."

I was going to kill him. And somehow I'd resurrect him just so I could kill him all over again.

Embarrassment was the mildest emotion raging through me when he stomped inside a few minutes later with a bundle of wood in his arms. What, were we playing house now? I couldn't directly look at him without picturing the way I'd woken—with our skin pressed together and my leg between his as I inhaled his scent.

Crap. This was so messing with my brain.

"We can't stay here," I rushed to say as he dumped the logs near the fireplace. Feeling fidgety again, my fingers dug into my hair, seeking knots to untangle. There were plenty to keep them busy and I briefly wondered how awful I must look. Probably like an electrocuted squirrel. "We're never going to catch up with Bren at this rate and—"

"I've lost his trail."

The admission didn't sink in at first. But when it did . . . double crap. Was he giving up? "We'll just follow that road we were on. I mean, he has to stop eventually, right? Otherwise Renold would have—"

"I don't think he's on that road anymore."

"If you'd just let me finish—"

"Aren't you hearing me?" he snarled, facing me fully. "I can't sense him anymore. We've failed our mission."

My fingers stilled, then slid to the bear tooth necklace and gripped it tightly. Not because of his attitude problem, but because of that *word*. Failed. Failure wasn't an option. "Are you a *quitter*, Ryker? Because you know what they say about quitters. They never win. Makes sense, actually. I *did* beat you in the Rasa Rowe Trial."

"I *let* you win."

"*What?*"

"You heard me," he said, taking a menacing step my way.

He wanted to fight? Fine. So did I. "My charger could have plowed yours over, but I held him back."

"Oh, how chivalrous of you." My feet moved, narrowing the gap between us. I casually dropped my hands, but they were ready to strike. "Remind me to thank you. When I'm dead."

His face twisted with disdain. "You think you're so clever, but you're not. Do you see me laughing? You're. Not. Funny."

I crossed into his personal space, straightening my spine so he couldn't look down his nose at me. My voice lowered, gearing up for the grand finale. "You *can't* laugh because you have a stick shoved up your—"

Knock knock knock.

We froze. My eyes widened while Ryker's narrowed.

I looked at the door, then back at him, silently asking if it was locked. He nodded.

"We know you're in there. Your lover's spat can be heard for miles. We just want a short reprieve from the cold, then we'll be on our way. Mind letting us in?"

I shook my head. Ryker was already on the move, not toward the door but away, making for the cabin's only window which surprisingly still had glass. I collected our packs and slipped on my coat, eyeing the unrolled sleeping bag we'd slept in. I hadn't wanted to touch the stupid thing and now regretted that childish decision since I wouldn't have time to grab it.

Ryker motioned me toward the window he'd managed to open without a sound.

The door rattled as a fist pounded on it. "Okay, time's up!

I know it's you, girl. I scented you all the way here and I'm tired of chasing you."

Air stalled in my lungs. No. Please, not *him*. Ryker lowered my pack out the window, and I grimaced when I realized that all my weapons were in there. It dropped into a snow drift with a light thump. He cupped his hands next and nodded at my feet. I almost ignored his offer of help, but now wasn't the time to indulge in bruised pride. I placed my boot in his palms and grabbed the windowsill.

"If you don't let us in, you're going to make me mad. There's no telling what I'll do then." The man's cackle sent a shiver down my spine. "Skerv dog wants in. I'm giving you five seconds. Five . . ."

"Skervvy?" Ryker hissed as he boosted me up. I perched on the sill and swung a leg over. "*That's* who you ran into?"

"Four!"

Ryker swore and ripped open his pack, pulling out a gun. "Get out of here, Lune."

"What about you?" My heart was galloping against my ribs now, trying to break free.

"Three."

He switched the safety off. "I'm not leaving until he's dead. Now *go*. He can't get ahold of you."

"But—"

Bang.

A gun roared, splintering wood. The door slammed open.

"Sorry for the early arrival, but that was boring," Skerv-vy drawled, then waved a gun in the air with his body safely tucked around the corner. "Don't make me use this. I'm coming in."

As his lanky frame filled the doorway, I caught my first glimpse of his face. Not only did he laugh like Lars, but he kind of looked like him too with his messy brown hair and dark eyes. Ryker lifted his gun and, at the same time, pushed me out the window. I was too shocked to scream as I fell, landing in the snow with an *oof!*

Scrambling for my backpack, I waited for shots to be fired. Instead, I heard Skervvy swear loudly, then, "Ryker Jones? *The* Ryker Jones? I thought you were dead, man!"

"Tom Skervlong. The man who inspired others to name him after a disease. Still not taking your vitamin C?"

What? They *knew* each other?

Skervvy chortled, and I belatedly realized that Ryker had cracked a joke. Had I hit my head? I was about to make my escape when Skervvy said, "Look, I'd love to reminisce and all that crap, but I'm looking for someone. Smells like apple blossoms as I'm sure you know. Where is she?"

"You can't have her, Skervlong."

There was a pause. I stopped breathing. "Oh?" The casual tone of his voice flipped my warning switch. As my stomach twisted, I slowly backed away from the window. "And why's that?"

"Because she's mine."

I sucked in air too sharply. The men fell silent. Then that vile man started cackling again.

"Looks like we've got a runner," Skervvy singsonged.

"She's fair game now."

"Lune, go!" Ryker shouted a second before gunfire went off.

For a moment, I couldn't decide what to do. Run or fight? Ryker needed help. *No, he's one of* them. *Run!*

I bolted.

Time slowed as I dashed for a thick stand of trees behind the cabin. My legs churned but weren't going fast enough. A volley of shots sent my heart into my throat. Faster. *Faster.* I had no idea where I was going. Judging by the brightness, it was late morning, but I couldn't see the sun. Couldn't get my bearings. Snow was falling again, slipping past the trees and smacking my face.

I jumped over a fallen log. My feet were still off the ground when something rammed me from behind, and I plowed into the snow face first. I immediately put up a fight, blindly throwing both elbows back at my assailant. Hands clamped onto my arms and jacked them up high. My muscles shrieked in protest and I cried out.

"Now this feels familiar, don't it, missy?"

Thane.

I growled my frustration. Of course Skervvy had back-up. He had said *we*. And I'd lingered outside the cabin like an idiot! The world spun as he flipped me over, then pressed me and my pack into the snow with his much larger body. Pinned me down like inferior prey. Helplessness was a boulder on my chest as light brown eyes set in a darker brown face peered victoriously into mine.

"Be a good girl and I won't hurt you," he crooned. His short beard scratched my face as he leaned close and breathed me in. He sighed and I recoiled at the sweet yet sour stench of his breath.

His hand reached up and I forced myself to hold still. To wait. He trailed a finger down my cheek and I let him. Made him think I was cowed. The finger veered toward my mouth. I made my move, sinking my teeth deep into his flesh. I fought my gag reflex as the taste of warm iron coated my tongue. He reared back and yelled several swears, but before I could wiggle free, his fist pounded my jaw.

Agony ripped through me.

"You're a nasty little thing, aren't ya?" His words sounded garbled to my ears, as if I was underwater. I blinked to clear my vision, but the black spots wouldn't go away. Thane's blurred face was still hovering over mine, though his attention had shifted elsewhere. I felt it then. Cold metal against my wrists.

Click.

"No," I groaned, jerking my arms away. But it was too late. My hands were cuffed. *Again.* Why did this keep happening to me?

"I tried to play nice, but I've lost my patience with you. See this?" He pointed at his wide nose. "The last time we met, you broke it. I had to reset it myself because there's no way I'd let Skervvy anywhere near my face, even if he *is* my partner."

He yanked me to my feet by the cuffs and I bit back a curse as pain streaked up my arms. It felt like he'd just ripped my hands off. At the mention of Skervvy, dread twisted my

84

insides. The thought of that crazy man anywhere near me while I was incapacitated sent determination rushing through my veins.

I jerked against my restraints, and the sharp action tipped Thane off balance. As he stumbled toward me, I aimed for a familiar target. Air whooshed from his lungs as my knee rammed into his groin. I tore free, only for him to retaliate by grabbing my hair. Instead of pulling, he shoved. And bashed my forehead against a tree.

Too many things happened next. I groaned as blood dripped into my eye. Grunted as Thane threw me to the ground again. Wheezed as his boot pressed down on my windpipe. Then he was gone. Where did he—? There. He was on the ground now too, wrestling with a tan and black beast. My heart pounded with fear, louder than the yelling and growling. A knife flashed. Fangs glinted.

I rolled, forcing my body to cooperate, to carry me upright and forward. I didn't dare turn to see if I was being pursued, to see if teeth or a blade were about to sink into my flesh. The only thing I could do was run, counting each new step a victory because I was still alive. Blood continued to blind me as it streamed down my forehead but I couldn't worry about that now.

Although, if the cut needed stitches . . . I brushed my panic aside and looked down at my hands. Crap. I couldn't survive out here with these cuffs on. The gunshots had stopped. Was Skervvy dead? Ryker? Panic simmered again.

Think. Think! Before you get yourself killed too!

I needed distance from this place so I could form a plan. Guilt poked at me for leaving Ryker to his fate, but I couldn't help him anyway. Without the use of my arms, I was simply that: useless. And if he'd lost Bren's trail, did I really need him?

Besides, I didn't trust his motives. He knew far too much about me, almost to obsessive levels, and his "because she's mine" line had been all sorts of creepy. I could tell Renold that one of his Recruiter Clan lackeys had killed him. Maybe he'd take out his anger on Skervvy instead of me when I returned without completing my mission.

My legs slowed as that realization finally settled into my bones. Giving up wasn't something I did. Ever. Hope was an incessant gnat in my ear and wouldn't allow me peace until I'd done everything in my power to achieve what I'd set out to do. Hope for a better future—it's what pushed me out of bed in the morning. And if I admitted defeat, what would happen to Iris? What if Renold took out his disappointment on *her*?

No, I couldn't give up. I had to find Bren. *Find Bren.* A fresh wave of adrenaline doused me and I picked up speed, not questioning my body when it silently urged me to change course. After several minutes of jogging, I became aware that I was going *up* again. My calves burned as the incline refused to level out. At this point, I was fairly certain Bren had driven his ATV contraption all the way to the mountain's peak and down the other side. Maybe I'd never catch up with him, but there was only one thing for me to do.

Follow.

BEAR

Hunger tore at my insides. Fatigue warped my vision. But after hours of travel, I didn't stop or rest.

I avoided roads so that I'd be harder to track, hauling my body over fallen trees, endless roots, and boulders taller than me. All with my hands cuffed and a heavy pack threatening to send me down the mountain at the first misstep.

Because, yes, I was officially climbing an entire mountain. And why not? Ever since I'd left Tatum City, there'd been nothing but obstacles between me and Bren. Ironically, that seemed to summarize the entirety of our relationship. Insurmountable odds, as if the universe were trying to keep us apart. Maybe the smart thing would be to head back, to admit that I wasn't cut out for the outside world.

The sky was already darkening and I didn't have the faintest clue where to set up camp. Without Ryker's keen senses, a beast was probably going to eat me in my sleep. I pressed on anyway. *No stopping. No turning around. Find Bren before you die of hunger or exhaustion or frostbite or . . .*

The list of possible ways to die out here was long and depressing. I thought of home instead. No, not *home*. Tatum City would never be my home, even if my sister and best friend were still there. Every day spent in that prison, I'd felt like a trapped animal. Like a part of me was meant to be wild and untamed, and no matter how many times they tried to break my spirit, that would never change.

I wasn't meant for walls. I was meant for endless possibilities.

But I could see now that life was simpler on the inside. There were still gruesome ways to die, but the environment was carefully controlled, as Ryker had said. Predictable, for the most part. Simple wasn't *me*, though. I hated being controlled as much as I hated losing control. Hated that I was so often afraid, and yet, sometimes I craved danger. The thrill of willingly drowning.

Did that make me crazy? Bren had said that I was important though. Different. Even Renold had. And Ryker had mentioned unique abilities.

I wasn't blind. Envisioning things before they happened probably wasn't normal. But was anything normal these days? Bren could see in the dark. Skervvy could track people's scent. Ryker could carry more weight than should be possible.

My mum had told me a story about aliens once. What if we were . . . ? I snorted. Nah.

Snow continued to pelt my head as I balanced on top of another felled tree. Halfway across, my foot slipped. With a cry, I tumbled off the side and into a gully. A shallow stream of water broke my fall. Sort of. I'd landed wrong on my left leg. I gritted my teeth against the pain, choking back a sob as I slowly sat up and peered through the growing gloom at my boot, which had punched through a gnarled mess of tree roots.

I lay there, panting, not sure what to do. Maybe this was the perfect time to rest, eat some rations, and cry my eyes out.

Maybe this was a sign to give up.

"No," I hissed, carefully bending forward to free my foot. The pain was terrible, but I'd felt worse. A couple years ago, I'd fallen out of a tree in the Arcus Point training cage and broken my leg. Needless to say, Elite Trainer Drake had unmercifully chewed me out, reminding me how weak and pathetic I was.

If he were here now, he'd shout in my ear, "If you don't get up and walk it off in two seconds, trainee, you're going to stand against the wall until sundown. Yes, that's right, you'll miss dinner. Suck it up. Strength, speed, precision!"

Thank the stars, no one in Tatum City could see me like this, sunken so low that I wasn't even recognizable. Tied, injured, muddied, bloodied, frozen, stuck. *Ladies and gentlemen, here lies the Elite Guardian of Tatum City. She will protect you, keep you safe . . .*

Lies. *I* was a lie. Over the last eleven years, even during the Trials, fear had paralyzed me time and again. How could I protect others when I couldn't protect myself? If not for Bren, a saber cat would have torn out my throat minutes into our final Trial.

If not for him, none of this would have happened. You would be safe and sound with Mum.

But would I really? How far did Renold's influence reach? How many Recruiter Clan members were out here right this moment kidnapping children and forcing them behind walls? A new thought slapped me across the face, and I inhaled shakily. Was that why Bren was out here? To kidnap more naive girls like me? Another thought punched me. Had he kidnapped Iris?

If he deviates from it, I want you to kill him.

I hadn't let myself dwell too long on that final command from Renold, but I did now as a surge of horror and anger rose at what Bren's mission might entail. This wasn't the first time I'd wondered how much Renold knew of Bren's past. Maybe he knew of the guilt Bren still carried for kidnapping me all those years ago. Maybe he'd given Bren an ultimatum too.

But I couldn't envision Bren as anyone's puppet. He had an uncanny ability to soothe a skeptical person into trusting him. Renold had even bent the rules for him, something I'd never seen him do before. Brendan Bearon was an enigma. If given the opportunity, I'd pry open his brain to see if magical powers oozed out. Maybe those golden eyes of his could hypnotize, like in the fairytales when the Sultan's Royal Vizier would use his snake staff to manipulate people's thoughts and actions, unraveling their strongest beliefs. It may only be a story my mum had told me as a child, but stories came from somewhere. Maybe they all held some form of truth.

Could Bren do that? Had I fallen prey to his charm and allowed him to use me as a pawn?

With a grimace, I freed my boot from the tangled roots. If only I could free my mind so easily. Maybe the key to ridding my thoughts of Bren was to stop him from completing his mission. Maybe then I'd feel in control again. Maybe even peace. A renewed sense of determination filled me. I wouldn't let him destroy another person's life.

I could play his game. Earn his trust. Then stab him in the back. Hopefully not literally—I didn't think I was capable of that, no matter how angry and bitter and hurt I was. But if I couldn't be an Elite Guardian to the insiders, perhaps I could to the outsiders.

Ding.

The suit's chime announced the end of the Faust Night Trial. I had drawn first blood. I had won. But my opponent wouldn't stop. Large hands reached for me, neatly flipping me over a broad shoulder. I landed on my back. Air escaped me in a giant *whoosh*. Pain should have followed, but I felt nothing. Only confusion. Because glaring down at me with a spear tip pointed at my chest was Bren.

I opened my mouth to speak, but no sound came.

His lips curved into a sneer. "You really thought I cared? Thought I'd sacrifice the win for you? Who do you think you are, Lune? Do you think you're strong? Because you're not. You're always afraid, remember? That makes you *weak*." Tears burned my eyes at his callous assault. He laughed at my pain. "You are nothing to me. Just a means to an end. Got that?"

Words refused to form on my tongue when he continued to look at me with hatred, something he'd never done before.

I choked back a sob as agony consumed me.

"Pathetic," he spat. "No wonder Renold asked me to kill you. He knows you're a failure, and now, so do I. Do the world a favor and stop *trying*." His spear bore down, skewering me to the floor.

I gasped, not from the blade piercing my flesh, but from the realization that he'd ripped through my heart without remorse. The pain I felt was from my soul as it splintered, as it broke under the weight of Bren's ultimate betrayal.

My suit dinged. Again and again. The high-pitched whine was an anvil to my temples, forcing me to close my eyes. I couldn't bear to see Bren's hate-filled expression a moment longer anyway. As the whining grew in volume, something nudged my neck. Gently. Then harder.

The sound of a deep *woof* had my eyes shooting open.

A fat snowflake plopped onto my nose as I scrambled to make sense of the massive form hunched over me. It definitely wasn't Bren. A plaintive whine came from its throat and a cold snout brushed my cheek. Fear, my constant companion, rushed through my veins as awareness kicked in.

I was still in the gully and must have dozed off. Now, a beast was about to end me before I could take a single step toward my new purpose. Stupid. *Stupid!* I barely breathed as the animal nudged me again, noting that a large tan paw sat on my chest directly over my heart. My wrists were bound, but if I could reach the knife in my pants pocket . . .

A warm, damp tongue licked my left ear. I squeaked and jerked my head away. The creature leapt back instead of lunging for my throat, giving me the time I needed to slide the blade free. I double-fisted the weapon, trying and failing to stop my hands from shaking. We eyed each other from opposite ends of the pit. The Pit. Would I forever be plagued with memories of the Trials?

When no attack came, I studied the animal. Then squinted as I caught sight of its markings. Beige paws and chest, black muzzle and ears. No way. Could it really be him? I whistled softly and the wolf dog cocked his head. A sigh of relief escaped me. My shoulders sagged and I relaxed my death grip on the knife. Had he followed me this entire week? I couldn't recall how many days I'd been traveling.

He must be hungry, but so was I. As I struggled to stand, the world threatened to tip upside down, confirming that I needed to feed myself. And find fresh water. But dusk had fallen while I'd slept, lowering the temperature to dangerous levels. Shelter was my number one priority. I did *not* want to lose any toes to frostbite.

I put away my blade, keeping one eye on the dog as I tentatively put weight on my injured ankle. Pain shot up my leg and I sucked in a gasp. Okay then. Possible sprain, but I didn't think the bone was broken. Climbing out of the gully was a messy affair. I scaled the side mostly by crawling, using roots to pull myself upward. By the time I hauled myself over the edge, my knees ached and a cold sweat peppered my skin.

Black emptiness crowded my sight and I took several deep breaths until my vision cleared. Rising to my feet was draining, but not as bad as when Catanna had stuck a knife in my back and I'd woken downriver near Tatum City's electric wall. I had used Bren as motivation to push past the pain and weakness, and I would use him now. Back then, he'd been an inspiration for strength, but today, he was a target for justice.

I didn't allow myself to use the word revenge. Because no matter how many times he'd betrayed me, I didn't want him hurt. My goal was simply to stop him, not see those honey-gold eyes glazed over in death. Envisioning such a sight squeezed my heart and snatched away my breath. I sighed. They were right about me. "Pathetic," I whispered.

My first task was to find a walking stick. Usually, I could push aside pain, but hobbling about on a sprained ankle without the full use of my hands would be incredibly stupid. *You can't be strong without first being smart.* Ugh. Why were Ryker's words coming back to me whenever I felt like a piece of crap? It was bad enough that I still felt pricks of guilt over leaving him. Now he was the voice of reason in my head?

After rooting around for a long and sturdy stick, I searched for a good spot to camp for the night. "Rocks," I mumbled. "Where are rocks when you need them?" Ryker had said they helped block the wind, and the higher I climbed, the stronger it became. Rocks served a dual purpose: lessened the air's impact and kept your scent from being carried to nocturnal predators. See, I was learning.

I could survive one night on my own.

Technically, I had a new companion though. Several yards off, the wolf dog, having climbed out of the pit without problem, silently trailed me. "You need a name if you're going to stalk me," I called to him through numb lips. "How about Pest? You did steal my bread after all." He sneezed, as if in protest. "Fine. Bear then. Because your paws are seriously like a bear's. You even look like one, did you know that?"

He didn't answer. I guessed that he approved.

We traveled in silence until darkness forced me to stop. I couldn't risk tumbling into another gully. With my luck, I'd crack my head wide open. Removing my backpack without being able to slip the straps down my arms took much longer than it should have. My frozen fingers struggled with the buckles—I could barely feel them. Alarmed, I pulled and yanked until a buckle broke.

I cursed, then tried to calm my erratic breathing. Panic would make things worse. To get the tent open, I had to use my teeth. The fabric snapped in my face, but I couldn't muster a laugh at my own expense. Crap, I was turning into Ryker. I couldn't help it though. The knowledge that my life was solely in my hands sobered me right up. And knowing that I was minutes away from frostbite terrified me. Maybe Ryker acted so serious all the time because he only had himself to rely on. I didn't even know if he had friends. I doubted Skervvy was one of them.

After zipping myself inside the tent, I wondered if Bear would let me snuggle against his thick warm fur. But he'd wandered off, probably to catch himself a rabbit or something when I'd failed to feed him. *Sorry, buddy. My rations are low as it is.* Plus, an empty hole had taken the place of my stomach. When was the last time I'd eaten? I managed to flick on the lantern and quickly wrapped my fingers around it. Long minutes passed before I could feel the tips again. I studied each digit, checking for signs of frostbite, then remembered my toes.

Ah crap.

The process of removing my boots was slow and awkward, my hands shaking with nerves at what I would find. My swollen left ankle made the situation that much worse. "Please, please look normal. Please," I whispered, wrestling one boot off, then the other. When I was staring at both bare feet, the tears came. My toes were red, not black. Sort of a good sign. I couldn't feel them though. Water. I needed warm water.

But all I had was the lantern. What if it gave out? *Then you'll die, idiot.* I could make a fire—I had matches. *Half frozen and with your hands bound?* "You're not helping," I hissed at my inner self. The tears wouldn't stop. They left icy trails down my cheeks, adding to my misery.

You cannot break me.

I sucked in a ragged breath and nodded. If humans weren't allowed to break me, neither was nature. I stuck my toes as close to the lantern as I dared, watching them closely for hours, praying that my one source of heat would last the night.

As the first fingers of dawn snuck into the tent, I was half delirious with hunger and exhaustion. But I was alive. I, Lune Avery, stared death in the face and didn't back down. I rolled my eyes at the dramatic thought. Switching the lantern off, I prepared to endure another day. There was a newfound sureness to my movements though. I could do this. Life had tried to crush me again but I had fought back. And this time, I'd won, all on my own.

"Who's tough?" I wiggled my toes, then watched them disappear inside dry woolen socks. "That's right, you are."

The boots went on next, but as I worked on lacing them up, I realized my grave mistake. My ankle had been warmed too much by the lantern instead of packed in snow to bring down the swelling. I called myself every stupid name I could think of, grimacing as I rose and tested the pain level. "Well, crap on a cookie, that really hurts." When did I become so chatty with myself? Was I that starved for companionship?

Ever since Bren, my inner voice helpfully supplied. But it was right. Spending every day with him for three solid months had ruined me. His silly jokes, witty comebacks, inane observations . . . I missed all of that. He had made life more than just bearable—he'd made it livable. I swiped the pointless memories away by repacking my sleeping bag and tent, then finally curbed my hunger with the last of my bread and a small handful of nuts.

My stomach still complained when I was finished, but I stored the rest and went in search of water. Snow would do if I couldn't find anything, but it wasn't fresh and could be contaminated—another thing I'd learned from Ryker. I didn't want to fall sick on top of everything. Bear wasn't in sight, but I had a feeling he was nearby. Was he hungry for companionship too?

I whistled, just in case he'd fallen asleep and didn't hear me leave, then took off. It probably wasn't wise to encourage his company, but the thought of being utterly alone up here . . . My lips twitched into a small smile as I heard the light patter of paws following me.

It was midday, the sun blazing bright overhead, when my senses went haywire. Until now, my gut had steadily tugged me northeast. And then, out of nowhere, my instincts told me to veer south. I blinked, stunned. No. No, no, no. All of this climbing for *nothing?* "Stars above, Bren, what are you doing?"

I didn't know how long I stood there, blankly staring at nothing, but it was long enough for Bear to come investigate. He sat a few yards in front of me, still as a statue. Waiting. Like he had complete faith that I knew where I was going. "I don't know what I'm doing, Bear. I'm . . . I'm lost."

The admission stung. More than stung. It gutted me. I wanted to collapse in the snow and never get up again. Let nature bury me whole. As my knees weakened, as my hope dwindled, a twig snapped. My head whipped up, searching for the source. A figure emerged from behind a tree. Before I could make out the face, before I could sense if the person was a threat or not, Bear charged.

My eyes widened. A split second too late, I recognized who it was. All I could do was watch as a growling Bear lunged at Ryker and brought him to the ground.

9

S E C R E T S

"Bear, no!"

In my haste, I put too much weight on my injury. The ankle collapsed under the pain, but my walking stick kept me upright, kept me hopping toward the vicious-looking dog intent on tearing out Ryker's throat. When I reached them, I didn't know where to look first: at Bear's wicked long canines inches away from ripping flesh, or at the crimson spatters littering the snow. Was I too late?

"Bear, no," I repeated, putting authority behind the words the same way I used to with Freedom when she got ornery. "Heel!"

And, holy wonders of the mystical universe, he obeyed my command. I didn't have time to speculate on it because Ryker's rapid breathing drew my attention. I quickly scanned his body, but his dark clothing made it hard to tell if he was bleeding.

"Bear?" he said, grunting as he slowly sat up.

I shrugged. "He wouldn't stop following me so I thought that was better than calling him 'Bread Snatcher.'" I hesitated as he remained sitting in the snow, a very un-Ryker-like position. Was he injured? I jangled the metal at my wrists. "I'd offer you a hand up, but they're occupied at the moment."

Ryker slowly rolled to a stand, his movements stiff and jerky. "I see that. I also see that you didn't take my advice."

And our three seconds of politeness died a sudden death.

"And what sage advice did I fail to heed, all wise one?" My snark switched back on, fully charged after a solid day of neglect.

His expression flattened as he tapped his forehead, staring pointedly at mine. I awkwardly brought my hands up and felt a dry, flaky substance there. Then I remembered. Thane had bashed my head against a tree and I hadn't bothered to clean the cut. Oops. Excuses formed on the tip of my tongue, but a fresh red dot plopped into the snow at Ryker's feet. I changed gears.

"Looks like you didn't take your own advice. Where are you hurt?"

He waved a dismissive hand. "I've got it taken care of. What happened to you?"

Deflection? I knew that game all too well. "Thane happened. I'm guessing you know who he is, too?" I would cross my arms if I had the ability. I settled for narrowing my eyes.

Sighing, he said, "It's not what you think." I didn't miss the way his hand hovered over the left side of his torso before it dropped. Injury located. "I used to work with them, but not anymore. I guess you could say our current interests lay on separate paths."

"And yet you're both interested in me, it would seem." Might as well be blunt. Get a reaction out of him.

His gaze remained steady and I struggled not to look away. "Yes," he admitted without inflection. "But for very different reasons."

"And what are those reasons? I should probably know in case I need to choose a side." Why couldn't he just spit it out? Was I doomed to spend my life with people who wouldn't be honest? Stars, I missed Asher with a vengeance. He had always been open with me.

"It's simple." Another drop of blood fell. "They want to enslave you and I want to prove my loyalty to Supreme Elite Tatum. And believe me when I say you wouldn't want to be their boss's slave. Elite Tatum treats you a whole lot better than he ever would."

I blinked, digesting the information, surprised that he'd actually given me a bit of ammo. "Okay," I drew the word out. "But this doesn't make us friends or anything. I'm only following Renold's orders because I have no choice. If it were up to me, I'd never step foot inside Tatum City ever again. That's not the life I want."

He watched me shrewdly, probably wondering where my chosen path lay. Well, he wouldn't get an answer—all of my paths were currently broken anyway. Without replying, he unbuckled his pack and rummaged inside until he'd produced a small case. As he flipped it open, I learned his intentions. A pick. He had a lock pick! The raw skin at my wrists tingled with anticipation.

His fingers wrapped around my forearm. The pick was inches away from setting me free when he paused. "On one condition." My hands tightened on the walking stick. "You tell me where you're going. Because you're obviously not heading back to Tatum City, something that I *thought* you'd do when I said I'd lost Bren's trail."

I refused to meet his penetrating gaze, staring at the hovering pick instead. "I'm . . . following Bren's trail." Crap. I should have told him I was running away. But I *really* didn't want to be electrocuted again.

"How?"

"That's two conditions."

"*How*, Lune?"

"My instincts tell me where to go, that's how," I snapped, hating the power he currently had over me. "I think about him and my gut tugs me in the right direction. That's all I know. Now unlock the cuffs."

The scrape of metal was the only sound for several unbearable moments. I dreaded knowing where his thoughts were taking him. Would he tell Renold? Of course he would. He was Renold's little pet. I needed leverage and fast. My attention fixed on the fresh droplets of blood near his boots.

Game on.

"What else can you do?" His tone was calmer now. Placating.

Nope. Deflection time.

"First, tell me about your injury. Did the beast that attacked Thane get you?"

"No. Don't worry about it."

Click. The cuffs unlocked and Ryker removed them.

As cool air washed over my tender skin, I had the urge to jump up and down, shouting, "I'm free!" Somehow, I resisted, instead saying, "I'm not worried."

He rolled his eyes. "All right then, where to next, *tracker?*"

Ugh. I knew he would go there.

"See, that's the funny thing. My instincts stopped working the moment you arrived, so I guess your presence has a cancelling effect." I started walking downhill as if to head back to Tatum City. Bear fell in beside me.

"Why are you limping?"

He wasn't asking the right questions! "Why are you bleeding?" I threw back. At his soft snarl, I smirked.

"Fine," he gritted out. "Will you try to find Bren again if I keep your little gut instinct trick a secret from your father?"

Now we were getting somewhere. "You actually *want* to complete the mission?"

"Of course I do. Why wouldn't I?"

"I thought your *real* mission was to get us back to Tatum City as soon as possible."

Silence followed. And there it was—my leverage.

I glanced behind me, noting that his shoulders were slightly hunched. "See, I can't naively trust that you'll keep my secret. I'm sure you understand given how you've ratted me out in the past. So tell me why you're *really* out here, and we can call it even."

He huffed, shaking his head at my attempts to trap him. "Bren and I . . . we've known each other for many years. We were forced to do a lot of unsavory things. When we parted ways, it wasn't on the best of terms. Probably why he pretended not to know me while we were inside Tatum City. Anyway, if I can help him complete his mission, maybe we can resolve some of the things left unsaid between us. Elite Tatum doesn't know any of this, and I want to keep it that way."

I faced forward again so he couldn't see my jaw drop. Did Bren and Ryker used to be *friends?* The world shrunk even more. Did Ryker know about my past connection with Bren? "This is so weird," I whispered. Louder, I said, "Consider us even, after you let me see your injury."

"I told you it's—" His pained gasp was unmistakable. I whirled around in time to see him slump against a tree. As he caught his breath, his eyes glazed over.

With a snort, I backtracked. "You're worse than me. 'I'm fine. Just a little blood gushing out of my body like a waterfall that'll magically heal without aid.'" I pointed at a fallen log in a very Bren-like manner. "Sit."

He looked ready to argue, but I poked him in the chest with my stick and he practically tipped over backward. He threw me a glare as he caught himself, then slowly lowered his body without comment. The tough guy didn't like looking weak? Too bad. I contemplated feeding him a Bren line, then thought better of it. We weren't friends—I didn't have to play nice. I also didn't want him to zap me.

I sat next to him, stretching out my injured leg as I fished the first aid kit from my pack. He unzipped his coat and I gasped. So much blood. A large dark stain covered the left side of his gray shirt. "What happened?"

"Skervvy happened." His hand trembled as he tried to lift his shirt. "The bullet didn't hit anything too vital though. It passed through cleanly."

Bullet? *Passed through?* I wasn't squeamish about blood, but the thought of a bloody hole in Ryker's stomach sent a shiver dancing up my spine. "Well, that's . . . good. Here. Let me." I reached for his shirt and he stilled. Was he going to push me away? I gingerly grasped the hem and, when he didn't stop me, lifted the material.

A large bandage that leaked blood was affixed to his left side just under the rib cage. I tried to remember the rudimentary lessons Drake had given us on anatomy so we'd know where best to strike our opponent. The stomach was on the left side of the midsection but further down. As I carefully peeled off the bandage, I remembered. The spleen. I swallowed the bile building in my throat. "When you say the bullet didn't hit anything *too* vital . . ."

"I mean that I'll live," he finished. "But I couldn't stitch it up properly by myself. And I can't reach the exit wound."

"Ryker," I breathed, moving to lift the back of his shirt. The material stuck to his skin. "How are you still *alive*? Isn't your spleen ruptured?"

"Careful. You almost sound worried."

"I'm not—" I glanced up to see him smirking. *Smirking!* "This is serious," I hissed, and panic edged my voice despite myself. I didn't know how to treat a gunshot wound. I would probably make it *worse*.

"Deadly serious."

My eyebrows scrunched together as I studied him. "Are you drunk?" Renold sometimes drank wine with dinner and an untimely joke would slip past his normally flawless control.

"I might have taken something for the pain." He shrugged. "So shoot me."

I pressed my lips together as a comeback formed on my tongue. This wasn't the time to indulge him. "Stitching you up won't fix this. You need a doctor or you're going to die." There. I said it. Maybe he'd snap out of the weird mood he was in and tell me what we should do now.

He sighed and grabbed the kit from me. "Just stitch me up, Lune. I'm a lot tougher than I look." With a bottle of disinfectant in one hand and a needle in the other, he paused. "Guess that makes me indestructible."

"Okay, this version of you is downright creepy. Give me the bottle." I didn't bother warning him of the inevitable pain to come—he seemed to have transported his brain to an alternate reality anyway.

"I can remember the day like it was yesterday," he mumbled, barely flinching as I began to remove the poor stitchwork he'd inflicted on himself. I ignored him as best I could, trying to steady my hands so I wouldn't cause more damage. Then he said, "I told Bren not to do it, you know." I paused.

"Do what?"

"Approach you that day at the lake."

I sat up straight, tugging the last of his stitches free too quickly. He groaned but my mouth had dried, shriveling up an apology. After several failed tries, I managed to say, "Wha—?

How?"

His eyes rose to mine, and for a moment, they were clear. Completely serious. My heart thundered as he said, "Because the day you were kidnapped, I was there too."

I gaped, frozen in place when those two-toned eyes rolled upward. Then he tipped over unconscious.

10

PROTECT

Leaving me hanging after that kind of announcement was beyond rude. I cut him some slack, all things considered, but Ryker had some major explaining to do when he woke up. While he slept—probably dreaming of the day he'd helped destroy my life—I worked on patching him up the best I could.

More than once, I contemplated driving the needle through his eye and being done with him once and for all. I wouldn't do it, but the thought was there all the same. Every time he revealed a secret to me, I felt further confused and frustrated. Maybe I'd hold the pain meds hostage, refuse to give him any until he spilled his entire life's story. I tied off the last stitch and surveyed my handiwork. Since the most I'd ever stitched was a hole in my training gear, I was quite pleased. Ryker didn't need to know that though.

He was currently laid out inside my very tiny, single-person tent. I had felt a shred of sympathy as I'd surveyed him spread-eagle in the snow without a coat on. The least I could do was drag his ridiculously heavy body a few feet into a tent so he didn't catch a cold next. Now, an hour later, he was still in dreamland as I debated what to do.

Pros to keeping him alive: he could tell me more about

my past and Bren's. And I couldn't forget that he was the key to getting back inside Tatum City, if that was the actual truth. Pros to letting him die: he couldn't blab any more of my secrets to Renold, he couldn't help Bren fulfill his mission, he couldn't stop me from running away, he couldn't slow me down as he eventually died from infection and a ruptured spleen.

I growled and swung my walking stick at a nearby tree. The stick snapped in two. Well, that was stupid. This whole mission was stupid. "What's the point?" I yelled at the blue, cloudless sky, wishing the answers were written there. Ryker was dying, that's all I knew for certain. The realization made me feel . . . helpless. Not relieved, like I'd hoped.

Bear padded into the small clearing with a limp rabbit in his maw. He eyed me for a moment, then silently approached, dropping the hare at my feet. Tears threatened to spill down my cheeks. So much had gone wrong this past week, but this loyal dog was the one highlight. His size still spooked me at times, but his quiet friendship eased my fears. Comforted me when I thought all was lost.

"Thanks, buddy," I murmured. "Guess it's time I learn how to build a fire."

We stayed put for the rest of the day. By sundown, Ryker still hadn't woken, and his skin was feverishly warm. I managed to tuck him inside my sleeping bag when I couldn't find his. It was probably still in that ramshackle cabin we'd holed up in. How the tables had turned. Now I was the one trying to save his life. Except I was doing a terrible job at it.

Might as well make good use of all that body heat, my

callous inner self suggested. But I had to agree. The adrenaline from earlier had worn off, leaving me bone tired. Careful not to jostle him, I slipped in beside him and waited for his warmth to penetrate my icy skin. The fire I'd managed to ignite crackled just beyond the tent, a welcome sound to dispel the utter silence. My belly was full for the first time in days, thanks to my new friend. And my body was slowly warming, courtesy of a dying Ryker.

The morbid thought punched me in the gut. I rose up onto an elbow and peered down at Ryker's face. Still unconscious. Still drenched with sweat. But the constant line between his black brows was gone. The brackets around his mouth were erased. Sleep suited him. Maybe it offered him peace, like water did for me.

My eyes drifted shut, but I quickly snapped them open. He needed to be watched over. What if he died in the middle of the night while I was fast asleep beside him? A shudder shook my shoulders. "Don't you dare die while I'm wedged in a sleeping bag with you, Ryker Jones," I whispered.

His moon and claw tattoo contrasted sharply with his too-pale neck. How much blood had he lost on his trek to catch up with me? Guilt gnawed at my insides. Our paths might be opposing, but he was trying to protect me for whatever reason. He had saved me from both man and nature. Maybe he wasn't entirely bad. Maybe, just maybe, I could give him a chance.

After a moment's hesitation, I trailed my fingers over the tattoo. "Thank you."

He didn't stir.

The last thing I remembered was tracing the edges of his tattoo, then jerking awake as a fierce growl ripped through the night. I scrambled out of the sleeping bag, too frantic to worry about disturbing Ryker. In a rush, I jammed my boots on, hissing as my injured ankle throbbed. Instead of my coat, I snatched up my bow, quiver, and a dagger.

I recognized Bear's growl as I burst from the tent with weapons raised, but a shrill cry drowned him out. Every hair on my body stood on end at the sound. Cat. My heart thumped madly against my ribs. And not just any cat. *Saber* cat. My worst nightmare.

Stars help me, let this be a dream.

Bright yellow eyes danced on the far side of the dying fire, squashing my hope. I almost bit off my tongue when I saw a large shadow near the flames. It was only Bear. I wanted to call him away from that hellish creature, but my throat closed. With his teeth bared, the dog inched around the campfire.

An image of a mauled body flashed before me, first a human's—not the girl who'd died in my Arcus Point Trial, but one more familiar, one that I tried so hard to forget—then Bear's. My chest tightened as I blinked both the memory and vision away. Flickering flames took their place. I grimaced when I realized the terrible mistake I'd made in building that fire. It was my fault the cat had found us, then *and* now. But I wouldn't let history repeat itself. I wouldn't let Bear be the cat's victim when it should be me.

I sheathed my dagger and readied my bow instead, the

familiar motion of fitting an arrow to the string a slight balm to my fraying nerves. As I forced my feet to move, not away from the horrific nightmare but toward, one word echoed like a shot through my head. *Protect. Protect. Protect.* Protect Bear. Protect Ryker. Protect myself. Running wouldn't solve this problem. Fighting would.

I filled my lungs.

"Over here!" I yelled and charged into the open where I'd have a clear view of the cat—and it of me. I couldn't think, only feel, relying on instinct to guide my body. My eyes adjusted to the darkness just enough to see the monster's outline. The shout must have given it pause, but now that I wasn't near the fire, now that I was a solitary human, unprotected and alone and weak, the cat pounced.

Fear almost destroyed me in that moment. It caused me to freeze for a second too long, to aim a little too high, to blink instead of jump aside as the beast barreled into me and took me down. But instinct saved me. I tore my dagger free and plunged the blade into the cat's side before I could blink a second time.

The animal screamed, its finger-length canines inches from my face. With a cry of my own, I shoved the dagger into its side once more. Then again. And again. I rolled as its body slumped into the snow. Heaving in shaky breaths, I stared wide-eyed at the massive creature, not believing that it was dead. My body tensed, ready for more.

Up until now, adrenaline had allowed me to forget my injured ankle, but as I stood, I felt the bones shift. A sickening wave of agony bolted up my leg and I fell to my knees, choking back a scream. *Push past the pain!* Now wasn't the time to show weakness. I was strong. I could protect.

What if there were more saber cats?

At the thought, I stilled. Then scanned the area. Dead cat. Campfire. Tent. Something was missing. Where was Bear? My heart skipped a beat. "B—"

A shape came running at me. I scrambled for my bow as the beast closed in fast. With seconds to spare, I pulled back the string, ready to shoot. My eyes widened when I recognized the tan and black markings. Bear. It was Bear! But he was coming right for me, his teeth flashing. Not knowing what to do and unwilling to hurt him, I curled into a ball, protecting my head.

Air stirred my hair as he leapt. And landed behind me.

Screams and snarls filled the clearing. When the fighting beasts almost barreled into me, I scrambled a safe distance away on my hands and knees. All I saw was a flurry of tan and black fur and razor sharp teeth. Bear must be one of them, protecting me from another saber cat. I prepared my bow again, but at the speed the animals were fighting, chances were high that I'd hit the wrong target.

My stomach twisted as Bear yelped. I focused harder, zeroing in on a patch of smooth beige fur. *Please don't miss, please don't miss.* When Bear emitted a high-pitched whine, I couldn't stand it any longer. My fingers loosened on the bowstring. At that exact same moment, the sharp report of a gun cracked across the night sky. I jerked in surprise and my arrow flew wide. The two animals leapt apart. As soon as they did, more shots filled the air.

The cat's cries as bullets pelted its body sounded too much like a human's. Chills washed over me. Afraid one of the bullets would hit me next, I didn't move. Then swallowed a shriek when fur brushed my side. It was Bear, shielding me from the new threat. I wasn't given time to wonder at his protectiveness as several masked figures barged into the clearing with weapons trained on us.

I dropped my bow and raised my hands, knowing that fighting would no doubt earn me a bullet to the brain. Bear pressed closer to me and growled at the approaching humans. Before I could comfort him, I heard a male voice say, "Shoot the wolf."

"No!" Without thought of how he would react to my touch, I threw my arms around Bear, trying to cover his body with mine.

Fingers dug into my shoulders and wrestled me away from him. Bear loosed a flurry of snarls. His muscles bunched as he readied to strike. Then he yipped sharply and whirled in a tight circle. He whipped around again, whining and stumbling. I watched with mounting horror as he righted himself only to collapse.

Struggling against my captor's ironclad hold, I shouted, "What did you do to him? What did you do?" No one spoke as Bear curled into a ball and closed his eyes. My stomach dropped. "No. Bear!"

The cry ended in a whimper as my bad ankle gave out,

forcing my captor to adjust their hold. "She's injured," a man said from behind me.

"I think the other one is dead," a female voice called from the direction of my tent. Time ground to a halt. The *tent*. Ryker. No. No, it wasn't true. He wasn't dead.

The world tilted. I blinked rapidly to clear my vision. Breathe. Just breathe. "He's not dead," I whispered. No one heard me.

A tall figure dressed head-to-toe in black with only a slit cut out for the eyes blocked my view of the tent. "Hold still," he ordered, then waved a blue glowing wand in front of me. Down. Up. Down again. Up. *Beep*. Pause. *Beep beep beep*. He swore. "She's chipped!"

The words didn't register. "He's not dead," I repeated, louder this time.

"The other one is too," the same female said, rounding the tall man to stand in front of me. "Who do you work for?"

"He's *not* dead," I told her, straining once more to be free of the hands holding me. I had to see with my own eyes that Ryker was still alive. He couldn't have died while I was out saving his life. "I need to see him. Just for a second. Let me see him."

The woman drew closer, halting mere inches away. There was enough light in the clearing to reveal her dark almond-shaped eyes as they glared at me threateningly. "You're not going anywhere. Tell us who you work for and maybe I won't shoot you."

Click.

I glanced down to see a gun level with my chest. At the moment, I didn't care. "Go ahead, kill me. I won't be enslaved by another madman. But let me see my friend one last time. Just for a second."

She studied me for a good long while, then shook her head and turned toward the tall man. As they whispered, I was given a window of opportunity. An impossibly small one, but if this was to be my last moment on earth, I would make it count. I bashed my head into my captor's face, then yanked my arms out of his grip.

The next part—the pain of putting weight on my ankle and avoiding several grasping pairs of hands—almost dragged me to my knees. But I didn't stop. I had to know. Only a yard away from confirming if Ryker still lived, someone tackled me to the ground. I yelled my fury and quickly unsheathed my dagger. "Just let me see him!"

The blade slid free only for a boot to stomp on my hand. My scream was cut short as a sharp object plunged into my neck. A *needle*. I coughed in surprise at the sickening *whoosh* that filled my head, then my limbs, slowing my blood. My eyes slammed shut. Sound warped, muted. But before I sunk into oblivion, I heard a female voice hiss in my ear, "You shouldn't have done that."

MY CONSTANT

Drip.

Drip.

Drip.

I had been listening to the incessant noise for what felt like years. But when I started counting the drips, I knew that only minutes, then hours had passed. Every five seconds, water splatted. Or maybe it was blood. Once more, I struggled to pry my eyelids open, but only managed a quivering slit. My whole body felt weird. Sluggish. Responding several seconds too late. I was forced to wait until my brain decided to cooperate again.

Sometimes I heard the rustling of clothes. The soft murmur of voices. One time, there was arguing. Loud enough to penetrate the bubble I seemed to be stuck in. "She's not a threat," yelled a voice. But my mind was playing cruel tricks on me. The owner of that voice had sounded familiar. I knew the person well, and yet, I didn't. I knew his deep voice had brought me a moment of comfort. The feeling popped a second later.

Who are you? I wanted to ask. But my tongue was attached to the roof of my mouth. For some reason, his name eluded me. *All* names did. Even my own. It was there one second, and gone the next. The only thing I knew was that counting calmed my mind. So I once again lost myself in numbers as the water—or blood—continued to *drip, drip, drip.*

"Why isn't she awake yet?"

"Give her time. With all she went through out there, then the surgery and unexpected complications, sleep is the best medicine for her body."

"But you promised that she would—"

"I'm a doctor, not a scientist. If you need help understanding the complex nature of this memory serum, I'd suggest speaking with Dr. Bradfield again."

That familiar deep voice, still a strange comfort to me yet clearly upset, muttered an indecipherable reply, then sighed. After a beat of silence, I heard retreating footsteps and the snick of a door shutting. I waited for the dripping to start. It didn't. After listening to the sound for hours upon hours, maybe even days, it was the only constant in my life. To have that disappear was frightening.

"It's okay. Take a deep breath for me." At the soothing female voice, I struggled to obey. "That's it. Just take your time. You're safe now."

Safe now? What did that mean? Was there a time when I wasn't safe?

My eyes moved. I managed to lift one lid, then the other.

Too bright. I shut them.

"You've been asleep for awhile. It'll take time for your body to adjust. Here, take my hand."

For a moment, my mind wrestled with her request. A part of me wished to disobey, to ball my hand tightly at my side. But a larger part heeded her words. I raised my arm, the movement much more difficult than I'd anticipated. My fingers touched smooth skin, then a hand wrapped around mine.

"We'll go slowly. Let your body adapt to its new surroundings." As the hand gently pulled me into a sitting position, something about the word "slow" bothered me. "There. How about you try opening your eyes again."

I did without question, because I didn't like being in the dark—I knew that much. The room was blinding white at first, but I blinked until colors and shapes appeared. There were light gray walls behind a round silver table, a charcoal sofa beside a slate blue door, and . . . a middle-aged woman. She was smiling. It took a second for my mouth to cooperate, but I smiled back.

"I'm glad you're awake, Lune," she said, releasing my hand.

I blinked. *Lune.* Was that my name? It felt . . . right.

A small sigh of relief escaped me. "Me too," I croaked, and she immediately handed me a cup of water. Over the glass rim, I searched her face for traces of familiarity but found none. Laugh lines surrounded her green eyes, though, which put me at ease. She wore a long white smock, and her brown hair was pulled back, revealing high cheekbones.

"Where am I?" I asked, glancing around the room again. There was a white-and-gray patterned rug on the floor, the only decoration. "Is this where I live?"

The woman hesitated. "This is your home for now, yes." Home. The word felt empty. Like this room. "But I'll let Dr. Moore answer the rest of your questions. He knows more than I do."

I nodded, settling against the bed's cushioned headboard. The back of my neck began to burn, causing me to wince. My fingers went to the spot and I frowned. There was a tender, raised mark at the base of my skull, just under the hairline. "What's this?" I looked at the nameless woman, trying not to show my alarm.

She must have seen the emotion because she gently patted my leg. "Something unpleasant, but I removed it. You're safe now. No harm will come to you."

There was that word again. *Safe.* Why did a part of me not believe her?

Rising from a metal chair next to my bed, she offered me her hand again. I took it after a quick moment of hesitation. "Now, let's get you on your feet. It might be difficult at first, but that's what I'm here for. I'm Dr. Stacey, by the way."

I slowly swung my stiff legs over the bed, taking in the pale blue, knee-length dress I wore. A hospital gown, maybe? But it was the color that gave me pause. "Do I like blue?"

"I don't know. Do you think you like blue?"

Without hesitation, which surprised me, I answered, "No."

"Hmm. Maybe you're experiencing a phantom emotion," she muttered, almost to herself. Her gaze cleared and a small smile graced her rosey lips. "There's a change of clothing in the bathroom. Let's go see what color they are."

This suggestion put a grin on my face. Getting out of bed sounded like a great idea. My feet hit the floor and I jumped up. Dr. Stacey caught me under the arms as my legs gave out. Pins and needles stabbed the bottoms of my feet and quickly worked their way upward. I groaned, flinching from the pain. "What's," I panted, "happening?"

"I'm sorry, dear, I should have warned you first." She positioned my right arm over her shoulders and let me lean on her as my legs continued to burn. "You've been in bed for the last two weeks, so it's normal for your legs to be weak."

Two weeks? What happened to me?

I glanced down at my trembling limbs and saw a strange boot on my left foot. How did that get there? I could have sworn both of my feet were bare. Was something wrong with my memory?

Dr. Stacey must have noticed my confusion. "It's just an ankle boot. You suffered a hairline fracture, but your ankle should be good as new in a few weeks."

Weeks. Why was I starting to dislike that word? I bottled my growing list of questions. Sealing them up would probably be easier than prying answers out of this nervous woman. Yes, that's what had been bothering me. The more questions I asked, the more nervous she seemed.

The trek to the attached bathroom took a few minutes,

which put an impatient frown on my face. My body craved something in there, though I wasn't sure what. My skin practically hummed with anticipation. When we finally reached the all-white room accented in silver, tears stung my eyes. Startled at the strong reaction, I blinked several times to clear my vision.

Dr. Stacey propped me against the white marble countertop, then rummaged inside a linen closet. She pulled out flared black pants and a forest green shirt. I nodded my approval. Next, she switched on the shower, saying something about sponge baths not being thorough enough. I stopped listening as my gaze locked onto the spitting showerhead.

Water.

It reminded me of the constant dripping that had kept me company over the last couple weeks. Somehow my body knew, even if my brain didn't, that I liked water.

I pushed off the counter and headed toward the shower stall, completely enraptured. The bathroom door softly clicked shut. Dr. Stacey must have given up on me responding. Whoops. At a more satisfying speed, I stripped naked and stepped under the downpour.

Hot!

Perfect.

No. *Heaven.*

Maybe I didn't just like water; maybe I *loved* it.

I couldn't stop smiling. I never wanted to leave this small square of utter bliss. Half an hour later, my skin tingled with cleanliness, but my legs started to complain in earnest. I was so *weak*. I really didn't like that word. Reluctantly turning the water off, I searched for a towel and found a fluffy white stack on the counter. I dried my now slightly pink self, then froze.

What did I look like? How could somebody forget their own *face*? For some reason, my fingers shook as they wiped away steam from the bathroom mirror. Was I hideous? But when my reflection appeared, I chuckled at the irrational fear.

"Not too bad," I murmured, wagging my eyebrows. I squinted for a closer look at a fresh scar on my forehead. It wasn't awful-looking, but would take time to fade. I turned my head. There was an older scar on my left temple in the shape of a C.

"What the—?"

I looked down at my arms, then my knuckles and palms. Scars. They were covered in scars. Unwrapping the towel, I found more on my stomach. Long ones, like something had raked open my flesh. I swiveled around and peered into the mirror at my back. Horror swamped me.

I screamed.

12

HIS VOICE

What happened to me? What happened to me? What happened to me?

"She's been in there for hours. I'm going to pick the lock."

"But Dr. Moore said—"

"I don't care what he said! He doesn't know her like I do."

I registered their words but they didn't sink in. I was too busy asking myself questions that I didn't have answers to. For the last hour, pressure had steadily built behind my eyes. My head felt ready to burst. I continued to rock myself where I'd curled up on the floor against the wall. I had lost track of time. My mind wouldn't stop circling like a vulture searching for prey. Every single time, it came up empty.

Empty.

My brain is empty of memories.

I choked out a strangled sob.

"Heaven help me, I'm going in!" a voice shouted. The door handle jiggled and I clutched the towel to my chest. Had I instinctively locked it? Did they give me these countless scars? Did they destroy the flesh on my back? I didn't know. I didn't know *anything*.

I heard a *click* as the lock unlatched. The door swung inward, slowly revealing the tallest person I had ever met. At least, I thought so. I couldn't remember meeting anyone other than Dr. Stacey. He took a step inside and I froze. He did, too. My gaze traveled up, up, up to his face, then ran over his handsome features—square jaw, full lips, dark brown hair that slightly curled on his forehead. And his eyes. His eyes . . .

They were gold.

A switch flipped on inside me, one born of self-preservation. Fear poured through my veins. Wave after wave. I was drowning, suffocating under the weight of his stare. So intense. So . . . predatory. My heart raced out of control. I gasped for breath as my chest tightened. Despite how scared I was, I couldn't tear my eyes from his.

Then I watched in disbelief as his expression crumbled. Pain etched deep lines into his face. He retreated, but not before I saw a sheen steal over those golden eyes, like he was holding back tears. Why did the sight make my own tears spill down my cheeks?

An hour later, when I'd calmed enough for Dr. Stacey to help me into bed, I lay awake, picturing the handsome man's face. I memorized every single detail. Because I never wanted to feel fear like that again—the all-consuming, controlling every molecule of my being kind. It was the first thing I knew that I hated.

Fear of losing control.

And now that my fear had a face, I was determined not to forget it.

Two days passed without another unexpected visit from the tall stranger. Dr. Stacey didn't mention the incident, so neither did I, despite my curiosity. I had been overwhelmed by the ordeal, and the thought of asking questions made me feel . . . vulnerable.

While my body used the time to heal and rest, I continued to scour my brain for memories that weren't there. When headaches formed from thinking too hard, I took showers, never growing tired of the warm water. Dr. Stacey brought me something called a puzzle, but by the third day, I couldn't sit on my butt for another second. As if in agreement, my leg bounced up and down at a rapid rate. I had acquired the new tic shortly after the bathroom debacle—at least, I thought it was new. Now, every time I sat, I bounced.

When my one visitor came in with breakfast, I was already dressed, leg bouncing away. Dr. Stacey prepared to greet me as usual, but I beat her to it. "I'm ready for answers. Can we go see Dr. Moore today?" I had planned my words carefully. I didn't want him coming *here*. More than anything, I wanted out of this room, even for a few minutes. It was starting to feel like a prison cell—not that I knew what a prison felt like.

She nodded, setting my food down on the silver table. "I'll let him know that you wish to talk. But," she continued, watching me carefully, "there's the matter of your guard."

"Guard?" My brows pulled together.

"It's for your safety. Because of your history, some of the people here are on edge. They think—" Her lips pursed as she focused on my glass of orange juice.

"They think what?" I asked softly, urging her to tell me. *I can handle it. No more meltdowns*, I almost added but didn't.

With a sigh, she moved to the bed and gently squeezed my shoulder as if to lend comfort. I tried not to stiffen. "They think you're dangerous, dear."

My mouth formed an O. It was safer than laughing.

"Anyway, I'll inform your guard to escort you to Dr. Moore's office. Be ready in an hour?"

I nodded enthusiastically and refrained from blurting that I was ready now. She left soon after, making sure I took pain meds for my ankle since I'd be walking around today. I still didn't know how I'd received the injury.

While I waited for my guard—whatever or whoever that meant—I paced. Every other step, my ankle boot thumped against the floor. Minutes before the hour was up, my fingers became fidgety as well, which reminded me that I hadn't brushed my hair. They kept busy by weaving a braid down my back. With nothing left to do, I sat on the bed and drummed my foot against the floor. *Tap tap tap tap tap.* The rhythm was oddly soothing.

"Well, that's new."

I whipped my head up to discover the door open. Leaning against the frame was a tall figure wearing boots, black pants, and a form-hugging gray tee. My eyes went straight to the powerful forearms currently crossed over a well-defined chest. Embarrassment scorched my cheeks at how blatantly I'd been gawking. There was no undoing it though. My gaze finally landed where it should have in the first place.

At the sight of his face, I sucked in a gasp and jerked to a stand. *Him.* The man with the familiar voice and predatory gold eyes. Didn't he know how to knock? Was that not a custom around here? Dr. Stacey did though. I almost told him so, but my mouth didn't seem to be working at the moment.

So I stared at him. What else could I do? Having memorized his facial features, I wasn't as afraid this time as I held his gaze, determined to control the emotion prodding at me. What was it about those eyes that had scared me so much? Should I listen to that instinct and scream for help? When I remained silent, he pushed off the doorjamb and took a step inside. Then another. The urge to run wrapped around me, but I held my ground.

A couple more steps and he was close enough to touch. I swallowed past the tense ache in my throat as his nearness, as his overwhelming gaze became too much. Control slipped through my fingers. Fear flooded in and I struggled to breathe. I squeezed my eyes shut and retreated until my legs bumped against the bed.

Trapped.

No, no, no.

"Breathe, little bird. Just breathe."

The combination of his familiar voice and the casual way he'd said the nickname startled me into inhaling shakily. My eyes snapped open. "What did you say?"

Something happened to his face then. It lit up, like he'd been granted his greatest wish. The most charming smile graced his lips—one side tipped up more than the other. At the sight, my stomach fluttered. Before I could make sense of the strange feeling, his large hands cupped my cheeks. Shocked at their warmth and his electric touch, every inch of me froze.

"You had me so scared, Lune," he whispered, sounding heartbroken and relieved in the same breath. His thumbs swept over my cheekbones. My heart skipped in response. Okay, this needed to stop. *Now.* My senses were overloaded and I couldn't think. I placed my hands on his chest to push him away, but he pulled me closer, saying, "Thank God, you're alright." Then he pressed his lips to my forehead.

For one heart-stopping moment, my body melted against his as if happy to be reunited. What was wrong with me? First he'd barged into my bathroom, then my room, then *kissed* me, and a part of me wanted to accept that without question? Anger sprang up like a roaring fire. I took control of myself and shoved him. Hard. He moved less than an inch. What the—? I wasn't *that* weak, was I? When his hands dropped and he pulled back a few more inches, I did what needed to be done.

I slapped his face.

The sound cracked through the gaping silence. My palm stung, but I felt a whole lot better, like I'd been wanting to do that for a long time. Was I a violent person? I didn't dwell on the worrisome thought. There was space between us and I could breathe again. That was what mattered.

And, more importantly, I was in control.

I crossed my arms, refusing to apologize for my actions. He had stepped over invisible lines and I'd clearly shown him where the boundaries were. His expression flipped from shock and confusion to hurt and sadness. I fisted my hands, determined not to feel bad.

He looked down at the floor. "I'm sorry. I thought . . . I thought you recognized the nickname, so I assumed . . ." He rubbed at his neck for several moments as he internally struggled with what to say next. Or maybe he was restraining himself from hitting me back? A spark of fear flared in my gut. There was no way I could defend myself against someone his size. He would crush me.

His eyes snapped to mine as if he'd felt my panic. When he reached for me again, I flinched away, almost toppling backward onto the bed. His hand froze midair. I watched with growing alarm as it curled into a fist. "Please, don't," he whispered, the same words that were on my own tongue. His arm lowered. "I would never hurt you, Lune. Ever. Please don't be afraid of me."

My thoughts tangled together. The words sounded genuine, but . . . "If I don't know you, how can I trust you?"

At the question, his expression fell even more. His fist now rubbed at his chest. No. At his heart. He was miserable and in pain. A small tug of sympathy urged me to comfort him, but I pushed the feeling down. He might know my name, but he was still a stranger who caused me endless confusion every time I looked at him.

He cleared his throat and the pain disappeared, replaced with determination. "You do know me—at least, you *did*. Not well, though. Not the way you or I wanted. Things were, *are* complicated, but I'll tell you everything I wasn't able to for the last four months. Please, Lune, just give me a chance."

A chance.

Did I give chances?

It was his voice that made my decision easy. The deep rolling timbre continued to comfort me for some odd reason. It was like a possession I valued but had forgotten about, yet still unconsciously searched for. The strangeness of it all should have scared me but didn't.

I awkwardly stuck out my hand as if greeting him for the very first time. "Hi, I'm Lune."

He stared at my outstretched fingers, then my face. Understanding dawned. A smile slowly widened his mouth as he took my hand and gave it a warm shake. "Brendan Bearon."

I smiled back.

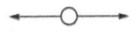

All too soon, I discovered why having a guard was necessary.

No one approached, but eyes tracked my every movement. Not in a curious, friendly way either. Maybe I should feel nervous, even afraid, but how could I when the most fearsome person I knew was walking beside me? Brendan kept peeking at my reaction, but when I pretended to ignore him in favor of viewing our surroundings, we continued in silence.

There wasn't much to see. Curved, pale stone hallways bearing simple, round light fixtures every handful of feet. Slate blue doors identical to mine. The rooms were probably exactly alike too. Something about this place felt off though, as if missing an important element. We turned a corner and I sucked in a quiet gasp, unconsciously slowing.

Straight out in front of me was air. Across the expanse, people strolled along the same waist-high metal and glass railing my hands had reflexively grabbed. There were actually several railings outlining the impossibly large man-made circle, all on different levels. I counted fifteen total.

As my eyes traveled upward, I expected to see blue for some reason, but found endless pinpricks of light instead, so intense I had to look away. Blinking to clear my vision, I realized now what was missing. Windows. The sky and sun. The outdoors. Instinctually, I knew about these things without having concrete memories of them.

Then I looked down and had to bite my lip as a grin threatened to split my face in two. Far below was a cluster of trees at the circle's center. Their color matched my shirt. But what sent a rush of tingles up my arms and legs was the deadly drop. I was so high off the ground. At least ten floors were stacked beneath this one.

I leaned over the railing. My braid slid over my shoulder as I took in the circular bottom with its bustling activity. Tiny people of all colors wove this way and that, like a chaotically coordinated dance I didn't know the steps to. From up here, their voices had dulled to a steady drone. Some sat at little red tables while others formed long lines to what looked like breakfast.

For many minutes, I was lost in the foreign sights and wonders of this place. I was pretty sure this was my first time seeing it. An urge to throw my arms wide and pretend I was flying stole over me. I laughed at the ridiculous feeling.

With a start, I remembered that I wasn't alone and quickly straightened. When I glanced at my guard, I found him watching me with a soft smile. My chest tightened. Before fear or who-knew-what emotion could take hold of me, he cleared his throat and casually placed both elbows on the railing.

As he peered below, Brendan said, "This is the Communal Circle, or 'The Circle' as most of us call it. The residents come here three times a day for meals. Community announcements are held here, too. Every person over the age of ten is given a job. Each position is valued, so we're all given the same rations and accommodations. We are all equal."

I immediately liked this place now that I knew how things worked. But . . . "Where is *here* exactly?"

"Blue Ridge Sector. A safe haven, I guess you could say. Welcome to my home."

That word again. Home. It didn't feel so empty this time.

"What's wrong?"

"Huh?" I side-eyed him as he studied my profile.

"Your nose did that flaring thing it does when you dislike something."

My jaw slackened. *What the what now?* Before I could

stop them, my fingers touched my nose. Brendan clamped his lips together to hide a grin. How well did he know me anyway? "Uh, I think it's the name. Did I used to dislike the color blue?"

"You *don't* like blue," he corrected. "You once told me it reminds you of . . . Wait, you remember?" His eyes did that lighting up thing again.

I forced myself to hold his gaze even as my pulse quickened. "I sometimes have likes and dislikes when things are mentioned, a feeling or emotion. That's about it though. No memories."

His expression fell. I was starting to hate that look. I had the craziest urge to tell a joke so that unmistakable pain would go away, but nothing came to mind. I must not have been a funny person before my memories disappeared.

THE SILENT WAR

"What's it called again?" I eyed the silver box suspiciously. He wanted me to get inside while it did *what*?

"An elevator," Brendan repeated, this time with a touch of laughter. "I promise it won't hurt you. I'll hold your hand if you want though."

My face and neck grew uncomfortably warm at the bold invitation. But it was the way he'd said the words, as if to challenge me, that captured my attention. My spine snapped straight and I marched inside the box, then whirled to face him. His brows ticked upward, nearly disappearing into his hair. I didn't know who was more surprised: him or me. Did I like challenges?

He smirked knowingly and strolled in to stand beside me. With a press of a button, the door slid closed, sealing us inside. It was just him, me, and a tiny box that seemed smaller than it'd been a moment ago. Out of nowhere, a cold sweat beaded my forehead. My stomach roiled.

The walls. They were closing in. Suffocating me.

I felt . . .

Trapped.

As I thought the word, deep-seated panic set in. My voice

shook as I said, "Brendan, I don't think I like—"

The ground jolted, throwing me off balance. With a surprised gasp, I fell backward. Before I could hit the wall, Brendan's arms surrounded me and pulled me close. His hand gently pressed my cheek to his shoulder. And instead of shoving him away like they did earlier, my hands latched onto his shirtfront as if he was the key to unlocking this moving nightmare.

"I've got you, little bird," he murmured against my hair. I could feel his warm breath, smell him as my nose brushed his neck. Sunshine. He smelled of sunshine with hints of leather and pine. The combination . . . I almost liked it. My stomach flipped uncontrollably.

No, not again, I was tempted to groan aloud. What was happening to me?

I flattened my palms against his chest and broke his hold on me, then grabbed a railing along the back wall. My fingers squeezed the metal as I tried to rid myself of his touch, his scent, his very presence that made me equal parts confused and exhilarated. The elevator ride lasted an eternity as I fought to slow my rapid pulse. I refused to look at him. He was watching me though. I could feel it. I could feel him everywhere. And if I had to be trapped in this box with him for one more second, I was going to—

Ding.

The door slid open.

My legs trembled as I lurched forward and deeply inhaled unboxed air that wasn't stuffed with tension. A second later, Brendan strode past, but not before I heard him mutter, "Thank heaven and earth."

We were on the very top floor now. I only caught a quick glimpse of The Circle fifteen floors below as we moved at a much faster clip than earlier. My ankle started to complain and I slowed, not knowing if I should call out to my "guard" or let him walk off whatever was bothering him. Because something definitely was. I was savvy enough to realize that something was *me*, but what could I do?

I didn't remember him even if my body did. My body wasn't allowed to call the shots, though. It was way too impulsive and needed to be kept on a short leash.

Brendan stopped and waited for me in front of a door with a sign above that said . . . I frowned as my mind stumbled over the letters. D-O-C-T-O-R. Okay, I understood that part at least. Why couldn't I read well?

Embarrassment heated my face and I studiously avoided his gaze when I caught up with him. I focused on a white eagle stamped on the door that held arrows in one claw and a branch in the other. Words circled the symbol, ones that would take me too long to read, so I didn't try. I snuck a quick peek at Brendan. Apparently, I wasn't the only one avoiding eye contact. He stared at the stone floor as he said, "Dr. Moore can be blunt. He means well, but mincing words isn't in his genetic makeup. He wants to help you though, okay? You have nothing to be afraid of."

I nodded. Blunt was preferable to Dr. Stacey's careful, placating words. I desperately needed to know why I had no memories. Brendan knocked on the door, and when a male voice answered from the other side, he motioned for me to enter first. I didn't know what to expect of the supposed leader of this place, but the man bustling around his desk to greet us wasn't it.

"Miss Avery! I'm so glad to see you awake and looking well. We were worried there for a moment." He stuck out his hand and I received a quick shake before he moved to clap my guard on the shoulder. "Any problems?"

Brendan shook his head, "No, sir."

Their exchange continued, but I was too busy studying Dr. Moore to pay attention. Not wanting to get caught staring, I pretended to inspect his office which contained a simple desk with the same eagle symbol on it, a few chairs, and three solid walls of books. The books piqued my curiosity, but their owner even more so.

The first thing I noticed was how incredibly short he was. Standing next to my guard, he looked like a child, except his face was anything but. Thick glasses rested on a balloon-shaped nose, enlarging light gray eyes that didn't linger on one spot longer than a second or two. His cheeks were ruddy, practically red next to a thick shock of white hair—"shock" because it looked like he'd stuck his finger in a light socket.

"Sit sit sit, Miss Avery," he said, waving at the metal chairs stacked against the right bookcase. "Your leg must be tired. You went through quite the ordeal out there on the mountain."

Mountain? Brendan grabbed two chairs and held one for

me as I sat. Before I could murmur a thanks, Dr. Moore was already speaking again, rapidly, as he took a seat behind his scuffed walnut desk.

"It's unfortunate you lost your memories, and I'm sure you have many questions, but I wanted to assure you that we're doing everything we can to create an antidote. When Dr. Stacey removed Bren's chip, there were no ill side effects, so it came as quite a surprise when yours contained a memory-erasing serum set to release at the implant's removal. I guess your adoptive father didn't want you revealing all the family secrets."

He chuckled, and I gave him a weak smile, not understanding the humor. In fact, I had no clue what he was talking about. I was adopted?

Brendan shifted in his chair. "Maybe you should start at the beginning. The *very* beginning. She wasn't taught much history while living in the city."

Dr. Moore folded his hands in front of him and I braced myself to be bombarded with a heap of confusing information. "Quite right, quite right. You've heard of the Silent War? Well, I suppose you wouldn't remember even if you had. Anyway, everything was quite different before the war one hundred years ago—The Tech Age, they called it. People could access the entire world with the press of a button and travel the globe in a matter of days. For the first time, unity and inclusivity were within reach.

"But that much power comes at a price. Bad people became more knowledgeable, dangerous weapons became more attainable. Soon, conspiracy theories and fear-mongering in-filtrated the news system of their time, whispers of war at the helm. People formed opinions before knowing the full truth, spreading the lies to anyone who would listen. They turned on each other, took sides—always hatred over respect. Dark out-shone light, hope in humanity was lost. Fear ruled the world. And fear has a tendency to turn into violence, wouldn't you agree?"

I blinked, belatedly realizing he'd asked me a question. "Um, I—I don't know."

He glanced at Brendan, saying, "I suppose it's a good thing she can't remember him." But Brendan was watching me—I could feel his stare like a touch. Curious how I was tak-ing this history lesson, maybe? But I didn't have an opinion yet. I needed the full story.

Dr. Moore plowed on. "The citizens of this country tried to overrule the government—they hated and feared those in power at the time. Anyone who opposed this takeover had the weaker voice, and as threats of violence grew rampant on every street corner, they feared leaving their homes. They quit their jobs, pulled their kids out of school. Word spread quick-ly and unrest formed in other countries as well."

He laid his palms flat on the desk and chuckled. "You're probably wondering why it was called the *Silent* War then. Be-cause as the world teetered on the cusp of anarchy, as the rul-ing governments threatened to nuke each other to obliterate the chaos, the end was already upon them and they didn't even know it. A mysterious airborne virus was released and"—his hands shot out as if holding an invisible ball—"poof. Ninety percent of all living things perished in an instant, and freedom of speech died with them. So, I guess you could say fear silenced the world."

My brain struggled to digest this unbelievable event of the past. "Who—who would do such a thing?"

He shrugged and leaned back in his chair. "Some say it was a secret military branch who wanted the world thrust back into the Dark Ages to more easily control the populace. Others say it was a terrorist attack led by mad scientists who wanted to see the world evolve into something other than hate and violence. But the real question is why a virus, and why *this* one? Did they know it would decimate so many? Did they know it would alter the seasons, make the cold temperatures colder and the hot temperatures hotter? Did they know that many of the remaining organisms would start to adapt, to mutate, to change into something . . . unnatural?"

"Maybe they wanted to throw chaos at the world so the world would stop its chaos. Change the chaotic outcome from violent individuals to group survivalism."

At my theory, his thin lips split into a grin, revealing a wide gap between his front teeth. "You're smart, Miss Avery, even without your memories. You'll be a fine asset to our community. Which brings us to our next topic: what to do with you."

My heart skipped a beat at the abrupt subject change. I looked down to see my leg bouncing. I still wasn't connecting the dots—how I had gotten here, why I'd been on a mountain, and what the world's devastating history had to do with it all.

Brendan placed one booted leg on top of the other, distracting my thoughts. My leg stopped moving. I snuck a glance at his face to find him smirking. Was he teasing me? I allowed my leg to bounce again. His smirk grew. "What the good doctor means is we won't be putting you on kitchen duty anytime soon. You have untapped abilities that shouldn't go to waste. Blue Ridge Sector isn't just a safe place—it's a program for people like us who adapted to the new environment and became something else entirely."

I turned to him. "Something else. As in, not human?"

"At our core, we are still human, just enhanced. No two people are exactly the same, but we've started to group abilities into categories for less confusion. Dr. Moore is an Intellect, I'm a Sensor, and you . . . well, I have someone for you to meet before we can know for sure what you are."

"Scientists have discovered the main component of the virus that mutated our genes," Dr. Moore added. "It's called CRISPR—clustered regularly interspaced short palindromic repeats. In other words, DNA fragments that can edit genes. The fact that this component was added to the deadly concoction makes me believe that whoever released it was hoping for survivors. The splicing had to be intentional, but how and why they formulated the mutations and abilities we see today is still a mystery."

His gaze turned speculative as he leaned forward once more. "It's also why the others are uncertain of you, Miss Avery. The virus changed so much of the familiar, mutating even the tamest of creatures. Have you ever stumbled across a wererabbit? Nasty little things." He grimaced as if reliving an unpleasant memory. "Fear of the unknown has been a curse upon this earth since the beginning of time. What we don't know can harm us, so we lash out first, ask questions later. But once we figure out what your abilities are, people should start to relax again."

"What if I'm . . . dangerous?" I glanced at Brendan again but couldn't read his expression.

"We strive to accept all individuals, Miss Avery, unlike the city you were raised in. Everyone deserves a chance to thrive in this new world, abilities or no. But if your abilities prove to be unstable," he said, his large gray eyes practically glittering with what looked like excitement, "we'll help you. Safety is our number one priority."

Our meeting ended soon after that, with Dr. Moore promising to answer any more questions I might have, but I had plenty to dwell on for the time being. Brendan offered to show me around Blue Ridge Sector—or "The Ridge", since apparently everything here had a nickname—but I declined. If they were going to test me for hidden abilities I knew nothing about, then I needed one more day of rest and solitude. Because after today, I doubted I'd be spending much time in my simple, quiet room.

MEMORIES

"What's your ability again?" I asked Brendan at breakfast the next morning. With so few memories to clog my brain, I shouldn't have forgotten this quickly.

"Ditching best friends for a pretty face, is what it's called."

My body tensed as the newcomer's voice blared directly behind me. When he rounded The Circle's dining table and plopped into a seat next to Brendan, I relaxed, wondering at the white-knuckled grip I still had on my fork. Why had I thought eating with the masses was a good idea? The surrounding bodies were almost worse than the elevator experience.

Brendan gave the young man a warning look. "You're gonna make her run for the hills, dude."

"Funny. I thought that was *your* job." The man's teeth flashed neon bright against his dark skin. He winked a hazel eye at me even as Brendan shoved his shoulder.

A comeback readily formed on the tip of my tongue, which surprised me. I had thought myself incapable of jokes, so why the sudden desire to knock this guy down a peg or two with a witty reply?

"Lune, this is Jaxon," Brendan said before taking a huge

bite from his apple which made my mouth water for some reason. "Don't let his strange fashion choices or goofy face fool you. He's smarter than he looks. Although, he gets these delusional dreams that we're best friends. Apparently they're so real, he can't help but dog my every step like a little lost puppy."

Jaxon guffawed, saying, "It's vintage," while straightening his faded yellow t-shirt. On the front, a helmeted man, dressed all in black with a floor-length cape, held a red glowing stick. Then, lightning quick, Jaxon had my guard in a headlock. "And you know the dreams are real, man. You and me for eternity!"

I froze with a forkful of scrambled eggs halfway to my mouth as I watched them scuffle. A part of me was alarmed that my guard had been overtaken so easily, but the other part was relieved. If Brendan had friends, maybe he wasn't so bad, even if my first instinct had been to fear him.

"Look there! She's smiling! My job here is done," Jaxon announced, jumping up before it could sink in that he was referring to me. He pointed at Brendan. "See you in training? Don't let your arms get flabby just because you're a pansy guard now. I bet they'll ask you to be a captain in the Abilities Competition. See you around, Lune."

And with that, he was gone, sucking some of the noise and energy from The Circle as he went.

"Sorry about that trainwreck," Brendan said, but couldn't quite hide a grin. "He says whatever pops into his head. It's an Intellect trait. Filters don't exist in their world."

I shrugged, finding that I didn't mind in the least. "What did he mean when he said it was your job to make me run for the hills?"

He groaned and muttered something about towel-snapping a little puppy. "That's not a conversation for nosy civilians. Walk with me?" He rose from the table and grabbed his food tray, reaching for mine. I snatched my uneaten apple from the plate, not wanting to waste it.

As I followed after him, munching away at the delectable fruit, so did dozens of stares. My senses sharpened and I became uncomfortably aware of every move my body made.

"Stay close to me and no one will bother you."

I glanced up to see Brendan watching me too, but his attention was different. Assuring. Comforting. As long as I didn't look directly into his eyes, I could let his words soothe the fresh flare of anxiety. "Why do they stare as if I'm going to throw butter knives at them?"

When he snickered, I frowned. "Sorry. It's just bringing back memories." We exited the dining area and I tossed my apple core into a trash bin. Despite the thinning crowd, he continued to speak softly. "Fear has a way of making us do foolish things. When something supersedes our knowledge or ability to control it, we retaliate, usually in violent ways. The Ridge is a safe haven, but our nature is to defend our home against foreign threats. Once upon a time, the people here looked at *me* the way they're now looking at you."

"Oh? You couldn't magically charm them with your smile?" As soon as the words left me, I wanted to bite my tongue off. I searched for a place to bury myself, but not a speck of dirt was to be found.

"Glad to hear some things haven't changed about you," Brendan said, sounding way too amused. I didn't dare look at his face. "But no, their first reaction was to fear me, kind of like—"

When he didn't finish, I peeked at his profile in time to see his jaw harden. Maybe it was a trick of the light, but a flash of pain seemed to shadow his features, then was gone as we rounded a corner. "Like me?"

His throat bobbed. "Yeah. I just . . ." With a sigh, he glanced down at me. I couldn't look away from the sadness in his eyes. "You've felt a lot of things for me in the past, but fear was never one of them."

My mouth opened, but I didn't know what to say. Did the old me not have self-preservation skills? Because everything about the man beside me screamed predator. His build, the way he walked, even how he watched me. Those golden eyes . . . they almost reflected light, appearing to glow when his gaze intensified.

Like right now.

"Crap," I breathed, shifting my focus elsewhere.

"You don't need to be afraid, Lune," he murmured. "I would never hurt you."

I stopped dead in the middle of the hallway which earned me a muttered curse from someone I'd unintentionally blocked. "Then who did?"

Brendan tried to nudge me out of traffic's way, but I

smoothly avoided his touch, too hyperaware of him at the moment. I crossed my arms and leaned against the stone wall, unconsciously protecting my back. "No one here wants to hurt you," he began, but I cut him off.

"How long have I been here?"

"Two weeks."

"Where was I before that?"

"Tatum City."

"Was I . . ." I almost clammed up. But the burning desire for answers had begun the moment I'd seen myself in the mirror three days ago. And the man before me was the only one who had the answers I sought. The questions I wanted to ask were hard though, uncomfortably personal. But I needed to know. My hands curled into fists. "Was I mistreated?"

He flinched, just a small tic beneath his right eye, but I caught it. "Yes."

"By who?" My voice shook, not with fear, but with rising anger. I dug my nails into my palms.

"Renold, your adoptive father, abused you for years."

My stomach lurched. What did he do to me? What had I endured? I needed to know. I needed to know *everything*. "Tell me. Hold nothing back. Have you seen the scars? The— the *claw* marks? What happened to me, Brendan? What—?"

I didn't realize I'd been close to shouting until he put a finger to his lips, sliding a glance at curious passersby. I opened my mouth to say I didn't care who overheard, but before I could, he grasped my arm and tugged me down the hall. My instincts balked at being manhandled, especially as thoughts of what my scarred body must have gone through ricocheted through my head. But, more than anything, I needed to understand. My mind practically begged me to fill it with memories before the vast emptiness drove me mad.

Brendan opened a door and pulled me through, closing it before bothering with a light. That split second of complete darkness sent fear skittering through my veins. A bare bulb flicked on overhead, illuminating Brendan's face in an eerie way. His eyes were in shadow, yet I could still see the golden glow of his irises.

"It's all right, little bird. Calm down. Just breathe for me, okay?"

My brows drew together. Was mind-reading part of his ability? I dragged in a trembling breath. As I worked on slowing my heart rate, I took in the room. Mops. Brooms. A shelf of cleaning supplies. The scent of lemon. A space that was way too small for Brendan and me to inhabit at the same time. "Maybe we should—"

He blew out a sigh before I could suggest we find a much larger room to talk in. "I've seen your scars. Maybe not all of them, but most of them. You were whipped for years."

"Whipped?" I hissed, horrified at the image that popped into my head. "My back?" He nodded as his lips formed a tight line. "And these?" I opened my fists, showing him my palms and knuckles.

The strangest thing happened then. His face softened and he reached for one of my hands. Too surprised to react, I didn't pull away when his fingers trailed the back of my hand, or when his thumb brushed over a scar on my palm newer than the rest. He chuckled quietly. "Self-inflicted. You were too stubborn to wear gloves and your charger's mane would slice open your skin like paper. Didn't faze you. Oh, and you like punching trees."

Half of what he said didn't make sense, especially when his touch grew bolder and his fingers slid through mine, thoroughly distracting me. At their warmth, at the jolt of familiarity, I retreated, tugging my hand free. "I—" I took a second to clear my tight throat. A faint smile tipped Brendan's lips, like he knew all too well what his touch had just done to me. I had a sudden urge to smack the look off his face. Which reminded me . . . "I like punching trees?"

He laughed, shaking his head. "You'll pretty much punch anything to avoid talking about your feelings." One of his eyebrows lifted. "So if you're feeling the need right now . . ." He spread his arms wide, almost knocking over a broom.

I snorted and took a small step back until a shelf poked my spine. "I'm not going to punch you. Was I really that violent?"

With a shrug, he lowered his arms. "You adapted to a harsh environment in order to survive. It's why you're here today. Don't be afraid of who you were, who you *still* are, Lune. We need that adaptive, resilient nature if we're going to save your sister and countless others from enduring what you did."

"Wait. Sister?"

For the next hour, maybe even longer than that, Brendan told me of my past life. My charger, Asher, Iris—the few souls I had cared about in the walled city—the Trials, my near-death experiences, the monster who called himself my father. But something was still missing. As I forgot about the cramped space we were in, too focused on all that I was learning, it hit me.

Of the many memories Brendan had shared, not a single one included him.

When asked if I'd rather tour Blue Ridge Sector or get right to discovering my ability, I chose the latter. The wary and oftentimes unfriendly glares of the residents were getting to me, making me jumpy. Even with Brendan always nearby, I wondered what these people would do if he left my side for more than a few moments. Better to put them at ease as soon as possible.

The Ability Center, where everyone with unique abilities trained, could be summed up in one word: enormous. There were several glass partitions dividing an assortment of obstacle courses, some containing physical objects while others appeared empty. I watched as a girl about my age wearing an odd device over her eyes entered a glass square.

"Virtual reality," Brendan said. I gave him a blank stare and he chuckled. "This is going to be fun."

A familiar dark-skinned man with short, springy black hair broke away from a group of young children and jogged toward us. "Bren, my man, miss me so soon? It's only been a few hours. But if you really need a Jaxie snuggle, just—" He paused, pretending to notice me for the first time. "Lune! I didn't mean to hit on your man. I have OCD and flirting with Bren helps with my anxiety."

"Um."

"Yeah, that's what my therapist says." Before I could so much as blink, Jaxon clapped his hands together and started talking again. "So, you two here to train? Did you know that your mall-cop guard graduated head of his class last year? Oh, how the mighty have fallen. All he needs is a doughnut and Segway."

"Dude, back the crazy bus up," Brendan interjected, coming to stand a little too close to me. Jaxon noticed and gave me a weird grin. "She wasn't raised around people who glorify a dead tech era and its bizarre culture. The references are lost on her. Go give someone else an aneurysm."

"Fine. My class of chicklets awaits my pearls of wisdom anyway. But when you get the itch for a moviethon, Lu Bear," Jaxon said, walking backward and stretching out his thumb and pinkie in a strange sign, "call me."

As he turned away, I noticed Brendan dragging a hand through his hair with an exasperated sigh. A wavy lock fell onto his forehead. "He insists that God made a mistake and put him in the wrong century. You can either love him or hate him. There's no in-between."

I shrugged as he ushered me forward. "He's the only one who's looked at me like I'm a normal human being, so I like him, I suppose."

Brendan's shoulders stiffened. "And how do I look at you?"

The answer didn't come readily. There were too many looks he gave me: sadness, hurt, hope, guilt, longing, resignation. All because I'd lost my memories, no doubt. But tucked deep inside his eyes, one look remained constant despite him saying I was an adaptable, resilient person. "Like I'm fragile glass about to break."

I waited for him to contradict my observation. He didn't.

By the time we arrived at the far leftmost corner where the activity level was drastically reduced, the silence between us had grown uncomfortable. Sooner or later, I'd grill him about our past relationship, if we even had one, but the sight before me pushed Brendan Bearon to the back of my mind.

A man in his early twenties was fist-fighting blindfolded. And winning.

As I stepped up to the glass partition the two men sparred in, I realized there was no sound. Not a single scuffle from inside reached my ears. Then I saw neon orange plugs obstructing the blindfolded man's hearing. I gawked as he swung a gloved fist and made contact with his opponent's gut. "How— how is he doing that?"

"His mind," Brendan answered so casually, I gave him a sharp glance, expecting to see a teasing smile. Instead, I found him watching the man with an expression of admiration. Maybe even reverence.

Five minutes later, the combatants broke apart and the blindfold was removed, revealing laughing gray eyes in a pleasant face. Maybe even handsome. Not ruggedly-intense Brendan handsome, but softer—a face you wanted to spill all your secrets to. Wait, what? Before I could dwell on the fact that I'd been comparing my guard's appearance to someone else's, the gray-eyed man exited the glass square.

"Bren, you made it," he said with a wide smile, light brown curls sticking to his forehead as he wiped the sweat away. His attention snagged on me next, and stayed put. Those eyes. They weren't electrifying like Brendan's, but they spoke to me, like they knew the innermost workings of my brain with a single glance. Feeling exposed, almost naked, I was about to look away when he whispered, "It's you."

ABILITIES

"Are you sure?"

Brendan was speaking now, drawing the man's gaze, but I still felt branded. The desire to hide behind the hulking body of my guard swept through me, but I resisted. I wasn't fragile glass.

"I'm positive. As soon as my ability brushed against hers, I saw the part she would play in all this. She's the chink in his armor, the linchpin."

Well, that all sounded particularly . . . invasive.

I must have made a sound—probably a snort—because those searching gray eyes found me again. "Forgive me, Lune. I know way too much and you too little. My name is Dominic Holland. I'm a Visionary."

He said the last word as if it would explain everything. Not knowing what to say, I stuck out my hand. Smiling apologetically, he took it, shaking once, then twice. Instead of letting go like any sane person, he held on, turning the moment from weird to creepy. The sweat on his palm threatened to leach into mine. Still holding my hand, he said, "Your memories are blocked."

Brendan stepped in close and Dominic finally released

my hand. "Blocked? So they weren't erased? Dr. Bradfield wasn't sure. He needed more time to study the serum's properties."

Dominic nodded, and while he wasn't looking, I carefully wiped my now sweaty palm on my pants. "Yes, I can feel the block. It's like a dam holding all the memories hostage behind a transparent wall."

"Can you tear down the wall?"

What the what now? Okay, that didn't sound safe. Hadn't they heard of brain damage?

"I don't know, I've never done it before. I could try though."

Time to insert myself into this deranged conversation. "That's okay. I like scrambled eggs, not scrambled brains."

Both men stared at me, stared like *I* was the crazy one. Then they burst out laughing. Well, then. I didn't know whether to be offended or say "screw it" and join in. I settled on crossing my arms.

When he'd somewhat composed himself after wiping a tear from the corner of his eye, Dominic said, "Your mind is way too strong for that. Think of it as a steel trap reinforced with titanium—it's stronger than any I've ever felt before. But you lack training. That's why Brendan brought you to me. He said you saw a vision of him getting stabbed before the event happened?"

Uh.

"Right. Memories. Thankfully, your ability isn't blocked, only your actual experiences. So even though you don't remember the details of your memories, the knowledge is still accessible to some extent. Dr. Stacey informed me you might be feeling phantom memories? Strong emotions, likes and dislikes of things for no apparent reason?"

I shrugged, sneaking a quick glance at Brendan. Hopefully she didn't tell everyone about my first encounter with him in the bathroom.

"It's similar to phantom limb syndrome," Dominic continued, "having sensations of the missing limb still being attached. With a little bit of training, we should be able to strengthen those phantom memories and figure out what you're capable of—plus the possibility of me unblocking your trapped memories completely. But first, let me tell you what I can do. You saw the fighting match?" I nodded and he beamed as if I'd won the match myself. I couldn't keep a small smile from slipping free. "As a Visionary, your abilities should allow you to do the same thing: predict what someone does before they do it because you've already *seen* it happen."

My brain officially exploded. "Wait, hold on. I may not have my memories, but seeing into the future? Really? That ranks up there with magic—impossible."

"Scientifically speaking, it's been probable for centuries but never confirmed. Seers were known to foretell the future and psychics claimed to read people's minds. More often than not, though, they were highly intuitive fakes. Then the Silent War happened. Animals mutated before we did, maybe a decade or so after the incident. But humans—call us stubborn, if you will—didn't easily give up their simple genetics."

"When did the first signs of change in humans occur?" I asked, shifting from one foot to the other. Brendan noticed my tic flaring and clamped his lips together. As if I didn't realize it was a pathetic attempt not to tease me. I rolled my eyes and shifted once more.

"Dr. Moore is actually the first known case at Blue Ridge Sector. We can't be sure—records aren't what they used to be without the internet—but he was born thirty-five years after the war, and he's now sixty-five, so the timing makes sense. As the name Intellect suggests, he has high intelligence, higher than any recorded in history. He designed much of the Ability Center as you see it today."

My next question came out of nowhere. But with all this talk of mutation . . . "Are there any side effects? To having an ability, I mean."

The men exchanged a glance, probably gauging how much information to dump into my breakable—or not so breakable—brain. "If you allow your . . . enhancements to control you," Dominic began haltingly, "they can drive you insane, literally. If left unchecked for too long, the genetics will eventually overwhelm your system and you become a slave to them. When this happens, you're labeled a Berserker."

"I'm pretty sure Lars is one," Brendan said. When I looked at him quizzically, he further explained. "While you lived in Tatum City, there was this guy who had an unhealthy obsession with you. He was violent and territorial, especially when he felt threatened by my presence. He—" Brendan's voice lowered as he clenched his jaw. "He was making plans to claim you."

Uh. "Claim? What does that mean?"

"It's a predator thing. Also a Sensor thing if not kept in check. He probably wanted to gain his alpha's favor by making you submissive to him."

Okay, I was going to throw up in my mouth now. "Do I even want to know who the alpha is?"

"Your adopted father," he admitted. At least he appeared as disturbed as I was.

"It's why we start training the children here as soon as they manifest, so they learn to control their foreign DNA," Dominic said, thankfully steering the conversation to safer ground.

"Manifest?"

"It's when you first show signs of changed behavior. Sometimes it's hard to catch, so Dr. Moore wrote a handbook on what to look for. But generally, when emotions are amplified enough, the symptoms will manifest."

"Like the first time I met you," Brendan quietly added. "Well, the *second* first time—our very first encounter is a bit foggy." He was staring holes into my shoes instead of my face, which was probably scrunched up in confusion. "Your emotions were high because you remembered that first meeting eleven years prior all too well. You projected your ability so strongly that I had to switch mine off."

A flood-gate of questions swarmed my mind. We had met as children? Was that before or after I'd been brought to live in Tatum City? If that day had been such a pivotal memory for me, why couldn't I feel a single emotion toward it now? I focused harder, trying to remember a young me and Brendan. Crap. I couldn't even picture *my* face, let alone his.

Pain bloomed behind my eyes and I squeezed them shut.

"Breathe, Lune." A large hand gently grasped my shoulder. I pried my eyes open to find myself leaning into Brendan's touch. Instead of pulling away, I sought out his face. His grown-up face. My brows pulled together. I so badly wanted to remember what a younger him looked like. "You were projecting just now, probably trying to access your blocked memories."

I straightened, immediately missing the warmth of Brendan's touch when his arm dropped. I managed to keep my next eye-roll inward. "Guess I shouldn't do that then." The thought tasted bitter. I had a gut feeling that I was too stubborn to give up without a fight though.

"No, you should," Dominic said, as if sensing my latest emotion. Was he a mind-reader too? "But you need conditioning first." He grabbed a handheld device from a cubby bolted to the stone wall behind him and tapped its glass-like surface. The screen brightened, and if my piqued curiosity were any indication, this was my first time seeing such an object.

With one final tap, he said, "There. Starting tomorrow, every day after breakfast, you're scheduled to train with me, plus meditation for unblocking those memories." He glanced at my ankle boot, then at Brendan. "When can she resume physical exercise?"

"Dr. Stacey said that by next week, light exercise should

be okay. Why? Have you seen something new?"

Dominic shook his head, shooting me a searching look. "No, but now that we have Elite Tatum's prized possession, the clock is ticking. The sooner she's prepared to do her part, the better."

My mind was reeling by the time lunch rolled around. If I overheard one more cryptic statement involving me and my mysterious past, I was going to lose it. Maybe I'd punch a tree. I eyed the cluster of trees standing regally in the middle of The Center like arrows stuck in a target. *Bullseye.* Strangely, the comparison made me want to smile.

Standing in the long lunch line with nothing to do but wait, I decided to test the water and see if Brendan would answer a few of my burning questions. He seemed lost in thought, so I spoke a bit louder than planned. "We knew each other as kids then?"

He flinched as if my voice had startled him. His arm jerked up and he rubbed the back of his neck, looking more than a little uncomfortable. "Uh, yeah. Briefly. I, um." With a sigh, he met my eyes. Something was definitely bothering him. A big something. "Look, Lune, maybe it's best if you don't know about our past—"

"Bren!"

A blur of wild, dark brown tresses and pale limbs streaked past me and smacked into Brendan. The impact would have tipped a smaller man over, but I already knew how hard it was to move that boulder. The image before me sharpened and I immediately stiffened. A pretty girl maybe a year or two younger than me had her arms wrapped around my guard's waist in a tight squeeze.

It was as if the hug were squeezing the air out of *my* lungs, not his. Feeling unsettled, I took a step back, promptly bumping into the person waiting in line behind me. They hissed incoherently and I muttered a quick apology, not daring to turn around. I couldn't bear an unfriendly face right now, not when my heart was beating off rhythm and I had an uncontrollable urge to bolt.

The girl was speaking, her hands on Brendan's sides and his on her shoulders. Her upturned face held a look of complete adoration. I wanted to wretch. "I know you said to keep my distance for a couple more days, but I couldn't stay away another minute! I've only had you back for two weeks and I miss you."

Okay. The pouty lip did it.

I turned tail and ran. Well, more like a wobbling fast-walk. This was weird. Really weird. Why was I having this absurd reaction? I made it halfway across The Circle when my name was called. His familiar voice was definitely not comforting right now. I picked up the pace, gritting my teeth as my ankle started to throb, but I was no match for his long strides. He caught up to me a moment later, halting my escape with a hand on my arm. I shook off his touch, but stayed put, scrambling for an excuse as to why I'd left. "I have to use the—"

A feminine gasp drew my attention. It was the girl again, standing a little behind and to the side of Brendan. Her hands were over her mouth. "I'm so sorry," I heard her whisper, then watched in shock as her amber brown eyes filled with tears. Her arms lowered, revealing a quivering chin. What was happening? "I—I know what you're feeling, but you've got it all wrong."

She looked at Brendan pleadingly. He put an arm around her, but she pushed it away, shaking her head in warning.

"What am I missing here, Bells?" he said with a frown. Even her *name* was pretty.

Sighing exasperatingly, she rolled her eyes. "Boys. So clueless." She turned my way again, and before I could stop her, she launched herself at me. Instinct warred with common sense as her arms pulled me into a hug. I ended up holding still, frozen as an icicle instead of maneuvering her into a chokehold. Was I capable of a move like that? When she stepped back, a gigantic grin stretched her full lips wide. "Let's try this again. I'm Isabella Bearon. Bren's sister."

To say this day was full of surprises didn't even begin to scrape the surface. It wasn't so much the bits of news that kept cropping up but my unexpected reactions to them. Especially when they pertained to Brendan. I was fairly certain by now that he was hiding our past history from me. Did we have a falling out? Did the old me hate his guts? Somehow I doubted that.

The more time I spent with him, the more I wanted to

know everything about him. About *us*. The past us. Because staring at the current him across the table as he teased Jaxon for viewing a "painful-to-watch" vampire movie for the umpteenth time was doing weird things to my insides. It made me feel out of control again, which was exactly what I didn't want, but I needed to know what he was to the old me.

"Which is why you made sure everyone calls me Bells and not Bella," Brendan's sister was saying as I tuned back into the conversation.

"Because I can't have my best friend's kid sister sounding like a brainless vampire wannabe." Jaxon pointed his fork at her and winked.

"Wait, I thought you *liked* those movies."

"No way, girl, they suck—"

"What sucks?"

Everyone stilled. Whatever was on Jaxon's extended fork plopped onto the table. He cleared his throat and sat ramrod straight. "Just the peas, my sweet. They have a weird chalky flavor today."

I glanced up to find dark, almond-shaped eyes glowering at me. I blinked, feeling the urge to look anywhere but at her. She dropped her food tray onto the table with a *clank* and sank into a chair next to Jaxon. As soon as she did, her expression changed to one of casual boredom. Flicking black strands of spiky hair out of her eyes, she said, "That's funny. It sounded to me like you were dissing my favorite movies."

Jaxon laughed nervously. "Now why would I do that, baby cakes? It's not like I have a death wish. Hey, I thought you were supposed to be on patrol all day?"

"I was. Control pulled us in when the weather got nasty. Said the blizzard should hold off any unfriendlies for the time being." She snorted, which made the piercing in her nose wink, then looked at me again. "Besides, I wanted to check up on our *guest*. She behaving herself?"

"Yukiko," Brendan said quietly, his voice laced with warning.

"Oh, that's right. The poor girl doesn't remember me or how she got here." The young woman sneered. Bells squeaked softly.

"Okay okay, let's all simmer down," Jaxon said, waving his hands in front of Yukiko's face until she snapped her gaze to his. "Crikey! You couldn't cut this tension with a chainsaw. Hey, Lune, this is my girlfriend Yukiko Chen. She's a Sensor and can smell fear, but they say staring into a predator's eyes shows it that you're unafraid, so I can't look at you right now. Did you know her name means 'happy child'?"

"Cut it out, Jaxon," his peach of a girlfriend said, whacking his chest. "Eat your peas." She picked one up and shoved it past his lips.

He grinned, flashing those star-bright teeth at her before throwing a wink at me. "And *that* is how you tame a beast."

CRAVINGS

I jerked awake, inhaling sharply as the bad dream fled my system. Details were obscure, but I remembered . . . a knife. A shiver shook my shoulders as I whipped my bed covers back and padded to the bathroom.

One week. One week had passed with no progress. My memories were still blocked, Dominic hadn't unlocked my abilities, Brendan wouldn't talk to me about his past, and Yukiko continued to hate-glare at me from afar. And with each day came an undeniable restlessness. At first, it was a simple tic, my leg jiggling away to its own beat. Then the feeling had hit my bloodstream, humming a tune I couldn't unhear. It called to me, begged me again and again to listen, to answer the cry.

Ugh.

I splashed cold water on my face, jarring any trace of tiredness from my limbs. Tipping my head upside down, I gathered my hair into a high ponytail, then slipped into a thin thermal shirt and black cropped pants. The only real progress I'd made was having my ankle boot removed yesterday. The injury still twinged on occasion, but I was pretty good at pushing aside the dull pain. Besides, I didn't plan on going for a run. During one of my tours of this gigantic place, I'd spotted a small workout room on the second floor that was hopefully not locked up at night like the Ability Center.

Just thinking of that room with its shiny exercise equipment made my body sing with anticipation. "Strange," I muttered, then tested the door handle. It was never locked from the outside, but I always expected it to be. Maybe I should start locking it from my end. What if someone, say Yukiko, felt like murdering me in my sleep? She never threatened me with actual words, but the looks she slid my way practically skewered me to the wall.

I shrugged the renewed thought of knives from my mind and cracked open the door. The hallway was blissfully silent. Without the sun to help me tell time, I could only guess at how early it was. Most of the people here had handheld devices that told the hour, but I hadn't been given one. Yet. I was sure they'd give me one once they knew the extent of my abilities. When they knew I was stable and that I could be trusted with their technology.

Bells let me play with hers sometimes when she saw me savagely drumming my fingers on any available surface I could find. The preprogrammed games helped soothe the itch under my skin. As an Empath, she could always feel when I was agitated. She would tease that it was because of Brendan, but whenever I'd ask her about his past, she'd groan and say, "That stupid fool needs to tell you himself."

Well, he hadn't. And I was *not* agitated right now because of him. It was that bad dream. Nothing more. Working up a fine sweat sounded like a great way to settle my nerves so I could face another day of disappointment. I barely made a sound as I glided down the hallway and stairwell instead of risking the elevator.

No one had explicitly said I couldn't leave my room in the middle of the night, but I didn't feel like explaining myself. What would I say anyway? "Oh, I just felt this incessant urge to punch something" might scare people, maybe even convince them I was crazy and should be locked up.

Nope.

Skulking in the shadows undetected was the right decision.

I arrived at the second floor landing and pulled the stairwell door open. One second I was walking and the next pressed against a stone wall with a callused palm over my mouth. I tried to scream but the sound was so muffled, no one would hear. Blind panic set in when my large assailant stepped close. I expected a knife to the heart would follow. I clawed at the bare forearm within reach, but no matter how much I scratched, the hand over my mouth didn't budge.

"Have you forgotten your training completely?"

The low, gravelly voice in my ear was all too familiar. Brendan. I froze and he pulled back, just enough that I could see his shadowed face in the dim lighting. I squinted. Was he smiling? I grabbed his shoulders and shoved, which of course did nothing. He took his sweet time removing his hand, brushing a thumb across my cheek before allowing me a foot of breathing room.

Yup. He was smirking. A clash of emotions wrestled inside of me at the sight. I wanted to smack it off, but I wanted to kiss it, too. *Holy crap, did that thought really just pop into my brain?* My eyes widened when his started to glow. It didn't scare me anymore, not after spending almost every minute of an entire week with him. What scared me now was how my body was reacting to having him so close.

And maybe I was imagining things, but Brendan seemed affected too. I could hear his unsteady breaths, feel his hand tremble where it rested on the wall next to my head. After what felt like a timeless eternity of staring into those eyes, wishing for something to happen but scared out of my mind that it would, he dropped his gaze and exhaled slowly. *"Num occidere me hoc est."*

"What?" I croaked, then carefully cleared my throat.

"Never mind." He pushed away from the wall, taking his body heat with him. Okay, I really needed to stop being a creep now. "What are you doing down here?"

"Am I breaking a rule?" I shot back, which only made his lips twitch. *Stop thinking about his lips!* I was blaming this on Jaxon and Yukiko. I had caught them kissing each other's faces off yesterday and couldn't get the image out of my mind. That must be it. Residual scar tissue from witnessing such a thing.

"No," he drew out the word, prolonging my torture. My foot rhythmically tapped at the ground. "Not technically. But you shouldn't go anywhere without me. It's—"

"It's not safe. I got it." My eyes narrowed. "How did you

169

know I was awake?" If there was a camera in my room, so help me . . .

He shrugged offhandedly. "I heard you. My room's right next to yours."

My jaw dropped. How come I hadn't known that?

"You never asked," he said, answering my unspoken question. "And when I saw what you were wearing, I put two-and-two together and took the elevator down here." His expression turned smug, and now all I wanted to do was make it disappear.

"Remind me what your ability is again? No wait, you're an Egomaniac, right? I've heard they're very rare, and highly dangerous. Their heads have a tendency to explode when they get too full of themselves."

He pressed his lips together, then barked a laugh. I tried to stay strong, but ended up joining him a few seconds later. "Lune Avery," he said, still chuckling, "I will never grow tired of that sassy mouth."

My laughter died. Crap. I was thinking about lips again. I needed to punch something. Like right now.

Thankfully, Brendan's state of mind was more stable than mine at the moment. He turned, crooking a finger at me to follow. "I'd rather just show you what I can do. It's more fun that way."

Why did that statement send heat flooding into my cheeks?

When we arrived at the gym, the lights were off. Instead of flicking the switch on, Brendan strolled into the pitch black room without pause, quickly disappearing from view. I stopped at the door, unsure what to do. "Brendan? Is this another attempt to scare the crap out of me?"

At the answering silence, I huffed and felt along the wall for a light switch. Argh, where was it? As I continued to sweep my hand along the stone, the air in front of me became heavier, the darkness denser. My heart pounded and, instinctively, I threw an arm out, expecting to hit flesh and bone. Nothing but empty air. Now I felt stupid.

"You missed," a voice whispered in my ear and I couldn't hold back a shriek. I whirled around, swinging a fist this time, but no one was there. Light flooded the room and I squinted as I searched for the person who had just earned himself a butt-kicking. Something tugged my ponytail and I whipped an elbow back. Nothing there. I turned, slowly this time, to find Brendan leaning against the wall near the light switch, an infuriating smirk on his face. "Don't feel bad, little bird. I can see in the dark and have heightened reflexes."

I crossed my arms. "I'm not the one who should feel bad. Who's the one picking on a helpless girl with an injured leg?"

He laughed softly. "You're anything but helpless. And the old you would smack the new you for playing the victim card, by the way." He pushed off the wall as my mouth fell open. Did he just chastise me? Well, now I was ticked off.

"Since you know so much about me, then how, pray tell, would the old me react to this situation?"

Snatching up two pairs of gloves, he put one on, then

tossed me the other. "She would have taken my words as a challenge and made me eat them by overcoming the obstacle I'd just put in her way."

"Huh. She sounds tough." I jammed on the gloves. "Or stupid."

With a sigh, he beckoned me forward. At first, I stubbornly held my ground, then realized how childish I was being and moved. Slowly. He waited until I raised my eyes to his, then said, "She was strong and brave." He lightly tapped the side of my head with his glove. "And she's still in there."

"What if . . . what if she isn't?" I asked quietly, admitting to a fear that had been squatting in the back of my mind.

"She is," he said with conviction, not a trace of doubt in his tone. "I won't accept anything else."

His words warmed me, filled me with a new boldness. *Ask. Now's your chance.* I bit the inside of my cheek, trying to ignore the prodding. But a moment later, I blurted, "What was she to you?"

There. I said it. No take-backs. But as his expression pinched and he looked down at his gloves, I squirmed with the need to run. Talking about personal stuff must not come easily for me—something he and I seemed to have in common.

The moment for his reply came . . . and went. Awkward silence reigned. The urge to drum my foot on the ground, to release some of this, this *tension*, zipped through me. Brushing past Brendan, I made a beeline for the punching bag that hung in the middle of the room. *Wham!* I poured all of my frustration into that punch, the impact a satisfying jolt of pain up my arm. Still, the heavy leather bag barely budged. I could do better.

I let loose a flurry of punches, not caring if I was doing it wrong. My blood was heating, pumping strong through my veins. That's all that mattered. For several minutes, I lost myself to the mindless rhythm of whacking the bag, unconsciously counting each hit. Sweat beaded my brow and rolled down my spine.

An insane desire to grin overcame me.

"It's the adrenaline."

I paused mid-swing, surprised he was still here. "What?" I said, maybe with a bit too much attitude. An image of his face appeared on the bag, swaying. Mocking. *Whack!*

"Your new habit—the restless leg thing. It's because your body was craving an adrenaline release."

I straightened, softly panting, then finally looked at him with a frown. "What does that mean?"

His lips twitched knowingly, which just made my frown deepen. "It means," he drawled, "that you're an adrenaline junkie. You've been training nonstop since you were ten years old. You're not used to inactivity."

"Are you calling me an addict?"

He shrugged. "There's no shame in it. I get cravings too. They're a bit different than yours though."

"Like what?" As soon as I asked the question, I knew he wouldn't answer. I could practically see his shoulder muscles go rigid. "You know what? Never mind." I about-faced and struck the punching bag with renewed vigor. One, two, three. *Whack, whack, wham.* Four, five, six—

"Hit me instead."

I grabbed the swaying bag and glared at him. "What?"

His lips tipped sardonically. "I said to hit me instead. I can always tell when you want to. And, boy oh boy, do you want to right now."

The goading undertone. The challenge flashing in those gold eyes. I bared my teeth and marched to him, halting a yard away. "And how can you tell? Do you read minds, is that it? You never did tell me exactly what your abilities are. Oh wait, is that a secret too?"

Yeah, I was challenging him. Taking the gloves off—figuratively. Daring him to play this game that I couldn't seem to back down from.

He approached, pinning me in place with a look that both thrilled and scared me. *Predator,* my mind screamed. *Run!* I locked my limbs. Even when he slowly began to circle me, I refused to move. Goosebumps skittered down my arms and legs as he came up behind me, as he whispered into my ear, "I can sense your anger. Smell it, taste it."

I couldn't breathe.

His arm brushed mine as he circled in front of me. "I can hear your thundering heartbeats. Smell your adrenaline and fear. Sense your ability trying to project." He paused, swallowing audibly. My hands shook with the need to . . . I didn't know what. But holding still right now was torture of the worst kind.

Behind me once again, I felt the moment his fingers, now free of gloves, met my back. My first instinct was to stiffen and pull away, but my body had other plans. I all but melted, unconsciously leaning into the touch. My eyes slid shut. "I could track you to the ends of the earth," he continued, his warm breath fanning my neck. "All because I can't resist your scent. Your ability calls to me, tugs at me, pulls me. It's my craving."

His hand fisted the back of my shirt, making my stomach muscles jump. I gasped softly, unable to move even if I tried.

He groaned, yanking gently on the fabric until my back met his chest. "Don't do that."

"Do what?" My voice sounded embarrassingly weak.

I could feel his chest expand, then contract. A shudder rolled through him, passing through me as well. "Don't torture me," he said breathlessly. For a moment, the world ceased to exist as I let the feel of him wash over me, consume me. I hardly knew him, and yet, I'd never felt so connected to someone. And right now . . . I wanted to be closer.

My face turned toward the warmth of his breath, seeking what it wanted. My body buzzed with sureness, more certain in its goal than anything I'd known since waking up in this place. I turned around fully, facing Brendan until a mere inch separated us. A small movement was all it would take to claim what I sought.

As my nose brushed against his chin, and he inhaled shakily, I knew why I wanted this so badly. He made me feel *alive*. He was my own personal spark plug. And I wanted to explode. I stood on tiptoe, determined to do just that, when he jerked upright. Swearing softly, he grasped my shoulders and eased me back a step. "I'm—I'm sorry. I shouldn't have done that. It's not right." He blew out a harsh breath and released me, creating more space between us.

My brain slowly clicked back on. I blinked, searching his face, hoping for something to make sense. But all I felt was—

"I know. I screwed up and made things even more confusing for you. It's just . . . we're not in Tatum City anymore, and . . . circumstances are different now. More complicated. I—I can't." With that, he strode out of the gym like he wanted nothing more than to erase what had just happened.

And now, all I felt was numb. And cold.

Polite detachment.

That was how Brendan handled our time together for the next three days. I told myself over and over that it didn't bother me, that spending my free time with his sister was good enough. But there was an ache, an empty hole behind my ribs that I couldn't fill no matter how busy I made myself, or how often I burned off excess energy.

If I was being completely honest with myself, it was a Brendan-sized hole. Nothing else could fill it. Was this a sign that I needed therapy? Because these feelings seemed . . . obsessive. But how could I ignore them when I spent several hours with him every day?

A thought whacked me upside the head and my eyes flew

open.

Dominic sighed, but not in annoyance. He was too good-natured for that. "You're still fighting my attempts at unlocking your memories. Your mind needs to be clear, focused. Where's it at this morning, Lune? It feels scattered."

"Sorry." I shook my hands out and uncrossed my legs. Meditation must not have been something my old self did. The position felt entirely unnatural to me. "Can we take a five minute break? I think I finally figured out why I can't focus."

His eyebrows rose but he unfolded his limbs and stood, offering me a hand. I smiled my thanks and quickly left the soundproof cubicle. It didn't take much searching to find my guard. He was leaning against the Ability Center's outer wall, his eyes already trained on me as I approached. Did he ever get bored of guard duty? How had he spent his time before Tatum City and the Elite Trials?

I was doing it again. Distracting my mind with thoughts of Brendan Bearon instead of focusing on manifesting my ability and unlocking my memories. I sighed through my nose. There was only one way to fix this problem. I stopped several feet away, making sure there was lots of space between us. Not knowing how best to say this, I went with blunt honesty. "I want a new guard."

He pushed off from the wall but didn't come closer. I noticed his jaw harden though. "Why?"

Ah crap. I hadn't thought of a proper explanation. "Because . . . because I can't have distractions right now." Ugh, nope. Try again. "Look, I don't think babysitting me is what you want. If your heart's not in it, then why not pass me off to someone else? I'm sure your ability is needed for far more important things anyway."

There. That was rational.

Then why did I feel terrible when his expression shuttered, like he was protecting himself from the blow my words had just dealt him? I opened my mouth, not knowing what to say but wanting to fix the look on his face. It almost looked like betrayal. Before I could speak, he cleared his throat, then said softly, "If that's what you want."

It wasn't. "It is," I replied, already mourning the loss of his future company.

He gave a curt nod and broke eye contact. "I'll speak with Dr. Moore, but for today, I'll ask Jaxon to watch over you."

By the time I willed my lips to form a thank you, he was gone.

BOYS ARE SO MUCH DRAMA

Two days later, I had a breakthrough.

With a wave of nausea, the vision hit me, then forced me to watch a little girl slip and crack her head on the ground. A large pool of blood grew beneath her as the mother screamed. I dropped my food tray, too stunned to cry out, and the scene vanished.

No blood. No screaming.

The girl was upright again, whole and alive. Running toward the slick spot that would make her fall. But the sound of my plate shattering startled her. She stopped and turned toward the noise. Everyone did. A tremor went through me and I doubled over, fighting the urge to throw up.

Jaxon, now my official guard, was calling my name. Maybe I went into shock then, because I straightened and walked all the way to the Ability Center without remembering the trip over. Dominic wasn't there. He must be at lunch. I curled into a ball in the farthest corner of the enormous room and switched my thoughts off.

That was how Brendan found me. I knew it was him when he knelt in front of me, but I knew that if I looked into his eyes, I'd lose it. My control was unraveling and I kept winding it back up, forcing myself to keep it together. A warm hand rested on my bent knee. *His* hand. No, no. Stop. He couldn't comfort me right now.

I'm not fragile glass. I'm not breaking . . .

Her eyes had been glassy.

Dead.

Pain speared through my chest. Then heat. The heat warmed my cheeks too. No, those were hands, tilting my face up, making me look at eyes brimming with concern. Alive. The eyes were alive. So were the girl's. *She's alive. It's okay. You're okay.*

I became aware of Brendan's voice telling me to breathe. I focused on the deep, rolling timbre, on the comfort the sound brought me. And then it all spilled out. "She—she tripped. The blood. So real. So much of it. I—she died, Brendan. Just like that. Gone." He stared at me and I couldn't read his expression. Did he think I was crazy? "What was it? A hallucination? I—I don't want it. I don't—"

My chin wobbled, cutting off my disjointed words. Brendan's face fell. He tugged me into his arms. My cheek ended up pressed to his chest, and I listened to the reassuring sound of his heartbeat. I allowed myself a moment of comfort that only he could give. It was selfish. But I fisted it tightly with both hands.

Then I let go, knowing I needed to pull myself together before anyone else saw. If this was part of my ability, I'd need to deal with it and fast before it swallowed me whole. Before I became crazy and dangerous like everyone here was waiting to see happen.

"What happened?"

I pulled away at the sound of Dominic's voice. "I'm fine," I said, peering at him over Brendan's shoulder. My legs trembled slightly, but I managed to stand on my own and smile, even though it was fake and lasted all of one second. At least I hadn't shed any tears. "I just—I wasn't expecting it. The vision, I mean."

Dominic's face split into a huge grin. "You had a vision? Tell me everything: what you were thinking about before it happened, what it felt like, how you reacted. The more information you can give me, the better I'll know how to train you."

So I did. I recounted the entire terrible event in detail, staring at my hands the whole time so I wouldn't have to see Dominic's exuberant expression, or Brendan's troubled one. Jaxon was there too, looking serious for once. By the time I finished, exhaustion weighed heavily on my shoulders and a headache pulsed at my temples.

Dominic turned his handheld off after he'd tapped in the whole story. Said we'd test a new theory he had on how to jump-start my ability first thing tomorrow. I couldn't muster any enthusiasm because there was only one thought clanging through my skull right now. This ability of mine was a curse. If it wanted to show me people dying, then I really *would* go crazy.

I begged off all activity for the rest of the day, saying I had a headache. I did, except I knew the excuse for what it was: a way to shut out the world. Maybe I'd take a long shower—

water always seemed to help drown my thoughts. But when I entered my room, my feet steered me toward the bed instead. A quick nap sounded heavenly, an activity that I bet the old me didn't indulge in very often. Just an hour . . .

Knock, knock.

Bells came barging into my room in a flurry of wavy dark hair and rustling fabric. After flicking the light on, she waltzed to my bed and dumped an armload of material onto my prostrate body. "What are you doing?" she said, hands on hips as she threw me a quizzical look. "Even my four-year-olds don't go to bed this early."

I huffed and yanked the blankets over my head. How long had I been asleep? "That's because they haven't manifested yet."

"Actually, one of the boys just did. He picked up a book of mine and started reading it to the entire class, marking him as an Intellect." She paused and I peeked over the blanket at her face. It was turning bright pink. "Anyway, the book wasn't age appropriate. I hope I don't get reassigned to another job."

With a sigh, I threw the covers back. "They wouldn't do that. You're so good with those kids." Which made me think of the girl who'd almost died this afternoon. Did Bells know her? She would have been devastated.

"I heard about what happened," she said sympathetically. She must have felt my mood, guessing at my train of thought. "When I first manifested, I cried a lot, like several times a day. Feeling another's emotions is scary and overwhelming, especially when you don't know how to turn the ability off. Sometimes it's so strong, I can hear people's thoughts, like they're shouting the words inside my head. My parents thought there was something seriously wrong with me."

I sat up and swung my legs over the bed's side. "Your parents?" Brendan's parents too, I assumed. Maybe they'd be more willing to answer my questions about their son. "Are they here?"

"Oh." She looked down and fiddled with her handheld. "They died when I was five. I barely remember them, but Bren tells me stories. He was eight when it happened."

At the news, a deep ache spread through my chest. Not expecting such a strong reaction, I rubbed at the pain clutching my heart. "I'm sorry to hear. I—" I swallowed past the lump in my throat. "I don't remember my parents. I, um, Brendan said I have a sister though. Iris."

Bells' face brightened. "Oh, I heard about her! Bren can't talk much about his missions—too many moving parts, he says—but he told me about you and Iris and your charger when he came home. Cleopatra, right? What's it like to ride such a ferocious beast?"

"Wait, back up. Missions? So Brendan left here to enter Tatum City and the Trials for . . . what reason exactly?" *Please know the answer, please know the—*

Her bottom lip poked out. "I'm sorry, Lune. I know you're hoping I'll have the answer, but I'm not privy to those details. All I know is that he leaves on mission for long stretches at a time. Has been doing so ever since he graduated. They're dangerous, I know that much. He's always done dangerous stuff though, so I'm kind of used to it. But," she said with a sly grin, "I know that this latest mission messed with his head. He's been abnormally quiet and contemplative since he got home. I wonder why that is?"

I gave her a flat look. "I have no idea. If it involves me, he isn't saying. That's why I asked to switch guards, you know. He was driving me insane."

Her eyes widened.

"Not literally," I rushed to add. "Well, maybe a little."

She snickered, then threw a hand to her forehead as her eyes rolled upward. "Boys are so much drama. I refuse to fall in love with one." Her hand lowered, cupping her mouth next as she whispered, "I can't help but be drawn to the tortured soul types though. They feel everything so intensely under all that dark brooding."

I shook my head, fighting a grin. Did I have a type? "All I want is to get my memories back. What if I have a boyfriend in Tatum City or something? And I don't even know what my favorite food is let alone my life goals."

"Life goals can wait," she said, grabbing a wad of fabric and plopping it into my lap. "You're too young to be so serious all the time. Tonight is about having a little fun! Now try that on."

I held the black sparkly material up with two fingers. "Um, where's the rest of it?"

She sighed loudly. "Don't tell me you've never worn a dress before."

"Do hospital gowns count?" I started to hand the slinky

thing back to her but she grabbed my arm and pulled me off the bed.

"We only get one community party a month. You're going, Lune!" When I stared at her dubiously, she batted her eyes. "You can be my date."

I wrinkled my nose. "What's a date?" When her mouth fell open in horror, I fisted the dress and headed for the bathroom, muttering, "Fine, I'll go. But if anything weird happens at the party, I'll leave and go to the gym instead. With this dress on."

Apparently getting ready for a party was supposed to be a mini workout session. There was the dress which, after several attempts at zipping it myself, I needed assistance putting on. Then makeup—who invented sparkly eyeshadow and lipstick? And hair—styled to curl loosely down my back. But when Bells pulled out black high-heeled shoes with a flourish—which were also sparkly—I snorted. "Not happening."

"Oh, come on," she groaned. "It's the one time a month tall guys can't look down their noses at us."

"I can look down my nose at them just fine, heels or no." Ugh. She could win a pouty lip award. I wrangled on the shoes after almost falling on my butt, then stood still for her inspection. Two thumbs up.

As we exited my room, Bells whispered, "Just don't bend over at the party."

"Why?"

"Um." I glanced at her sharply as she fiddled with her handheld. "You fill out the dress better than I do, that's all."

She gave me a syrupy smile. "Oh, and I asked Jaxon to meet us there. You know, in case . . ."

"In case someone goes crazy on me for thinking I'm crazy?"

She laughed, but it sounded slightly nervous. Was I making a mistake by going to this party? I hadn't the foggiest idea what to expect. My steps faltered and I considered turning back, but Bells' unwavering confidence pulled me onward.

I heard the party before laying eyes on it. The *thump, thump, thump* was like a heartbeat, but one that shook my entire body. I stopped in my tracks, uncertain if I liked the foreign feeling. A door in front of us whipped open and sound poured out, blasting my eardrums. I took a step back and bumped into something.

Before I could turn and apologize, a hand settled on my lower back, guiding me forward. "Ladies," a voice said loudly. Jaxon. I allowed myself to be steered through the door. "Yukiko's gonna be jealous of how gorgeous my company is this evening. Don't tell her . . ."

His words were lost to the overpowering swell of the music. Sounds I couldn't put a name to joined the beat in a wild clash of noise that somehow felt synchronized. I was deaf to everything but the pulse pounding in my head, my skin, my very bones. My heart could stop and I wouldn't even know.

Somehow I kept moving, one teetering footstep after the other. We passed through a dim hallway and swept aside long strands of beads dangling from what I assumed was the party's entrance. And then my world *really* exploded. With colors. Pinks and greens and blues shot through the foggy gloom in streaks, highlighting a bobbing wave.

No, those were people, swaying to the music. Dancing.

"Dance with me, Lune!" Bells shouted in my ear, and grabbed my hand. I didn't protest. I was in too much shock to do anything but let her drag me into the shifting bodies. A shoulder bumped into mine. Hair whipped my cheek. A hand whacked my arm. Everywhere—up, down, all around—there were people. Moving. Touching. Breathing.

Crap. I wasn't breathing. I forced in air, immediately tempted to expel it when I tasted salty sweat and fruity body spray on my tongue. The room brightened enough to reveal Bells facing me now with her arms in the air, the chunky silver bracelets on her wrists flashing under the colorful lights. Her head whipped side-to-side and her lithe body, clad in sparkly dark purple, undulated like a snake. I worked on gathering my vocal chords which had found their way into my stomach. "Are you okay?" I yelled.

Her eyes popped open, but she kept moving. "You've never danced before?"

I gave her an exaggerated shrug. Maybe, but I doubted it had been anything like *this*.

She grabbed both my hands and raised my arms, waving them back and forth. "Move to the beat. Shake your hips."

What?

She shimmied once more, showing me how it was done, and I couldn't help it. I busted out laughing. But she wasn't offended. In fact, she joined me. That's when I decided she was my friend. The thought made me so giddy, I let her teach me how to move my body in ways it'd probably never moved before. In no time, I was as sweaty as the rest of the crowd, damp curls sticking to my neck.

If I was an adrenaline junkie, then dancing was my fix.

"I have to go pee," Bells said as the fast-paced song switched to a slower one. She waved her handheld in the air. "I got you a new dance partner though, so don't move." With that, she was gone. *Blip.* Leaving me alone in the middle of a swarm of strangers.

No problem, I told myself. Jaxon would come any minute now and make me forget that the people brushing up against me could be planning my demise. *Dramatic much? Yep.*

One minute and twelve centuries later, I was struggling not to panic. Where was Jaxon? Maybe they'd taken him out first so it would be easier to get to me. The faces around me spun, a sickening blend of blue, pink, and green. Someone tapped my shoulder and I whirled, coming face-to-face with
. . .

Brendan.

I gasped, the sound smothered by the music's slow beat, but I think he heard it anyway. *I can hear your thundering heartbeats.* Could he hear them now? "Where's Jaxon?" I tried searching for his best friend, but it was no use. Even with heels on, Brendan was half a foot taller than me and blocking my view.

He bent his head so he didn't have to shout in my face. "Dancing with a put-out girlfriend who didn't get the memo that he'd be here until only a few moments ago."

My mouth formed an O, but I couldn't resist snickering, even if I did feel sorry for Jaxon. I finally took in the rest of Brendan, hiding my inspection by smoothing the front of my dress at the same time. He wore a black collared shirt with the sleeves rolled up to the elbow and dark slacks. My gaze got stuck on the vee of tan skin above his unbuttoned collar though. I kind of wanted to stare at it forever, but someone knocked into me from behind and broke my concentration.

I pitched forward and practically nose-dived into that strip of skin. If it weren't for Brendan's fast reflexes, I would have. Stupid reflexes. I snorted at how loopy my mind was acting, even giggled a bit. Someone needed to punch some sense into me. His hands on my shoulders dropped, but not in the way I expected them to. They traced the bare skin of my arms, then slowly guided my hands to rest on his shoulders.

My eyes rose to his, which were much, much closer now. He lowered his head farther and my breath caught as his cheek came up alongside mine, as I felt the graze of his stubbly jaw. "Dance with me?" his voice rumbled in my ear.

I laughed softly, more nerves than anything. "Do I have a choice?"

He froze, then pulled back to look me in the eye again, this time with a line bisecting his brows. Mine scrunched up too, in confusion. He blinked a few times and cleared his expression, smiling faintly. "Someone who I admire greatly once told me that you always have a choice."

I tipped my head to the side, wondering at the

whimsical look on his face. "That's good advice. I'll remember that." The tempo of the music changed then. Still slow, but the notes were long and almost languid. Crap. Things just got awkward. "Confession: I have no idea how to dance to this kind of music."

I watched his smile transform into that devastating, lopsided smirk. "Good thing I do then," he said, giving me no warning as he grasped my hips and pulled me closer. Warmth immediately ignited every part of me that brushed up against him. But when he started to move, his hands guiding me into the rhythm, I wanted to burn. My arms slid around his neck, drawing us impossibly close, until all thought scattered.

Him. Me. Our bodies moving as one. Intoxicating feelings and emotions overwhelmed my senses and stole my control.

Control.

I was losing it. This was what drowning felt like.

My arms stiffened as my breaths came in harsh pants. Air. I needed air. I needed—

"Let go," he said, resting his forehead on mine. "I've got you." As if to punctuate his words, he pressed a hand to my back, fitting me more securely against him.

And maybe that was the last thing I should have done, but I did. I shut my eyes and let go of my fear, my control, my every thought. I let it all go. And in their place, I let him in. A rush of uncontrollable energy filled me and I drank it whole, feeling more alive than I'd ever felt before. I felt delicious warmth on my cheek. Felt it moving, exploring. Tasting.

I tipped my head back and the warm pressure kissed my neck. Again and again. *Kiss.* Those were lips on my skin, trailing over my jaw, nipping at my ear. I moaned his name. I dug my fingers into his hair and brought his head around until his mouth was inches away from kissing mine.

Then my stomach twisted violently. A force shoved me backward and an image blocked my view of Brendan. I stared at someone's back. No, it was *my* back, and that was Brendan's hand holding me close. Out of nowhere, an arm thrust into the space and jabbed something into my spine. With a yank, the arm retreated, but not before I saw a thin blade coated in red disappear into the crowd.

Blood. That had been blood. *My* blood.

I tried to scream, but only a wet gurgle came out.

No. No!

I jerked forward and my eyes shot open to see Brendan inches from my face, about to kiss me. With a strangled inhale, I tried to push away, tried to untangle my tongue so I could tell him of the vision. But words failed me and Brendan was lost. Lost in the moment that I had succumbed to. And now . . . and now . . .

Not knowing what else to do, I gripped his hair. Hard. His eyes flew wide, glazed and confused. My mouth opened, but instead of a scream or something intelligent coming out, I said, "My back."

It wasn't the words that clued him in, but my expression. I knew stark terror was written there. He looked over my shoulder and I saw the moment he became aware of the threat. His

191

eyes intensified and his jaw hardened. But instead of running, or yelling, or throwing us to the ground, he crushed me to him and twisted, reversing our positions.

I felt the moment the blade sunk into Brendan's back. Felt him jerk against me. Heard him grunt as the blade was ripped out. Cold fear swept through me. He slumped forward but the weight of him was too great. I cried out as he slipped from my arms and crumpled to the ground. I yelled his name as his golden eyes rolled upward. As he stilled.

No, no, no, no.

"Don't you dare die on me, Brendan Bearon!"

Something inside my head snapped then. Cracked. An image leaked through an invisible shield, one where I was holding Brendan's face like I was doing right now, telling him not to die. I choked on a sob, and let my tears fall freely.

A memory.

I had just seen a memory.

DON'T YOU DARE

"Did you see the person's face?"

"No. The—the angle was all wrong. I wasn't even in my body, more like a spectator in the crowd."

"And why didn't you turn around and defend yourself the moment the vision ended?"

My mouth opened, and stayed open. I knew it was normal for Dr. Moore to be blunt, but the thought of telling him that I'd practically plastered myself to Brendan's front and his grip on me hadn't allowed for movement . . . I'd rather jump off a cliff.

So, of course Jaxon, not having any qualms with being open, did it for me. "She was a willing prisoner at the time. Of Bren's arms. The dude's grip is stronger than an octopus's, if you know what I mean."

The Ridge leader's bushy eyebrows bunched together which made his glasses slip down his nose. No, he didn't seem to understand the meaning. "When Dr. Stacey is done with him, I'll ask Bren if he saw anything. I want a full report of your story before we start the investigation though, Miss Avery. Use Jaxon's handheld. In the meantime, all of your extracurricular activities need to be approved by me first. We need to get to the bottom of this before someone gets killed. And Jaxon, I'm sure you don't need to be told to keep this on the down-low. Mass panic would be most unpleasant to deal with."

There were too many things I disliked about his instructions, but instead of speaking my mind and making things worse, I responded with a curt nod. He was in charge, not me, and his primary goal was to protect his people. My only goal was selfish—to see Brendan again and make sure he was all right.

When we left Dr. Moore's office with explicit orders to engage the lock on my bedroom door, I made a beeline for Medical. I had been forced to leave Brendan there, not knowing the state of his condition while Dr. Moore peppered me with questions. If he died and I hadn't been there because of some stupid—

"Whoa there, Lu Bear," Jaxon said, purposefully slowing his gait to discourage me from running down the hallway. I bit back a few choice words. "I'm just a lowly Intellect, but your rage is coming through loud and clear. Even a regular human could feel it."

"Feel my fist," I muttered, punching the elevator button. Three seconds later, I ditched the waiting for a much faster method: the stairs. After wrestling off the high-heeled shoes I'd managed to hobble around in all night, I all but leapt down the stairs. My ankle barked a protest, but I barked right back. I was in no mood, *no mood* to be told what to do right now.

"Lune."

"What?"

"Hey, don't bite off the messenger's head. Lots of important information has gotten lost because of that rash decision."

I blew out a breath and worked on a less murderous tone as I rounded the thirteenth floor landing. "What is it?"

"We're coming up hard on our destination. You might want to put on the brakes."

"We have eleven floors to go, what are you talking abou—?"

"He's been released."

I grabbed the railing and jerked myself to a stop, almost causing a bodily collision with my guard.

"Crikey, you need taillights, girl." When I turned my gaze on him, his eyes widened in mock terror. Then he grinned. "You forget who my girlfriend is. No one can shoot hellfire out of their eyes like she can."

"Jaxon," I warned through gritted teeth.

He huffed dejectedly. "He's in his room. Lion-boy is too stubborn to stay in a hospital bed. He messaged me during our meeting with short-stuff."

My mouth had many things to say in response to Jaxon's latest bits of revelation, but it settled on, "Lion-boy?" I began moving again at a slightly slower pace.

"Yeah, his abilities have been compared to a mountain lion's. Saber cat too, but 'cat-boy' isn't manly enough, you know? I, on the other hand, am like a panther. At least, that's what I'm telling everyone."

I briefly paused, digesting the information. "Interesting.

I'd say you're more like a goat though. Always bleating, always underfoot. You even have that empty stare thing going on, like nobody's home."

He yelled in outrage, saying I was one headbutt away from facing his wrath, but I left him behind as I raced down the last flight and banged open floor ten's stairwell door. When I reached Brendan's room, I froze just shy of entering as my nerves finally caught up with me. There were so many things, so many *feelings*, and I didn't know what to do with them all.

"Should I go in first and make sure he's decent?" Jaxon whispered from behind. "Maybe he likes to sleep in the nu—"

I whipped up a hand and he stopped, thankfully.

"Okay, but don't say that I didn't warn you. Things are already plenty awkward between you two without adding in . . ." At my glare, he added, "Shutting up now."

After rolling my neck and loosening my shoulders, I decided to knock. I mean, he *could* be naked. And maybe the door was locked.

"Come in," I heard Brendan say. "But if you've come to finish me off, can it wait till morning?"

I didn't know why my fingers trembled as they cracked open the door—which was stupidly unlocked—but when I saw him, saw the way he smiled as if relieved, I wanted nothing more than to run my shaking hands over his face and assure myself that he was alive. My limbs seemed to have petrified though.

"You okay, man?" Jaxon said over my head. Brendan gave a thumbs up. As he nudged me into the room, Jaxon whispered in my ear, "Make sure he doesn't overexert himself tonight."

The door clicked shut before his words could sink in. And now I was alone. With Brendan. *Please say he didn't hear that.* By the look of his expression . . . Ah crap. He heard. At least he was clothed.

He crooked a finger at me. "Come here, little bird."

The way he said the nickname, so casual like it was the most natural thing in the world, awakened butterflies in my stomach. Their wings beat at my insides as I approached, all too aware of the way his gaze lingered on my bare legs. I tugged on the dress's short hem self-consciously.

His room was identical to mine, but his table held books and, most interestingly of all, the walls were covered in colorful, rectangle-shaped metal. I squinted, trying to read what was written on them. None of the words made sense except one: H-O-T-T-I-E.

"License plates," Brendan said, as if I'd understand what that meant. "I just need to find seven more states before I've collected all fifty. I probably won't find Hawaii though."

I hummed like I was impressed, but I was still clueless— and maybe felt a tiny bit stupid for knowing so little. Shyness stole over me when I dropped my shoes and stood near the foot of his bed, not knowing what to do with my hands now that they were empty. They didn't want to be though. Double crap. He said he couldn't read thoughts, but . . .

"Are you all right?"

His visible concern stilled my agitated movements. I

nodded, kicking myself for being flustered when I should be helping him. "Are you?"

He nodded, smiling slightly as though amused. "Just a little sore. The pain meds here are awesome though."

"Do you need anything?"

His head started to shake, paused, then slowly nodded. When he remained silent, I searched his face for an answer. And found it. I didn't know how, but in that moment, I knew exactly what he needed. My heart tumbled in my chest, and I moved, not giving myself time to overthink things.

He was propped up by pillows, half lying on his side so as not to disturb his wound. I didn't let him reach for me and risk pulling at his stitches. I gingerly climbed onto the bed and wrapped my arms around his shoulders, burying my nose in his neck. Breathed in the warmth, the life in him. The sunshine. His hand slid to my back and held me to him, his grip trembling slightly with fatigue. We didn't speak, simply soaked in each other's presence.

I pressed my mouth to his skin, closing my eyes and opening myself up to the feel of him. This moment could last forever and still not be long enough. But I had to break the spell. I wanted him to be the first to know. "I had a memory. When I thought you were dying, I yelled something, a sentence similar to one the old me said to you."

His breath hitched and the fingers on my back loosely fisted my dress. "Which memory?"

"I remember that it was dark and cold. I felt panicked because the Trials would begin the next morning and we could both die in them. I—I grabbed your face and said, 'You can't die, Brendan Bearon. You just can't.'"

He laughed softly, then flinched in pain. He trailed his nose down my neck, making me shiver. "That was the best night of my life," he murmured, pressing his lips to a sensitive spot just below my ear.

My body arched against him, and in my growing haze, I almost forgot about his injury. "Sorry." I tried pulling away but his grip on my dress tightened. He kissed my neck again and I melted, too weak to resist. As his mouth continued to explore my skin, that question came back to me, the one he had refused to answer a week ago. But now . . . now . . . "What was she to you?"

What am I to you?

He paused, his mouth still warming my neck. I held my breath and waited for him to shut me out, to push me away like he had in the gym. But maybe it was news of my memory or his close brush with death that made him say, "She's everything I'm fighting for. Redemption. Hope. Peace. Joy. All the things I can't have until I right the wrongs I've made."

And now he pulled away, leaving behind a dull ache in his absence. Sighing quietly, he took one of my hands in his and rubbed a thumb over my knuckles. He stared at our joined hands as he said, "But I've been selfish and weak. I want those things *now*, and in pursuing them, I've put you in danger time and again. You've been through so much because of me, and instead of keeping my distance, keeping you *safe*, I—"

His face contorted and he gripped my hand tightly. "You

almost got stabbed. *Again.* You could have—" He hissed sharply through clenched teeth. "I even failed to identify the assailant. All I saw was that knife coming at you. And now they're still out there, still a danger to you. Getting too close to me is a bad idea, Lune. You'll only get hurt—"

I placed my finger over his lips, needing to stop his words before they shredded my heart. I couldn't stand hearing the pain behind them any longer. The guilt. The burden he was shackling himself with. I couldn't bear seeing him suffer like this. Because after I'd been given that small sliver of memory back, I remembered the emotions that came with it. The way I had felt about Brendan at the time. The desire to make him forget about tomorrow and live in that one moment. With me.

"But what if I want to be close?" I whispered, my breath catching as his mouth warmed my finger. Desire trickled through me. An overwhelming need to press my lips to his.

And maybe I too was selfish and weak for wanting peace and happiness right now, but so be it.

I kissed him.

A soft brush of lips to ease the pain. A tender caress to distract the mind. With a gasp, I pulled back, shocked at what I'd just done, scared senseless that I'd ruined everything between us by forcing this on him. "I'm s-sorry," I stuttered, slipping my hand from his.

Before I could jump off the bed and flee the room, he caught my fingers again. Startled, I met his eyes. What I saw in their depths rooted me to the spot. "Don't you dare run," he breathed, slowly looping my arm around his neck once more.

"Don't you dare stop."

A small noise escaped me and my limbs threatened to liquify. He leaned forward as if to kiss me, but paused a breath away. Waiting. Challenging me. Holy crap, I was going to die. No, I was already dead. My body took charge then, pushing past my frozen state of shock. One hand grasped his neck while the other ran over the stubble on his cheek, guiding his lips to mine.

When our mouths joined, my control began to slip. All I felt was his soft lips eagerly returning my kiss. All I felt was the warmth, the fire, the passion stirring my blood. His fingers slid into my hair and tugged none-too-gently, sending electric jolts racing along my scalp. I repaid him in kind, making him gasp sharply.

He rose up, bringing me with him, and somehow I was straddling his lap, molding my body to his. My lips parted as new sensations flowed through me. His mouth opened, and I moaned weakly as his tongue touched mine. Any control I was holding onto snapped as we danced to a rhythm only our bodies knew. Warmth built in my core and I trembled. I ran a hand down his neck, his defined chest, skimming over rigid, unforgiving muscle.

Brendan laced our fingers together, halting my movements. I broke our kiss and dragged my lips over his jaw, his neck, his . . . "Lune," he panted. "I need to tell you about my past. About what's going to happen. I—"

"Please," I breathed, then kissed his mouth again. How could anything feel and taste so perfect? "Not tonight. Later."

He gently grasped the back of my neck and pulled away enough for me to see the desire in his eyes. But there was more than that, and I knew there was so much more in mine, too. I let him see it. He blew out a shaky breath and slowly lowered his head, brushing the softest, most tender kiss to my lips. "Soon."

I nodded, whispering, "Deal," then smiled as I grazed his mouth teasingly. He leaned forward with a low growl and I laughed as he nipped at my chin.

When he learned that I needed to fill out a report about last night's incident, Brendan helped, using my inexperience with handhelds as an excuse to tap in the story for me. But I wondered if he already knew that I could barely read, let alone write. Had the old me told him? It was awkward enough re-telling the event to him, but since we were using Jaxon's hand-held, we had company. Very nosy, very suspicious company.

"Something's different today," Jaxon mused, rubbing at his jaw as he glanced at Brendan still propped up in bed, then at me shifting from foot-to-foot in the middle of the room. I stilled my antsy legs and gave him what I hoped was a neutral look. His face split into a megawatt grin. "You two kissed."

My lips parted. What the—? I threw an accusatory glare at Brendan who wasn't bothering to hide a satisfied smirk. "Don't look at me, I didn't tell him. You don't have a very good poker face, is all."

Huh? What did that even mean?

"And after I gave you strict orders not to overexert the invalid last night." Jaxon tsked at me in mock disapproval.

"That's not what you—" I stopped when he snickered. My cheeks burst into flame. This was *not* happening right now. Carefully avoiding eye contact with either of them, I marched for the door. "Now that you have the *full* story, I have training to do."

I was scrambling down the hallway with Jaxon squawking at me to wait up before realizing I hadn't said goodbye to Brendan. My steps slowed, then renewed their clipped pace. Nope. He had been enjoying that torture way too much. When I arrived at the Ability Center, my skin felt a couple sizes too small.

"Don't be mad," Jaxon said, coming up alongside me.

"I'm not." Though I wanted to smack him.

"Embarrassed then. Like a kid caught with their hand in the cookie jar."

"Jaxon," I barked, my face heating all over again as we neared Dominic.

"Hey, no judgement, sister. I openly take from the cookie jar all the time. I know you've seen it at least once."

For the next few hours, I pretended he didn't exist. Which was hard considering he kept giving Dominic unsolicited advice on how to coax my ability out. But the older man listened intently, digesting last night's newest incident with rapt interest. At least he didn't smirk when Jaxon described the way Brendan and I had been dancing. In fact, I was pretty sure his cheeks darkened a bit.

Great. Just great.

Somehow I'd get back at Jaxon for this.

"I want to try something, Lune. I'm hoping the newness of it will heighten your senses and allow your ability to manifest," Dominic said, ushering me into the usual glass cubicle. He held up a silver opaque band—virtual reality, I remembered Brendan saying. When I couldn't fit it to my face correctly, Dominic made sure it was securely in place, deftly attaching a round sticker to each temple—a sensory pad and feeling receptor, he explained.

"You'll need space for this exercise, so I'll leave you alone in here. I'll see what you see on a separate viewing screen." I felt him drop something into my palm and I blindly grasped it between my fingers. "An ear communicator. So you can hear and talk to me."

I heard him leave the cubicle then, sealing me inside. "Can you hear me?" I said loudly when I'd slipped the communicator in.

A voice chuckled in my ear, making me flinch in surprise. "Clearly. You don't have to yell."

Inwardly, I grimaced. Oops.

"Okay, I'm going to turn on your headset and feeling receptor. If the images are too overwhelming, close your eyes and recenter your body. Tap your temple twice if the receptor becomes too much. It may take a few tries before your brain accepts two realities at once."

Well, that sounded . . . weird.

"You can do this, Lune," he added more quietly. "If you can master your ability, maybe you can stop whoever is out to harm you."

My chest tightened. I hadn't thought about it that way. Instead of being the helpless victim, waiting for the next time someone tried to kill me, I could be one step ahead. Even save others I cared about from getting hurt. I felt something then that I'd almost given up on. Hope. I finally had a reason, a purpose for navigating unfamiliar waters that up until this point had terrified me. Maybe facing that fear would be worth it if I could stop death in its tracks.

As soon as I nodded, the world fell away under my feet. I squeaked, backpedaling for solid ground. My back rammed into something hard, briefly knocking the air from my lungs.

"You don't need to move," Dominic said, sounding apologetic. "That's what the sensory pad is for. If you walk in place, you'll move where you want to go in the virtual world."

"Where—where am I?" I struggled to keep my eyes open as a wave of dizziness swept through me. Everywhere I looked . . . darkness. And yet it wasn't. There were muted blues and greens and purples. Pinpricks of light scattered as far as the eye could see, some clustered together to form speckled patches.

"You're an astronaut in outer space. Look at your hands."

I did and immediately reached for the bulky white gloves I was wearing. How did these get on my—?

"I wouldn't do that," Dominic warned as I attempted to pry one off. "Your hand will shrivel up in seconds."

"What?" I yelled, flattening myself against the glass

205

partition. Real. The glass was real. Not floating in outer space.

"In space, any exposure of skin would result in frostbite. It's extremely cold up there. But remember, you're not actually there. Your mind is playing tricks on you. It wants to believe what it sees is real, so it's relaying that message to your brain. The mind is a powerful thing, Lune Avery, and yours is willing to believe in the impossible."

"My visions."

"Yes. Maybe even more than that. Based off what Bren can sense, your ability to project energy is so intense that he thinks you're more than just a Visionary. You're something new—at least to our records. I'm hoping that this practice today will shed some light on what that something is."

Okay, then. No pressure. But outer space was probably a safer place to learn my ability than earth. No knives. No slippery floors. No people dying in front of me. I carefully took a step forward, then another, firmly planting my feet on solid ground even though I couldn't see it.

I nodded that I was ready.

19

GUNS & ALIENS

"Lunge faster! Don't forget to check down below. They could be coming from any direction."

I was wrong. Outer space was *scary*, not safe.

An alien horde had found me floating all on my lonesome and was attacking from all sides. My mission: envision their moves before they made them so I didn't get shot. Then, shoot *them*. No problem. Except my visions weren't working and apparently I didn't know how to shoot a gun. Oh, and I kept dying. The pain from the feeling receptor wasn't as intense as the real thing, but every time my virtual body was knocked back with a sharp zap and blood gushed out of me, I ground my teeth together.

A blue sizzling bolt shot for my face and I ducked. Another slammed into my arm and I spun around, then lost my balance. My shoulder and hip bone collided with the ground and I squeezed my eyes shut, cursing myself for losing touch with reality again.

"You okay?" Dominic asked, concern evident in his tone.

"Yeah," I panted, forcing my legs to bear my weight. The image of space had paused when I pried my eyes open again.

"Maybe we should call it quits for the day. You've been at

it for two hours."

"Just one more try. One more." I readied myself, raising my virtual weapons.

"Okay." Dominic sounded hesitant, but I knew he wanted me to manifest as much as I did. "This time, pick a target. Only one. Open yourself up to that target with your emotions. Let go of control but stay focused. Let your mind immerse itself in the target. *Feel*, don't think."

I nodded, shifting onto the balls of my feet.

Feel, don't think.

I could do that. Letting go of control would be the hard part.

"And make sure to pull the trigger this time!" Dominic added.

The virtual world sprang into motion. Dozens of enemies surrounded me. I zeroed in on one—the closest. Its long, tentacle arms undulated grotesquely, threatening to distract me. But I let myself forget everything around me, just like I had last night dancing in Brendan's arms. Let my mental guard down inch by inch as if opening a door. Feelings rushed in— fear, dread, determination, adrenaline, excitement. I focused on projecting those emotions at the alien, strangling its gangly body with them.

My gut lurched as the alien's weapon discharged and a blue static ball whipped for my heart. I braced for the pain, but none came. When I blinked, the image of my impending death was gone. The alien hadn't fired yet. My stomach bottomed out, but I forced myself to remain calm. To wait a beat.

The alien's bony finger squeezed the trigger.

Zip.

I leaned to the side, just enough to avoid getting hit. Then unleashed myself on the creature, bellowing a war cry as I pumped its sickly bulbous belly full of virtual lead. *Zap, zap zap.* With a shriek, it flew backward into its comrades. Who were preparing to return fire. Crap. My concentration broke.

But Dominic must have known I'd manifested because the image blipped out of existence, leaving me in the dark. I heard the glass door whoosh open, then hands were removing the silver band from my face. The brightness of reality was a punch to the eye sockets, but I blinked away the hazy spots and searched out my trainer's expression. When I saw it, I knew I had guessed right. He was grinning from ear to ear, happier than I'd ever seen him.

I smiled back, even let myself laugh. "I did it!"

"You did it," he reaffirmed, squeezing my shoulders. Then he pulled me into a tight hug. I hugged him in return and laughed with relief.

I had successfully projected my ability. On purpose this time. The thought filled me with a heady sense of control. If only Brendan had been here to see, to know firsthand that I could stop whoever was out to harm me. And maybe that knowledge would give him a tiny sliver of peace.

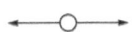

A week flew by. Every day—even my free day of no duties—was spent training, each longer than the last until I was skipping my afternoon exercise routine in favor of more hours with Dominic. He didn't seem to mind the extra time with me, even insisted that I was his number one priority per Dr. Moore's instructions. My memories were still blocked except the one, despite Dominic's continued attempts at freeing them, but my visions during virtual reality practice were coming more frequently, and my reactions to them were more steady.

There was one thing I was truly awful at though: shooting a gun. And if I wanted to compete in the bi-annual Abilities Competition in a couple weeks, I needed to up my game. Supposedly, with my experience contending in the Elite Trials, I excelled at wielding all sorts of weapons, plus several other useful survival skills. But apparently I'd never trained with a gun in any form, which put me at a huge disadvantage.

Jaxon was currently teasing me on my terrible aim, comparing me to a trooper of some kind I'd never heard of. He pointed at the white-armoured figure on his black tee for emphasis. "These dudes. They never hit their target. Although, in their defense, I don't think they were ever given proper shooting lessons."

Brendan abruptly stood from our lunch table and grabbed our trays. "Message Dom that Lune won't be training this afternoon, Jaxon," he threw over his shoulder as he slid our trays onto the washroom conveyor belt.

I frowned, surprised and maybe a touch annoyed at his

bossy command. But when he turned and graced me with a mysterious smile that all but said *Are you up for some trouble?* I followed him without comment, a twinge of anticipation shivering through me. Since the night of the party, we hadn't kissed again. Not that I didn't want to. Crap, I wanted to so badly. But I knew that something still bothered him involving his past—maybe even his future. He was obviously having a hard time telling me, but instead of *asking* him like any well-rounded person would, I clammed up.

Because what if the thing that was holding him back ruined our relationship? I wasn't even sure what we were. Friends, yes. But we'd kissed. And not just a quick peck to test the waters. No, we dove in head first. Where we stood now, I was content with. Perhaps I was selfish for not wanting that to end, but the thought of this sliver of peace vanishing froze my tongue.

If he wanted to change the dynamic, then that was his decision to make.

"Our schedules are all cleared," Jaxon said, coming up alongside us. "What daring plan have you concocted, brave leader?"

"An extracurricular one," Brendan replied.

My brows rose and Jaxon gasped. "You rebel, you. The tallest man in The Ridge going toe-to-nose with the shortest man. I love it."

I snorted. "Can't we like, I don't know, get in trouble?" My assailant from the party hadn't been captured, after all. He or she was still roaming these hallways, perhaps waiting for another unguarded moment to strike.

Dr. Moore said they didn't have any leads yet but to proceed with daily activities as normal. "We don't scare easily, Miss Avery," he'd assured me earlier this week. "Terrorists thrive on fear, so we won't give them anything to feed on."

"I don't think you realize how much clout Golden Boy here has with the big—I mean, *small*—man. He can practically do no wrong," Jaxon said. Brendan sighed in mock exasperation.

We passed by the Ability Center as I asked, "And why is that?"

"Girl, don't you know anything about your boy?" Jaxon's voice rang out. Before I could point out that technically Brendan wasn't my anything, he added, "Boy Wonder is a freaking DNA detector. Yeah, he's also a Sensor with cat-like reflexes and superhuman strength, blah blah, but he can tell when someone has an ability and how potent it is. With him around, you can skip all the guesswork and go straight to dropping said mutant human into a category."

"Jaxon," Brendan groaned, rubbing the back of his neck. "You make it sound like a science experiment."

"Isn't that what we are, my good man? What normal human can bench press half a flipping ton? Or hear thoughts? Or see something happen before it's happened? And don't forget that you were stabbed last week and now almost healed. This place may be our home, but you have to admit, they welcome people like us with open arms because of what we *are*."

Brendan didn't confirm or deny, but a muscle jumped in

his jaw. Which had me thinking.

"What if someone wanted to leave The Ridge?" At the question, both men zeroed in on my face. *Okay, this is awkward.* I hurried to add, "I haven't seen the sun yet. I just . . . I have this strange urge to feel it, if that makes sense."

A hand brushed mine, then Brendan was lacing our fingers together. My heart skipped a beat at the public display, the first he'd initiated since our dance. "I'll see what I can do," he said quietly.

We took a left and walked to the end of a hallway I'd never been down before. As soon as the door opened, I recoiled at the sharp *bang, bang, bang.*

Jaxon started laughing. I threw a glare at him but he was too busy thumping Brendan on the back. "I like how your mind works, man," he shouted over the repeated banging noise. It was then that I noticed a long row of human-shaped targets.

I couldn't help groaning. "Really? Guns?"

"They're my weapon of choice," Brendan said in a way that had me peering up at him quizzically. He winked. Was I missing something? That look he was giving me though, like a little boy barely containing his excitement. I pressed my lips together so I wouldn't grin like an idiot. "If guns are your weakness, then I'll help you fix that."

A man ushered us through when he spotted Brendan, passing him and Jaxon black handguns and a case of bullets. He side-eyed me warily. Apparently word hadn't spread that I wasn't a threat. Or maybe it had, but they didn't like my abilities. They seemed to accept Dominic just fine though . . .

"They don't know whose side you're on," Jaxon whispered in my ear even as he gave the man an extra friendly wave. "They think you followed Bren here to exploit their home."

"I—" What was I supposed to say to *that*? What if they were right? "Why did I leave Tatum City? Why did Brendan?"

"The Supreme Elite sent me on a mission," Brendan explained. "Said it was a chance to prove my loyalty and worth after we—after I failed to follow the rules." When we reached the far corner of the room where curious ears couldn't eavesdrop, he continued with, "Apparently he sent you on a mission too. To spy on me, actually."

Jaxon snickered and I frowned at him. "Sorry." He cleared his throat and unsuccessfully smoothed his expression. "Highly classified inside joke that I can't talk about."

Brendan shot him a warning look. Okay, weird.

"So we both failed our missions then?" I asked Brendan.

He sighed, then began loading his gun. "No. I'm not done with my mission. Here, you should learn to do this." He placed the gun's cold handle into my hand. My first instinct was to let go, but he wrapped his fingers firmly around mine. "First rule: don't drop your gun."

"I thought it would be 'don't shoot yourself in the foot' or 'don't stare down the bullet chamber.'"

His lips twitched. "Smarty-pants. Just for that, I'm not gonna make this easy for you."

"I don't want you to go easy on me," I couldn't help saying, gratified when he threw me a wicked grin.

"Well, can you two go easy for my sake?" Jaxon said with a grimace. "'Cause this flirty ooey-gooey stuff is making me nauseous. I'll be in the booth next door, drowning out any noises you decide to make. But can we keep this episode PG-13?" He didn't wait for a reply, already slipping on noise-canceling headphones and sauntering around the partition.

Right on cue, heat rushed up my neck and scalded my face. I tried to pull away but Brendan wasn't having it. The hand not currently grasping mine reached around me, effectively trapping me between his arms, then finished loading the chamber. Slowly.

"That was the magazine," he murmured, his mouth brushing the shell of my ear. "Slide to engage the firing mechanism." His fingers guided mine to the right spot and I struggled to pay attention. His chest pressed against my back, thoroughly distracting me. "Trigger." Our fingers moved again to who-knew-where. I wasn't paying attention to the lesson anymore. His scent surrounded me and before I knew it, I was leaning into him with a soft sigh.

He chuckled, then slid away, leaving me cold and alone with the gun. "I told you I wasn't going to make this easy. Gun pointed at the ground, newbie."

I gaped at him. Did he just use his charm on me as a—a *test?* My eyes narrowed. "I hope you know that two can play that game."

"I'm counting on it," he purred, then twirled his finger at me to face the target. I did, gladly, as my cheeks reddened further. He didn't touch me again, which helped with focus at least. And even though he warned me about the gun's kick, I still chomped down on my lip, holding back a curse when it jolted in my hands.

"I don't think I like guns," I muttered under my breath, but Brendan still heard through our synced noise-cancelling headphones and chuckled. I checked the target for a hole. Brendan peered over my shoulder and shook his head, saying there wasn't one. Ouch. I was even worse at shooting in real life than in virtual reality.

"Keep practicing. You'll be a crack-shot in no time."

Planting my feet the way I'd been instructed, I lined up for another shot. "Why are you teaching me to shoot anyway? Will I be using a gun anytime soon other than on aliens?" *Bang!* Crap on a cookie, I hated the recoil.

"With your luck, probably."

When I looked up at him, I was expecting a teasing expression, not a serious frown. "What?" I lowered the weapon like I'd been taught and flicked the safety on. "You said you're not finished with your mission, but what about mine? Am I supposed to go back?"

With a sigh, he picked up the discarded gun and leveled it at the target. *Bang, bang, bang.* I couldn't help searching for holes. And found three dead center. I rolled my eyes. Of course he was good. Wasn't he good at everything?

He excels at kissing, that's for sure.

I struggled to erase the images popping into my brain, focusing on crossing my arms and jutting out my chin instead. Answers. I needed them and he had them. I wouldn't be brushed off this time.

Brendan must have seen the determination on my face because he put down the gun and scrubbed a hand through his hair. "Yes, you were meant to go back, Lune. But I can't send you into that lion's den without your memories. Even if you *did* have them, you're finally safe from Renold. You're finally *free*, just like you always wanted. The old you wouldn't want to return."

I mulled over this new information about myself, about what I had wanted in life. But one thing was bothering me . . . "What about my sister Iris? Would the old me just leave her there?"

He pressed his lips together as if frustrated by my line of questioning. Too bad. When my eyes narrowed, he grunted, replying, "Of course not. Before I left Tatum City, I told you about her to make sure someone was protecting her. But you're here now. When I return, I'll keep her safe. I promise."

"When will you return?"

"Soon," he said evasively, reminding me that I still knew practically nothing of his past or future plans. My teeth ground together. "I can sense your annoyance, little bird, but everything's changed now that you're not in the middle of all the danger. This is a complicated mission and only a few people are allowed to know about it. If we don't play this right, a lot of innocents could get injured, or even killed."

"Then why do it? Why did you enter Tatum City in the first place?"

He looked down at his hands, which slowly curled into

fists. His forearm nearest to me flexed, drawing my eye, and I wondered at an oval scar there. Who had bitten him? Finally, he answered, "Because I'm righting my wrongs. And because I'm the only one foolish enough to enter while knowing I may never come out."

My lips parted. So if he returned, there was a chance he wouldn't be able to leave? That I would never see him again? Out of nowhere, fury rushed through me. My fingernails gouged my palms. I wanted to shout at him, scream that he couldn't go back. Because . . . because a terrible pain was crushing my heart, and . . .

"That's the stupidest thing I've ever heard," I choked out, then whirled, marching for the exit.

EXPLANATIONS

I managed to avoid Brendan for the rest of the afternoon, and when he didn't show for dinner, I assumed he was avoiding me too. My fork stabbed at a mound of mashed potatoes. "Why? Why does he do the missions?" *Stab.* "Aren't any of you upset that you might not see him again?" *Stab stab.*

Jaxon, Yukiko, and Bells all stared at me with mixed expressions—Jaxon with sympathy, Yukiko like I was insane, and Bells looked . . . guilty. "I'm so sorry," Brendan's sister began, tears forming in her eyes. Jaxon held up a hand, then stood, gesturing at me to follow suit.

"It's okay, Bells, I've got this," he said, a rare softness in his tone. She nodded but continued to stare at her plate. I opened my mouth, wanting to apologize for upsetting her, but Jaxon grabbed hold of my shirt sleeve and tugged me after him.

I had no idea where he was taking me, but when the elevator stopped on the third floor and he had to key in a special code before the doors would open, curiosity overrode some of my anger.

"Did you know that this place was built before the Silent War?" Jaxon said as we passed door after door, each carefully labeled. L-I-V-E-S-T-O-C-K, read one of the signs. "This is the Agricultural floor, dedicated to keeping our community alive. Homeland Security, back when they existed, was prepared for an apocalyptic outcome such as this. Good thing, too. Thousands of people have been saved from a life like the one you were forced into."

Forced. I was forced? Brendan hadn't mentioned how I'd initially entered Tatum City. We arrived at a door labeled C-O-N-S-E-R-V-A-T-O-R-Y and Jaxon pressed his hand to a dark panel on the wall. After a beep, the door slid sideways. I blinked, not expecting the quiet area to be so high-tech.

"Perks of being born here and having both parents work on this floor," he went on to explain. "Plus, my other job—not the teaching chicklets one that I do when I'm off guard duty—makes me a part of the esteemed 'inner circle'. Stick with me and you'll get a free pass to all the high security spots in no time."

With anyone else, the words would have sounded like bragging. With Jaxon, they sounded like genuine pride for his birthplace. I liked him and The Ridge even more now. "So how many jobs *do* you have?"

"Eh, I kind of tinker in everything. Helps tire out my brain so I can sleep a few hours at night." At my raised eyebrows, he added, "Downside of the Intellect ability. My racing thoughts drive me cuckoo if I don't control them. It's why Bren volunteers in Medical once in awhile and reads poetry. Keeps him in touch with his humanity so he doesn't go wild animal. All Sensors have an affinity for animals though. Yukiko smuggles in little creatures and stashes them in her room. Don't tell her

I told you."

"Uh . . ."

When the door whooshed shut behind us, several bursts of air hit me. I yelped, leaping sideways into Jaxon. He steadied me, then draped an arm over my shoulders as he belly laughed.

"S-sorry," he wheezed, clutching at his stomach. "De-de-contamination chamber."

Did he think I would know what that was? I huffed and threw his arm off me, surprisingly okay with his touch despite my actions. "Isn't this an extracurricular activity?"

"I got the green light." He waved his handheld in the air with a sly grin. "Because I'm a good boy, unlike that tall drink of water you're currently drowning in."

I wrinkled my nose. "Please don't ever call him that agai—" My mind blanked as an inner door slid open and I caught sight of what lay within. A sea of green. Not paint or metal or material, but the purest of shades that only nature could create. Above was a transparent tarp of some kind that slightly dimmed the multitude of lights dotting the ceiling. The air was thick, tasting of earth and rain.

"Welcome to the Garden of Eden," Jaxon said with a hand flourish. "It's obviously not the real thing, but pretty close. There's even a huge apple tree at the center. Everyone who eats the fruit gains immortality."

When I continued to silently gape at our surroundings, he huffed and tugged me out of the doorway so it could close.

"I swear you don't understand a word I say, Lu Bear.

What did they teach you in that city?"

"Um. I know how to count and tie my shoes." I was only half-joking. There were so many things I didn't know, especially without my memories. Only my subconscious saved me from complete ignorance. But I wanted to know more. I wanted to know *everything*, starting with what made Brendan Bearon tick.

Thankfully, Jaxon was in the "let's chat about my best friend" mood. He stuffed his hands into his pockets and began strolling down a stone path, saying, "I met Bren on one of my top secret missions three years ago. In fact, I almost shot him. Well, he probably would have shot me first, but anyway. He was being hunted by the Recruiter Clan boss who valued him more than all of his goons combined. The man thought his prized ability detector must have come to harm, but in reality, Bren was deserting. Did he tell you any of this?"

I shook my head. All of this information felt new to me and I yearned for more, even taking my eyes off the plant life around me so I could better capture his words. "Who is the Recruiter Clan and why would he leave them?"

The path forked and we went left, the distant sound of trickling water reaching my ears. "That particular clan claimed Asheville, the old city outside of Tatum City. It used to be vibrant, rich with history and eclectic lifestyles before the Silent War. Now it's broken, used as a waystation for human trafficking. Anyone unfortunate enough to step inside the old city's borders doesn't usually come back out a free person."

I grimaced at the image he'd just painted. "And Brendan

used to be a part of all that?"

"Not willingly. But . . . there was Bells. She was their blackmail piece. If he didn't cooperate, she was punished. Don't ask me to elaborate on that." My throat tightened as I struggled to stop my mind from forming awful conclusions. "After witnessing his parent's deaths, he knew how serious they were, too. He endured that life for eight years, working as their human ability detector. But there came a point when he couldn't protect Bells anymore. She was budding into a young woman and . . ."

At his uncomfortable shrug, I put the pieces together. Oh no. "Was she—is she—?"

"No, he got her out in time," he reassured, pausing to pick a few dead leaves off a flowering plant. "He knew they wouldn't just let him go though. So before he left, he made it seem like there'd been a fight. Blood, broken furniture. A lot of the clan members were jealous of his standing with the boss, so the idea that one of them would kill him wasn't farfetched. But then there's the boss's son."

Jaxon turned to me, studying my expression. I raised my brows, confused at the wariness in his eyes. Did he think it was a mistake telling me about Brendan's past? "Please, Jaxon. I need to know."

After another moment of hesitation, he nodded. "I'm only telling you this because I've never seen the dude so conflicted. I know it's because of you, and that distracted state could get him killed. It's against protocol to disclose what he does for The Ridge, but I can tell you what he used to do for the Recruiter Clan. Are you sure you want to know?"

No. "Yes. I want to understand why he would willingly lock himself inside a city that might never let him out." And why he would leave his friends and family, everyone he *cared* about behind.

"There's a simple answer for that, but it's hard to swallow." He held up a finger, then jogged backwards around a corner. Uh, okay. I trailed after him, and when I rounded the bend, I sucked in a gasp. Stone gave way to lush grass, and in the middle of the clearing was a shallow pool with a fountain at its center. Next to the water was a voluminous willow tree, its branches drooping so low, they brushed the grass.

Jaxon was nowhere to be seen, so I inched forward, even went so far as to remove my shoes and sink my feet into the soft grass. A grin pulled at my cheeks. Before I knew it, I was inches away from the pool, staring in wonder at the gold and white flashes rippling beneath the surface.

"Koi fish," a deep voice said next to me, and I suppressed a squeak of surprise. "I'm assuming you didn't have any of those in your city based on the puckered, fish-like look on your face." I whacked Jaxon's chest. With a loud crunch, he bit into a shiny red apple, then tossed one to me.

I held up the perfectly ripe fruit. "So this will give me immortality?"

"No, I put a spell on that one. Spoiler alert: it puts you into a deep sleep and only tall, dark, and handsome can wake you with a kiss."

Shaking my head, I took a big bite. I liked Jaxon, but holy

crap, I really *really* liked apples, spelled or not. Maybe apples were my favorite food.

"Should I leave you two alone?"

My eyes popped open—okay, maybe I liked apples a little *too* much. "Shut up," I mumbled, taking a seat at the pool's edge. "So what's the simple answer?"

He sighed, like he'd hoped I would have forgotten why we came here, then sat beside me. For several moments, the only sound was the soft rush of water falling into the pool's center. I waited, feigning patience by leisurely twirling a blade of grass and wiggling my toes in the water.

Just as I was about to press further, Jaxon quietly said, "He's doing penance. Over the years, he's destroyed many lives. They haunt him still—guilt eats at him every day. So now, the only thing that keeps him going, the only thing that lets him sleep at night, is saving lives.

"Of course we're upset at the thought of never seeing him again when he goes on his missions, but an aimless Bren isn't a Bren you want to see, trust me. I'd rather he live his life dangerously than not at all. My only worry is that he won't stop until he's sacrificed himself in the process."

At that, unease stirred in my gut, along with a deep ache in my chest. I let silence settle between us again, too afraid to pursue the next question. What had Brendan gone through that would drive him to continually risk his life?

The moment for answers dispelled a minute later when Jaxon checked his handheld, then jumped to his feet with a whoop. "They caught your dance killer. Found the knife hidden in his room and everything. Let's head back. I gotta be there for the interrogation 'cause, you know, my 'other job.'"

I blinked, trying to wrap my brain around the news as he hauled me upright. We were nearly to the elevator when I finally muttered "dance killer" with an eye roll. A little on the nose, but funny.

The shock wore off a couple hours later.

I was safe. *Really* safe now. Relief hit me like a shot of adrenaline. I hadn't realized until this moment how tense I'd been all week. Knowing that the person who'd wanted me dead couldn't harm me again was a terrible burden lifted. I could breathe easier. I could stop peering over my shoulder.

Jaxon hadn't said if he was going to swing by my room after the interrogation, and I grumbled at my continued lack of a handheld. Too hyped up, I couldn't fall asleep. And I couldn't visit Bells' room without a guard. Brendan must have been out as well because every time I pressed my ear to the wall separating our rooms, there was only silence.

Did that make me a creeper? Oh well.

He was probably at the interrogation too if he was as important as Jaxon said he was. Or maybe he was simply trying to stay as far away from me as he could. And who could blame him? The last words I'd said to him had been ugly. I might as well have spat on him while I was at it.

Guilt gnawed at my insides, further ramping up my energy. As soon as I saw him again, I'd apologize. Thanks to Jaxon, I knew him a bit better now. Knew that he carried a burden so much bigger than the one I'd just removed from my shoulders. Still, I had so many burning questions. Pacing the room grew boring, so I opted for a shower. Water would help soothe away the persistent buzz beneath my skin.

A half hour later, steam curled around me as I towelled myself dry, then stepped out of the shower. I slipped on a black tank top and yoga pants, my muscles completely relaxed for the first time all day. Maybe the first time in weeks. As I opened the bathroom door, I ran my fingers through my wet hair, working out any remaining knots.

When I reached the middle of my room, I frowned. Something felt . . . off. The air was thicker out here, even without the shower steam. My eyes lifted and that's when I saw it. Bold, red letters on the wall. My chest tightened, heart thundering as I slowly read the words.

We don't want you here. Leave now.

Crap. Oh crap.

There were others. And they'd been in my room. *My room.*

I could feel the blood draining from my face at the realization. Brendan. I had to get to him. I lunged for the door, but something snagged my hair. Yanked me back. Before the pain could register, before I could scream, an arm snaked around my neck and squeezed.

For an unbearable moment, fear froze me. The arm tightened. Air escaped my lungs. I wheezed, unable to draw breath. Unable to think. Fire burned my throat. My eyes widened as dark spots blotted my vision.

Then I reacted.

My heel slammed onto a booted foot and my assailant grunted, loosening their grip a little. Enough for me to create some distance between our bodies and ram my elbow into their rib cage. I heard a hiss of pain, which fueled me onward. As my attacker curled around their injury, we tilted forward. I went limp and my dead weight pitched us even more off balance.

We tumbled to the floor. I rolled so that I was on top, staring at the ceiling, then snapped my head back into their face. After a muffled shout, the arms fell away and I dragged air into my lungs. Coughs racked my body as I rolled again, seeking out the intruder. A dark hoodie and mask hid their identity, but my burning desire to know who they were overrode common sense.

I reached for the mask. My fingers grabbed the material. A sharp bite of pain pricked my neck. I dragged the mask off, but just as I caught sight of pale skin, the world tilted. The floor rose up to meet me and I was once again rolling onto my back, staring up at the ceiling. But there was something terribly wrong this time. I flexed my muscles—or tried to.

My body didn't respond.

I couldn't move. The only part of me still responsive was my eyes. They widened as my attacker, with their mask once again firmly in place, loomed over me with a syringe in hand. I opened my mouth to scream, but even my lips refused to move. My heart pounded wildly as I helplessly waited for my impending death, for a knife to stab me. No one was here to stop them this time. No one would find me until morning, and by then, I'd have bled out.

I'm going to die. I'm going to die.

The wait was the worst. The anticipation of pain. I just wanted it to be over. *What are you waiting for?* I wanted to yell. The masked figure stepped out of my line of sight. My panic grew, a thundering beat inside my skull. Would they prolong my death? Torture me? *Wake up, body, wake up!*

Thoughts of being flayed alive consumed me. The need to defend myself was a raging fire that grew hotter and hotter the longer it was trapped within my unresponsive body. A minute passed. Then two. Nothing happened. More time slowly ticked by, and not knowing where my attacker was ate away at my mind. I could feel the anxiety like a heavy rock on my chest, pressing the air from my lungs.

If I didn't calm down soon, I was going to pass out.

Brendan. Think of him.

My instincts rebelled against closing my eyes, but I squeezed them shut so I could picture his face. *His voice. Think of his voice.* The deep, rolling notes that always brought me comfort for some inexplicable reason. If I could just hear him, maybe the hand gripping my heart would loosen so I could breathe again.

Exhaling through my nose, I focused all of my energy on seeking the sound of that voice. My name on his lips. His teasing drawl. Concern on his tongue like a gentle touch. The rare anger that further deepened his voice, kind of like right now as he spoke to someone I couldn't see.

"He swears that the knife isn't his, that he's being framed, and I believe him. I've known him for years and he wouldn't jeopardize his family like that. I still think it's our traitor trying to instill fear throughout the community."

"I agree, which is why I've allowed Miss Avery to roam about the premises without much protection this last week," another voice sounding like Dr. Moore said.

"So you're using her as *bait?*" Brendan hissed.

"You know how long we've been trying to catch this traitor, Bren. First the rumors to cause unrest, then the theft of our high tech. Now attempted murder? You know the stakes more than anyone if this spy is working for Renold Tatum. Besides, she can take care of herself. Dominic says her visions are becoming stronger, faster, and more accurate. She would make a valuable asset on this case."

"No. Absolutely not. She didn't sign up for this. She wouldn't want—"

Brendan's words abruptly cut off. No, I needed to hear *more*, I needed to understand how I was doing this. Was this real? I opened my mind to him and shouted into the void. *Brendan.* No response. Panic swirled through my thoughts again, but I shoved it down, projecting my desperation for him to hear me instead. The feeling rushed through me and I immersed myself in it, sensed it gather into a writhing ball just behind my closed eyelids. I pushed the emotion into the dark silence.

Brendan, I need you.

The words echoed along a corridor I couldn't see, but could feel. I directed them to him, not knowing where he was, but believing that I would find him anyway. The sound bounced around in my head for a moment more before all went silent again. I inwardly sighed. This was stupid. No one could—

"Lune?"

My heart slammed against my chest and I wrenched my eyes open, expecting to see him standing above me. There was nothing but the white ceiling of my room. I started to cry then, frustrated and scared. Except tears wouldn't come. They were frozen too, burning behind my eyes with no way to get out.

More time passed and a new worry wormed its way into my mind. What if I was stuck like this forever? I wanted to thrash and wail but could only manage a weak flutter of my eyelashes. The need to expel my fury drowned out the fear that my attacker was still nearby, ready to chop up my limbs piece by piece so they could better hide the evidence of my murder.

Just wait until I got my hands on them. I would chop off their—

The door banged open and I inwardly jumped, a scream building in my throat that couldn't find release.

"Oh, God. Lune!"

Blessed relief shuddered through me at the sound of his voice. *Please, let it be real.* His face, so worried, so beautiful, filled my vision, and the tears burned hotter. I formed his name on my tongue, but it stuck there. I felt his hands on me—my face, my arms, my stomach, my legs, back to my face—searching for injury. Finding none.

"Lune, speak to me," he said, running his fingers through my hair. "Where does it hurt?"

I blinked slowly, not knowing what else to do.

"Okay, I got it. Blink once for yes, two for no. Are you in pain?"

Blink blink.

"Good. Good," he said, but the deep groove between his brows remained. "Can you move?"

Blink blink.

He stared at me, mortified, then his face fell. "I'm so sorry," he choked out. "This is all my fault." His agony was so intense, I could feel it in my bones. A tear escaped my right eye. Then the other. He caught them, carefully wiping my cheeks dry. "I'll fix this, little bird. I will."

As he pulled out his handheld and hurriedly typed in a message, I wanted nothing more than to comfort him, to wrap my arms around him and hold him close. To tell him over and over that *I* was sorry. That this wasn't his fault. I wanted to kiss away his guilt and sorrow, erase the worry lines on his brow.

But all I could do was blink.

And silently cry.

NO MATTER WHAT

"The effects of the drug-induced paralysis should be out of your system by morning," Dr. Stacey said, unwrapping a blood pressure monitor from my arm. "Unfortunately, there are any number of people who could have stolen the drug from our medical supply wing. We haven't needed to worry about that sort of thing until now."

She looked down at me sympathetically, but her thin smile seemed forced.

"So you haven't noticed anything *strange* lately?" Dr. Moore asked from his position near my feet. "Abnormal requests, lower than usual supply count?"

She stood, shaking her head. "Try asking Dr. Bradfield. His team makes the drugs, after all."

Dr. Moore lowered his voice, glancing around before saying, "Do you have any reason to believe Dr. Bradfield would want Lune gone from Blue Ridge Sector? It's almost been a month and he hasn't created an antidote for the memory blocker serum. Maybe he hasn't even tried."

Dr. Stacey's eyes widened. "No. I don't know. I haven't heard anything. Have you discovered the reason behind the threats on her life?"

"We thought so about an hour ago, but now I'm uncertain. We think it's more than some misguided fear of her abilities."

"Oh? What else could it be then?" Her gaze rested on Brendan who was leaning against the wall opposite the bed I was stuck in.

His golden eyes never left me as he said, "I'm not sure yet. I think it involves Tatum City though and her connection there." He shared a quick look with Dr. Moore. "Can I take her back to her room now?"

The Ridge leader nodded, gesturing at the door. "We'll talk more tomorrow."

When Brendan crossed the small private room and bent over me, Dr. Stacey was ready with a wheelchair. "No need," he said, carefully lifting me into his arms. Even if I *could* complain, I wouldn't have. All I wanted was to be near him. I just wished that I could turn my head an inch so I could bury my nose in his shirt. The hallways were empty, which I was grateful for. If people saw me this way, helpless and weak, would they finish me off at the soonest available opportunity?

I suddenly wanted to be on my own two feet. But no matter how much I struggled, not even a finger would move.

Brendan peered down at me, probably sensing my heightened emotions. "You all right?"

I wanted to lie and say yes. I wanted to see his shoulders relax and the brackets around his mouth disappear. But maybe it was everything Jaxon had told me or my steadily growing feelings for him that made me tell the truth instead.

Blink blink.

He didn't speak again the entire walk back to my room, but his arms tightened around me, fitting me closer to his chest.

Safe, my mind hummed. With all my heart, I believed that.

After nudging open my bedroom door, he took one look at the writing on the wall and turned around. When we entered his room, I breathed a sigh of relief. I doubted the attacker would attempt another pass at me in my room, but the thought of sleeping there sent chills down my spine.

He gently placed me on his bed, then fussed with the pillow behind my head and tucked a blanket under my chin. If my muscles would cooperate, I'd have a big goofy grin on my face right about now. He caught me staring at him—what else was I supposed to do?—and cracked a small smile.

I wanted to bask in that smile forever, but he was moving again, stripping his shirt off as he went into the bathroom. It was only a few measly seconds of glimpsing the long length of his spine and perfectly bronzed skin, but heat flared up my neck anyway. How could the shape of skin and muscle be so . . . attractive?

I rolled my eyes. At least I could still do *that*. When he was gone for over a minute, my attention strayed to the bedroom door. Had he locked it? Anyone could enter and stick a knife in my chest even with Brendan only yards away. I was *that* helpless. Crap. Did the handle just turn? My heart rate soared and I strained to pry my mouth open.

"Lune, what's wrong?" Brendan burst into the room wearing nothing but sweat pants. He crouched next to the bed, scanning the room for threats. "I could smell your fear. Did anyone come in here?"

He fixed his attention on me, waiting for a response, but I was too busy soaking up the sight of him. Crap, he looked good. Could his shoulders be any broader? My jaw would have dropped under normal circumstances. *Get your hormones under control, idiot,* my mind wisely hissed at me. I met his eyes and quickly blinked twice. Then focused on the door.

"You want me to lock it?"

Blink.

He straightened, and as soon as I heard the *snick* of the lock engaging, I sighed. It might be a false security measure, just like hiding under a blanket at night, but it calmed my thoughts all the same. Although, a half-naked Brendan Bearon standing in the middle of the room wasn't going to allow me any sleep. How did I convey with my eyes that he needed to sit down and put a shirt on?

When he raised a hand to rub at the back of his neck—a habit that I was beginning to think meant he was feeling embarrassed or uncomfortable—I was equal parts fascinated and amused. His bicep flexed and I couldn't look away. The ridges of his abdomen tensed and hardened, demanding my full attention, so I obliged. If only I could—

"You gotta stop staring at me like that," he said, and when my gaze flew to his, I inhaled sharply at the look of want there. My pulse shot through the ceiling. Something strange had come over me, this blatant boldness, and apparently it wasn't finished yet.

Blink blink.

His eyes rounded, then he laughed in surprise. "Is Lune Avery flirting with me?"

Blink.

"Wow, um." He ducked his head, still chuckling. "This may be the craziest but best conversation I've ever had."

When he peered up at me through those impossibly dark lashes, I rolled my eyes. His face split into the most gorgeous grin I'd ever seen, and my heart melted into a pathetic little puddle. I would do just about anything to keep him smiling like that.

His attention shuffled over the room before landing on the gray couch behind him. "You should get some sleep. I'll, uh, take the sofa." I waited for him to look at me, then blinked twice. His brows rose. "Do you need anything?"

Blink.

"What?"

Of course I didn't answer, but I spoke with my eyes just the way he had when our situations had been reversed. Even as I did, my mouth dried. The thought of him next to me while I was so vulnerable . . . Crap. It thrilled and scared me. But I didn't care that my heart was beating so hard it almost hurt. Not when I desperately wanted him as near as possible. So I continued to hold eye contact despite the heat flooding my cheeks.

He swallowed, then nodded, no longer smiling. But I

didn't mind. Because I could tell he was feeling the exact same thing I was—an incessant need to be close. "I'll just, um, put a shirt on," he said, his voice low and rough, making my stomach flutter.

Double blink.

Crap, did I just do that?

He paused midstep, searching my face for clues to what I was thinking. He wouldn't find any. I was purely running on instinct and hormones right now. Thoughts had fled me long ago. And maybe he saw that. He pressed his lips together to suppress a smile. I would have suppressed a ridiculous giggle if my vocal chords were functioning.

I didn't look away as he approached, not even when he crawled over me and fitted his body next to mine along the wall. Propping himself up on an elbow, he stared down at me. Then reached a hand out to graze his thumb over my bottom lip. The touch awoke my senses, sent sparks sizzling through my veins. I wanted more, so much more, but he settled in, tucking me close against him. My head rested in the crook of his arm and I breathed him in, letting my eyes drift shut.

Just before the heaviness of sleep blanketed me, before my string of consciousness dimmed, I felt his lips press a kiss to my forehead and heard him whisper, "You're my everything."

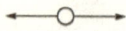

I didn't know how long I'd slept, but when I woke, my

muscles responded to my commands. A little stiffly, but I relished the rusty feeling in my joints. *I can move.* Wiggling my toes, I grinned, then realized my cheek was pressed to something deliciously warm. The view that greeted me when I opened my eyes was . . . nice. More than nice. My hand, which was resting on a chest, began to explore. The hard planes were foreign to my fingers, but that didn't stop me. They traveled south to those distracting abdominal ridges I'd seen last night.

Brendan's breathing pattern changed then and so did mine. My body was fully awake now, tingling with the desire to keep moving. And maybe it was my close brush with death that erased all shyness, but I wasn't going to pass up this opportunity.

I rolled, wrapping a leg around his as I laid partly on top of him. His hands shot up, grasping my hips, and I gasped softly. At the noise, he jerked awake. Shock, confusion, then desire warred within his golden irises. I bit my lip to keep from laughing.

"*Scala ad Caelum,*" he murmured gruffly, sliding his hands up my sides. I shifted, pressing myself closer to him, and he groaned. My stomach clenched tightly as the sound rumbled through me.

I ran a hand up his chest. He shivered under my touch, then dipped his fingers beneath my tank top. The warmth of his palm on my bare back made me want to take things further. I rubbed my thumb over his bottom lip, once, twice, until he was leaning up for a kiss. With a wicked grin, I arched away from him. At the look he shot me, like a predator who'd been told to chase, excitement jolted through me.

He growled and flipped our positions, pressing me into the mattress. I gasped as his mouth hungrily came down on mine. Our last kiss had been intense, but nothing like this one. This one was . . . ferocious. All teeth and nipping and tugging. I wound my arms around his neck, sucking his bottom lip into my mouth. He pulled away, only to claim my mouth again, breathing raggedly as he kissed me over and over like he would never get enough.

My fingers slipped down his neck, digging into his shoulders. His kisses became even more demanding and I opened my mouth, letting him slide his tongue inside. The taste of him was sheer bliss. Memories from last night, of my desire to apologize for the awful thing I'd said to him, flitted through my thoughts. I shoved them away, angling my head so our kiss deepened. Every inch of me burst into flames. Grabbing his face, I dragged my teeth over his lip. His stomach flexed over mine as he rose up, bringing me with him.

He curled my legs around his waist, then slid both hands beneath my tank top. My back heated under his touch and I pressed myself against him, kissing his jaw, the thundering pulse at his neck, the hollow of his throat. *Why do it? Why enter Tatum City?* I paused as yesterday's words replayed in my head, then trailed my fingers down his neck.

To right the wrongs I've made.

I flattened my palms against his chest, feeling the rapid beat of his heart. *That's the stupidest thing I've ever heard.* Grimacing, I leaned forward and pressed my forehead to his shoulder. I struggled to breathe past the ache building in my throat.

He's doing penance. It's the only way he can sleep at night.

Brendan's touch became comforting circles on my back as he sensed my shift in mood. My chin wobbled. He was lending *me* comfort, after what I'd said? I had ridiculed his purpose, his reason for facing a painful existence filled with regret. I couldn't imagine what he must have gone through to protect his sister. And instead of offering a sympathetic ear, I'd shamed him.

When he whispered, "What's wrong?" I broke.

A strangled sob left me. The sound unleashed a flood of tears. He tried to pull back, probably worried that he'd overstepped boundaries and was riddled with more guilt. I threw my arms around his neck and clung to him. "I'm sorry. I'm so sorry. I didn't know." The words hurt to say, like apologizing wasn't something I often did or allowed myself to do, but once I started, I couldn't stop. The stress of last night must have gotten to me. Or maybe subconsciously I'd been wanting to do this for awhile now.

"I've been self-centered ever since arriving here, thinking only of my wants and needs. And all this time, you've only thought of others. You let yourself get stabbed so I wouldn't. You let people use you so they wouldn't hurt your sister." His muscles tensed at that, but I wasn't finished. "When I thought I was going to die last night, I poured all of my energy into calling for your help, and you—you came."

He ran a soothing hand over my hair. "I'll always come

for you. No matter what. I'm drawn to you in ways that I don't understand. I heard you in my head, crying out for help, and there was nothing, *nothing* that would have kept me from getting to you."

I hugged him harder, but after a moment, he carefully grasped my arms and lowered them to my sides. His thumb tipped my chin up so that I met his eyes. Mine were probably red and swollen, but I didn't care, not when he was looking at me that way. Not like I was fragile glass about to break, but something rare. And precious.

Then his expression changed. Saddened. His mouth formed a smile a second later, but I'd still seen.

"Come with me," he said, rising from the bed with my legs still clinging to his waist. "Well, I didn't mean that so literally, but this works." I quickly disentangled myself and set my feet on the ground, taking a step back. Brendan leaned forward, whispering in my ear, "You're adorable when you blush."

I wasn't sure if I wanted to shove him or kiss him for teasing me. Before I could do either, he held up a finger and unlocked the door, disappearing down the hall. I stayed put, but really wanted to lock the door, just in case. He was back a minute later with boots and a coat I hadn't worn yet. Or maybe I had—I'd been on a mountain when they'd found me. Wait. "Where are we going?"

Placing the bundle in my arms, he made for the bathroom. "You'll see," he said with a wink. When he entered the room again dressed similarly to me, my fingers started to tingle with anticipation.

As we walked down the hallway, Yukiko appeared out of nowhere, also wearing warm clothing. She took one look at me and my barely restrained excitement, then rolled her eyes. "She'll need to be blindfolded."

"Is that really necessary?" Brendan said.

"Dr. Moore's orders. And mine. We don't take chances, Bren, you know that. Just be glad I'm not throwing a bag over her head."

His lips thinned, but he didn't argue. I didn't say anything, too busy wondering if Yukiko hated me enough to stab me in the back or strangle me in my room. The attacker's skin *had* been pale . . .

As soon as we stepped foot in the elevator, she handed a black swath of fabric to Brendan who glanced at me apologetically before tying the blindfold securely behind my head. Everything went dark, but when he laced his fingers through mine, I couldn't stop a small smile from leaking through my false composure. Several minutes of beeping doors, elevators, and stairs later, we stopped.

The air felt . . . chilled. I shifted in place, unable to hold still. Brendan's hand squeezed mine and he laughed softly. "Are we there yet?" I asked, itching to take the blindfold off.

"Not yet. There's one more thing we gotta do first. But you're gonna need to trust me."

I tilted my head, curious at the amusement in his voice. This better not be some elaborate prank. He chuckled as my nose wrinkled with suspicion, but I didn't balk when he tugged me forward, or when my legs brushed up against a hard and bumpy object. My fingers blindly felt along its surface, which was smooth one second, then leathery the next.

"Hop on," Brendan said, and I heard him pat something. My frown of confusion became a squeak of surprise as a hand wrapped around my right leg and lifted it up and over the large object. I pitched sideways, but an arm circled my waist, stopping my fall. I really hoped that was Brendan and not Yukiko.

"Be back in one hour. You know what happens if you get caught," Yukiko said from somewhere behind me, and I relaxed against the grip that wasn't hers.

"Probably more than anyone. Ready?" Brendan said directly in front of me.

Was I? Maybe if I knew what happened if we were caught. Or what I was currently straddling. I tentatively settled onto the leathery surface beneath me. It felt solid enough. The arm around me disappeared and the seat I was perched on roared to life. Literally, figuratively, every sense of the word. The sound was deafening. Okay, maybe not *that* bad, but loud enough for me to shriek and clutch at Brendan's coat for dear life. His body shook. Was he laughing?

"Here, put this on. Safety first," he said over the noise. Something pressed into the sides of my head and I retreated, batting away the intrusive object. "It's a helmet. And no, helmets don't make you weak."

That was a weird thing to say. I grabbed the bulky headwear and wrestled it on while Brendan made sure my blindfold didn't slip. Now that I was officially uncomfortable and clueless about everything that was happening, I signaled my readiness. *Game on.*

I felt him lean back and murmur, "Better hold onto something, little bird," with an incredibly amused tone, then the object we were on jolted forward. Instinct had me curling my body around his. Even my legs lifted, trying to fit their way onto the seat. He was definitely laughing now. His whole back was shaking.

Oh, I was so getting him back for this.

AN IMPOSSIBLE DREAM

Sharp wind tore at my clothing. Air froze in my lungs. The ground felt a million miles away. I should have been panicking, or at least nervous. I should have demanded that Brendan remove the blindfold. But all I did was press closer to the man I trusted and grin like a fool.

The growling machine beneath us crested what must have been a hill and went airborne. My heart launched into my throat. That split second of weightlessness, when the only option was to give up control and simply live in the moment, barreled through me. I laughed, the sound breathless and unchecked. I almost threw my arms wide, but stopped myself just in time.

"I want to see!" I yelled, the wind practically snatching the words out of my mouth.

We rolled to a grumbling halt a minute later. The machine switched off. I all but bounced off the seat, tugging on Brendan's coat impatiently. "Hold on, wiggle worm," he said with a laugh.

"Did you just call me a worm?" I scowled as he removed my helmet.

"It's an expression, like calling someone a worry wart or

cranky pants . . ." He didn't finish upon seeing my face as the blindfold fell away. Sunlight pierced my vision, so intense I almost squeezed my eyes shut, but I kept them narrowed on Brendan. Worry shadowed his once jovial look. "What—?"

I pounced. Wrapping my arms and legs around him, I threw my weight to the side. For a second, he didn't budge. But I'd caught him by surprise so, with a grunt, he tipped off the machine. *Crunch!* We landed in packed snow at least a foot thick. When my head popped up, it was to see a stunned, slack-jawed Brendan splayed out next to me, half buried in a drift.

Laughter burst out of me. As my body spasmed uncontrollably, I crawled to him. I drank in his utter confusion, knowing the best was yet to come. I almost collapsed into the snow in a fit of giggles, but somehow, I held it together.

"Here," I gasped. "Let—let me help y-you." As I reached a hand out to haul him up, I darted the other toward his face. Reflexively, he blocked me, but that was okay. I had a different target in mind.

My loaded fist wiggled under his shirt collar and released its cold contents. He yelped, shooting up faster than I thought humanly possible. I cackled and rolled onto my back, rocking back and forth as he shook the snow out of his shirt.

"Payback," I singsonged. His eyes, flashing with wicked intent, swung my way. I pointed a finger at him. "Hey, we're even now. I call a truce."

An evil grin swept over his face. "Let me help you up, little bird. You look cold." He took a menacing step toward me.

Crap.

I scrambled to my feet and fled down the hill, not getting very far before his arms wrapped around my waist and swung me in a circle. My head fell back as I laughed some more, too happy in the moment to care if I half froze to death out here. When had I ever felt this . . . free?

Never, my mind whispered.

I stopped struggling and Brendan lowered me to my feet. He looked as happy as I felt and the sight stole my breath. Rising up on tiptoe, I pressed my lips to his cheek. "Thank you," I murmured.

He pulled back and graced me with the sweetest smile, making my heart ache. "For what?"

"For this moment." I let myself stare into his eyes for the sole purpose of memorizing their shape, their color, the way they were watching me now. "I'll never forget it."

Because I was so close, I saw the shadow that passed over his expression, saw the sadness return, the indecision. A faint line formed between his brows. His mouth opened, then closed. "I—" His voiced cracked, and he cleared his throat roughly. "I have something to show you." He threaded his fingers through mine and I followed as he led me uphill.

The climb was fairly steep, and even though I'd exercised nearly every day for the last couple weeks, I started to huff and puff after a handful of minutes. Brendan glanced back at me, fake concern pulling the corners of his mouth down.

"Shut up," I muttered, which only made him smirk.

As we rounded a sharp bend and the trees fell away,

revealing a large clearing blanketed in sparkling snow, Brendan said, "Close your eyes." I looked at him skeptically. But when he added, "Don't make me blindfold you again," I did as instructed with a groan.

The more we climbed, the more intense the sun became. My eyelids were bathed in a warm red and I ached to open them. Brendan's back was to me. I could just take a tiny little peek . . .

"Don't you dare."

"What?" I said innocently.

"I know you're thinking of peeking. You don't follow orders very well."

"Oh? Then maybe you shouldn't order me about." Made sense to me.

One second he was in front of me, the next behind, his breath stirring my hair the only warning. Before my eyes could fly open in surprise, he placed a hand over them. "Or I could just do this," he whispered into my ear. His arm wrapped around my waist and he nudged me forward.

All I could do was press my lips together to keep from smiling. I was doing a lot of that this morning. My cheeks were starting to hurt. As we progressed, the ground leveled almost too perfectly, making me even more curious. We slowed, and my next step was blocked by a hard object. I reached out and felt rough stone beneath my chilled fingertips.

"I wanted to show you this because I need you to remember what you've been fighting for," Brendan said quietly. A small tremor shook the hand covering my eyes. I heard him swallow, heard his unsteady breaths. "And—and you should know that I took it all away."

Then his hand was gone and I was blinking away brilliant sunlight. And . . . and . . .

Tears pricked my eyes.

I was standing on top of the world.

"How? Where?" I couldn't formulate a full thought, not when the expanse of sky above was endless blue and the floor below was a vast sea of snowy mountains and trees. Words couldn't describe this level of beauty. A tear slipped down my cheek and emotion clogged my throat, which surprised me. I didn't know why my reaction was so intense.

"This is the tallest point of the highest peak on the eastern half of North America," Brendan said, coming to stand beside me. "When I first saw you in Tatum City, you were staring up at this mountaintop. I think the old you wanted to climb this mountain someday."

I cleared my throat and wiped away a tear. "I think so, too." My eyes devoured the view for another minute, then glanced up at a pensive Brendan. "How did you take all of this away from me? I don't understand."

A puff of air curled from his mouth as he released a long sigh. He grabbed hold of the stone wall in front of us and bowed his head, as if what he was about to say was a heavy weight pressing down on him. "I'm not the good guy, Lune. I—I steal people's freedom. I've stolen lives. At first it was hard. Seeing their faces when they realized I'd betrayed them. Then it got easier. I can—I can manipulate and lie. Make people trust me. Make *you* trust me." His grip on the stone tightened, whitening his knuckles.

With each word, my heartbeat grew louder, until my head pounded, until I couldn't think past the roaring in my ears. But he wasn't finished. "My parents' deaths were my fault. I led the Recruiter Clan straight to our doorstep with my recklessness and—" He stared at his trembling hands. "The price was to watch them drown. First my mom. Then my dad."

"Brendan," I whispered, reaching to comfort him even as horror filled me.

He shook his head, freezing me in place with his stare. "That's not all. I've killed, Lune. When a mission went wrong, to escape the Recruiter Clan—I've ended lives to spare my own. You're not safe with me and you'll never know freedom when I'm near. You should run far away. The old you knew that—I just convinced her otherwise. But I can't be selfish with you anymore."

He stepped close to me, looking for all the world like the deadly predator he was making himself out to be. A part of me wanted to run, I couldn't deny that. My first instinct was always to flee. To fear. But I knew him. *Knew* him. The man standing before me wasn't a cold-blooded killer.

So I erased the space between us. Placed my hand on his cheek. Watched a single tear track down his face. "That's *not* you. I know you were forced to do things to survive. I know about Bells. You made the choice to protect her, to fight for a better future. Don't give up *now*, Brendan. Don't throw your life away, don't throw *us* away."

His jaw hardened under my touch. "There shouldn't *be* an us, that's what you've forgotten. When I left Tatum City, you weren't even speaking to me. I had stolen your chance at freedom yet again and you couldn't stand it."

I frowned. "Again?"

"Yes," he hissed. "Again. I *kidnapped* you. Stole you from your mom. Don't you remember?"

I jerked back, dropping my hand.

He barked a self-deprecating laugh. "Now you're getting it."

Pain tightened my chest at the revelation, at the tone of his voice—like he was trying to slam down a permanent wall between us. My quivering lips only allowed one word to escape. "Why?"

As if my agony was too much to bear, his gaze fell. "You said it yourself. I did bad things to survive, using Bells as an excuse to do them. I made my choices and now have to live with them."

"No," I said forcefully, grabbing his chin and making him look at me. "That's not what I'm asking. Why tell me this now? Why push me away when we're finally becoming *happy?*"

"Because it's not *real*, Lune," he replied with equal intensity. "You begged me to be real and I swore that I was, but I lied, okay?" His fingers circled my wrist and pulled his face from my grip. "Listen carefully because I'm only saying this once. I'm a *spy*. There's nothing real about a spy. Spies lie. I am a lie."

I stared up at him blankly. "What?"

"You heard me. It's impossible for us to be together, no matter what *we* want. I never should have selfishly pursued you—it's not fair. There's no future for us where I'm going. My job is to find humans with a high potency of mutated DNA and rescue them before the Recruiter Clan discovers their existence. But thanks to people like me, most of them are already locked up, so I infiltrate and report the weaknesses of that establishment.

"Tatum City? It's not a city at all but a military compound. The Elite Trials? A smoke screen. A ruse to lull the citizens into thinking they're special for entering them. Everything you've been taught is a lie. Everything you've been fighting for is a lie."

"Stop!" I yelled, yanking my arm free. My heart was hammering so wildly, I couldn't breathe. Too much. Too *much*. I couldn't put together all the pieces. Only one word rang true. *Lies, lies, lies.* My voice shook as I said, "Message Yukiko."

"Why?"

"Just do it! I need a ride back." With that, I stormed off the stone platform and followed the set of tracks we'd made to climb up here. I didn't take a last look at the mountains. Didn't fill my lungs one last time with the cleanest air I'd ever breathed. Not when my vision blurred with tears. Not when my throat squeezed shut. What would the point be anyway? It was all a dream.

A beautiful, impossible dream.

"Whoa. I legit got chills just now watching you shoot ice daggers at Bren's back. Trouble in paradise?"

"I don't want to talk about it," I said stiffly to an over-observant Jaxon. Was I *that* obvious? I set my dinner tray on the conveyor belt with a little too much force. Another thing I wasn't good at: hiding my feelings.

He held up his hands in mock surrender but peered over my shoulder at Bells. "What do you think, Empath? Intervention time?"

"Definitely," she agreed, then shrugged with a little smile when I frowned at her. "You joining us, Yukiko?"

The girl who had begrudgingly come to my rescue earlier today snorted loudly as she pushed past me. "Does it involve junk food?"

"Only the best for you, babe," Jaxon purred in her ear. When she smirked at him, a pang of sadness hit my chest. I looked away.

The four of us ended up in Jaxon's room, which was over-flowing with . . . stuff. "He's a pack-rat," Bells said, plopping onto his couch and patting the spot next to her.

"That hurts my feelings," Jaxon called from near the bathroom where a hazardous stack of what looked like thin books was climbing the wall.

"That's funny," Bells said with a tilt of her head. "I'm only picking up giddy anticipation vibes from you."

"I'm not giddy. I'm completely calm in my excitement. Your ability is getting rusty, Isabella."

"Dolls?" I mouthed at her, discreetly pointing to a shelf

lined with dozens and dozens of upright figures, some tucked inside clear cases.

Jaxon practically shrieked as his keen eyes narrowed on me. "They're action figures, not dolls! I want one of Bren, but he said he'd tear off the head and burn the body." He held up two of the books. "Dystopian or romantic comedy?"

Bells rolled her eyes. "How about a superhero one where the character has mind powers?"

Then she looked at Yukiko and they said together, "Chick flick." Jaxon groaned, but he was pushed aside as his girlfriend rummaged through the pile. I heard her mutter something about mean girls and Jaxon groaned again.

"It's a classic!" Bells said, jostling me as she bounced on the cushion. "We need snacks, Jax."

"On it. And then maybe I should go sulk with Bren. My eyes can't handle all that pink."

I soon discovered that instead of reading a book, we were watching a movie. Judging by my slack-jawed reaction, it must have been my first. Life-like images were projected on the bedroom wall, and as astounding as that was, the people in the movie were even more so.

"Did people our age really dress and act that way before the Silent War?" I asked, grabbing another handful of popcorn before Yukiko could eat it all.

"Pretty much," Jaxon said from his wedged position against the other side of the couch. "Their biggest concerns in life were zits and bad hair days. And instead of labels like Intellect and Sensor, they called themselves geeks and jocks."

The more I learned about the past and how different it was from our way of living, the hungrier I became. We ended up watching another chick flick about a girl who discovered she was a princess and got a complete makeover. After that one, Jaxon insisted he get to pick the movie before his brain exploded. He chose an action movie that had me on the edge of my seat—despite Jaxon reciting every line of the movie before it happened. Bells told me that people couldn't actually fly like that or shoot lasers from their hands, but it looked so *real*.

All too soon, Yukiko switched the screen off and stood, stretching her back until it popped. "It's past midnight, we should get some sleep. I'll walk Lune to her room."

I glanced at Jaxon whose eyebrows had climbed halfway up his forehead. He shrugged and silently mouthed what looked like, "I'll pray for you."

Oh great. Was this the part where I, lulled into a false sense of security, let my guard down only to be stabbed in the back or strangled, then left for dead in a hallway closet? I blinked, shaking away the thought. Maybe I shouldn't have watched a violent movie right before bed.

My room was on the other side of The Circle, same floor as Jaxon's along with most of the single residents not living in a family unit. Despite having parents, he and several of the recently graduated young adults had opted for their own space. It wasn't a long walk, but making the trip with Yukiko? An eternity would be shorter.

Then she actually spoke to me of her own free will. "He's protecting you from himself. But more than that, he's protecting himself from you. You're his weakness, and he's afraid that he won't be able to follow through with his missions if he allows himself to get too close. He'll be thinking of you and your safety instead of others."

At the candid way she dropped those words into the void, I completely blanked. My mouth was probably rounded like a fish's. "What—what are you talking about?" Really? I was going to play dumb?

She gave me a sidelong look. Okay, I deserved that. "I'm a lot like him." My brows started to raise in disbelief, but she added, "We handle our demons differently, but we have similar pasts—and struggle to forgive ourselves. Now, we have an insatiable need to save and protect what is ours.

"There's only one problem with that," she went on dispassionately, as though unaware of how thoroughly her words were warping my perception of her. "Who will save us from ourselves? Having a hero complex forces us to distance ourselves from the ones we love, but what kind of existence is worth living alone?"

She stopped several doors down from mine and faced me. It took me a second to realize she was making sure Brendan couldn't overhear our conversation. Crap, now I was feeling a bit of respect for her. She flicked her spiky bangs out of her eyes, giving me a once over. Determining if I was worthy of her sage wisdom?

Whatever she saw made her finish instead of leaving me to walk the last few yards alone. "You only need one person to fight for you, to remind you that life is about taking chances, especially on the things that matter most. Jaxon, the persistent idiot, forced me to see this. And I think it's time someone did that for Bren."

I was pretty sure I'd never been so speechless in my entire life. She didn't wait for me to reply, simply took off for my room again, even checked inside for unwelcome visitors. When she turned to go, I finally found my voice. "Yukiko." She paused, but didn't look my way. "Thank you."

With a nod, she silently closed my door, and I made sure to lock it. I then spent the next hour sprawled on my bed, staring at the ceiling and wondering when the girl who hated me had become my friend.

A POINT TO PROVE

I readjusted my night goggles, then flicked them back on. The darkness became several shades of green, but my eyes adapted quickly. Ever since Jaxon had told me of the bi-annual Abilities Competition, I'd practiced nonstop getting used to this headwear. Although I'd only been in the ability program for a month and a half now, I was allowed to enter the contest based on my past training experience.

"Is your gun working?" Yukiko asked, so softly that I barely caught the words through my ear communicator.

"Yeah," I murmured. "Tested it earlier."

Despite my lack of memories, I had discovered something recently: instincts and muscle memory couldn't be erased. So I had trained hard, even practiced shooting a gun on a daily basis. My skills were still subpar, but my visions made up for what I lacked. Most of the undergrad competitors were Sensors who naturally enjoyed challenges and the thrill of the hunt, but there were a few Empaths and Intellects.

Bells didn't want to compete, saying it wasn't her thing, but Yukiko and Brendan had been selected as the graduate team captains. As luck would have it, I ended up on Yukiko's team. Fitting that I was pitted against Brendan considering we hadn't patched things up between us since the mountaintop debacle. Ten days of barely speaking to each other. As painful as the silence was, hurt and pride had me trapped in their vicious snares.

He wanted to keep me at arm's length? Well, I wasn't going to beg for his attention. Funny how the old me had pushed him away, but now it was him trying to create distance between us. Maybe we were doomed from the start. Maybe there were too many painful memories for us to overcome.

I checked my handheld for the time. I'd finally been given one thanks to Jaxon pulling some strings. Three minutes until the competition would begin. It was held in an underground level below The Circle. The ceiling soared high above which allowed the massive indoor space to be converted into a replica of the outdoors. Except it wasn't winter down here. Cold, yes, but a false wind and rain pelted us, making the whole experience quite miserable.

"War games. Gotta be prepared for anything," Yukiko had explained when the elements had first kicked on twenty minutes ago. I wasn't entirely sure what she meant by that. All I knew was that entering this competition might not have been the smartest idea. But if my comrades could stand around in the freezing pitch black without complaint, then so would I.

Besides, I had a point to prove.

This was my chance to show everyone that I wasn't a danger but an ally. That I took their way of life seriously and could be trusted not to jeopardize it. I wanted to be understood and accepted, and I'd do whatever it took to make them see the real me.

But I had something even bigger to prove to myself. And Brendan.

I had confided in Yukiko, who admittedly had rolled her eyes at first, but she was on board now. Ever since that night she'd walked me to my room, we'd called an unspoken truce. Whatever grievances she'd held against me when I'd arrived at Blue Ridge Sector were now a thing of the past. I wasn't sure what had changed her mind about me, but we were almost friends now. *Almost*, because she still looked at me like I was a waste of air sometimes.

Not at the moment though. Every member of our team was important and had a purpose. The end goal was to find the enemy's diabolical plans and cross back into friendly territory before being captured or "killed." My job was to spy on the opposition using my ability and find out where the plans were hidden. I had argued for a more proactive role, but Yukiko had quickly shot me down. I was too valuable to be running out into the open with guns blazing. Plus, everyone else had better aim than I did.

I wasn't bitter or anything. Maybe just a little.

Because of my ability—and being who I was to Brendan—Yukiko predicted that he would send his Sensors to sniff me out. So I had traded jackets with a teammate who'd insisted the rain wouldn't wash away my scent entirely. She was to be my decoy, and also watch my back so I could focus on my visions instead of my immediate surroundings. I didn't like feeling vulnerable and dependant on someone I barely knew, but Yukiko had muttered something about teamwork and relying on others, so I'd agreed.

As soon as my handheld buzzed, I was to take our team's plans and find someplace to hide them. If the enemy came near, hopefully my ability would keep me one step ahead so I could whisk the plans off to a new location. There was only one flaw to the plan: the more I used my abilities, the more Brendan would detect the energy. So Yukiko's mission was to distract him, draw him out into the open with an aggressive frontal attack.

Only twenty seconds to go until the competition started.

"Remember," Yukiko breathed, bending her knees as she prepared to spring. "Run first, shoot second. Stay toward the back of our territory."

I nodded, knowing she could see the movement despite not wearing goggles. Another reason why Sensors excelled at this competition. Debating the pros and cons, I wedged our team's plans underneath my heavy black vest. The rolled-up paper crinkled against my shirt. If I was shot and eliminated while carrying the plans, the game would be over, but if I could predict the enemy's moves before they made them, what safer place for the plans to be than on my person?

My handheld buzzed. Decision time was over.

Yukiko and several others jumped from their hiding spots, fanning out just as our captain had ordered. They each wore a red band tied around their left bicep so we'd know not to shoot them. Brendan's team all wore yellow bands on their right arms. At least they were on opposite arms since night vision made all colors green. As soon as I made certain the area was clear, I turned the opposite direction, planning to lose myself in the depths of our territory.

The playing field was so massive, I could literally get lost in it. Maybe if I did, no one could find me or the plans. Wishful thinking. If a Sensor didn't sniff me out, an Intellect would decode our team strategy and report it to the ranks. The entire host would bear down on me. I spotted my decoy several paces to the right and breathed a bit easier. At least I wasn't alone.

My eyes landed on a two-story structure that hardly counted as a building—I could clearly see the inner skeleton of the thing. But the inside stairs looked intact and there was also a metal ladder on the outside that reached the rooftop. From up there, I'd have a great vantagepoint of my surroundings and more than one way of escape.

A gunshot rang through the air and I instinctively ducked. The sound was farther away though, close to enemy territory. The battle had begun. After a quick moment's hesitation, I peeled off my borrowed jacket and rubbed my cheek over the material. Maybe I should pee on it too, dowse it completely in my scent. The ludicrous thought would have made me laugh if I wasn't so desperate for this to work.

I propped the jacket against a trash can sitting just outside the building, then reattached the red team band to my thin thermal shirtsleeve. If I chose the ladder for my ascent, a Sensor might be able to pick up traces of my scent where I gripped the rungs. Inner stairs it was. I took them two at a time for good measure, noticing that the wind and rain couldn't reach me here. Too bad I couldn't linger.

On the second floor, I made for the room I hoped had a window that would give me access to the outer ladder. When I found it, I itched to do a victory dance. But there was no time to waste. Sure enough, Yukiko's voice crackled in my ear a second later. "Find anything?"

"Not yet."

"Keep me posted."

"Copy that," I responded, and she switched off our line.

As I stuck my head through the gaping hole that passed for a window, more shots rang out. Closer this time. I grasped the ladder and tugged, making sure it was solid. Did anyone ever die in these competitions? A shiver slid up my spine. This had better be worth it. I swung onto the ladder and made for the rooftop. Within seconds, my shirt was soaked through. Now I was *really* shivering. At least the vest didn't retain water.

When I reached the top, a grin split my face. Perfect. There were several obstacles to duck behind in case someone came up here, giving me a greater chance of escape. Gunfire close by broke the silence and I flattened myself against the roof. Shouts followed, a yelp of pain. My heart beat an unsteady rhythm, partly from nerves, but mostly from anticipation.

Brendan was right. *I'm an adrenaline junkie.*

Carefully, I crawled toward the lip of the roof and peered over the edge. No movement below. I wanted to check all sides to be sure, but Yukiko was counting on me to find those enemy plans. So, going against every instinct, I trusted my decoy to have my back and squeezed my eyes shut.

Focus on the plans. Where are the plans? I had never tried searching out an inanimate object until now. Was I capable of doing such a thing? Only one way to find out. I pictured the rolled-up shape, the waterproof bag they were sealed inside of. *Focus. Focus. Open your mind. Open your . . .*

An invisible force yanked me forward and I flew off the roof at breakneck speed. Instead of splatting on the ground, I skimmed over it, hurtling past debris, a rusted car, another building, then stopped. In front of me was Brendan, sneaking along a crumbling brick wall. He paused and his eyes shot in my direction. Impossible. There was no way he could see me. And he wasn't. He was looking *through* me, tilting his head as if listening to something.

Then his nostrils flared and a wicked smile turned up his lips.

Ah crap. He sensed me.

I snapped back to my body so fast that when I found myself on the rooftop a second later, I loosed a sharp gasp. Double crap. Brendan was coming for me. What should I do? Contact Yukiko? Have her dash back to rescue me? *No. Take him down. This is your chance.*

Movement from below erased my thoughts. I squinted, trying to make out facial features through the rain. Not Brendan. But they had a band on their right arm. An enemy, nonetheless. My heart thudded as I maneuvered my gun to poke over the roof's edge. The enemy, who appeared to be male, was staring at the spot I'd dropped my borrowed jacket, completely oblivious to my position. As he came within shooting range, I hesitated, not wanting to give up my location—and the plan's. Just as I was about to shoot anyway, another figure appeared behind the first, gun raised.

Zip. Splat.

The enemy cried out, whirling around, but it was too late. His vest lit up so bright, I had to look away. I recognized my decoy as the shooter and gave her a little salute, not sure if she could see me. She nodded, but a moment later dove into a forward roll and scrambled behind a trash can. Shots were fired as she aimed at a spot I couldn't see. I crouched low and hurried to the other side of the roof only to arrive too late.

My decoy grunted loudly as her vest was pelted numerous times. She doubled over, but I could still see her vest glow like a mini sun. Crap! Who had shot her? I worked on slowing my erratic breathing so I could better hear what was happening down there. Quietly, I returned to my old spot and peeked over the edge.

No movement. There was nothing except an overturned garbage can.

Wait, where was my jacket?

"Looking for this?"

At the deep voice directly behind me, I stifled a scream. Then threw myself into a roll. *Zip. Zip.* Shots splattered where I'd been a second before. I scrambled upright and blindly fired at the enemy, but didn't stop to see who it was. I already knew. Shots followed me, nipping at my heels. I ducked behind a metal box just in time as a flurry of shots pelted its side.

Run first. Shoot second.

I had a terrible itch to disobey orders right then. But Brendan was an expert with a gun, and I was . . . I was crap at it. Ugh! When the shots eased up, I made a break for it, aiming for the ladder. Right before I reached the ledge, my leg buckled as a stab of pain tore at my calf. Stunned, I dropped my gun and it clattered onto the rooftop. But it didn't stop there. Rain had made the cement slick and the weapon sailed off the roof with a faint *whoosh.*

No!

I didn't have time to mourn the loss though. I was shot, but not in the vest. The game wasn't over yet. I clambered down the ladder, daring to pause for a split second to see how close Brendan was. With a small shriek, I ducked as he shot for my head. *My head.* He was so dead. Instead of climbing all the way to the ground and probably getting peppered with gunfire on the way down, I slipped through the window again, shoes squeaking as I slid onto the second floor.

As if demons were chasing me, I bolted through the room and into the hallway. If I could sneak through a first floor window, maybe I could outfox Brendan and find a new hiding spot. I would need to find a new gun though. I couldn't go back and—*Wham!* I slammed into an obstruction that hadn't been there before. I bounced back with a groan.

Then glanced up. To find Brendan smirking at me. Crap, he was fast. I hadn't even reached the stairs.

First, he waved my gun in the air. Then my jacket. "I can't tell if dropping stuff is part of your plan, or . . . ?" As he chuckled, I stayed rooted to the spot.

I slowly crossed my arms over my vest, an action that he noted with amusement. I could feel the outline of our team's plans still pressing against my stomach. I allowed a smile to form. "My plan is to take you down, so yes."

"And how are you going to do that?" he taunted, stepping toward me. "You're weaponless."

Yukiko chose that moment to interrupt. I all but leapt out of my skin as her voice filled my ear. "Lune, Bren must have slipped past us. I can't sense him in their territory. I think he's heading your way. Have you found their—" I plucked out the communicator and pocketed it.

Brendan raised his brows. "Not following orders again? You should have called for backup. You're going to need—"

I lunged for my gun still dangling from his fingertips. As soon as my hands wrapped around it, he pressed his gun to my chest and shot me point blank. Paint splattered my vest and neck before I could register the pain. My stomach lurched and I was once again standing before him, not a drop of paint on me. Vision or not, I couldn't believe he had shot me. The knowledge made what I was going to do next that much easier.

This time when I lunged, I changed my approach. With one hand, I grabbed for my gun. The other stopped Brendan before he could train his gun on me. Then, with a war cry, I brought my knee up into his groin. As his face twisted in agony, he curled forward and I struck again, clocking him upside the head with my gun that he was still holding. Then I bashed his hand against the hallway wall, forcing him to release the weapon.

He grunted, stumbling back a step, and I snatched up my gun. When it was pointed at his chest, I said, "Drop your gun." Instead of complying, he gaped like he'd never seen me before. So I shot him in the leg.

A curse or two flew from his mouth as he reached for the injury.

"I said drop it." I aimed for his chest again. This time he did, letting the gun fall with a clatter. "Hands behind your head."

Grimacing in pain, he did as instructed. His eyes brightened in my night vision as he said, "Is this the part where you shoot me in the heart now?"

Was that supposed to make me back down? Feel guilty? My nostrils flared as I stepped into his personal space and glared up at him. "No. This is the part where you see that I'm not weaponless. This is the part where you realize I don't always need to be rescued. I can protect myself, I can *save* myself. I don't need you to be my hero all the time. I just need *you*."

I placed my free hand over his heart and watched as his lips parted. He didn't move as my hand slid down his vest, then quick as a snake, darted underneath and yanked out his team's plans. The look on his face. Pure shock. I slowly grinned, whispering, "Now this is the part where you learn that I don't take prisoners."

And then I shot him.

My night vision burst into victorious light.

24

DON'T COME BACK

"I can't believe you kneed him in the stones," Jaxon groaned, then threw his head back as he laughed. He held out a fist. I stared at it blankly. "It's like a high-five. You're supposed to—never mind. The moment is gone now."

"Do you think he got the message?" Yukiko asked, peeling off her vest. Her fingers remained steady as she rehung the heavy equipment in the small room used to prepare for competitions.

My fingers trembled with cold as they attempted to unzip my vest for the second time. Taking off my waterproof jacket had been worth it, but I really needed to warm up, not chat about the person I'd just taken out my frustrations on. "I'm n-not sure. I was too busy stealing his plans and sh-shooting him to ask qu-questions." Crap. I was going to get sick at this rate.

"There's a shower room right through that door if you wanna—"

I didn't wait for Yukiko to finish. "Th-thanks," I stuttered, still wrestling with the vest as I forced my stiff limbs toward the door. When I entered, the room was empty, so I didn't bother with decency. One of the showerheads spat to life as I

ADAPTIVE

cranked the handle to a near scalding temperature. I shucked off the vest and let it thump to the floor. My shoes and socks were next.

I had my sopping shirt halfway over my head when the door squeaked open. Startled, I froze with my arms awkwardly in the air. The shirt blocked my view of the newcomer so I tugged it down around my neck.

Air stuck in my throat at the sight of Brendan standing just inside the doorway. He was frozen too. Staring at me. Intensely. Then I remembered my state of undress. Apparently he did too because his eyes traveled south and landed on my bare midriff. His gaze inched higher, gliding over my black bra and exposed skin. A kernel of warmth bloomed in my stomach at his heated look.

I slowly lowered the shirt and covered my nakedness. His eyes tracked the movement, then raised to mine. Breathing became a chore. The room filled with steam, either from the shower or from the tension building between us. Probably both. I waited for an explanation as to why he was here, but none came. He simply clenched and unclenched his hands, watching me like he was searching for something.

The tension stretched taut and I struggled to hold still. My body, chilled to the bone, yearned to draw closer to his and soak up the heat it knew forever radiated from him. His nostrils flared, as if scenting my struggle. Then he was moving. Eating up the space between us. Cupping my jaw. Tilting my face up to his.

My lips parted in surprise and he pressed his to them,

271

inhaling deeply, breathing me in. I clutched at his shirtfront as a wave of feeling swept through me, threatening to buckle my knees. He curled an arm around me and we shuffled backward, back, back, until hot water was pouring over us and I was pressed against the shower wall.

I gasped into his mouth as the planes of his body molded to mine, as pleasure streaked through me. Our lips, now warm and wet, crashed together messily. Perfectly. Like our relationship so often was. My hands slid up his chest and gripped his neck. He grasped my thighs and lifted me up. My legs squeezed his waist as he pressed me more firmly against the wall.

A moan rolled up my throat when his fingers slipped under my shirt and warmed my sides. His thumbs brushed along my rib cage, sending my heart thundering.

"I need you too," he said shakily, placing a lingering kiss to the corner of my mouth. "So much. I don't . . . I don't want this to end."

My chest tightened at the open admission, at the vulnerability in his voice. The time for games was over. This moment was about truth, raw and painful. But real. *Finally*, I inwardly sighed. I slid my lips over his, once, then twice, until his body trembled against mine. "Then don't push me away. Ever again."

"I won't."

"Promise me."

"I promise." He exhaled, taking several breaths before hoarsely whispering, "I'm scared."

I ran my fingers through his damp hair, letting him feel the comfort I could give. "Of what?"

"That I'll destroy you."

"You won't."

"You don't know that. I've caused you so much pain already."

I tugged on his hair so he'd lean back. When he opened his eyes, I said, "You told me I was strong. So let me *be* strong. Don't stop believing in me just when I've started to believe in myself."

He searched my face, saw my certainty, then blew out a sigh, folding me into a hug. "You're stronger than me in the ways that matter most, Lune Avery." I buried my nose in the crook of his neck, a smile pulling at my mouth. Maybe we were going to be okay after all.

My handheld pinged a second after his did. We both ignored the sound, unwilling to let go of this fleeting moment of blissful peace. Brendan's lips found mine again, gently nibbling, teasing, until I grabbed his face and crushed our mouths together.

Ping.

Ping.

I felt him fumble for the handheld in his pants pocket. He swore softly as it clattered to the shower floor. I snickered, kissing his chin before wiggling to be let down. Not that I wanted to—I could happily stay here forever with my two favorite things—but it wasn't often that I received messages. Maybe Jaxon needed help picking out his outfit or something.

When I saw the message, I frowned. The words were confusing, though I understood the first couple. "Report to . . . C-o-m-m—" My face flushed, not from the water, but from embarrassment.

Brendan stroked a finger down one of my no doubt beet-red cheeks. "It's okay, little bird. It's not your fault." My heart kind of melted and dribbled down the shower drain at that. He tipped the screen his way. "It says, 'Report to Communications.'" He bent and picked up his handheld, showing me an identical message.

I assumed he knew where that was since I'd never been there before. "Should we change first?"

After a quick stop on the tenth floor for dry clothes, we rode the elevator to the top, bypassing Dr. Moore's office. Brendan led me to a stretch of rooms similar to the ones Jaxon had when we'd visited the Conservatory. There were signs and handprint scanners next to the doors. Brendan paused in front of one and pressed his hand to the black screen. Huh. I guess he *was* important.

Inside the Communications room was a vast network of technology unlike anything I'd seen before—not even the Ability Center had this much stuff. The space wasn't that large, but the open floor plan made it seem so. Several rows of desks and screens stretched from wall to wall, and most of the chairs were occupied. The air was filled with the sounds of clicking keyboards and droning voices. What could they possibly be doing?

I was distracted by a waving hand and caught sight of

Jaxon. He really *did* have access to all the top secret places. Next to him stood Dr. Moore, Dr. Stacey, and, surprisingly, Dominic. "What do you think's going on?" I whispered to Brendan as we approached.

"Any number of things," he whispered back, which didn't help settle my nerves one bit. His knuckles brushed against mine, an attempt to reassure me. But if I were being allowed in here, something big must have happened.

Dr. Moore quickly shook our hands, then ushered the entire group inside a small private room. When the door closed, he turned to me. "So glad you could join us this evening, Miss Avery. There have been some rather startling new developments and your instructor, Mr. Holland, thinks you can help us better evaluate the urgency of this situation."

It took me a moment to realize he meant Dominic. I glanced at my teacher and he smiled kindly. None of them looked nervous, but that didn't stop my palms from sweating and my mouth from drying. I swallowed carefully before saying, "I'll do what I can."

"Good, good. Mr. Manly, if you will play back the message we received." He gestured at Jaxon who was sitting at the room's lone desk, typing something onto a screen.

When I caught his eye, I mouthed, *"Manly?"*

He made a face, mouthing, *"Shut up,"* then leaned back as he clicked a button.

The screen remained blank, but a male's voice came from the speakers. "Testing. Testing. Crap, I hope I'm doing this right. This is Asher Donovan, sending a message to Bren

Bearon. My last correspondence was one week ago, and since that time, the unrest in the village has increased significantly. I'm continuing to plant seeds of doubt, reminding them that the Elite Trials are rigged and that the Supreme Elite hired people to kidnap children so they can contend in the Trials. They believe you and Lune have disappeared at Renold's hand because you dared to fight together in the Arcus Point Trial. They're scared, but they're also listening and want answers."

The voice crackled and, for some reason, I gritted my teeth, willing the young man to continue. Was this *the* Asher? The one Brendan had said was my best friend? When he spoke again, I exhaled in relief. "I really hope Lune is out there with you right now, Bren. When the people saw the scars on her back that night at the village dance, it didn't take them long to form conclusions. Her bravery was the spark needed to start this revolution. Getting them to believe my words wasn't hard when they saw with their own eyes what a monster Renold is."

My throat tightened and I crossed my arms as if that would help ward off the prickling sense of vulnerability poking at me. I had shown everyone my scarred back? Had I really meant to start an uprising inside Tatum City?

"But before anyone wonders where I've gone," Asher continued, "I need to tell you why I'm communicating today. Iris went missing. Two days ago, she didn't stop by the stables to see Lune's charger like she usually does. I thought she might be sick, but when she didn't show up yesterday, I suspected something was wrong. I—I snuck into the barracks, Bren. I know you said to stay away from there, but with you and Lune gone, there's no one to protect her. Anyway, she's not there. You said she was important so I thought you'd want to know right away. I just, I don't know what to do. She's Lune's sister. After everything Lune has done for my family, I have to find her. I'm sorry for not sticking to the plan, but I need to know where people are disappearing to. I'll let you know what I find.

"And, Lune?" I leaned forward as Asher's voice softened. "If you *are* out there with Bren, know that I miss you. But, please . . . don't come back. Signing out."

Thick, stifling silence settled over the room. The message had been for Brendan but was directed at me, almost like an apology. And although I had no memories of Asher or Iris, the thought of them disappearing or getting hurt . . . tears burned my eyes. But I wasn't given an opportunity to dwell on the two people that supposedly meant so much to me.

"Bren planted several nearly invisible voice communicators throughout Tatum City while he was there," Dr. Moore said, nudging his glasses higher as he turned my way. "Most are for spying purposes, but he left one with Asher, his inside man. He wasn't able to tell your friend much on account of the restraining chip we'd injected beneath his skin—it's not pleasant once triggered, but it assures he can't be interrogated if caught. Still, he managed to communicate well enough. It helped that Asher is probably an Empath."

Restraining chip? *Inside man?* Why did I suspect the old me didn't know about this and wouldn't like it? I looked at Brendan, not quite masking a troubled frown. If his facial expression were an indication—part guilt, part "I'm so dead, aren't I?"—my assumption was correct.

He cleared his throat uncomfortably and rubbed his neck. "Asher wants to make a difference, Lune. Always has. The only reason he never signed a Trials contract was because you asked him not to, but he wants a better future just as much as you do. As much as *any* of us do. Which is why I have to go back. I have to help."

Although he'd already told me that he was returning, the reminder was a fresh slap to the face. Especially after our latest confession to each other—that he needed me and I needed him. The thought of never seeing him again was a level of pain I didn't want to live with. So I squared my shoulders and said, "Then I'm going too."

His jaw slackened. Several people in the room sputtered at my declaration, but all sound dimmed as Brendan's expression hardened. He leaned into my personal space and softly growled, "Over my dead body."

My eyes briefly widened at the aggressive tone, then narrowed to slits. "Try and stop me." I settled onto the balls of my feet as if I'd make a dash for the city right here and now.

His breath fanned over my cheek as he hissed, "You'll never get past the airlock."

"Oh?" My hands formed fists. "So I'm a prisoner now? Is that why you pushed me away so many times? Because you knew all along it would come to this and I wouldn't be able to *stand* it? How many times are you going to betray me, Brendan? How many!"

At some point, my voice had risen to a shout. I hurled

the words at him, using them as weapons. I knew they hurt—I saw the pain in his eyes. But I was hurting, too. How dare he leave me behind! How dare he steal my choices after everything we'd been through, after how far we'd come. My heart pounded, heating my blood.

As I continued to glare at him, refusing to back down, my mind prodded me. *Poke. Poke. Poke. You have an audience.* I tuned into the rest of the room. Utter silence. I ran my eyes over the occupants. All gaping at me. Ah crap.

Dr. Moore cleared his throat and Brendan straightened reluctantly. "You're not a prisoner, Miss Avery, but you're too dangerous in the hands of Renold Tatum."

My brows pulled together. "What—why?"

"Based on the data we've collected—from Bren and the hidden voice communicators—we believe your adopted father is amassing an army, and the Trials are a test of some sort toward that goal. Although his methods and motives are unclear, we know that he's stealing children with abilities, then forcing them to contend in the Trials by unorthodox means. The physical abuse you endured over the years? We think that was his way of controlling the outcome of your decisions. He *wanted* you to contend, he *wanted* you to be afraid and emotional about anything and everything. He wanted to break your control."

How come everyone knew more about myself than I did? Ugh, I needed my memories back! Was he saying that I'd been forced to become crazy? Who *did* that?

"As I'm sure you're figuring out," Dr. Moore went on,

"Renold Tatum is a madman. But it wasn't just him. Apparently he'd been groomed by his father and grandfather to continue the family work. He confided that much to Bren before sending him on his mission. The man is completely devoted to whatever it is the Trials stand for, and kidnapping children from the surrounding area is nothing compared to what he has planned. Lune," he said more quietly. "He wants to use you as a weapon."

"I—" My eyes darted around the room as I tried to swallow this heavy dose of information. A *weapon?* "How?"

"It's your abilities he wants. He knows they're strong and is obsessed with unlocking them. When Bren felt compelled to check on you the night you were injected with that paralyzing drug, you telepathically communicated with him, didn't you?"

The question was laced with so much certainty, I didn't bother denying it. "In my mind, I told Brendan that I needed him and he came. But . . ." I hadn't told Brendan the other part, mostly because I was afraid of what the penalty would be for eavesdropping on such a private conversation. That felt silly now, especially under the circumstances. I just hoped they didn't think I was unhinged after this. "But I also overheard him talking to you."

There. I said it. I was so screwed.

Dr. Moore's gray eyes brightened. Instead of angry, he looked excited. That almost seemed worse. "And what did you hear?"

"Um, you were talking about the man you caught, the

one who tried to stab me. Brendan said he thought the man was being framed and you agreed."

Dr. Stacey stepped forward from her position against the wall. She had been so quiet, I'd almost forgotten she was there. Her face was animated as she said to Dr. Moore, "Why didn't you tell me about this, Carl? You don't think he did it despite the knife being in his room?"

"I . . . let's calm down here for a second. First, that was classified information," Dr. Moore replied with a pointed look my way. Crap. "Second, nothing's been confirmed. We're still working on the case. And third, can you do it again, Miss Avery?"

"Wait, what?"

Instead of elaborating, he turned to Dominic. "Mr. Holland, have you received any new impressions on Lune? Can she project from here or does she have distance limitations?"

Dominic squeezed his eyes shut and pinched the bridge of his nose as if attempting to do just that. "Unfortunately, no. Whether she has an actual hand in Renold's downfall or simply has a premonition of what will happen is still hidden from me. I don't know the range of her abilities yet."

"Dom can predict major event outcomes in uncertain detail," Brendan explained to me. I nodded but refused to look at him, as childish as that was.

"It's why I was out on a mission the day I met Bren," Jaxon said. His chair squeaked as he leaned back and stuck his feet on the desk. "Dom predicted that I would convince Bren to join us—because no one can resist my witty charm—and the rest is history."

Well, that would explain why Brendan seemed to have Dominic on a pedestal. He had saved him and Bells from being recaptured by the Recruiter Clan. But wait . . . "So how long have you known about me and my abilities?" Months? *Years?* The realization suddenly made me angry. Had they even tried to rescue me during that time?

Dominic's expression turned apologetic as he scrubbed a hand through his sandy brown hair. "I've known about you for over a year now, but I didn't know it was *you*, just a girl with an exceptionally strong ability who was the key to ending Renold's reign. The details are always obscure."

Okay, I could understand that. Sort of. My emotions still threatened to overrule any rationale. "I guess what I really want to know is why I'm being told all of this stuff. Why trust me with such sensitive information if I'm so dangerous?"

"Because we need you, Miss Avery," Dr. Moore said with a focused urgency that sent goosebumps crawling up my arms and legs. "We need you to make contact with your sister. If Renold Tatum has discovered her abilities, which we believe are identical to yours, he will force her to become a weapon possibly even more dangerous than you."

25

ADRENALINE

After enduring that crapload of information, you would think I'd be given time to sort everything out. But apparently, now that I was a part of the inner circle, my duty to Blue Ridge Sector was more important. Dominic spent all evening trying to help me focus my ability so I could attempt a long-distance connection with my sister. But although Brendan said she looked like a ten-year-old me, I felt no link, no bond.

I needed something to work with. A memory. An emotion.

It wasn't like with him, whose presence was so strong in my mind, thinking of his face, his voice, his scent was as simple as breathing. Finding a girl I knew nothing about was proving to be impossible. We had stayed up past midnight, but the only thing I'd managed to acquire was a wicked headache.

Now, it was ridiculously early in the morning and I was back at it per Dr. Moore's instructions. Unable to concentrate with so many hovering bodies nearby, I'd asked for someplace quiet to focus. Jaxon had been insightful enough to offer me access to the Conservatory again. As soon as I'd reached the pond and willow tree, he'd made himself scarce, and I curled up against the tree's trunk, hiding from the world.

Instead of concentrating on what I should be doing though, my mind strayed to last night's conversation and all that it implied. So I really *was* dangerous. It was in my DNA, something I couldn't change. My past dreams of freedom, of living a quiet and simple life—preferably next to a body of water bigger than this pond—were slipping through my fingers. If I were being completely honest with myself, the dream I had of me and Brendan was slipping away too. And maybe the old me wouldn't have been torn up about that fact, but the new me ached all over from the pain of it.

Why did it have to be *him* who returned to Tatum City? I still didn't know the full extent of his mission, but if Renold knew of my ability, wouldn't he know about Brendan's? He could be used as a weapon too, could be forced to kidnap children with abilities again. I groaned and rubbed at my gritty eyes.

Someone touched my arm. Expecting Jaxon, I startled when I saw Brendan instead. His face . . . Ugh. Why couldn't I stand it when he looked sad? Why did I want to press my thumbs to his forehead and smooth away the worry lines? I focused on my bent knees before muttering, "I'm still mad at you."

"I know," he said softly, but sat next to me anyway. His arm and leg brushed mine, instantly warming my skin. I didn't pull away. After a beat of silence, he sighed. "From the moment I first saw you in Tatum City, I hoped the girl in Dom's vision wouldn't be you. I didn't want you to be a part of all this. It's messed up and dangerous and, before it's all over, there will be casualties. Did you know that there are more cities like the one you were trapped in?"

My head whipped his way. "What? No. Really?"

"Yeah." He slowly reached for my hand, hesitant, like he expected me to pull away. But he looked so tired, so resigned to what was ahead of him that I didn't resist when his fingers threaded through mine. He sighed again, the sound lighter this time. "We think these cities were planned out even before the Silent War. Whoever unleashed that airborne virus must have known it would change the footprint of the world. And now, humans with mutated DNA are being herded into these compounds masquerading as safe cities. Most believe everything they're told too because they aren't allowed to think for themselves. Opinions, knowledge—they've been erased. Silenced."

"Is that . . . is that why I can't read very well?" The truth of those words tasted sour. What else had I missed out on?

"Your mom probably taught you some as a child, but books aren't allowed in the cities. I snuck one in though." At my raised eyebrow, he chuckled. "Jaxon dared me to. He wasn't being serious, but I never back down from a dare or challenge. It's sort of a flaw of mine, I guess, a Sensor weakness. Which reminds me." He jumped to his feet, tightening his hold on my hand so I was forced to join him.

Surprised, I stumbled upright. Into his chest. For the life of me, I shouldn't be feeling a blush creep up my neck, but it was there all the same. I leaned back to see an insufferable smirk on Brendan's lips. "A little warning next time?"

"No promises," he said, his voice smooth as honey. "I quite like you there." My mouth fell open and more heat burned my cheeks, but he didn't leave me room to reply. Or whack him. "So I learned something appalling about you while we were in Tatum City."

"What?" I squeaked, pushing away from him.

"Once again, it's not your fault. Renold is a cruel, sadistic monster." Even as I tried to disentangle our hands, he pulled me forward, chattering away like a lunatic who must not value his *stones* very much. When we reached the path leading out of the Conservatory, he said, "If my flaw is experiencing too much, then yours is experiencing too little. We're gonna change that. Jaxon!"

As if he'd been waiting for this moment, Jaxon popped his head out from behind a potted tree. "You bellowed?"

"You're such an eavesdropper."

"It's my job, man! Blame it on the system."

"What *do* you do, Jaxon?" I couldn't help but ask, though I doubted he'd tell me.

"I listen in on everyone's conversations from afar. I'm like a sleek, state-of-the-art drone. Like I said, just doing my job."

"He tries to piece information together and better understand what has come of the world," Brendan further explained.

"*Tries* is the word. The world's gone to crap, I know that much. My theory is that your fake daddy wants to create a brainless, robotic cult that wields pointy objects. Oh, and you're his little fortune cookie. And don't forget the carnivorous horses. Anyone who resists will probably get fed to them." He shivered dramatically. "Imagine riding off into the sunset on one of *those*."

"She has," Brendan said with a straight face.

I did?

"She did? For freaking real? Sick, girl, you're like a beast-taming, kick-butt warrior princess. All you need is metal armor and a cape."

I pinched my lips together, which made the snort that came out my nose even louder. Beast-taming, kick-butt warrior. I liked the sound of that actually. Maybe not the princess part though, especially if I had to get a makeover. "What else have I done?"

By the time we made it to The Circle, the three of us were in stitches. "I really flipped you over my shoulder?" I asked Brendan, no longer mad at him—for the time being.

"Mmhmm. But I got you back. Oh, and I made you drink tree bark," he said with a wink. "Twice."

"Gross." I shoved him, but the effort was pathetic since I couldn't stop laughing.

"Talking about drinks . . ." He scanned the mostly quiet space. Only a few early-risers were shuffling about, waiting for the breakfast line to open up. "You two stay here. I'll be right back."

As soon as Brendan left, Jaxon settled onto a dining table and snuck covert looks my way. After the fifth one, I rolled my eyes. "What?"

"Oh, nothing. Just checking how you're handling the news of being a weapon of mass destruction."

"A *what?* I'm not a—" I stopped when I noticed the teasing light in his hazel eyes. "Maybe the first thing I'll do is destroy your movie collection."

He gasped, clutching at his heart. "Now that's plain demonic. You think you know a person." His feigned shock fell away as he gave me a rare serious face. "We've got your back though. I hope you know that."

I nodded, managing a small smile of appreciation. "I do. But . . . who will have Brendan's?"

A hand covered my eyes and I flinched. "I've got my own back. Always have," Brendan whispered in my ear. The words were meant to soothe, but they had the opposite effect.

"I realize overconfidence and a big ego go hand-in-hand," I said, trying to pry his fingers off my face, "but then there's idiocy. I think you might have that too. Scratch that. I *know* you do."

He tsked, tightening his hold. I was debating whether to stomp on his foot or elbow his gut when I caught a whiff of something incredible. It was unlike anything I'd ever smelled before. Warm, rich, earthy, nutty.

I hummed my interest, reaching for the source.

"Nuh-uh. Blind taste test for calling me an idiot."

"Dude, you were going to do that even before she ripped you a new one."

"Whose side are you on, *best* friend?"

"Hers."

288

"Righteous," I said, forming a fist like he'd done yesterday. Was it really only yesterday that my greatest concern had been to beat Brendan at his own game in the Abilities Competition? So much could change from one blink to the next.

"You two have spent way too much time together," Brendan mock-complained as I felt Jaxon bump my fist with what I assumed were his knuckles.

"Don't burn her tongue off."

"I won't. I put an ice cube in it."

"What are you two talking about?" I asked, trepidation making me cringe back from the heavenly scent. "Is this thing even food?"

"No. A drink."

I went silent for a moment. "Is it tree bark?"

"What? No! You think I'd do that?"

"Yes! Third time's a charm, right?"

As we argued, I could hear Jaxon cackling up a storm. So much for having my back.

"Look," Brendan said, lowering his voice to a placating level. "I made a promise to you while we were in Tatum City. This is me honoring that promise. And you obviously need it."

"What's that supposed to mean?"

"Boy, you gonna get kneed in the stones again," Jaxon crowed. A loud thump came from his direction. Did he fall off the table?

"Just try it, okay? You can knee me later," Brendan said with growing impatience. Jaxon started coughing so hard, I worried for his lungs. "Jax, man, you know I'm getting you back for this, right?"

"Okay, okay!" I raised my hands in surrender. "Let's get this over with."

"This is so not how I envisioned this happening," Brendan muttered. I bit the inside of my cheek to keep a smirk at bay. Served him right. As the glorious scent became stronger, he said, "Just take it nice and easy. I'll do all the work."

"Stop, man, stop!" Jaxon wheezed between spasms of laughter. "My mind is so in the gutter right now."

"Ignore him," Brendan said. Did I detect a note of embarrassment? I felt the cup's rim touch my bottom lip. "He's off his meds."

I wasn't allowed to reply as he carefully tipped the cup a second later. Hot liquid, but not too hot, filled my mouth. I didn't taste it right away since the heat and scent were overpowering, but once it settled on my tongue . . . I spewed it out of my mouth in a rush. Gagging on the bitter flavor that still coated my tongue, I whirled out of Brendan's grasp and glared at him. "You said it wasn't tree bark!"

He gaped at me, and after a moment, I realized Jaxon was too. The latter spoke first, indignation pitching his voice higher than normal. "Girl, you did *not* just spit out liquid gold."

"Liquid what?"

"It's coffee," Brendan said, chuckling. Jaxon looked at him as if he'd lost his mind too. "I should've known you'd be the 'I take a little coffee with my sugar' type."

After two cups of much sweeter coffee, I decided that I actually liked the stuff. As we left The Circle, I asked for a third, but Brendan wouldn't let me—said something about cravings, addiction, and neurotic-like symptoms. I was wide awake now, my blood alive with a buzz similar to adrenaline. "And you think this'll help me find my sister *how* exactly?"

"Because every time you have a vision, adrenaline seems to be the thing that triggers it," Brendan explained as the elevator doors closed. Jaxon was still eating breakfast with Yukiko and Bells so it was just him and me now. He punched the tenth floor button, not the fifteenth to Dr. Moore's office like I'd expected.

"Where are we going?"

"To your room. I've been given permission to try something. We're going to take a trip down memory lane in hopes of unblocking one or two of them. An Iris one if we're lucky. Then maybe you'll be able to find her."

I chewed on the inside of my cheek, wondering what his plan was. "How did Iris end up in Tatum City? Was she kidnapped too?" I tried to keep my tone neutral, but a hint of accusation still coated my words.

Brendan noticeably winced. "I think she was, yes. Not by me though. I sensed her project, and when her energy levels were similar to yours, I suspected that you two were sisters. Seeing her face only confirmed it. Being in close proximity to the two of you can be overwhelming, to say the least. But I learned a long time ago how to switch off my ability when it becomes too much."

"Huh. I seem to have the opposite problem," I muttered as the elevator dinged and the doors slid open.

We walked in silence for a few moments before Brendan said, "I think you've been subconsciously repressing your ability for fear of losing control."

I shrugged casually even though I knew he'd hit way too close to the mark. "Maybe some of the visions I've had weren't very fun."

"You're right, you've had some terrible ones." From my peripheral, I saw him glance at me. "But you've saved lives. That little girl in The Circle. Yours. Mine."

"Wait, hold on." I stopped in front of my bedroom door and faced him as anger stirred my blood. Not anger at him, but at myself. "I didn't save your life, I got you *stabbed*."

"That was *my* choice, Lune. But I'm talking about a past event you don't remember. We were training after dinner hour at the lake near the barracks. Lars and his goons showed up, looking for trouble. They had Iris and were trying to get a reaction out of you by drowning her. At the same time, they had me pinned down and Lars was about to stab me in the heart. You stopped it from happening, even as you were rescuing Iris. In fact, I think she might have had the same vision. The energy coming from you both momentarily stunned me. And when you screamed, it was as if time itself stopped."

At the detailed description of such a horrific memory, my heart thudded against my chest. Adrenaline surged. My eyes slammed shut and I curled forward, clutching at my head as images flashed before my closed lids. Rapid. Intense. Emotions followed—fear, desperation, confliction over an impossible choice. A scream of rage and heartbreak. A girl.

A girl who looked like me but wasn't.

Iris.

I clung to her image, trusting Brendan to watch over my body as I opened my mind. I immersed myself as if diving into that lake, collecting every single drop of memory that I had of my sister. I saw her, wet and afraid, pointing at a figure in the distance. Before I could focus on the person, she whispered, "Bren."

At the sound of her voice, I felt a connection form. Over and over, I replayed the soft-spoken way she'd said his name. *Bren, Bren, Bren.* The familiarity—not only of Iris's voice and what she meant to me, but of the name itself—settled into my bones. The bond solidified, allowing my mind to reach out toward her. To travel along an invisible tether. Down the hall it soared, punching through stone, barrelling through the mountain until it burst into open blue sky.

My consciousness continued to stretch, racing faster, traveling farther than should ever be possible. Panic bloomed. Fear of losing control, of losing touch with reality. But that single word—Bren—kept me centered. I wasn't alone. He was right there with me. I simply had to trust that he wouldn't let me fall.

Minutes passed by along with a thousand trees. I shot over a looming gray wall, briefly registering it as Tatum City's. Then I was plummeting. Down, down, through cement and walls. The connection stretched tightly. Tighter, tighter. Pain pricked at the edges of my awareness. Abruptly, my mind slammed to a halt.

Silence surrounded me.

In the stillness, in the darkness, I couldn't see her. But I could feel her. Fear, confusion, pain. The emotions were hers, not mine. *"Iris,"* I whispered.

She stirred, as if woken from a troubling dream. "Please, don't. I didn't do anything, I promise."

Her words echoed through me weakly, like she had no hope of being listened to.

"Of course you didn't, dear," a new voice said, one that sent shards of ice scraping across my mind. "But you will."

26
THEN STAY

"Lune. *Lune!* Come back to me!"

The stark urgency in the words snapped me back to my-self. I sucked in a ragged breath as my eyes shot open. A wave of coughing racked my body. Bile pushed against my throat. I shivered, forcing my lungs to expand and contract. Wait, why was I shivering?

I blinked away water, squinting as white tiles filled my vision. A groan left me as I registered the headache pulsing behind my eyes, then I croaked, "W-where am I?"

A shuddering sigh directly behind me warmed the top of my head. A set of arms drew me closer to a hard chest. "We're in a cold shower. Definitely not as pleasant as our previous one. Whatever stunt you just pulled, can you never do that again? Your temperature spiked out of nowhere and I couldn't wake you up. This was the only thing I could think of."

Clarity returned then. The vision—or whatever it was. Holy crap, I had traveled to Tatum City and back again with my mind. I wanted to laugh. And cry. Then laugh some more. But more than that, I wanted to say a name. A name I hadn't uttered in far too long. "Bren."

"Did you hear anything I just said? You freaked me out,

Lune. I thought you were—" He paused. His muscles went rigid. Then, in shock and disbelief, he whispered, "What did you say?"

I slowly twisted, grimacing at the ache in my bones, but needing to see his face. With each memory given back to me came a new awareness of this man. How much he had meant to me. How much more he meant to me now. I met his eyes and took a moment to soak in their golden color. So rare. So beautiful. Like the rest of him. I straddled his hips, giving in to the urge to brush damp strands of hair off his forehead before exhaling his name again. "Bren."

His chin quivered, then a tremulous smile lit up his face. "I wanted to hear you say that for so long."

I bit my lip, but couldn't hold back a smile of my own. "Why didn't you tell me? Why let me call you Brendan this whole time?"

He skimmed a thumb across my cheek. "I needed a reminder of what I lost. And what I've been trying so hard to get back."

"After pushing me away several times first," I deadpanned, tugging on a lock of his hair.

He laughed softly, the sound part relief, part embarrassment. "I didn't think it possible that you'd forgive me a second time for stealing your freedom and ruining your life. For all the secrets and lies. I kept you at a distance where it's safe so I wouldn't lose you completely.

"But," he continued, watching me intently, "I couldn't stay away, despite knowing how uncertain my future—*our* future is. While in Tatum City, I embraced the idea of being stuck there so long as I was with you. But now that you're here and I have to go, I'm afraid I'm going to lose you forever, and . . . I can't stand it. Because every new second I spend with you, I fall in love all over again."

My lips parted as I struggled to make sense of his words. He couldn't possibly have said what I thought he'd just said. "You . . ." I croaked, then swallowed past the tightness building in my throat. "What?"

Bren brought both his hands up and cradled my face. My eyes started to burn when he leaned down and pressed a tender kiss to my forehead. Tears spilled down my cheeks when he said with a slight catch in his voice, "I love you, Lune Avery. Foolishly. Desperately. And I can't bear to be apart from you."

My heart. It expanded inside my chest until I thought it wouldn't fit anymore. Was it possible to die of happiness? I wanted to say the words back—they were on the tip of my tongue, pushing against my lips. I hadn't known I felt that way toward him, but I did now, and I knew without a doubt that it was real.

Despite how certain he'd sounded, worry lines formed between his brows when I remained silent. I longed to erase them, ached to tell him how I felt. But something stopped me. Instead of saying what my heart wanted, I replied softly yet firmly, "Then stay."

I might as well have shot him. The pain that shadowed his face hurt to see. But I wouldn't take the request back. I needed him. *Needed* him. He was the closest thing I had to a home. When he was with me, I felt safe. Alive. He made me look forward to an uncertain future, one where I wouldn't be alone. Together we could find a way to help those trapped inside Tatum City. But apart? Every bone in my body rebelled against being separated from him, as though warning me that he shouldn't leave alone.

So I steeled my spine and said again, "Stay, Bren. Please."

His mouth twisted as if he too were fighting with his heart. At the turmoil clearly written in his eyes, my heart sank. I already knew what he was going to say. "I can't. I'm so sorry, little bird."

"Then let me go with you."

"You're killing me, Lune. I can't let you go back there knowing what Renold wants with you and what Lars has threatened to do. I have to finish this on my own."

"Why? Why *you*, Bren? What you're attempting to do is . . . it's suicide, okay?" My teeth chattered as my voice and emotions rose. I was now gripping his wet shirtfront, halfway between shoving him back and dragging him closer. Couldn't he see how impossible this mission of his was? Being allowed to leave the city once was a miracle, but twice? Fear sent goosebumps skittering across my skin. "If you go back alone, something tells me I'll never see you again."

"You will."

"You can't know that. What if my—what if Renold discovers that you're a spy? What if he tortures you for information? What if he—" I sat up straighter. "I saw Iris."

"What?" His tone changed then, filling with purpose.

Almost faster than I could blink, he had us both on our feet. He switched the shower off and, after wrapping a towel around me, said, "Where is she?"

"Underground. She's still in Tatum City though. I don't know what building it is—I can't remember the city's layout—but she was surrounded by cement. And . . . I can't be sure, not with my memories blocked, but I think Renold has her."

Bren swore under his breath. He left a wet trail behind him as he exited my bathroom in a rush, stripping off his shirt in the process. "Get dressed, Lune. Dr. Moore needs to hear this."

I stared at the wall over his shoulder so I wouldn't get distracted by all that sleek golden skin. "Bren," I called before he could slip out of the room. With a hand already on the doorknob, he shot a distracted glance my way. "If I'm so important to Renold, why did he allow me to leave?"

His gaze shifted to the floor so I couldn't read his expression. Ah crap, what was he hiding *this* time? Before my anger could ignite, he replied with, "I don't think there's a clear-cut answer to that question. I think he wanted to test your loyalty and further draw out your abilities. But . . . I also think he's jealous."

"Wait, what?" I definitely didn't expect that last one. *Jealous?*

Bren huffed a laugh. I watched in surprise as he began rubbing at his neck. "Yeah. He's never let on, but I think he knows about our past connection. I spun a convincing story about seeking asylum from the Recruiter Clan, saying I'd do anything to avoid being used by them any longer. They might be loyal to *him*, but that doesn't mean the sentiment swings both ways. He welcomed me with open arms. Of course, I had my own set of rules to follow once inside—one of them being to sign contracts with all three Trials. To keep me in line, he threatened to hand me over to the Recruiter's boss. Anyway, I think his real reason for allowing me entrance was you."

"Me?"

"Mmhmm. He counted on you remembering me so your emotions would stay heightened and unbalanced. All of that anger and hate and fear was supposed to make you project your ability. I didn't come to these conclusions until two nights before the first Trial, when I could sense the anger pouring off him after discovering we had feelings for each other. The fact that you didn't hate me anymore, that you actually considered me an ally . . ."

He barked a laugh and shook his head. "I wish you could have smelled his jealousy when he realized your loyalty had been given to another."

I raised an eyebrow. "I don't see how this is funny."

"It's not," he said, trying unsuccessfully to wipe away his grin. "Maybe just a little."

My eyes narrowed on him. "Is this like some male dominance thing where you pee on your *territory*? Because that crap is so not going to—"

"I swear it's not. I swear! Stop looking at me like that. Besides, I think the point of letting us both leave the city was to see if we'd run off together or betray one another. If we ran,

I'm betting our brains would be fried right about now." He twisted, tapping at the base of his neck where a small scar lay. "That nut job has an obsession with electricity."

I felt for the slightly raised scar on my own neck, fighting off a shudder. "So if we fail our missions?"

His face turned serious. "Others will take our place. They'll be the ones enduring whatever torture techniques that madman comes up with next. That's why we need to get Iris away from him. Now that the citizens are aware and questioning the system, Renold will be desperate to retain control. If I prove myself loyal to him, if I complete my mission, he'll trust me. I could find his weakness—and the city's—then discover the safest way to wrestle power from him and free the people from their slavery to the Trials."

"And if he doesn't trust you?" I clenched my teeth so I wouldn't beg him to let me go again, so I wouldn't shout in his face that if he was willing to sacrifice himself for this cause, why couldn't I?

"If he doesn't trust me, then I'll do whatever it takes to sabotage the system from the inside before it can be stopped. One way or another, Renold Tatum and the Elite Trials will be destroyed."

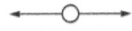

That hum. That *buzz.*

I couldn't get the sickening sound of electricity out of my head.

When I woke from the nightmare—which no doubt manifested after further speculation on Renold's penchant for torture earlier today—I blinked in confusion, wondering why I was standing in the middle of my dimly lit room. My muscles were still tightly wound as though warding off additional agony. The feeling lingered, that blinding jolt of white hot pain, so intense that my limbs had shaken, then stiffened. Deadened.

But I hadn't been the one receiving the barbaric affliction.

Bren had.

His screams had rung through my skull, and I couldn't help him. That helplessness traveled through me now, leaving me breathless and weak. I needed to see him! I stumbled, but caught myself on the arm of the couch. After a moment of clearing my vision and calming my galloping heartbeat, I opened the door.

And there he was.

The unexpected sight startled me and I flinched back, instinctively coiling my body into a defensive stance. But I was so overcome with relief to see him upright and unharmed that, a split second later, I launched myself at him. He uttered a surprised grunt when my arms tightly squeezed his neck. I pressed my nose to his warm skin that always smelled of sunshine, a scent that I decided was my favorite.

When he pulled me closer, I exhaled shakily. *Safe. He's safe*, I assured myself.

"You all right?" he asked, his voice husky from sleep. "I

heard you cry out."

Why did I feel like crying right now? There was something so real about that dream. I couldn't shake it. And why had I been *standing* when I'd woken up? Still, I nodded. "Just a nightmare."

"Want to talk about it?"

I should. Maybe if I told him, he'd realize that returning to Tatum City would be the death of him. Or maybe he'd bring me with him so we could take down the system together. But would he believe me? That my dream had felt like a . . . a what? Premonition? Was that part of my ability? Or was it just paranoia? Ugh. I didn't know. Maybe if I waited until morning, my head would be clearer. So I simply said, "No. Just . . . please don't go."

I had meant to the city, but Bren was focused on the present. In a breath, he was carrying me into my room. The door snicked shut behind us as he laid me on my bed. From above, he watched me with an expression that held so much at once. Love. Caring. Adoration. My chest ached at the sight. But there was a troubled look in his eyes too. Indecision. Regret.

No. Not tonight. I wouldn't allow pain tonight. If everything were to change tomorrow, the least we could do was live this moment together. So I set aside my insecurities, my fears and doubts. And rose up onto my knees so my face was level with his. "Stay," I breathed, grasping his shirt and tugging him closer.

He didn't resist, intent on my every move as I trailed my fingers lower, as I fisted the shirt's hem. Before my mind could catch up with my actions, I lifted the material, exposing his abdomen, his chest, until he was helping me remove the shirt completely. My breath hitched as I allowed my gaze to wander, to take in the shadowed swells and dips of his muscles.

Heat crawled up my neck at my boldness, but I held onto my resolve. He needed to know. He needed to know how I felt about him. If words continued to fail me, then all I could do was show him. And so I didn't falter. I didn't stop my body from leaning forward, didn't stop my lips from pressing a kiss to his heart. The feel of his skin against mine was soft and warm and perfect. Shyness evaporated. My hands found his bare waist. He tensed under my touch, sucking in a sharp breath. A thousand butterflies fluttered inside my stomach at the sound.

I kissed a path across his chest, slowly, taking my time. His fingers dug into my hair, clenching as I ran my palms up his spine. When I lightly traced my nails over his skin, shivers racked his body. I could do this all night, touching him, marveling at his reaction. But he moved then, tugging on my hair so my chin lifted. His mouth, hot and needy, fell on mine.

Heady warmth ignited my blood as he released my hair and grasped my hips, pressing me tightly against him. I whimpered and scraped my nails down his back, just to see what he'd do. He growled, for starters, then deepened our kiss. Our tongues touched, and in a matter of seconds, I was drowning, aching to be nearer.

As if sensing that desire, he lifted one of his legs and slid it between mine. "Bren," I moaned, digging my nails into his skin as heat barrelled through me. I didn't know it was possible to feel this much—with someone, for someone. I couldn't breathe under the building pressure. "Bren," I said again, trembling as I struggled to speak. I was going to explode into a million stars. But I desperately needed to tell him. I needed so badly for him to know.

I drew in a ragged breath and bared my heart. "I'm in love with you."

At first, nothing happened, like he was deaf to sound, lost in the feelings coursing through him. But then the muscles of his back tensed. My pulse raced as our labored breaths stretched between us, as all other movement stopped. His eyes remained firmly shut. Had he changed his mind? He'd looked so certain earlier today. The words had felt *real*. My face heated for a completely different reason now. Right when I decided to lock myself in the bathroom and never resurface, a tear slipped down his cheek.

Before I could panic, before I could convince myself that I'd screwed everything up, he crushed me to him. I could barely breathe as his arms wrapped around my rib cage and held me tightly. A tremor went through him. Like he was breaking down. Like he was crying. I felt it then. Tears in my hair where his cheek was resting.

What did I do? Did I *break* Brendan Bearon? I had meant to take away the pain, not heap on more. I didn't know how to handle this sort of thing, so I blurted, "I'm sorry."

He huffed a quiet laugh, squeezing me tighter, if that were possible. "Never apologize for loving someone. It's the greatest gift you can give them."

Gift. I liked the sound of that.

It made me realize something. He said he'd stolen my freedom, but the gift of his love right now felt a whole lot like standing on top of a mountain, free of past horrors, free of future uncertainty. All I had to do was accept what he offered me freely.

So I did. Without a drop of doubt or hesitation.

ALWAYS, BREN

The soft weeping that drew me from a deep, dreamless sleep was definitely not Bren's. My hand swept over the mattress beside me, expecting to meet his warm body, but the space was empty. Cold. A frown tugged at my mouth, which turned into a lazy grin a second later as I imagined him re-entering my room with a cup of coffee. I could practically smell it now.

A sniffle broke through my sleepy haze and my eyes popped open. As I suspected, I was alone in bed. So where was the crying coming from? I rolled over and blearily scanned the room. A curled-up figure was on my couch, too small to be Bren. Alarmed, I quickly rubbed my eyes and sat up. When Bells' face came into focus, my shoulders relaxed, but my frown returned.

"What's wrong, Bells?" I disentangled myself from the sheets and placed my feet on the floor. Was I not the comforting type? Because, once again, I had no idea what to say. The skin around her eyes was red and splotchy, her hair disheveled as if she'd run her fingers through it several dozen times. Fear slowly gripped me. Had someone died?

Before my brain could form a multitude of terrible scenarios, she glanced up at me with the saddest expression I'd ever seen. "Bren's gone."

My heart stopped.

A fist must have wrung the air from my lungs because I could no longer breathe. My mouth opened, but nothing came out. The world paused, taking in my state of utter shock as if the moment warranted extra attention.

Only one word played through my head.

How, how, how, how, how?

I had been with him all night. It was barely morning. What could have happened in such a short amount of time?

"Sorry," Bells moaned, clutching at her head like she had a migraine. "He does this every time and it never gets easier. Just . . . just check your handheld, Lune."

The pain in my chest almost made movement impossible. When I stood on shaky legs, the room tilted. I slumped against the wall, forcing myself to inhale, just enough to make the black spots go away. Passing out wasn't an option. I needed answers. *Now.* I found my handheld on the table where I'd left it the night before, but next to it was a coiled object. Brown. Leather?

My trembling fingers picked it up. A necklace. And attached to the end . . .

A bear's tooth.

I gasped and dropped it as image after image assaulted me. My eyes weren't able to stay open as memories poured to the front of my mind, memories of a younger Bren, memories of the moment he gave me this necklace, memories of never taking it off no matter how many times I'd wanted to. And somehow, after everything, here it was. Bren was giving it to me *again*. But why?

A moment later, I had my answer as I opened a message on my handheld. I struggled with some of the words, but after reading them, each one sank deep into my bones.

"You told me once that the price of freedom was pain. You were right. I confess that I can endure your anger and hate, but not the pain that saying goodbye would bring. So please forgive me for leaving this way, but I've reached my pain threshold. We will see each other again, Lune Avery, I swear it. Stay safe. You have my heart. Always, Bren."

Oh, Bren. "What have you done?" I whispered brokenly, willing the handheld to reply. It did. Or rather, it buzzed. I checked the screen to see that I'd received a message from Dr. Stacey, asking me to meet her in Medical as soon as possible. *Now* what? My brain was about to explode.

I remembered dressing and giving Bells a hug, at the last minute slipping on the bear tooth necklace, but everything else was fuzzy. Walking, the trip down the elevator, entering Medical—all done on autopilot. Belatedly, I realized I should have messaged Jaxon to escort me. Too late now. I could see Dr. Stacey heading my way. I would message him later.

"Lune, thank you for coming so quickly," she said, ushering me down the aisle toward the back of the long room. She stopped at the last partitioned-off space and gestured for me to sit on the bed. I did so mechanically, only faintly curious as to why I was here. "How are you holding up?"

"Hmm?" I blinked up at her without expression.

She gave me a sympathetic look. "Dr. Bradfield completed his memory blocker antidote just last evening," she said gently, and I saw then that she held something in her hands. A needle. No, a syringe with yellow liquid. I noticed her fingers tremble slightly. Was she nervous about restoring my memories? Excited? "Bren wanted me to wait to give you this until after he'd left. I think he was afraid to face you once your memories were back. All of that animosity right before leaving for his mission would have been hard. This was easier, I hope you understand."

I nodded even though what she said didn't sit right in my gut. When had Bren ever run away from a challenge? *He just did*, I reminded myself. *When he failed to say goodbye.* Maybe I didn't know him as well as I thought. But with my memories back, maybe I could find some closure. Or at least answer a few of the questions currently swarming my brain. I took a calming breath and strengthened my voice before saying, "I'm ready."

I was given a mild sedative first since the injection site was to be the same place I'd received the chip from Renold. "For the best results, the serum needs to be injected close to your brain stem," Dr. Stacey said almost apologetically. "You will feel a sharp pinch."

As the needle bit through my skin, several warnings slapped me. What if the serum made things worse? What if I was better off without my past memories of torture and imprisonment? What if I changed? The new me had adapted to this environment. Would the old me be able to do the same?

Too late, too late, too late.

My muscles locked as the syringe was compressed. Cold fluid rushed through my system. The needle retreated. I expected the old me to pop back into existence at any moment, but nothing happened. I glanced up at Dr. Stacey, shrugging when she asked if I felt any different.

"The memories might come back gradually, not all at once. I'll message Jaxon to escort you to your room. Expect some lightheadedness and disorientation for the next twenty-four hours." She patted my arm, then said she needed to check on another patient, leaving me with my doubts and anticipation.

Thoughts of Bren crowded in now that I was alone. Of the danger he was willingly walking into all because of a guilty conscience. I tried not to be mad, tried to focus on the message he had sent me, on the pain he must be feeling. On the love. But old resentment ate at my newfound happiness. He had left me. Again.

I'm real. I'm right here, he whispered to me.

"No, you're not," I said out loud, clenching my teeth.

It's going to be okay, little bird. Just wait and see.

I squeezed my eyes shut as his voice amplified inside my head. As his words tore at my false calm. *I can't wait around,* I shouted back at the ghost of him haunting me. *I'll go insane if I do. You can't leave me like this. You can't!*

My breaths came in gasps as voices assaulted me, voices

from the past. Renold and Rose, Lars and Catanna, Asher and Iris, Ryker and Mum. I inhaled sharply. Ryker. Mum! I clutched at my head as the images came, vibrant and terrifying. They overloaded my senses, leaving me blind and weak. I curled into a ball on the bed before I could fall over from the weight of the memories pouring into my mind.

Pain.

Fear.

Hate.

Rage.

My past was a swampland of misery.

I knew that I was crying—the salt of my tears leaked into my mouth—but I couldn't stop. I couldn't stop the memories from tearing at the solid ground beneath me, from ripping away the blindfold, from forcing me to see what I'd been missing.

Where was Ryker?

Where was my mum?

What was Bren's mission?

My past collided with my present, forging a disjointed, conflicting future. My goals in life, my *mission*, had been erased. The old me didn't want life inside The Ridge where decisions were made for me, where secrets and hidden agendas were just as plentiful as Tatum City. Would they ever let me leave? Or was I a prisoner, furthering their mysterious plans under the guise of helping others?

The past me had wanted to stop Bren from completing his mission. Not to save him, but to save *others* from what I'd endured. And I'd failed. He was beyond my reach now. I had exchanged one prison for another. But the thing that hurt the most, the thing that dug into my chest and twisted my heart to shreds was that I loved him.

Even with the old me and new combined, *stars above*, I loved that insufferable idiot to the point of obsession, and it scared the crap out of me. A part of me hated myself for it, thought me weak and pathetic. But I was stronger than that now. I knew my mind. My heart. Knew what I wanted. And I wanted *him*.

After I sabotaged his mission, saved Iris, and found my mum.

Piece of pie.

Someone nudged my shoulder and I flinched, struggling to keep still when all I wanted was to hiss at the intruder. Now that my memories were filtering in, I remembered how reactive I could be. How I would lash out, then apologize later if they hadn't meant me harm. Years of conditioning were hard to break, but I forced my fingers to loosen one at a time, quickly wiping away tears before facing Jaxon.

But it wasn't hazel brown eyes I saw. Instead, intense blue and black ones peered down at me as if questioning my sanity.

I hiccupped in surprise. "Ryker."

"What are you doing?" he whispered in reply, scanning my prostrate form. "Are you injured?"

And suddenly, it was as if the last two months had never happened. I shoved aside my tangled memories and focused solely on the man who was supposed to be dead. Ignoring his questions, I whisper-yelled, "Where have you *been?*"

He scowled. "Rotting in a cell, that's where." He thrust a backpack at me. "We have a short window of escape. Come on, let's go."

"What?" I squeaked, attempting to sit up. They had locked him away? And didn't bother *telling* me?

"Quiet," he growled softly, then grabbed my arm without warning and hauled me off the bed. My knees immediately buckled as the room rotated nauseatingly. Ryker caught me before I hit the floor, uttering a curse. "What did they do to you?"

My forehead dropped to his chest as I fought to keep my stomach where it belonged. "They gave me," I panted, "my memories back. I was . . . sort of . . . sedated."

He swore impressively, then slung my arm over his shoulders, bearing most of my weight. "Escape first. Explain later."

I was in no shape to push him away, but did I even want to? He wanted out and so did I. After that, I'd have to improvise until the rest of my memories returned. I couldn't remember our final moments together before I'd woken up inside The Ridge. Only that he should have died from his wounds. Had this all been a setup? Was Ryker in on it? Was *Bren?* I didn't know who I could trust at the moment, which made me drag my feet as we slipped through Medical's rear exit.

Ryker grunted under the added weight, shifting his hold for a better grip on my waist. I recognized his clothing as the ones he'd worn outside Tatum City. Unease crawled up my spine. "How did you get out of your cell?"

He paused, looking both ways before crossing an intersection in the hallway. It was early enough in the morning that traffic was still minimal. Someone was bound to notice us though. "Less than half an hour ago, I noticed my cell door was unlocked after the guard delivered my meal. Sitting right outside was our backpacks and gear, even our weapons. I didn't question it."

We reached the stairwell and he opened the door like he knew it would be there. "How do you know where to go?"

He held up a slip of paper. "Someone drew me a map to your location and then the exit. And it says that if we get lost, you'll know the way out." His expression was dubious, yet curious too, as he waited for my reaction.

Oh. Crap. The people who'd threatened me, who didn't want me here. Was this *their* plan? It could be a trap then. We could be playing right into their hands. Double crap. "Uh. Yeah." I straightened as best I could, grimacing as the stairs before us rippled like water. "Up or down?"

"Up." Ugh. At the sound of approaching feet, Ryker grasped at pieces of my hair and partially hid my face. "Keep your head down."

I did, feeling like a fugitive from one of those action movies Jaxon loved. Jaxon. He was probably looking for me. Should I message him? Could I trust him? My sudden doubt sent a bolt of agony through my chest.

When the passing resident was out of earshot, Ryker whispered, "How well are you known around here?"

"Um . . ." Did I dare admit to being a part of the *inner*

circle? No. Definitely not. "I've made some friends."

He snorted softly.

I took my eyes off the stairs to glare at his face. "What?"

"*You* made friends?"

My lips pursed and I focused on climbing again. "Shut up."

"My point exactly," he muttered.

If I didn't need his support so badly, I'd shove him down the stairs. He would survive. Probably. By the time Ryker had us exit the stairwell on the twelfth floor, my body was screaming at me to rest. A headache throbbed at my temples, behind my eyes, and at the base of my skull. I stopped trying to think about what I was doing and concentrated on not blacking out.

We somehow passed through doors that required a handprint, navigating stairwells and hallways I'd never seen before. No one paid attention to us, as if they were so confident in The Ridge's security, they'd never thought of the possibility that two people could be breaking out. When we hit a dead end, Ryker swore and backtracked. Several minutes later, he crumpled the map in frustration. "You're up, Lune."

I squinted at our surroundings, then slumped against the nearest wall. "I don't know where we are."

As his jaw hardened and his fingers curled into fists, I remembered why I used to fear him. He was downright scary-looking when mad. But I was too exhausted to feel anything other than mild amusement. "I suggest you rack your memory and fast before someone spots us," he hissed, "or it won't just be me who gets locked in a cell."

Oh stars. I hadn't thought of that. For all they knew, I was helping a prisoner escape. Technically, I was betraying The Ridge, throwing away their trust in me—if anything they'd told me had been real. I groaned and closed my eyes. How had this become so screwed up?

I had a choice to make. I could cry for help and pretend that I didn't know who Ryker was, that my memories hadn't resurfaced yet. Ryker would be locked up again and I could continue my life here at The Ridge. Or I could use my ability and search for the way out of here, then finish what I started two months ago. Neither choice was ideal. Without Renold's chip tying me to him, I could choose a third route.

I could choose freedom.

But it wasn't just about me anymore. I had friends and family who needed saving. I had someone I loved walking to his death. What was the point of freedom if I spent it alone? I doubted my mum was stashed away in a cell somewhere in The Ridge, which meant there was no guarantee I'd ever see her again. At least I had my ability. Someday, I would find her, I promised myself. But right now . . .

I had a mission to complete.

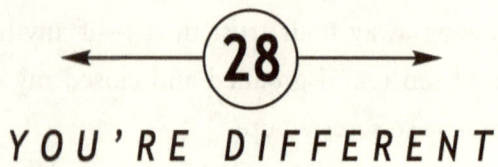

YOU'RE DIFFERENT

"Take a left."

"You're sure?"

"Trust me on this, okay?"

"I don't trust anyone," Ryker groused, sounding way too much like me. Why had I never noticed how similar we were? And if I allowed pessimism to eat me alive like he obviously was, I'd become as cranky as him too.

Stars, please say I'm not already like that.

"Well, if you want out of here, you're going to have to, grouchy pants."

I felt his shoulders stiffen. "I'm not—"

"Yes, you are."

His eyes narrowed on me. "You're different. The same and yet . . . not."

I pressed my lips together. "Um, thanks. I guess." I stopped talking and focused—conversing with Ryker took way too much energy. Every few minutes or so, new memories would surface and throw off my balance. Sometimes Ryker had to all but drag me until the ground would stabilize again. To find the exit, I'd conjured an image of the machine Bren and I had ridden up the mountain on. The outdoors was just beyond where the machine was kept.

We were almost there. Maybe a handful of minutes away. Adrenaline stirred in my blood, dulling the throb of my head-ache. *So close, so close.* We rounded a corner and I collided with something. Instinctually, my head whipped up. When I met the startled eyes of what looked like a guard, I bit back a curse. "Sorry," I murmured, glancing down. Not quickly enough. Suspicion had colored his face.

He let us pass by, but unease shot through me. I walked faster.

"What's wrong?" Ryker said quietly.

"I think he might have recognized me," I said, peeking over my shoulder. We were alone. For now.

He swore under his breath, then doubled our speed.

"That one." I pointed to a red door at the end of the hall-way. "It leads to the outside."

Tugging myself from Ryker's hold, I broke into a less than graceful jog. *Almost there, almost there.* I reached the door first and grasped the handle. When I yanked and felt the re-sistance of a lock firmly in place, fear coursed through me. In a panic, I slapped a hand to the black print reader on the wall. It flashed red, rejecting me.

No. *No.* We were so close!

Ryker nudged me aside and tried the handle without suc-cess. I gaped as he reached behind him and pulled out a gun.

"What are you—?"

"Stand back," he said, aiming at the door.

Bang!

He blew the lock open, then ripped the door wide. We sprinted inside, and that was when an alarm went off. The ear-splitting screech was worse than a hammer striking my skull. I covered my ears, but the pain was so intense, tears blurred my vision.

Ryker grabbed my shoulders and shook. I groaned as the action set my head on fire. But he didn't stop. "How do I get the tunnel door open? Is there a button? Lever? Lune, snap out of it!"

Tunnel? There was another door? I scanned the room through bleary eyes, noting that it wasn't a room at all, but a massive cavern. At the far end was a wide, steel door barring the way out. A bullet wouldn't be breaking through *that*. I didn't know how to open it. I didn't know!

"Freeze!" a voice shouted from behind us.

Faster than I could blink, Ryker whirled us around and banded an arm across my chest. Every part of me froze when I felt the cold steel of a gun press to my temple. "Don't move or I'll shoot," Ryker said loudly, his voice echoing in my ears.

My stomach bottomed out when I saw who'd entered.

Yukiko.

Her expression was hard, intent on Ryker, not me. But her gun . . . it was pointed at my chest. "What makes you think I care?" she responded coldly, widening her stance.

Without warning, the gun at my temple cocked. I flinched, but Ryker's grip only tightened. "Open the steel door or I *will* shoot."

For a moment, time slowed. The choices I'd made hovered

before me like a movie screen and I couldn't look away. Leaving with Ryker. Mistake. Breaking out. Mistake. I had made the wrong decisions and would now pay the price with my life. Something in my expression must have caught Yukiko's attention. She grimaced, then slowly walked to a keypad on the cave's wall and punched in a code.

Despite not being able to see it, I knew the door was sliding open when bright sunlight spilled inside, illuminating Yukiko's irate face. Her gun was still trained on us, tracking our every movement as Ryker walked us backward toward one of the four-wheeled machines. When the engine rumbled awake, she took a step forward. Even with a gun still pointed at her, she continued to advance inch by inch. Ryker growled a warning and she paused.

He fisted my shirt, dragging me sideways until my butt plopped onto the machine's seat. He joined me a second later, barking at me to drive since he refused to turn his back on Yukiko. I had no clue how to work one of these things, but when I'd been plastered to Bren, I felt the way he'd twisted the handles and pressed on the lever at his feet. My fingers briefly squeezed a handle lever. We jerked forward, then stopped.

I was about to do it again when Yukiko yelled, "Stop!"

"Go, Lune. Go *now*," Ryker growled, wrapping an arm around me.

My body went rigid, not from his touch, but from the effort of not looking back. Guilt gnawed at me, tugging and pulling until I couldn't help but glance at her one last time. Stars. I shouldn't have. Tears were streaming down her face, tears of betrayal. The sight crushed me. My chin wobbled and I opened my mouth, needing to explain, to apologize. *Something.*

But the opportunity was there and then gone as a shadow passed over her eyes. Determination. Regret. She'd made her own decision. "You know I can't let you leave, Lune," she called out. Her voice shook, but remained steadfast. "I have to protect what matters most. You know that."

I stopped breathing when her eyes narrowed, when her gun raised level with my head. Every part of me screamed at her not to do it, but I couldn't speak. I couldn't move. The shock was too much. She was going to kill me. My friend. Was going to shoot me.

Bang!

I jerked. Stabs of adrenaline burrowed under my skin. I waited for pain to register, for darkness to take me. Instead, I watched time slow to a crawl as Yukiko fell back, landing hard on the ground. My brain didn't understand. Didn't *want* to. But when Ryker turned around and I saw the deadly focus in his eyes, I knew.

"No," I whimpered, looking again at Yukiko's unmoving form. "No. No, this can't be happening. No."

Wake up, wake up. This isn't real.

Ryker's body pressed heavily against mine, blocking my view of her.

I snapped.

"Let me go. Let me go *right now*, you cold-blooded killer!" I shrieked, clawing at the arms boxing me in. In response, his foot knocked mine aside as he took control of the machine. He grabbed onto the handles and we lurched forward. I howled in rage, trying to pry his fingers free as we picked up speed. But his grip was a vise. I remembered his words to me, spoken with so much surety.

I can see better than you, smell better than you, hear better than you, but more importantly, I am faster and far stronger than you.

No. No! Was he a Sensor like Bren? If so, I wouldn't be able to get away. Not now, not when my body was weak and he held the weapons. We burst into the morning's light just as shots were fired from behind. More guards must have arrived a moment too late. My throat tightened when I thought of Yukiko lying lifeless on the ground, so I switched off everything. My mind, my emotions, my body. Any more pain and I'd automatically shut down anyway. At least this way, I'd be awake.

The world streamed by as we shot down the mountain at breakneck speed. There was no road, only thawing dirt and rocks. The land wasn't white anymore but brown and budding green. It was all a blur as we swerved around trees and navigated the rocky terrain. I clutched at the machine—an ATV I remembered now—as we veered sharply to avoid a tree stump, doing my best to stay out of Ryker's way.

He was practically on top of me, breathing down my neck. I wanted so desperately to shove him off me and watch him tumble down the mountain, but I'd probably join him a second later. And at the speed we were going, I wouldn't survive.

Just as I was going to yell at him to slow down, I heard the roar of another ATV. Ryker glanced back and swore. The machine jolted forward, pressing me further against him. Shots fired. The tree next to us splintered. Ryker curled himself around me, making a smaller target as he wrenched on the handles, changing course.

When more bullets zipped past, Ryker grabbed my hand and forced me to grip the lever. "Drive," he barked.

"No!" I shouted, struggling to pull free.

"They're shooting at *you*," he growled, slapping my other hand onto the handle. "If you want to live, then drive the blasted ATV!"

I ground my teeth together but did as instructed. After only a few moments of guidance, he let go. I almost crashed the machine a second later, narrowly avoiding a tree. I should have known what Ryker's intentions were, but when he returned fire, I startled. Then wanted to scream my frustration. They were my *friends*. This shouldn't be happening!

We bumped over gnarled roots and loose rock, the jarring motion sending spikes of agony through my head. My eyes wouldn't open more than a squint, so I saw what was ahead too late. I only had time to shout a quick warning before the rocky ground fell away, leaving us airborne. With my heart in my throat, I screamed all the way down in terror and, stars help me, elation. Something must be wrong with me because I had missed this thrill of danger charging through my blood.

But when we landed and every bone in my body shrieked at the impact, common sense returned with a bang. No, that was the sound of us still getting shot at. Ryker faced forward again and wrapped his hands around mine, taking over the steering. "Are you crazy?" he yelled in my ear, then clutched the lever until we were once more playing a deadly game with gravity.

"You already know the answer to that," I replied as I checked on our pursuers. Three human silhouettes on ATVs were perched on top of the embankment we'd just fallen from. I ducked as one shot at us, but we were quickly traveling out of range. They must not have liked the idea of dropping to their deaths. Couldn't blame them.

Despite the danger shrinking into the distance, Ryker didn't slow. My fingers ached where he continued to grip them, my back stiff from hunching over. But I didn't say a word. I was conserving my energy, because when the time came, I only had one chance at escaping this heartless monster.

When we found a road, I wanted to sob in relief. Although cracked with age and riddled with potholes, concrete was far smoother to ride on than roots and rock. But the ATV sputtered and died about three hours later. At least we'd made it to the bottom of the mountain. Ryker went so far as to hide the machine off the road, saying we needed to cover our tracks.

Like they didn't already know exactly where we were headed.

I refrained from rolling my eyes, instead acting docile and obedient. Maybe a bit *too* agreeable since he kept shooting me quizzical looks. But every time he did, I made a show of rubbing my temples and cringing in pain. I *was* in pain, but I still had enough strength to do what needed to be done.

We set off on foot after he pulled my coat and boots out of my backpack and told me to put them on. I didn't protest. The air was no longer freezing with spring just around the corner, but I had fled The Ridge in a thin cotton shirt and shoes that wouldn't hold up under such conditions.

I allowed several minutes of silence to drag between us. Well, *this* felt familiar. The view. The tension. I didn't miss the fact that he hadn't offered me my weapons. I was staring at my bow now, strapped to his back. But I didn't need it. I had something else in mind.

My boot snagged in a root protruding from the road and I pitched forward right into Ryker. Before I could enact my plan, he twisted around and grasped my shoulders, holding me at arm's length. I let out a moan and closed my eyes, squeezing the bridge of my nose for good measure. After a moment, he released a guttural sigh of pure annoyance and dropped our packs. He bent and retrieved his first aid kit, popping out two pills from a bottle.

"Take these," he said, also handing me a water bottle. I did as instructed, glad to listen for once.

I waited until he was bent over again and zipping up his pack before I sucked in a weak gasp. "Ryker," I breathed, letting my arms fall limp. My eyes rolled upward as I tipped forward in a dead faint. He caught me. His guard was completely down, his position awkward, unprepared. I quickly snaked a hand behind him and yanked his gun free. Then I whipped my head up, ramming my forehead into his chin. His teeth clacked together.

My vision spotted from the sharp impact, but there was no time to clear my sight. I brought the gun up and clocked his skull with my depleting strength, shoving out of his arms before he could pin me down. I had expected the escape to be harder, so I almost fell on my butt as I regained my balance.

When I'd blinked away the remaining flashes of light, I knew the moment of surprise had ended. I had to act. Now. I pointed the gun at his chest. "Don't. Move."

The look in his eyes. His irises chilled to a crystal blue, their edges blackening even more. That was intimidating. He sneered, but I saw his hands trembling. In rage? Fear? "What's gotten into you?" he said, his voice deathly soft. Crap. Rage, then.

Well, I had some of my own. My hands were shaking too as they gripped the weapon tightly, but my aim didn't waver. "You killed my *friend*," I hissed through clenched teeth.

His brows lowered. "I did not."

"You did! I saw her hit the ground. I saw her *blood*." My palms began to sweat as I tried not to remember what she'd looked like.

"You saw a shoulder wound, nothing else. I had to stop her from putting a bullet in your head, Lune!" His voice rose in anger.

So did mine. "You're lying! This isn't the first time you've murdered someone who stood in your way. When I've lived out my usefulness, will you kill me next?"

He bared his teeth. "Don't tempt me. And I'm not lying. I only kill when I have no other choice." I wanted to scream at the casual way he said it, like killing another human being was a natural part of life. He must have read something in my expression because he added confidently, "You won't shoot."

My nostrils flared. "Oh?" I cocked the hammer and sighted down the barrel. "Wanna bet?"

For a split second, alarm shone in his eyes. Then his face blanked. And he charged. I had one painfully clear moment of indecision. To shoot or not to shoot. But if I fought like him, would I become him? Cold, callous. A monster. Exactly what Renold wanted. My instincts were to pull the trigger, end the threat. But what if I was wrong about him? What if he hadn't killed Yukiko?

I blinked and the moment passed. I made a new decision. With only a handful of feet between us, my aim shifted and I squeezed the trigger. The shot knocked him back, but he didn't fall. I wasn't sure who was more shocked, him or me, as he staggered to a halt within reaching distance. But he didn't lunge for me. Or the gun. Instead, he stared down at himself and slowly peeled back the right side of his coat, exposing his shoulder. There, a dark red stain spread over his shirt.

His mouth soundlessly opened and closed. Then, "You . . . you shot me."

I swallowed hard, trying not to gape at the blood or I'd throw up. I made myself shrug and say, "It's just a shoulder wound."

Disbelief colored his face. The emotion remained fixed in place as he looked me up and down several times. And then he did something I'd never heard Ryker Jones do before. He laughed. A *real* laugh. "You," he wheezed, then grunted in pain, "really have changed."

My brows lifted. "You do realize I've shot at you before, right?"

"Yeah, but this time you thought it through first. And won," he said, gesturing at the gun still pointed at him. Did I detect admiration in his voice?

Now probably wasn't the time to tell him I had terrible aim with a gun.

Instead, I whispered, "You're insane."

He shook his head and huffed a laugh. "That makes two of us."

Were Ryker and I having a moment? Like some bonding thing where sworn enemies discovered they had something in common and . . . Ah crap. The last memories I had of our time together before we'd been separated chose to click into place right then. I remembered patching him up after he'd risked his life for me, I remembered Bear. *Bear.* Oh no. Had the guards killed him? I remembered Yukiko tackling me to the snow when I'd swiped at her with my dagger. Well, that explained why she hadn't liked me at first. I remembered the panic, the fear that Ryker was dead. In our final moments together, I had

329

considered him my friend.

And I remembered the last words he had said to me.

The day you were kidnapped, I was there too.

STORY TIME

I grimaced as the needle slid through Ryker's flesh.

"This is definitely bringing back memories," I muttered, finishing the last stitch. At least I didn't want to stab his eyes out this time. Maybe a little, for Yukiko's sake. But resisting the urge was easier now, like the new me had tempered the old somehow, granting me more control of my reactive body.

Ryker frowned. "How so?"

"You don't recall the time I stitched you up when you should have been *dead*?"

"Oh. That. The memories are hazy. Too much blood loss or something."

I rolled my eyes. "That's putting it mildly. So you probably don't remember what you said to me either." I chewed on the inside of my cheek, wondering if I should even bring it up again. But now that my memories were back, I wanted to fill in the many gaps of my sordid past. Needed to make sense of it and figure out once and for all who were allies . . . and who were enemies.

When Ryker shook his head, I shoved caution aside and blurted, "You said you were there. The day I was kidnapped. That you tried to stop Bren from going to the lake. What were you doing there? Why don't I remember seeing you?"

As I fixed a bandage over his wound, I felt his muscles tighten. I paused. Maybe he hadn't meant to disclose that information to me. Oops.

I leveled him with a look. "You might as well just tell me. I'm not in the dark anymore about what's been happening around here. I know about the human trafficking and the mutated abilities. I know that you're a Sensor like Bren. Were you forced to kidnap kids too?"

His face hardened. For a second, I wondered if he'd kill me for possessing such information. Maybe I should have kept my mouth shut, but it was too late. I narrowed my eyes in return, waiting for his reply. Finally, just as my eyes began to water from holding his intense gaze, he looked down. I let out a slow breath. Staring contest challenge: two points for me, none for Ryker.

"I was born into it," he began, his words clipped as if saying them was the last thing he wanted to do. "The Recruiter Clan. Asheville. They were my home up until two years ago. When Bren came along, things changed. I saw his innocence, something I'd never known, and when I saw it destroyed, piece by piece . . . I tried to stop him."

He shifted uncomfortably, rearranging his shirt to cover the bandage. "Since I was old enough to walk, I've been taught to listen but not be seen. It's why you never saw me at that lake. It's why you didn't see me in Tatum City until I wanted you to. I know many things, things I'm not supposed to, so I've made a few enemies over the years. It's why I was handed over to

Renold who gladly took me in for my skills. If it weren't for him, I'd be long dead, so I owe him my loyalty."

So many things about Ryker made sense now. He had only been nine or ten when I was kidnapped that day at the lake. I didn't want to feel kinship toward him, but I sort of did. He had tried to preserve innocence the way I had with Asher and Iris. There was only one thing that troubled me. "Why do *you* remember me from that day, but Bren didn't?"

His face cleared of emotion as he looked me in the eye and said, "He tries to forget, that's why. The memories are too painful." With that, he stood, wincing as he slowly rotated his shoulder. "Story time's over. We need to find Bren if he's still out here. If not, we better head back to Tatum City and explain what happened to us."

Even after everything he said, I still had so many questions. I needed to know one more thing before we continued on. "Ryker, what do you know of the place you were imprisoned in for the last couple months?"

He shrugged, then grunted, pressing a hand to his injury. "The guards weren't very chatty. They enjoyed interrogating me though."

A lump formed in my throat that felt a lot like guilt. I had been treated like royalty in comparison, completely oblivious that Ryker was locked away. Or even existed, for that matter. Did this mean he had no clue that I'd found Bren? That Tatum City's Elite Guardian was a spy? But *I* knew, which was probably why Yukiko had been willing to kill me. To protect those she cared about. At the same time, she'd been crying. For me.

Stars, I really screwed things up.

I swallowed past the ache. "Did they . . . did they torture you?"

"No, not physically. They used this serum though—"

Ding.

Suddenly, his expression darkened. "Lune, what's that?"

"What?" I followed his gaze to my front pants pocket. My handheld! I couldn't believe it still worked this far away. Maybe Jaxon was trying to reach me. At the realization that I hadn't said goodbye to him or Bells or Dominic, that they'd probably been told I was a traitor, my heart sank. I pulled the device out. "It's for messaging. I'm sure they're just wondering if—"

Without warning, Ryker lunged at me. I shot to my feet, but before I could do anything else, he snatched up my handheld and threw it to the ground. "Hey," I protested, bending to pick it up. He was faster. The heel of his boot came down on the device with a sickening *crunch.* I stared at the splintered wreckage, first in shock, then sadness as I remembered Bren's final message to me. I would never get to read it again. Next came hurt and anger. My hands curled into fists as I yelled, "What did you do that for?"

He was in my face now, glaring daggers. "It can track our location. Either you're ignorant or working for them. Which is it?"

My mouth opened, but I was completely speechless. What was I supposed to say to *that*?

"Answers. Now," he barked. When I remained mute, his

hands fell on me, searching, grasping. I hissed and knocked them away, but he yanked me close with that viselike grip of his. Warm breath gusted over my face as he said, "Did they chip you? Are you *chipped*?"

"Let her go," a new voice growled, low in warning. We both froze at the sound of a gun cocking.

But the voice. That *voice*.

I slowly turned my head and there stood Bren.

A very *angry* Bren. The furious look in his eyes was solely trained on Ryker who hadn't released me yet. I drank in the sight of him, for a moment forgetting the danger I was in. He was alive, and I didn't see him hauling along a string of kidnapped children. I could still stop him. I could *save* him.

"Bren," Ryker said calmly, *too* calmly, and finally let go of my coat. He didn't step away though. "I'm surprised to see you still out here and not safely tucked inside Tatum City. What are the odds that you're *here*, at the very spot that was drawn on a map for me to find? You wouldn't happen to be double-crossing the Supreme Elite, would you?"

My heart skipped a beat at the bold accusation. Bren's face gave nothing away. He took a step closer, but didn't lower his gun. "And why would you think that?"

"Because you've double-crossed before. And because I think your loyalties have recently shifted," he said, sliding me a glance. It was barely there, but I saw a corner of Bren's mouth twitch. Recalling what Ryker had revealed about his past, how he was trained to *notice* things, my stomach flipped. What was he up to? I thought he'd wanted to make amends with Bren, help him complete his mission. I was thrown for a loop once more at his next words. "How's Isabella?"

Bren stilled. So still that my eyes widened in alarm. Crap. I was missing something here. He lowered his gun, then stuck it into the waistband of his pants as he sauntered even closer. The way he walked, as if approaching trapped prey, put me on edge. When he was a yard away, he simply said, "Don't ever say my sister's name again," then unleashed himself. His fist plowed into Ryker's jaw, sending the shorter man reeling.

I sucked in a gasp as he did it again. And again. With a fury I'd never seen before. "Bren," I shouted, springing into action. If he kept this up, he would kill Ryker. I couldn't let him for so many reasons, the greatest being that I knew he'd never forgive himself. "Bren, stop!" I threw myself between them, knowing the move was stupid, knowing he wasn't in his right mind, but it was the only way.

His fist struck my cheek.

The pain was instant, spreading over the entire left side of my face as I fell back into Ryker. The salty taste of blood filled my mouth where I'd bitten my tongue. Everything stopped then. There was only pain and Bren's expression. They were one and the same in that moment. The horror bleeding onto his face hurt to watch. I reached a hand out in reassurance, wanting him to know that it was okay, but was distracted by the feel of Ryker's gun slipping free of my waistband.

No, I silently screamed as Ryker pushed me aside and raised the weapon. I could do nothing, *nothing* as the gun whipped through the air, bludgeoning Bren's skull. I managed to yell Bren's name as his eyes rolled upward and he crumpled to the ground, but I made a grave mistake. I lunged for him and not Ryker. The cock of the gun was loud in my ears as I pressed shaking fingers to the pulse at Bren's neck.

"I'm sorry, Lune. I was hoping for a different outcome than this," Ryker said, then ordered me to get up.

My lips quivered, in anger and hatred. I wanted to rip his heart out for this betrayal. "You can stick that fake apology up your—"

Cold steel pressed against the back of my head. "Up. Now."

I did, never taking my eyes off Bren, even when Ryker forced me to stand in front of a tree. But when he produced familiar-looking wrist restraints and a length of rope, my attention snapped to him. My muscles coiled, preparing to strike.

"Don't even think about it," Ryker warned and raised the gun again.

"You won't shoot. You're my *Keeper*, remember? You're supposed to keep me alive," I taunted, trying to gauge his reaction, his ultimate goal. I shifted to the side. A shot fired. The sound exploded in my ears, momentarily stealing my hearing. Wood splinters pelted my face and I bit back a yelp as one sliced open my cheek.

Ryker slammed me against the tree a second later, knocking the wind from my lungs. "You're right, I won't shoot you," he growled in my still-ringing ear as he slapped the restraints onto my wrists. "But I'll do to you what I did to Bren if you don't hold still."

It only took him a few minutes to have me firmly trussed to the tree. I prayed that Bren would wake up and save me, but Ryker tied his hands together too. Then he disappeared into the woods. By the time he returned, my wrists were already sore from trying to free themselves. I blinked stupidly when an ATV rumbled to a stop next to Bren. Had Ryker pretended that our machine died for this very scenario?

But no, another backpack was slung over his shoulders. The possessions must have belonged to Bren. I watched, curious despite myself, as Ryker unzipped the pack and produced a simple brown box not much wider than a book. He glanced at Bren's unconscious form, then at me, before slowly opening it. I held my breath as a feeling settled into my gut. A certainty, that whatever was in that box was important.

As he flipped the lid back, Ryker's eyes widened. He looked at Bren again, and something like indecision crossed his face. Maybe, just maybe, I could get through to him then. "I thought you were going to help him complete his mission. I thought you were going to resolve things left unsaid between the two of you."

He stared at Bren a moment more, then closed the box. "I am," he replied softly, all of his earlier fire gone. "This is me completing what he started. But you don't know everything, Lune. If you did, you would understand why I have to do this. We're not so different, you and I."

My chin wobbled as I fought to keep tears from escaping. I told myself that they were tears of rage, but I couldn't lie.

Stronger than the hate and anger was a deep-seated hurt that he would do this after all we'd been through together. "I was wrong about you."

"How so?" He refused to meet my eyes.

"I thought you were my friend."

His entire body stilled. For several silent seconds, he blankly stared at the box in his hands. Then he carefully zipped it inside the pack once more and whispered, "I'm no one's friend."

He left me.

After lugging Bren's limp body onto the ATV, he freaking left me tied to a tree. He didn't take the backpacks though. My eyes were drilling holes into all three of them just out of reach. I assumed that he would come back, at least for the packs, but when?

"Man, I thought they'd *never* leave," a voice said from behind me. I jerked against the ropes in surprise. "I can't believe Ryker found the legendary Brendan Bearon. At this point, I wouldn't be surprised if the Easter Bunny popped out of the ground and planted a wet one on me." The cackling sound that followed sent a cold sweat racing down my spine.

No. It couldn't be. Life wasn't *that* cruel. Please, no. Gritting my teeth, I yanked against my bonds with everything I had.

There are worse things than death.

Ryker's words decided to haunt me at the worst possible moment, when my nightmares were materializing and I couldn't escape them. Sure enough, the two men who had chased me through a city and up a mountain strolled into my line of sight, identical expressions of glee on their faces. Thane was sporting a grizzly new scar right above the beard line on his cheek and Skervvy walked with a slight limp. Maybe Ryker hadn't been the only one shot that day at the cabin.

What had felt like a lifetime ago now came rushing back.

"Those boys have it *bad* for you," Skervvy went on and casually removed a throwing knife from his belt. My heartrate kicked up another notch as he deftly flipped the blade in the air, catching it over and over. "What makes you so special? I can't put my nose on it."

Thane snickered at the lame joke. "I'm willing to sniff test her and find out."

"Get anywhere near me with that heinous thing and I'll chop it off," I said menacingly, but when they both crowed with laughter, I struggled not to wet myself.

"Let's get going before Ryker returns for his pretty package," Skervvy said, making a beeline for the backpacks. That left Thane to untie me. I hadn't forgotten our last encounters and how he couldn't seem to keep his hands to himself. Sure enough, as the ropes loosened, his knuckles brushed my chest. I didn't react. Not yet. He needed to free my legs first. When the last of the rope fell and I felt groping fingers on my thighs as he slowly straightened, I attacked.

Wham.

Knee to nose. The satisfying crunch of bone breaking was almost better than cutting the ugly thing off. He needed to learn not to get so close. Before I could push him away with my still-cuffed hands, fire speared through my arm. A scream lodged in my throat, but I choked it down, glancing at the source of pain to see Skervvy's throwing knife embedded in my bicep. Shock rendered me immobile, long enough for Thane to regain his sight and shove me against the tree.

He wedged his leg between mine, then grabbed a chunk of my hair, forcing my head back. I knew what would happen next. Every cell in my body railed against the impending violation. I would rather die. Ryker was right. Some things were worse than death. As Thane's head lowered, I squeezed my eyes shut and tried to switch off my thoughts, my senses, escape to a place where no one could touch me.

Then he let out a loud yelp, his grip falling away. Growls and screams filled the air. I tore my eyes open in time to see a large tan and black beast take him down, immediately lunging for his neck. Blood sprayed. Skervvy yelled, brandishing a gun, but the flurry of rolling bodies held him in check.

I was hypnotized. In shock, more likely. I could feel myself shutting down. The strain of the day had worn me ragged. Everything that had happened. I felt like fragile glass about to break.

The beast gained the upper hand, trapping his prey beneath him. Bear. I knew it was Bear. He had come to rescue me again. How he'd found me after all this time, I could only guess. Thane let out a wet gurgle as Bear sunk his teeth into the man's jugular, then tore out a chunk of flesh. Oh, stars. The spurting blood . . .

My stomach roiled. I wretched, shaking uncontrollably as the action pulled at the blade still in my arm. After wheezing in a breath, I looked up to find Bear staring at me. His ears pricked forward as if to say, *Are you all right?* That moment. That split second of time when clear devotion shone in his bright yellow eyes—maybe even love. I would remember it forever.

The gunshot came a second after, obliterating that look.

I watched, helpless and heartbroken as Bear's eyes dulled, as he slumped on top of Thane. Dead. I cried then. Fell to my knees as my strength gave out. I wished for oblivion, especially after Skervvy shot Bear two more times, just to be sure. I wished for nothingness to take me far far away when he yanked the knife from my arm.

But I remained awake through it all.

I was forced to shoulder my backpack and trudge behind my captor, hands tied and a rope around my neck as he led me into Asheville, the Recruiter Clan's den of nightmares.

Into hell.

ONE LAST TIME

The darkening streets were alive.

Celebratory.

The air stank of their excitement, their euphoria at having captured new prey. I was paraded up one street, down the other, until I could have sworn we'd trekked the entire city. Exhaustion couldn't even begin to describe what I was feeling. Not only physically, but mentally and emotionally. I was unraveling.

Rest. I needed rest before I passed out in the street. Maybe that was what they wanted—to see me broken. I wouldn't give them that pleasure.

Up ahead, the dull brick buildings shown brighter. Laughter and catcalls rose into the night, sounding like wild, untamed beasts. I hadn't spotted a single woman, and that was the worst sight of all. If they weren't in the streets, then where were they? What was the clan going to do with me? The possibilities sent shivers racing through my body. I bit my lip to hide a pained groan as the action pulled at my still-bleeding arm.

Skervvy hadn't bothered to clean the knife wound. He'd simply tied some material around my bicep to slow the blood flow. What mistreatment would I endure next? I had dealt with plenty of torture over the years, but at Renold's hands, it had been controlled and precise. I doubted I'd get that courtesy here.

The last thing I was prepared for though, the very last thing, was the sight that awaited me up ahead. A roaring bonfire, twice the height of a man, dominated the clearing we walked into. Several people, mostly teenagers, threw objects into the fire, whooping whenever one exploded.

A solitary figure, removed from the action but still close to the fire, stole my attention. There was something odd about his pose, like he was reaching toward the sky . . .

I felt the rope around my neck tighten as Skervvy picked up the slack. He tugged me to a stop and I closed my eyes, relieved to have a small break. "Looks like payback came early, girly. Recognize anyone?" he said, his voice slick as oil and full of wicked amusement. He jerked on the rope, and the sudden pain forced my eyes open.

The flickering flames made the figures around it dance in unnatural ways. I squinted at the shadowed faces, but my mind whispered at me to ignore them, to seek the one figure that stood out from the rest. Because it knew before I did who that figure was. I couldn't clearly see his face—not when it was cast down in what looked like defeat. I couldn't make out his clothing since he was naked from the waist up. I saw then that the man's wrists were tied, his arms stretched between two posts. And the people weren't just throwing objects into the fire, but at him as well.

My heart beat wildly, spurred on by the knowledge of who that man was. I wanted to shake my head in denial, pinch myself until I bled, until I woke up from this living nightmare. Because the man slowly lifting his head, the man turning my direction and opening golden eyes I would never again forget . . .

Was Bren.

Please. Stars, please.

This couldn't be real. They would kill him, *kill* him for having deserted them. I could see it in the way they circled him, the way they spat insults I was too far away to hear. His suffering called to mine, devastating in its intensity. I answered it without hesitation, regardless of the consequences.

With a cry of pure heartache and desperation, I swung my bound fists at Skervvy's head. They connected. He had been too busy gloating to expect an attack, so he stumbled sideways and tripped over his own legs. The impact sent a fresh wave of agony through my injury, but I clenched my teeth and charged toward Bren. I swerved as someone tried to tackle me. I was yards away now. Close enough to make out the panic on Bren's face. The fear.

He grasped the ropes above him and pulled, his biceps bulging from the strain. As I continued to run, a part of me knew that we would lose this battle. Weak and injured as we were, greatly outnumbered, there was no way we'd escape this. But if I could just reach him. If I could just wrap my arms around him, kiss him one last time, it would be enough. I could handle the rest knowing that I had lived. Knowing I had *loved*.

I would cling to the moments we had stolen from a cruel world. If I could just steal one more . . .

My head whipped back as the rope jerked me to a halt. My feet flew out from under me. I hit the ground with a sickening thump. Air couldn't breach the fire searing my throat where the rope dug in. I rolled onto my side, reaching both hands toward my neck as I struggled to breathe.

Through a dense fog, I heard my name being shouted over and over. My limbs shook as I turned toward that voice, the voice that never failed to comfort me. If he kept speaking, maybe I could endure whatever was to come. I managed to fill my lungs, to blink away the darkness crowding my vision, only to hear Bren scream. My heart seized at the terrible sound. I sought him out. He was still tied up, but . . . but . . .

"Holy crap," I whispered rawly.

He cried out again as he pulled against his restraints, the veins in his arms and neck protruding from the effort. The ropes snapped. In a rush, he crossed the space between us and gathered me into his arms. I allowed tears to fall as I pressed my face to his chest, soaking up his scent, his warmth, his nearness. I felt the rope stretch taut, tugging me away from him. My bound hands grabbed the rope and yanked hard, allowing us one final moment.

Our lips found each other, the kiss filled with all the fear and despair coursing through us. But more than that, it was filled with an endless hope. Because we wouldn't stop trying to be together no matter how many times this world tore us apart. I would find him again. And with that hope burning inside me, I managed to say, "I love you, Brendan Bearon. Now *save* yourself."

The agony that twisted his face was unbearable. So I made it easier for him. I let go. Without my resistance, the rope dragged me back several feet. His mouth formed the word "*No.*" I saw the way his muscles bunched to run toward me. Silhouetted by the roaring fire, shadowy figures surrounded us in a loose circle. They hovered, shifting as though nervous, unwilling to bridge the gap. Were they afraid of Bren?

My eyes narrowed, focusing on his as I willed him to listen. To fight for a better tomorrow. "I dare you to run," I whispered, but I knew he could hear me over the chaos. "And don't you dare stop."

Disbelief and pain etched jagged lines into his skin, carving tears down his cheeks. He shook his head, but my stomach twisted when I saw that my words had sunk in.

I'd dared him.

His body trembled as he warred with himself and the impossible thing I'd asked him to do. When I couldn't stand it any longer, I opened the connection between us, forming the bond almost immediately in my desperation.

I know you'll come for me, no matter what, I spoke into his mind. He sucked in a gasp. *And if you love me, I need you to go. Now!*

For one heart-stopping moment, I thought he would back down from the challenge. I thought he would give up and let them tie him again. Kill him. All because of me. Then, with a roar I could feel in my bones, he leapt to his feet. He narrowly dodged a fist as the clan finally closed in, avoiding several more swings as they converged, blocking his way of escape.

He was actually doing it.

He was saving himself.

I couldn't breathe as he bellowed his fury and fought to be free. For a split second, the way cleared. For a split second, my hope soared.

Then the ear-splitting ring of a gunshot destroyed my dreams.

Bren fell.

I gathered the ragged pieces of my heart and screamed his name into the night. Again and again until my voice gave out. The rope took me away from him, farther and farther until the mob swallowed him whole. I didn't know if he was alive or dead.

Skervvy sidled up alongside me and hissed, "Now we're even." And when he prepared to knock me unconscious with the gun that I knew, just *knew* had shot Bren, I knew the pain would be nothing.

Because the agony of not knowing if Brendan Bearon had survived.

The not knowing . . .

It was the most excruciating thing I'd ever feel.

———◦———

Cool, gentle fingers slid across my brow. The touch was soothing. I almost decided to keep my eyes closed and pretend to be asleep just so the fingers would stay. Why did I want someone touching me? The old me, who would have grabbed and twisted the offending hand, warred with the new as I continued to lay still. But at the soft whispers, at the light straining against my eyelids, telling me it was morning, I pried them open to slits.

Someone, dressed in a pale print dress, was hovering beside the bed I laid on. Instead of peering up at the face I assumed was female, I scanned the airy room. Lacy curtains covered the many windows, which I noticed had black bars over them. Women dotted the room, most older than me. Some conversed in small groups while others were curled up with a book or other solitary activity.

My eyes slid shut again as confusion assaulted me. All of those horrible memories pushing at my brain that were demanding to be let in, to be *felt* . . . were they a dream? Maybe I'd had one of my waking nightmares. It had been so *real* though. They always were. But this one—the agony, the rage, the feeling of my heart being ripped out of my chest. I would never be able to scrub those emotions from my memory.

That kind of pain—the anguish of losing a part of your soul—couldn't be forgotten.

The fingers feathered across my forehead once more and, for some reason, I didn't question their presence. I welcomed them. *Needed* them. Especially after everything I'd—

"LuLu? Are you awake?"

At that soft-spoken, musical voice, my eyes shot open. I tried to look everywhere at once, frantically searching for that voice, a voice I hadn't heard in so long that I'd forgotten what it sounded like.

And now everything came back with painstaking clarity.

I was a little girl again, waking up on the morning of my seventh birthday.

Only, when I found the owner of the voice, she didn't look the same. She was older, maybe by a decade or so. Fine lines outlined her mouth and eyes. Her cheekbones were sharper. But her hair was still a dark brick red. Her smile was still teasing and kind. Her eyes. They still looked like mine. I reached up and, with a trembling finger, touched her face. Real. It was real. *She* was real.

How? How was this possible?

My voice shook in awe and wonder as I whispered to the woman I hadn't seen for eleven long years, "Mum."

ACKNOWLEDGMENTS

God knows I needed to tell this story. With each book, I put a little bit more of myself in, and I'll be forever grateful that God gave me the ability to articulate the words that I wanted to share.

But I wouldn't have been able to get the message across as clearly without the help of my incredible critique partners and beta readers! Tyffany Hackett, Grace Kathleen, and Melissa Mc-Murry, thank you for always reading my work and giving me honest feedback! Your comments give me life, but also challenge me to make my work better. Oh, and thank you for being my friends. I so value that! I'm also super grateful for Virginia See's keen eye. I'm always shocked at the stuff you find, lol! And I'm so happy to have added two new betas, Haven Holt and Kate Anderson, who both "get" my storytelling. Nothing makes me happier!

And to my critique group—Stephanie Moore, Lyn Hawks, and Russell Johnson—thank you for pointing out that I forgot to add Lune's name to chapter one, ha! You guys keep me grounded and focused, and I always look forward to our meetings!

I also wanted to thank my long-time friends and family for your support. I am overwhelmed by your enthusiasm and willingness to follow along on this journey!

Lastly, I want to thank my readers for continuing on this adventure with me! You are making my author dreams a reality. Stick around for the epic, heart-stopping conclusion to this series!

ABOUT THE AUTHOR

Becky Moynihan is the award-winning author of *The Elite Trials* trilogy (a YA dystopian romance), and co-author of the *Genesis Crystal Saga* (an NA urban fantasy series), with author Tyffany Hackett. She lives in central North Carolina with her family.

Find more info on Becky's website: www.beckymoynihan.com "Be the first to know!" Sign up for Becky's newsletter to receive the latest deals and releases!